THE
AWFUL
TRUTH
DAWN

I0587025

Book I

Gerry and Sam Conrad

This is a work of fiction. All names, characters, places, and events are the product of the author's imagination or used in a fictitious manner. Any resemblance to actual events, locales or living or dead, is entirely coincidental.

Copyright © 2023 Gerry and Sam Conrad

All rights reserved. No part of this publication may be reproduced, distributed, or transmitted in any form or by any means, including photocopying, recording, or other electronic or mechanical methods, without the prior written permission of the publisher, except in the case of brief quotations embodied in critical reviews and certain other noncommercial uses permitted by copyright law.

Library of Congress Control Number: 2023916716

ISBN   978-0-9758710-2-7
eBook ISBN 978-0-9758710-3-4

Cover design by Gerry and Sam Conrad
Butterfly Artwork by Gerry Conrad

First Edition

Knowing your own darkness
is the best method for dealing with the darkness of other people.

~ Carl Jung

EVENING AND MORNING ~ APRIL 10, 2090

*C*aroline was the one who walked into the cave.

She didn't care whether the droplets on her face were from the sulfurous mist or the tears from her broken heart. Caroline stumbled through a jagged maze of dripping stalactites, cradling a threadbare blanket and a worn canvas backpack. The light grew dimmer, and a craggy stalagmite reached up, tripping her, ripping her thin cotton dress. Sounds of trickling water echoed louder across the slimy frigid chamber, mocking her.

Caroline brushed her long gray hair from her wet face and descended further into the cave. A flat rock, large enough to rest her age-touched body, beckoned her like an old friend. With solemn reverence, she spread her faded navy-blue blanket across it and removed her soft white dress to cover the coarse blanket. She stashed her backpack behind the rock with her shoes and reclined on her side, curling into a ball, knees tight against her chest. Caroline was beyond fatigue, beyond fear. It was time. The man she swore to love forever was now gone forever. All the souls she loved—forever gone. It was like a death, because this time she'd forget her shattered past and all her grave losses. He was her life—yet her purpose remained....

She slept.

Caroline walked into the cave, but a child walked out.

Angel, 2090

CHAPTER 1

Odd-shredded bio-fibers cling to my body, so I grab the blanket, find a clean spot along the edge, and wipe off the shriveled matter. Something smells musty sweet, like rotting leaves.

A canvas backpack peeks out from behind the rock alongside a hidden pair of old, worn shoes. I remove a simple, folded white dress from the backpack and slip it over my cold, exposed body. It's far too large and hangs like drapes until I tie its matching cloth belt tight around my slim waist. My feet swim in the shoes, making walking difficult. The damp blanket rips with ease, allowing me to tear strips of fabric to stuff into the shoes for a better fit. The backpack holds a disappointing few morsels of food, but a wrinkled red apple looks edible, so I grab it and sling the backpack over my shoulder. A bluish-white shaft of sunlight guides my way out of the dank cave.

Morning rain bequeaths the forest with welcome sweet, fresh air, and the sun warms my chilled flesh as I hike to an unpaved road near a clearing. Birds chirp their morning chorus, and I pause when a monarch butterfly catches my attention, circling me before flying away. A fragrant breeze caresses my long brown hair, like scented butterfly kisses. I dodge puddles trudging my way to the road, hoping to reach my destination before nightfall. The route runs east and west, so I follow the sun.

§

My dry mouth is dusty, tasting like dirt road, and my legs ache to rest. The overhead sun blazes on my face and shoulders, my arms are turning a rosy pink, and the road ahead never ends. Floral and earthy smells of the forest and her vibrations surround me, creating a canopy of perfume and music.

3

Peppered with a woodpecker's *rat-a-tat-tat*, branches in the breeze rustle sublime counterpoint. But the sweet scent and murmur of babbling water tempt me off the road. My sore feet beg for a place to rest and to adjust the wads of padding in my shoes, so I descend the slope toward the stream.

Terrifying thunder silences the forest, and I freeze. A jeep veers from the road, crashing through the foliage, shearing off branches, barreling toward me, and slams into a ditch, flipping on its side with a thud a short distance away. The driver, ejected from the vehicle, smashes against trees as he tumbles, landing on his back, a splintered bone protruding from his leg. I rush to his side.

He moans in agony, blood gushing from his horrific injury. But first things first. Kneeling at his side, I remove my cloth belt and secure it tight around his leg above the wound. His khaki uniform turns crimson, as does my white dress. The bleeding abates, but his face contorts as he groans and grits his teeth.

His anguish touches me, and by instinct, I wipe my bloody hand on a blood-spared section of my splattered dress and rest it on his forehead. A warm rush of psychic energy ripples from deep inside me, and on impulse and Knowing, I draw it up, transferring it to his mind. It baffles me how I know to do this. I can't remember.

He sleeps for me now.

The forest restarts its interrupted symphony. I untie the belt to release blood to his lower leg. Bleeding resumes, and I wait. I try to apply pressure to his gaping wound to prevent hemorrhaging but allow blood flow. The jagged protruding bone is gruesome. Unsure what to do, I re-tie the belt. At least he won't bleed to death. I peer around, searching for help. Was he alone? I can't fix this.

Another sudden hush permeates the forest, and I glance in every direction for signs of human intervention, for help. Unfamiliar sounds reverberate through the forest, their source hidden. Another jeep?

Male voices grow closer.

At the top of my lungs, I scream, "Over here! Help!"

I repeat my distress calls until, above me, a jeep screeches to a halt. Five uniformed men scurry down the berm to the crash site. I stand and step out of their path as they race to their injured comrade and tend to his leg. One soldier takes charge, yelling orders while pacing and wiping his forehead. He calls to the wounded man, "Hang in there, Buddy. You're gonna be fine."

Helpless, standing at a short distance, I watch them secure Buddy's leg and prepare to lift him. Four soldiers carry Buddy out of the ditch and into their jeep. Two soldiers speed off with Buddy, and the others scramble back down to rejoin their leader.

The leader inspects me, noticing my ruined dress, a bloody hand smear under my breast, now blood-soaked from the waist down and clinging to my legs.

"Are you hurt?" he asks. He exhibits the same fear and concern he showed for Buddy.

I shake my head.

"What's your name?" he asks. "Where did you come from?"

I don't remember my name, and I can't mention the cave. He surveys our surroundings, his face apprehensive. He squints, scanning the countryside for something, but for what?

Another soldier whispers loud enough for me to hear.

"Sir, we're not aware of villages in this sector. She shouldn't be out here."

The leader furrows his brow and tilts his head while looking me over, but I say nothing. He spies the small mountain stream nearby and grasps my hand, leading me to the creek.

"Name's Dan Matthews," he says. "What's yours?"

I don't speak to the tall, sandy-haired, sun-bronzed soldier.

At the stream's edge, I remove my shoes, hike my dress, and wade into the water midway to my knees. Dan removes his shoes and socks, rolls up his pant legs, and joins me. He strips off my blood-stained dress and tosses it to the ground, away from our shoes. I wash Buddy's blood from my hands and scoop a handful of clear water, letting it slide down my parched throat. The surrounding water turns blood red, so I scoop another clear handful before it's tainted.

Dan also cups handfuls of water to wash away Buddy's blood, then inspects me to make sure I'm not hurt or bleeding. I squat and cleanse my upper body with the water, watching the slow-flowing stream filter Buddy's blood away in reddish ribbons. Dan watches me like a protective parent and offers his hand to help me out of the water.

He removes his shirt and undershirt to dry my arms and back. When he moves to my front, he hands his undershirt to me and gestures for me to dry myself. I dab it against my chest.

With his outstretched hand, Dan requests his undershirt and trades his shirt, which he wraps around me. He watches me wiggle my arms into the sleeves and waits while I button it. It's long enough to cover my bottom. He dons his damp undershirt and slips on his socks and shoes. The insides of my shoes squish from my wet feet. He leads me, gripping my hand, to rejoin the others.

We scramble up to the road and wait.

The soldiers eyeball me, so I stand a little closer to Dan. *What now? Am I free to go?* My bloody dress, ditched near the stream's bank, is unwearable, and its belt remains tied around Buddy's leg. My backpack with scarce food? Somewhere on the ground, out of sight. My legs burn with fatigue, my feet hurt, and I'm still wearing Dan's shirt. If I return it, what will I wear?

We wait until another jeep arrives, which we greet with a collective sigh of relief. Tension among the soldiers evaporates like water on a wet road in sunshine.

The jeep faces the oncoming sunset, so this may be a faster way to reach my destination. My legs can rest since we're headed in the same direction.

Dan directs me to climb into the backseat next to a soldier with chestnut brown hair like mine. Not knowing what else to do, I hop in beside him, leaving room for Dan, who jumps in next to me. Sandwiched between the two soldiers, I move close to Dan. The soldier beside me inspects me, his eyes on Dan's shirt like he's afraid I might steal it. I follow his gaze to the damp cloth clinging to my small breasts. After pulling the fabric away from my body, I inch closer to Dan. I smile and glance up at him.

"Looks like you made a little friend, sir," my seatmate says.

Dan smiles.

The jeep backs up and turns around, heading in the opposite direction. Change of plans.

§

The jeep speeds along the bumpy dirt road, with the soldiers quiet and somber, monitoring their surroundings and I sense their apprehension again. I read their thoughts and detect their fear of getting caught outside by the Overlords. Do they mean the Captors? I know I must avoid them, but I can't remember why, yet it's important.

I decide I am fearless.

We bump along on the same tree-lined road, its scenery unchanging until we round a curve. In the far distance, an immense circular fortress appears built into a mountain, with a solid stone exterior, except for the very top, where windows glint in the sunlight. Bright yellow wildflowers grow in a verdant meadow surrounding the complex.

"Shangri-La," says my seatmate, smiling but appearing tired and haggard.

"Yep, that's where we're headed," Dan says. "We'll get you some proper clothes, find out where you belong, and get you something to eat. Are you hungry?"

I stare at Dan. It's like he's reading my mind. Can he do that too?

I nod and smile. My tummy growls at the mention of food, and it sounds like a wonderful plan. I lean back, resting against Dan. I don't know where I'm going, but I'm on my way.

Everyone becomes quiet again, yet I sense relief among the soldiers, and the cloud of nervous tension that has accompanied us dissipates.

Shangri-La remains in the distance, but the jeep swerves from the road into a hidden tunnel in the mountainside. As we travel through the tunnel, its height, width, and ability to hold three jeeps widthwise, and as many stacked as high, is astonishing. The tunnel ahead looms darker than night, but dim amber lights grow brighter as we advance, illuminating our passage. I turn around in my seat. Darkness follows behind us now, like magic. The tunnel moves us along by lighting the way with soft glowing golden lamps that fade after we pass them.

We slow to a stop, and Dan announces our arrival at the base.

"Westview," he says, nodding at a huge sign bathed in soft light. "Come with me."

We march through a garage-like area with aromas of oil and grease and turpentine hanging in the air, yet the spotless parking bay sparkles. Several jeeps and trucks, painted in camouflage, sit parked around a loading dock, where soldiers dressed in khaki uniforms like Dan's scurry about, busy as bees.

We weave through a maze of passageways with clean, polished floors to arrive at the medical wing to check on Buddy. Dan and I stop at the hospital reception area, where Dan informs me they'll examine me to make sure I'm not injured. He touches my shoulder.

"I'll be right outside waiting for you. You'll be fine," he says. "I'm going to check on Andrew." His eyes reassure me as he turns to leave. Who is Andrew? Does he mean Buddy?

While Dan checks on Buddy Andrew's condition, a nurse shows me where to shower. The windowless room with bare walls has a hospital bed, a small nightstand, and a bathroom. The nurse opens the bathroom door, nodding for me to enter.

"You need to shower. This is shampoo." She holds a bottle marked "shampoo" and addresses me like a small child or an idiot.

"It's for your hair, to wash it. You put some in your hair and lather it like this." She scrunches her fingers over her head near her hair like she's washing it. She hands me the shampoo bottle and bar of soap.

"You use this to wash your body. It's soap. You rub it on and then let the water wash it off. You can use this if you want," she says, handing me a washcloth.

After she turns on the shower water until it's warm enough, she orders me to undress and step into the forest-green tiled stall. She must believe I'm a feral cat that's never washed, yet even a cat knows how to clean itself. What did they tell her about me, that they found me in a cage? I humor her and remove Dan's shirt, but when I enter the shower, it appears she intends to watch and direct me.

"I can handle this myself," I say, glaring at her and waiting until she realizes I'm not moving until she leaves. The nurse closes the clear plastic shower curtain and steps away, but she's still there. I take my time washing my stringy hair and my stream-bathed body.

After finishing my shower, I towel off, under the nurse's watch, without instruction. My damp, tangled hair smells sweet, like strawberry shampoo. The nurse hands me a brush, but before she can tutor me on its use, I brush my long hair.

The nurse shows me clean clothes like a nurse's uniform, saying they belong to me now, but first, I must put on a hospital gown. I grab Dan's sweaty shirt. The nurse struggles to take it from me. I resist. She yields, and I dress in the hospital gown, clutching Dan's shirt.

"The doctor needs to examine you," the nurse says. She shepherds me to an examination room, measures my height and weight, then orders me to climb on the exam table. A skeleton hangs from a metal stand on wheels in the corner. The doctor enters and follows my gaze to the human skull.

"Alas, poor Yorick, I knew him," I say in a whisper.

"Where's that from?" the nurse asks.

"Hamlet," the doctor says. Unfazed, never looking at me, he snaps on latex gloves. "Act five, scene one. Odd. That's what I was thinking."

The doctor inspects my mouth, under my arms, and listens to my heart with my gown pulled down to my waist, exposing my chest. He instructs me to lie back, scoot down, and put my feet in cold metal stirrups. I'm so exposed. Why do I have to do this?

"How old are you?" the nurse asks. She stands near my head, peering down at me with expectation, but I don't know, so I don't speak.

The doctor's gloved fingers probe me. You can discern the age of a tree by counting its rings. But don't you have to cut it down first? What's the doctor counting? His hand moves further south. The instant he tries inserting a finger, I scoot away from him, grunt a warning, wiggle out of the stirrups, and scramble to a sitting position. *Okay, enough. I'm done here.*

Without care, I tear off the hospital gown and throw on my new clothes, pushing past the indignant nurse. My loose-fitting new clothes cover me better, making me less conspicuous. Dan's shirt remains safe, tucked under my arm.

Dan waits for me, as promised, and grins when he notices my new clothes. He wears a crisp, clean shirt and appears to have showered too.

"Follow me," he says.

We march through several spotless passageways until we reach a spacious area with maybe twenty cots lined up in perfect order. Neatly fitted with olive-green blankets and fluffy pillows covered in bright white pillowcases, each cot sports a small olive-green footlocker at its foot.

We continue our tour through a smaller space boasting a gleaming white stove, fridge, sink, and several counters and cupboards, all blinding white. Bright red coffee cups hang from hooks near a jet-black cylindrical urn. The aroma of fresh-brewed coffee fills the air.

Our destination, an enormous open cafeteria, bustles with uniforms everywhere. Aromas from freshly baked bread blend and delight my nose, exciting my growling belly. In line, Dan helps me select from unfamiliar dishes, all smelling delicious and so much better than the abandoned food in the backpack. Dan finds us a table by ourselves, where I inhale everything on my plate. Many soldiers stare at me, but I don't care because I'm starving. After stuffing my neglected stomach, I ask him about the different colored uniforms. He explains the uniforms have different meanings, and the white shirts outrank the khaki shirts. They call men with white shirts officers.

"Why are you afraid of the Overlords? Will they hurt you?"

"What makes you say that? They are our benefactors. They provide us with food, shelter, and everything we need or want," Dan said. "Why would you ask that?"

An officer approaches Dan. They speak for a moment, and then Dan excuses himself, stepping away for a private conversation. Meanwhile, I watch the crowd in amazement. Various soldiers congregate in the vast cafeteria, mostly men and a few uniformed women, all knowing where they fit in—yet here I am, lost. Dan turns back to me and beckons me to come with him.

He ushers me into a large, bleak room with a long wooden table, several chairs—and three officers. An imposing older officer with a deep tan, and short dark brown hair, sits near the table's far end, with the others standing nearby.

"I'll be right outside," Dan says. He tells me to sit across from the seated man, pats my shoulder, and heads for the exit. He's leaving me, but I don't want him to. I'm not afraid. My stomach tightens. I don't like these men. I clutch Dan's shirt in my lap with both hands.

"My name is Major Jim Nadler," the seated officer says. "We're here to find out where you belong."

"What's your name, child?" asks a standing officer. A scary long scar etches across his chin. He moves toward me, and I lean back, clasping Dan's shirt to my chest.

I won't speak.

"Do you understand what we're saying?"

Nadler frowns.

I nod. I understand them, but I have nothing to say. Frantic, I stare at the closed door, willing my newfound friend to come back and rescue me.

"Look, young lady, we're here to help you," says another officer. His voice is softer, but his menacing beak-like nose and black, close-cut hair scare me.

"Where are your parents ... your family ... your home?" asks Scar Man.

"Where do you live, child?" Black-Haired Man asks.

I wear an expressionless mask as they shoot questions at me like a firing squad. As soon as they hit me with one question, they fire another, and I can't answer any of them. I don't know.

"We want to help you," Nadler says. His words, now gentle, don't reassure me. Something disturbs me about him. I focus on the door. Did Dan leave? Will he be there when they finish questioning me, as he promised?

"How did you get off base?" asks Scar Man.

"Were you alone?" asks Black-Haired Man.

"Look at me," Nadler says, glowering.

I grant him my full attention.

"I can find out where you belong," he says. "But ... it would require considerable time."

"So, why don't you tell us so we can send you home?" asks Scar Man.

"Can you speak, child?" asks the Black-Haired Man.

I glance at the door, then back at Major Jim Nadler with pleading eyes until he understands my message.

Nadler commands Scar Man, "Get Sergeant Matthews in here."

Scar Man leaves, returning with Dan, and I smile and release a deep sigh. Dan pulls up a chair and sits beside me.

"It appears our young lady here won't talk," Nadler says. "Without you."

"Now, young lady," Nadler says, "Tell me your name and where you came from?"

When I turn to Dan, he nods, but I have no answers.

"I don't know, and I can't remember," I say, whispering and sounding like I'm on the brink of tears.

I don't remember yesterday. Memories of my entire past no longer exist. I have Knowing. I'm not sure how I know, but I understand I must keep my secrets.

"Permission to speak, sir," Dan says, addressing Nadler.

Nadler nods.

"She's been through a traumatic experience," Dan says. "She must be in shock. We found her covered in Sergeant Jenkins' blood, and she witnessed the broken bone sticking out of his leg." He pauses. "I'm sure it's overwhelming for a child. Someone must miss her. With more time ..."

I read Dan's uneasiness. He's unsure if his opinion is welcome. Nadler's face is hard like stone.

Rescuing him, I blurt out my first thought.

"They're all dead. They're all dead. I can't remember."

I stare at the floor, praying they'll stop their questioning.

"Okay, Miss, you're safe here," Nadler says. "You're safe now."

His voice is soothing.

"Who's dead? Your family? Your people? Can you tell me what happened?"

I shake my head, trying to force tears. "I can't remember, and I don't know. It's gone …"

"What's gone?"

"All my thoughts. I can't remember."

I peek to see the officers trading blank stares. Dan shrugs. Nadler sighs again and stands.

He believes me; this, I'm sure. After all, it's true—I can't remember anything. The truth doesn't bother me. It's a fact I remember nothing, and I accept that fact.

§

After Dan and I finish dinner, a nurse arrives to settle me in the nurse's quarters.

"No. I won't go. I'm staying with Dan."

"Look, princess, I'll stop by to get you in the morning. I'm a grown man, and you can't sleep in the barracks with me."

"Why not?" I say, raising my voice in pitch.

"Listen, princess, you catch a good night's sleep, and I'll take you for breakfast in the morning. We'll visit Andrew together, I promise."

"No, don't make me go. I'm scared. What if I need you, or you leave, and I won't even know? What if someone tries to hurt me?" That should work.

Dan looks defeated and tired. The nurse sighs.

"There's a Comfort Room we occasionally use for visitors. We can add another cot for tonight. It will give the child another day to acclimate to the base. I hate the idea, but she's afraid of everyone except you," she says.

I switch on my poker face.

"Ok, princess, one night, and tomorrow we'll move you to the nurse's quarters. You've had a tough time today, so I guess we can make an exception for tonight. But you must go right to sleep. Understand?"

I nod in agreement. It worked.

§

My mouth tastes like peppermint from the toothbrush and toothpaste the nurse provided, and it's a welcome improvement over the taste of dirt road. She also furnished me with a plain nightgown and more underclothing. They placed my cot as far away from Dan's as possible in that modest Comfort Room. Dan prepares for bed in his undershirt and sweatpants,

11

tucks me in, turns the lights down low, and crawls under his covers. After a few minutes, I sneak out of my cot and slip in next to him. Dan sits up straight.

"No, no, princess, you have to stay in your own bed. Come on, you promised."

"No, I promised to go to sleep." I turn away from him and pretend to be asleep. I doubt my soft snoring convinces Dan, but he gives up and settles behind me. It takes a while until his even breathing tells me he's fallen asleep. I do the same.

CHAPTER 2

My eyes open wide. With no windows, it's hard to tell if it's day or night so I turn the light up brighter, then slip back in bed facing Dan, who's still in dreamland. A little gold cross hangs from his neck on a thin gold chain. I take it in my hand to examine it and turn it over. Engraved at the top is a tiny letter "D," and at the bottom, "5/5." Maybe Dan's first initial and a date? His birthdate? An anniversary? I'm studying the cross necklace when Dan opens his eyes. He checks his watch.

"Is it morning yet?" I ask.

"Yeah. How long have you been up?"

"I just woke. Why is this called a Comfort Room? It's not very comfortable."

"Well, princess, they're for officers and women to … get better acquainted. And you'd probably be more comfortable in your own bed."

"Like friends? Or lovers?"

Dan lifts his eyebrows.

"Are we better acquainted?" I ask.

"Get dressed. I'm hungry, are you? We have a lot to do today."

We eat breakfast, then head to the hospital section of the base to visit Andrew. He's groggy but smiles when we enter his room. I notice his kind hazel eyes, short black hair, and high cheekbones.

"There's my Angel of Mercy," Andrew says.

A pulley hoists his leg with an attached rope to elevate it. I walk over to him and read him to assess his condition. His pain is manageable, and I'm aware they've given him something to make him more comfortable. He gazes past me at Dan, and sadness covers his face.

"I guess you'll have to carry on without me."

"Hey, I'm sticking around for a while. You'll be up chasing skirts soon

13

enough. I'll save you a couple."

I squint at Dan. Chasing skirts? Why would he do that?

"There's a child in the room," Andrew says in a whisper.

Dan nods. "Yeah, we need to find where she belongs. We found this child out there stranded on her own. But lucky for you, this smart little girl put a tourniquet on your leg."

Andrew reaches out to me, so I hold his hand.

"Thank you, my angel. You saved my life."

I like this Andrew, this Buddy.

§

I spend my days learning my way around, eating meals, and visiting Andrew. Our initial visits with him had to be short, but we increase our stays each day. Doctors say it speeds up his recovery.

On our way to visit Andrew this morning, I ask Dan, "What is this place, and why do they call it Westview? Who are all these people?"

"It's a military base. We're called the Peace Force, and it's our mission to protect civilians and enforce the law. The Overlords must have named it Westview a long time ago."

Overlords? My stomach ties in knots. I wish I could remember.

"Are there other bases?"

"Besides an unknown number of Overlord base clusters, we have six military bases, including this one, and six civilian bases in our cluster."

"What's a cluster?"

"Several bases connected by tunnels."

"Who lives on civilian bases?"

"Well, everyone was born on a civilian base and grew up there. Those who join the Peace Force, most likely transfer to a military base, although civilian bases retain a military presence. Do you remember anything yet?"

"No. Why did you join the Peace Force?"

"To make a difference. To make sure we're all safe."

"From what? Overlords? The Boogeyman?" I ask. I giggle.

He doesn't respond.

"Is that why you were out there?" I ask.

"Did anyone ever tell you, you ask too many questions?"

"I don't remember." I wink at him. "Asking questions is how I learn."

When we reach Andrew's room, I notice well wishes plastering his cast, and Dan hands me a pen. I sign it "Get better, Angel" in red marker.

§

Sometimes Dan has other obligations, ones that can't include me. At first,

14

he was unsure what to do with me, but after I expressed my love of reading, he began taking me on trips to the library. It's always deserted and becomes my private sanctuary. Dan always promises to return for me, and he does, even though I've learned my way. Sometimes I bring books back with me, and during my visits with Andrew, I read to him. He enjoys that and was surprised I didn't struggle with most of the big words. I asked Dan if I could get a sketch pad and drawing pencils, and he promised to see what he could manage. The next morning, he surprised me with a medium-sized sketch pad and a cache of charcoal pencils.

§

Westview has been my home for two weeks now, and today I sense a foreboding. Dan and Andrew seem uneasy, trading guarded glances. Dan sits me down, telling me he must discuss an important matter with me.

"Princess, my unit ships out tomorrow, and I'll be leaving with them."

"Take me with you."

"You can't go with me. Major Nadler hasn't heard from all the civilian bases. You belong with your family. You can't stay here, and you're not allowed where I'm going."

He wraps me in his arms and comforts me.

"I'll be alone. Who'll I sleep with? Who'll protect me?"

I sleep on my cot now, but we still share the Comfort Room.

"Stay here with Andrew and keep him company until they figure out where you belong. It's the best thing for you. Princess, you're too young for military life. You must stay strong. I'll miss you, but I'll know you're safe."

He kisses my forehead, and I'm already missing him.

"Promise you'll say goodbye before you leave."

"I promise."

He's right about Andrew needing me. Pain overwhelms him sometimes, and I've made it my job to ease his suffering. And I'm a great distraction. I sing or read to him or dream up stories, often silly ones, making him laugh. They move my few belongings and my cot to Andrew's hospital room, and I spend my first night there. The next morning, Dan stops by for our goodbyes, but I'm not ready to let go.

"Buddy, you get better fast because we have plans. And take care of my little princess for me," he says with a wink.

"She's my Angel," Andrew says.

Andrew calls me Angel, so I guess that's my name. It doesn't fit, but he likes it. Andrew isn't in any shape to take care of me. I'll be caring for him, but it gives me a strong purpose. After all, I am strong and fearless. I tuck my sadness and despair down deep inside me and present a brave face. Dan will not see me cry.

15

"Goodbye, Dan. You better not forget me because I'll never forget you," I say. I kiss his cheek and give him a long hug and a forced smile. "Have a safe trip."

"I won't forget you," he whispers in my ear. "You behave yourself."

No promise from either of us as to the future.

§

My pillow muffles my sobs. I miss Dan so much already. My tears fall fast and hard, soaking my pillow. Andrew doesn't need to know, and I'm allowing only one night for my grief.

CHAPTER 3

Dan left a few days ago, so I sit alone in the cafeteria, killing time while nurses bathe Andrew. Military personnel congregate, eating, drinking, talking, laughing, and circulating. Nadler was nowhere in sight when I sat to eat lunch, but now he stands before me, gesturing toward the empty seat across from me. I nod, and he sits.

"How are you getting along? I understand they gave you a name. Angel, is it?" Nadler stares like a dog watching a squirrel to see if I'll answer.

"I'm fine. Yes, Andrew calls me Angel, and I like it."

"We've been trying to discover where you belong. No record of missing children from any of our bases. It's impossible to leave a base—except through the tunnel, and they're guarded extremely well. It's improbable for anyone, much less a child, to slip past guards."

His eyes stay on me as I swallow another bite.

"The doctor thinks you're at least thirteen. Have you remembered anything yet? Were you born in the outside world? In a village? Are you a member of the Overlords?"

Overlords. I shudder at their mention.

"No, I don't know, I doubt it, and I'm not."

Dan spoke of the Overlords with reverence as if they were Saviors, but they sounded more like Captors. They rounded up citizens and mandated them to inhabit the bases. He said it happened a lifetime ago—around 2030. He supposed everyone alive now was born on civilian bases and experienced no other way of living. To me, the Overlords are The Enemy. Nadler doesn't need to know. Nobody does.

Nadler's strange gaze spooks me.

"Sergeant Matthews reported finding you near a village."

My body tenses with a warning. He's lying.

"Why are you lying to me?"

"What makes you think I'm lying?" He tilts his head and grins.

"I sense when someone lies, and you are lying." Did I offer too much? The rest of my lunch elapses without words.

§

Andrew wakes in a foul mood, irritable, snapping at the nurse, complaining about pain, exhibiting intense sadness, refusing dinner, and not wanting me to read to him. With my hand on his shoulder, I sense his darkness, so I slide into bed on his good side and lay my head on his chest, and he allows me. Reaching over, I place my hand above his cast and search for the precise spot. I apply pressure, not too hard, but enough to send my energy to block his pain. Like I did for him in the forest after his jeep crashed.

"What are you doing?" Andrew asks. He relaxes, sighing in relief; his pain recedes now.

"I'll sit with you in your darkness until your storm passes and you find the light," I say.

I share the warmth of my body and the comfort of my caring. He remains silent and soon falls asleep, so I'm careful to leave his bedside without disturbing him. Preparing for bed, I sense him watching me. I turn to witness a grin flash across his face before he closes his eyes again. He appears pleased I'm here to help him. The storm has passed.

§

Today Andrew and I spent the afternoon talking, laughing, and being silly. I sketched several drawings of butterflies, flowers, a turtle, and a picture of a window with trees and birds outside. I'm taping them to his bare, beige windowless walls.

Andrew understands I've lost my memory, so he shares stories from his past and his friendship with Dan. He, Dan, and two others had enrolled in the same training camp and had become best friends in their two years of training. Their instructor favored them, and they remained in close contact when they graduated. They're his family, his brothers, and they plan to serve together on the same military base once they master their area of interest. For Dan and Andrew, salvage runs are the big draw, and they're gaining experience from the ground up.

Andrew removes his cross necklace, holds it up, and stares at it.

"It'll never happen, now," he says, lowering his head, shaking it, and frowning like someone who's lost everything.

I take the cross necklace from him, turn it over, and notice the letter "A" at the top and the fraction or date "4/5" near the bottom. Identical to

Dan's, except for the engravings, his necklace must have significance.

"You'll be successful once you're back on your feet, and I'm sure there's a reason this happened. Look, it brought us together. Everything happens for a reason, and we're guided to our destiny. I don't know how I know this, but I do. I call it my Knowing."

"Knowing? How?"

"I'm not sure. Often, things pop into my mind. I simply know things."

"What are your dreams, Angel? What is your destiny?"

"When it's time, I'll know. You need me to stay and help you, so this is where I belong."

Andrew's bewildered expression fades into acceptance. With his depression at bay, warm feelings wash over me, knowing I'm able to bring him back.

§

Over the past few weeks, Andrew has needed me to join with him to quell his darkness several times and help him deal with his pain by applying my energy. He doesn't understand it but believes my story that there are pressure points that control pain. When he asked why the doctors weren't aware of it, I convinced him it was a different type of healing that should remain our secret. It frees him of his suffering, so he accepts it.

As his healing shows signs of progress and Andrew becomes more mobile, he doesn't require my help as much. His bouts of depression occur less often, and the pain is more manageable. Andrew's need for me changes in other ways. Whenever a pretty nurse pops in, he's uncomfortable with my presence, and that's my cue to excuse myself.

§

The busy cafeteria provides an excellent opportunity for people-watching, and I regret leaving my sketchpad behind. I'm almost finished eating when Nadler finds me.

"Mind if I join you?" he asks.

I nod and he sits. What does he want this time? Nadler has found me in the cafeteria several times, asking me more questions or engaging in banal chit-chat. I'm not sure I like him, but Andrew advised me to be courteous to high-ranking officers like Major Nadler.

Another officer joins us, and he and Nadler engage in a brief conversation beyond my understanding, but he is deceitful. He rises to leave, and Nadler turns his attention to me, seeming to expect something, and I soon realize he's testing me.

After several minutes of playing dumb, I extend my hand. He takes it.

"You know he was lying."

It isn't a question or a challenge. It's a statement of fact.

Nadler appears surprised but pleased somehow.

"You knew he was lying, so why didn't you say something?" he asks.

"It's not my concern. The fact you're testing me is."

"What else can you do? Can you read minds?"

"I Pay Attention, that's all. If you Pay Attention, people reveal their secrets. I'm uncertain how it works, but it does. Can't you do it?"

"If only I could, it would make my job considerably easier."

"What's your purpose here?" I ask, curious for the first time about Nadler.

"My purpose, Angel, is to uncover people's secrets and discover what they're hiding. Sometimes individuals commit crimes, and it's my responsibility to unearth the truth and see justice served. I protect decent people from those who break the law."

That sounds like a respectable job to me.

"Did you think I was a criminal? Is that why you questioned me?"

"No, of course not, Angel. We found you, lost and traumatized, and I wanted to help you figure out where you belong, but I'm starting to think you belong right here. How do you feel about that?"

I shrug. It appears I'm here to stay. It's been several weeks. I'm happy being Andrew's companion and enjoy the prospect of belonging. They don't allow anybody under the age of eighteen on a military base, so I'm an exception, special.

The afternoon flies by, and Andrew sleeps soundly. Bored, I head back to the cafeteria for people-watching, to study how they act and treat one another. Certain men command and others respectfully follow, but their treatment of women is most curious. Men only speak to women when asking them to accompany them. Once I questioned Andrew about that, and he claimed they visited Comfort Rooms to play nice together, assuring me I'd understand when I'm older.

This time I bring my sketch pad and pencil and draw officers one table over. Three officers eat their meals while carrying on a conversation, so I save a still picture in my mind so that if someone leaves, I can finish my drawing. I'm engrossed and concentrating hard.

"You're pretty good at that, aren't you?"

Nadler sits at the table across from me.

"How long have you been sitting there?"

"Not long. How did you learn to draw like that? I'm impressed."

"It's easy. I store a picture in my brain, imagine it on paper, and draw what I see."

"You take a picture with your mind?"

"Yes, of course. Can't you?"

"No. I'm not aware of anyone who can, besides you."

He stares into the distance for a moment.

"You have a photographic memory. It's rare, but I've heard of that. Are you able to read a book and then recite what you read?"

"Sure. I can remember one page at a time."

"What else can you do?"

I shrug.

"May I see your other drawings?"

I've filled several pages in my sketchbook with artwork. I pass it to him, and he examines my first drawing, taking his time. It depicts Dan from the waist up. It was fortuitous of me to create the drawing, now that Dan has gone. I keep it to remember him. My drawing and his shirt are my treasures.

The next drawing shows Andrew in his hospital bed, also from the waist up. He was watching me while I read to him when I captured the picture in my mind. It shows him smiling, enjoying the story.

The third drawing displays a butterfly emerging from her cocoon. The half-human butterfly has long, dark hair and struggles to free herself. Halfway out, her graceful wings unfurl behind her. She can't take flight until she's liberated. Nadler studies this drawing with great interest.

"You snapped a photograph of this butterfly girl with your mind?"

My laugh erupts in a loud burst.

"Of course not. There's no such thing. I made her up in my imagination."

Nadler, appearing pleased about making me laugh, examines the remaining drawings. They're doodles and designs without meaning, some might be flowers, and others could pass as birds, while some doodles resemble nothing in nature. He scrutinizes my current half-finished drawing. One officer left their table earlier, but the illustration shows all three officers, although shading and details remain unfinished. Nadler nods in approval.

"These drawings are fantastic. Well done." Nadler stares at nothing in deep concentration. Before I can read him, he turns his gaze to me with a strange expression. "Stay here. I'll be right back to try an experiment."

I continue drawing until he returns.

§

Nadler says, "I'd like to try something."

He pulls a card from a deck of playing cards, studies it, and holds it up, hiding its face.

"What card am I holding up?" he asks.

I read him to figure out his game, then I touch his arm and say, "She's a queen like her upside-down twin sister."

Nadler smiles, takes another card, holds it up, and fixes his eyes on me.

"You must look at the card first."

He peeks at the card.

"Number three on its upper left side, and inverted number three, on its bottom corner."

"Amazing! Do you know what I'm thinking?"

"That I'm amazing." I giggle.

He laughs, and then gets serious. "Can you … tell me what I'm thinking?"

"No, it doesn't work that way."

He needs reassurance. It's true, I can easily enter his consciousness, but I'm smart enough to know the danger of revealing that. Instinct warns me to let him think it necessary to touch him, to read him, and that my skills are limited.

"How does it work, then?"

"I'm not sure. You must concentrate on an object before I can picture it or sense it. It's difficult to do. Generally, I catch an odd feeling without details, but you intend for me to see, so it's clear."

He doesn't need to know what happens when I Pay Attention.

§

Four months have passed with me gaining weight and growing taller. A military woman ushers me into a small office where she and her associate measure me for clothes I'm told will be civilian wear. They inform me they'll make my clothes somewhat bigger and expandable.

"Why?" I ask.

"Because you'll grow more." The woman speaking stands behind me, out of my view.

"Why can't I wear clothes like yours?" I ask the military woman tending to me. She wears the same uniform, dark blue pants with a light blue blouse, that all military women wear. She's recording my measurements and stops to glare at me.

"Because you're too young, and you must earn it. We undergo very difficult training and earn our right to wear the uniform of the Peace Force."

She throws her shoulders back and thrusts her chin forward. Her comrade moves to my side, straightens herself, hands on her hips, chest out in agreement. They spank me with their tone for being presumptuous, but I desire to blend in, not stick out, and not always be different.

§

Plenty of empty tables in the cafeteria make it easy to grab one by myself, and Nadler is nowhere in sight. I sit alone, drooling over my plate full of noodles in a creamy white sauce and green peas with little chunks of white meat that taste like chicken. After savoring each mouthful, I soon join the Clean Plate Club.

Finished with lunch, Nadler finds me and asks to join me. I nod and he takes a seat.

"I haven't seen you for a few days. You aren't avoiding me, are you?" he asks.

"Nope. I've been busy, that's all."

"Busy doing what?"

"Stuff."

"I've been thinking you might need a female guardian. I want you to meet Miss Elly. She'll help with any problems you might have … you know, girl stuff."

"I don't need anyone. I have Andrew, and he has me."

"Okay, but let's meet her, anyway. You've been on the base for several months now without real supervision. You need a female caretaker to monitor you and help with matters Andrew can't, matters that might embarrass you to discuss with him."

Nadler escorts me to his spotless outer office and introduces me to his receptionist, Miss Elly. She looks around thirty, with short, military-style hair and muscular like all military women since they expect them to exercise too. I sit in a cold metal chair in front of her tidy desk.

"Where do you sleep, child?"

"My name is Angel, and I sleep at the hospital with Andrew in his room."

"Well, we'll fix that. I'll find something in the women's quarters."

"I need to stay with Andrew to help him."

"It's inappropriate for you to share a room with a grown man. I'll remedy that. My job is to teach you how to be a woman, keep yourself clean and hair brushed, manage manners, and protect yourself from men. You have enough clothes?"

"Yes, ma'am. The nurses found me extra clothes to wear. They measured me for more clothes, but they haven't arrived yet."

Miss Elly nods in approval. She walks around her desk and picks up my long ponytail with an air of disdain.

"We'll have this cut shorter. Make it easier to manage."

"First, I've shared a room with a grown man for longer than four months now and nothing inappropriate happened. Second, there's nothing wrong with my hair. I take care of it, and I keep myself very clean, and I always brush my hair and my teeth. And third, I can't stay away from men. They're everywhere."

I stand, ready to leave. We're not going to get along.

Miss Elly shakes her head.

"Do the nurses provide you with feminine hygiene products?" Miss Elly makes a face I don't understand.

"What for?"

Miss Elly softens. She sits me down to explain something she calls periods, and Nadler excuses himself.

§

It takes a month for my clothes to reach Westview. They're nicer than the clothes I've seen civilian domestics in the cafeteria wear. Although a significant improvement, I'm still different. Last week, Miss Elly found me quarters near her. That's one battle I lost, but I'm keeping my long hair. She hasn't proven to be a problem, although she's strict, and it's obvious to me I'm a burden. Lucky for me, I'm not required to spend much time with her.

Andrew is sound asleep when I enter his hospital room, so the book I bring to read to him will wait. Instead, I turn on my CD player. My music may be over a century old, but it's fresh to me, and I love it. I've learned that after the Overlords transferred everyone to bases, no new music discs were produced, so all recorded music is over fifty years old. I chose this music CD with the title *"City of Angels,"* because of the word angels in the title, clearly meaning it should be mine. With headphones on, I sing softly to myself, so I don't disturb my sleeping Buddy. My song speaks of God sending his angels and asking if everything will be all right.

My feet move with the music as I sashay and sing to myself. Andrew wakes and watches me, so I sing out loud and continue dancing. His big smile shows he enjoys my company. When the song finishes, I turn off the player.

"Did I wake you? I didn't mean to."

"It's okay. I sleep too much anyway. Where did you get your music and player?"

"I asked Miss Elly if I could have some music, and she brought me the player. Major Nadler took me to an enormous room where salvage crews unload their bounty. He let me select a few compact discs. I chose three."

"Do you believe in angels?" he asks.

I shrug. "I know nothing about them. Are they real?"

"You're an angel, and you're real, aren't you?"

That makes me smile.

"I brought a book to read to you. Are you in the mood?"

"Sure."

After reading for a while, Andrew's soft snoring tells me he's fallen back to sleep.

§

Six months have passed since the day I arrived at Westview.

"Angel, sit down. I have some news," Andrew says.

Nadler walks in, and my stomach somersaults. This can't be good news.

"I'm recovering, and they're transferring me to a rehab facility."

"Okay, great, take me with you. You know I can be a tremendous help."

Andrew's pained expression means sorrow heads my way.

"You can't go with me. Rehab will be tough, but there'll be nurses to care for me."

Nadler puts his arm around me. "I'll be looking after you, and Miss Elly and I will tend to all your needs."

I'm not afraid to stay, but I can't stand to lose Andrew.

Andrew nods. Nadler pats me on my head and leaves us alone.

"Please, take me with you. Don't leave me here alone. I'd miss you too much. You're so important to me." I refuse to cry—but I'm grieving already, and my hands shake.

"Angel, I'll see you again soon. When I'm finished with rehab, and I'm walking on two sturdy legs, first thing, I'm gonna find you and take care of you. It's my turn."

He lifts my face to make eye contact and removes his cross necklace.

"I want you to hold on to this for me. It's not a gift. It's a loan. I need you to take care of it for me; its magic will keep you safe. When you miss me too much, hold it tight in your hand and remember I'm coming back to take care of you, my Angel. When that day comes, you can return it to me."

Andrew secures the necklace around my neck. I don't believe in magic, but it seems he does. I must trust his decision and believe his promise, and I can't make it harder for him to leave because he needs rehab. It's true, I need him, but for his sake, I must let go. This, our last evening together, I must stay strong.

§

I sob into my pillow, muffling my cries. I'm not afraid someone will hear me in my room, but I don't want to hear myself.

CHAPTER 4

My living quarters are quiet and cozy—now that I've taped my favorite drawings on the bare gray walls. Nobody enters without my consent, but it's best to allow Miss Elly entry, though it doesn't happen often. My room came furnished with a comfortable single bed, a writing desk with a chair, an adequate bookcase, and a private bathroom. Nadler found me more drawing paper and pencils, which store nicely inside my old lift-top wooden desk. I stocked my bookcase with library books on history, science, math, geography, and philosophy. Plus, a fictional book about a girl following a talking bunny down its rabbit hole into a peculiar world.

I'm almost fourteen, I guess, according to the first doctor. Miss Elly takes me to see another doctor because I still haven't had my period. I don't understand why that's so important because I don't want one, and somehow, I understand I'll never have one. It's the Knowing.

The doctor seems confused when he examines me. My small breasts and slightly rounded hips give me the shape of a young woman, but I lack hair under my arms or covering my legs. He seems to think that's important. They still view me as a child. The doctor says all my permanent teeth have come in, including my wisdom teeth, something rare, based on his reaction. When I ask him if having my wisdom teeth means I'm smart, he ignores me, but he asserts only adults have all their teeth. It seems I'm a medical mystery. I don't see what difference it makes. I'm just me.

It would have delighted me to spend my days in my quarters reading, learning, and drawing, but Nadler had special plans for me. I spend part of each day in Nadler's spacious office, where he tutors me in the rules of conduct and his expectations of me. Nadler says our work is particularly important, and whatever happens must stay between the two of us. Classified, he calls it. I'm never to breathe a word to anyone about my role, not even Miss Elly. Not anything I see, hear, or do. I must speak solely to him about my work. Nadler calls himself my handler, and I am a Civilian Asset. That sounds important. I already keep my secrets, so this should be easy. We repeat my lessons daily, and he tests me at random times.

Sometimes we meet in an anteroom off Nadler's office for my lessons. It's modest, with a leather couch and a small wooden side table. Today, I'm sitting up straight on the couch while he repeats my lesson on the proper way to address the officers. He advises me not to speak unless spoken to, and to limit my answers to yes, sir; no, sir. To always be polite. He says it's of paramount importance to never talk about what I do. Lie if I must. He says sometimes it's okay to tell a little lie—except to him. Never lie to him. I can handle this.

Every time we meet, he reiterates these points, making sure I fully understand them.

Today, Nadler explains the ranking system. On all military bases, except Central Control, the highest-level officer is the Commander. His team comprises several Majors; at Westview, that team includes Major Nadler. Majors command First Lieutenants. Second Lieutenants are special officers who hold an array of responsibilities, including lawyers, doctors, and other specialists, who aren't considered upper echelons. Below First Lieutenants are Staff Sergeants, Sergeants, Corporals, Privates, and Specialists in that order. A soldier has the starting rank of Private, the lowest male military ranking unless they're chosen for an officer's track. Military females have but one rank, Specialist, and can never earn a higher rank.

I'm told the highest-ranking officers in the Peace Force reside at Central Control, the largest military base, and it's improbable I'll ever meet any of them. Everyone outranks me, even the civilian domestics, because of my age, so I must always be respectful and follow protocol. I'm allowed to call military women by their given name, but I must always address men by their rank and surname. I ask Nadler what my rank is, and he says that as a child, I have no ranking.

"You know you're very important to me." Nadler's voice becomes soft, and he gazes at me with tenderness. Today's lesson has ended.

"You'll belong to me, be my girl. Anything we do together is okay. Do you understand?"

I nod.

Nadler sits next to me on the couch, close, with our knees touching.

"I need you to do me a favor."

I shrug. He unzips his pants.

What? He tries to push my head down. I squirm, pushing away from him. My legs feel like rubber stumbling out of the room. I can't tell anyone, not even Miss Elly, who warned me about men. I keep my word.

§

Several days have passed, and Nadler has spared me his intentions. I need information on what Nadler wants. Was that sex, and was it okay? The library lacks books about sex, and I have little knowledge. I search everywhere, and I'm ready to abandon hope when an officer strolls into the library, but I can't discern his rank. I must be especially polite to high-ranking officers. He might be familiar with books on sex or health, but rules dictate I must wait until he speaks first—to be safe. So, I stand, wearing an expression begging him to acknowledge me.

"Well, who are you?"

"I'm called Angel. Can you show me where the books on sex are?"

"Well, I doubt you'll find any out here," he says, smiling. "We keep sexual materials beyond this door. What do you want to know?"

"Everything. Because … I know nothing." I grasp the doorknob.

"You can't go in there. You're too young, and not allowed." He pauses and says, "I suppose we could take a brief look, but we can't tell anyone."

"I can keep a secret. Do they have books in there?"

"They have movies, which are better because you can watch them in action, and it's faster than reading."

He slips the door open after ensuring privacy and quickly ushers me in. Boxes, movies, and magazines fill gray metal shelves along a wall. The officer sets up a video player, sits in a chair in front of it, and instructs me to hop on his lap. He starts the video, and right there on the screen, naked men and women perform acts I've never seen. It's fascinating.

I see what Nadler wanted of me. I close my eyes and gag, fighting the urge to vomit. Nope, I will never, ever do that. My eyes remain clamped shut until the officer announces it's safe to open them.

The movie continues showing other acts, but when another woman does the gross act, I'm ready to leave, so I slide off his lap and stand by the door. The officer cautions me to keep this secret.

"If you tell anyone I let you in here, they'll punish us both. They'll strip me to the waist."

"Then what?"

"Whipped," he says. "They won't do that to you, but they'll punish you. They'll spank your behind hard with a strap."

My stomach threatens to expel its contents. I break out in a cold sweat.

"We did nothing wrong," he says, his voice now soft as if to console me. "You asked about sex, and I showed you. But they'll think it's wrong. They won't understand."

I don't understand. Why would they punish us? It sounds worse for him, and he's been nice, teaching me about sex, and I'll never betray him.

"I'll never tell a soul. I don't want them to punish either of us, but I

28

should leave now."

The officer opens the door, makes certain the coast is clear, and lets me out. He must have liked the movie because he stays inside.

§

After a two-day break, Nadler sequesters me in his antechamber for one of our instruction sessions. This lesson is brief, reviewing past lessons. He studies me with a softened gaze, and class is over.

§

In my room, I discover a tinge of blood on my panties. I guess it's my period that Miss Elly warned me about, but it's a tiny amount of bleeding. Nadler says I'm a woman now, he loves me, and I'm special. It's our secret.

§

I've been in training for a month now and I'm looking forward to field work with my handler. We're planning to meet later, but I want permission to explore the basement so I'm hunting him down.

Nadler isn't in his office, but I know he sometimes works in the prison area, where I'm never invited. When I pass through the gray steel doors of the prison, it's clear why. Whipping sounds echo through the prison chamber, causing my heart to race. A male voice groans in agony, followed by more whipping sounds, and gut-wrenching moans. Inside one of the prison cells, a shirtless detainee stands shackled to the wall. An officer raises his arm to strike the tormented man's raw back. His suffering rips through me when the strap hits his flesh. I rush to the bars, falling to my knees.

I scream and scream and scream.

Holding on to the bars, as if that would magically end this, with eyes closed, I screech.

"Please stop. I hate this. It's wrong. Why are you hurting him? I can't stand this."

Hands pull at me, trying to force me to leave, but I become dead weight and crumble to the floor. Then a hand cups my face, bringing my head up.

"Angel, open your eyes. Look."

Nadler's gentle but firm voice commands my attention, and I obey his order. The horrible officer wielding the strap steps away while another officer removes the shackles from the beaten man. They put him in handcuffs and lead him away.

"Where are they taking him?"

"To the infirmary to dress his back."

"Why did they do that? They hurt him so bad." My terror rises.

Nadler squats to my level, his voice calm. He answers, saying the prisoner has information they need, and he won't talk. I remember my first day. I didn't talk at first, either. My stomach heaves, and I taste bitter bile. I take deep breaths to keep from vomiting.

"Would you hurt me like that?"

The movie room officer warned me what would happen if I revealed our secret. They'd whip my butt. I wasn't sure I believed him, but I do now.

"No, Angel, you're a child and very special to me. I'll never hurt you."

Comforted somewhat, I allow Nadler to pull me up and walk me to his office. I glare at three other cruel officers, feeling safe with my guardian, indicting them, guilty of complacency. They regard one another like I spoiled their fun time, some shaking their heads. If they feel terrible over a child witnessing a senseless whipping, then fine, I want them to feel awful.

Back at the office, Nadler provides a glass of water and sits with me.

"The detainee is a spy. Somehow, he breached our secure base. We must learn what he was doing, and to whom he reports."

These matters are beyond my experience, but it's clear to me there's danger in this.

"A spy? For the Overlords? If he's spying for them, then they're aware he's at Westview and would intend to get him back. If we hurt this man, the Overlords might seek revenge and hurt us far worse. What happens to him now? If you release him, it'll be dangerous for us, and if you keep him or kill him, it'll be equally serious. This is wrong."

"Angel, please. You must leave this to me."

"I can discover whatever you need to know without hurting anyone. Give me a chance. It may take longer, but I'm sure it's the best way."

§

I befriend the spy, and we spend several hours together, first in the prison infirmary and then in the prison. After many such visits, he learns to trust me and tells me his name is Scott. The officer who whipped him has stayed away as Nadler promised, and Scott's back has healed. He has a kind face, reminding me of Dan.

"Whipping you was horrible." I cringe at the memory. "We're not all cruel, and if I could make amends would you forgive us?"

He leans forward and crosses his arms.

"You're a child—what could you do?"

I lock eyes with Scott.

"Say yes, and I'll show you."

He bites his lip.

"Yes."

§

I secure a key, unlock his cell, and distract the guard long enough for him to escape. There's no possibility of escaping through a tunnel crawling with guards, but Scott claims to know a way, so I follow him through a hidden passage. Once we're inside a concealed corridor, he turns to me.

"Come with me, Angel. It's the only way out. Your people will punish you, but we'll welcome you with open arms."

There's no doubt I'd be welcome, and that it would be my end. They are The Enemy, and I feel this on a deep level. But this poor soul has suffered. Beating him was wrong and setting him free is the only reasonable course.

"I can't. They won't hurt me. I'm a child. Please, remember your promise. Hurry."

I pray to all gods I'm correct. Nadler promised. The thought of a strap hitting my bottom makes me tremble, so I won't think about it. What's right is right, after all.

§

Back in my quarters, Miss Elly bangs on my door and proclaims I must report to Nadler's office. A prisoner escaped, and Nadler wants me with him. She escorts me to his office. I have never seen Nadler so livid. He clenches his fists and punches the air, and a vein in his neck bulges like it wants to burst.

"Angel, a prisoner broke out, and the entire base will remain on lockdown," he pants, "until we catch him and we're all safe. I want you to stay close to me."

I draw in a deep breath and cast my gaze on the floor.

"We're safe because Scott's gone. He left an hour ago."

Nadler stares at me with utter disbelief.

"His name is Scott, and he came from a village nearby looking for food and needed medicine." It's not true, but it's necessary to lie sometimes.

"He wasn't a spy. He wouldn't talk—to protect the other villagers." My lies compound as I invent new ones. "Scott told me his wife and children are waiting for him. I felt awful for what we did to him, so I helped him."

It's a giant leap of faith, taking Nadler at his word that he won't punish me. What will I do if I'm wrong? Nadler's face turns beet red, and I can't tell whether it's anger or contempt on his face. I took the moral road, no matter my fate. He needs to understand.

He calls in others to discuss the turn of events.

Nadler shakes his head in disgust. "I'm confining you to quarters."

He glares at me. "Until further notice."

"Yes, sir."

CHAPTER 5

As punishment, my quarters become my provisional prison when I'm not taking meals with Nadler or working with him. Today, he initiates me with my first interview assignment, where I'll inform him if the subject is truthful. Our strategy includes me pretending to be slow, timid, and uncooperative. Nadler will make a case for my presence, and while he questions the subject, I'll Pay Attention, determine his truthfulness, and discover whatever he's hiding. I'll sit close to him and touch his arm if he allows. That's our plan.

The small interview room contains four chairs and a table displaying a hook secured on one side to permit handcuffing the subject if required. Handcuffed to the table sits a rugged, weathered fellow in his thirties with a five o'clock shadow. He appears unkempt and unclean but shows no signs of torture. Nadler promised me he would harm no one, and I'll prove to him it's unnecessary.

Nadler orders me to sit next to the subject and roughly nudges me into the seat, making it easier to pretend I dislike him and don't appreciate being here. I squint at my seatmate, looking him over. Nadler sits across from me, and a familiar officer joins him to his left, across from the subject. He's the cruel officer who used his strap on Scott, and that intimidating strap, now in front of him, coils snakelike on the table in a threatening pose. Shackles hang from the far wall, and I shudder until I remember Nadler's promise. I take small comfort in knowing I'm not a subject.

"I'm Major Jim Nadler and this is Lieutenant Daemon Fischer. You both should understand the importance of telling the truth. If we catch you in a lie—there will be consequences. Lieutenant Fischer here is exceptional at getting at the truth—if necessary."

For effect, Fischer picks up the strap, fondles it, and sets it back down. The subject shifts in his seat, so I read him and sense his fear. Nadler promised me no harm would befall the subjects, and I need to remember that—and *breathe*. Trust is everything. Nadler told me so.

"If you're truthful, this will be easier on you. We caught both of you outside. Do you know each other?"

"I don't know her. Never saw her before," Rough Man says without turning my way.

I shake my head no.

"Why were you outside the base?"

"Scouting for food. I've heard the bases receive regular supplies of food, and I was hoping to grab some. I thought I could distract the soldiers and take a few rations."

"Were you working alone?"

"Yes."

Wrong, he's lying, and he's protecting someone. I signal with a slight motion to let Nadler know.

"If you're after food, we'll provide it, but you must be honest."

I touch the man's arm to learn his truth.

"I'm his child, and I was with him. My task was to distract the soldiers so my Poppy could steal us some food. I made noises near the truck and lured the soldiers away. That's when they caught my Poppy. He's all I have." I act scared and willing to say anything to save us. I'm channeling his son, a boy about twelve, who remains stranded alone out there.

The interview is over.

Rough Man looks at me in disbelief. I nod to him.

"Wait, she's not my daughter. Okay, my son was with me, but he's just a boy. Now he's out there alone, waiting for me to return. Honest, all we wanted was some food, I swear."

The subject squints, stares, and whispers to me.

"Poppy? How did you know?"

Nadler and Fischer exchange knowing glances.

§

I'm preparing for my next interview. Nadler reveals what happened to the first subject. They took him to the location where his son was hiding and waiting, gave them food, and sent them away. This happened a few days ago and was an easy and painless interview.

My second interview parallels my first experience. Same interview room, same table with handcuff hook, same seating arrangement, but this subject is military, one of their own, so he's not handcuffed. Daemon's present, but not threatening this time, and his sinister strap is nowhere in sight. There's no threat to be truthful because military personnel fully understand the punishment for lying to a superior officer. Nobody explains my presence.

"So, Alex, how are the salvage runs going?" asks Nadler. He's cordial, but it's obvious he wants answers.

"Excellent, sir."

"It seems a case of spirits came in with the latest haul and disappeared. Know anything?"

Alex hesitates. "No, sir. I heard about it, but I don't know what happened to it."

I give the signal—he's truthful.

For Nadler's benefit, I touch Alex's shoulder and peer into his eyes. He appears baffled. I read him and discover he's unaware of what became of the case of alcohol, but he knows the person who does. And now, so do I.

I ask Nadler to be excused, so he walks me out. In the hallway, I provide Nadler with the name of the person who knows the whereabouts of the alcohol, and I'm dismissed.

§

For the last six months, Nadler has given me dozens of assignments, training and testing me with each interview, and I faithfully deliver even when it's uncomfortable. He trusts me again, and I've regained my freedom to explore. We make a good team, and my ability to read Nadler and the subjects makes our interviews run smoothly. We always get to the truth. Nadler says he enjoys working with me and that I'm invaluable. I like that.

§

Several officers gather to use the showers after their P.T. The men's shower room fills with stinky men in all stages of undress, hiding their rank. After showering, they stand around drying off, horsing around, oblivious to their nudity—and oblivious to me. My little corner behind the lockers affords a full view but hides most of me. As in the women's showers, their nude physiques appear in various shades of coffee, from latte to mocha.

I peer out to observe their well-built bodies, with ripped muscles everywhere—torso, legs, and arms. Military personnel must exercise at least three times a week, but some officers must work out more often. Everyone on base, at least military people, seem like clones of each other. All are tall and similar in body size, except for differing skin tones and hair colors.

An ape-like shadow looms above me. Busted. A wet, naked hulk towers overhead, glaring down.

"So, what do we have here?"

His voice is gruff. Another officer, with a towel wrapped around his waist, joins him.

"Hey, that's Nadler's little girl. How'd she sneak in here?"

"I don't know, but she's leaving. Keep her here while I dress."

"Yes, sir."

Dressed, Gruff Man returns, grabs me by the arm, and we're on our way to Nadler's office. I'm sure my guardian won't be happy. He knocks on the half-open door, and Nadler grants us entrance. Gruff Man waits for Nadler to address him.

"What is it, Porter?" He appears worried, glancing from Porter to me and back again, but not angry.

"Found this little squirt hiding in the men's showers."

"Is that so?"

I nod and stare at my shoes. Why is it wrong? I guess I caused some excitement, so it must be. Nadler never let me see him naked.

"Thank you, Porter. I'll handle this."

"Yes, sir."

Porter leaves. Nadler laughs, shaking his head. Everything will be okay.

"What were you doing?" he asks with an incredulous expression. "The men's showers?"

"I was curious what men's bodies look like without their clothes, and everyone undresses in the showers. I wanted to check them out."

"You must stay clear of the men's showers. They don't allow females in there. Those are the rules. They don't allow men in the women's showers. Everyone likes their privacy."

How private is it with countless other naked individuals walking around? Indeed, I never saw men in women's showers, only women staring at me like I'm strange, even though I have the same lady parts they have.

"I promise never to do it again." I keep my promises.

"Good girl."

It appears Nadler was truthful when he said he would never punish me.

§

Miss Elly pulls me aside as I enter Nadler's office.

"Angel, today is Major Nadler's birthday and we'll be celebrating with my father in the Commander's dining room, but you won't be attending," Miss Elly says with a dismissive air.

I know it's his birthday and I don't expect an invite to Jim's celebration with Miss Elly and her father since I wasn't invited last year. She need not remind me her father is the Commander. I know.

Nadler and I have worked together for a year and a half now, and based on the doctor's estimation, I'm fifteen. I don't have birthdays, so every spring, I simply add a year.

My assignments have become more serious and sometimes questionable, but my loyalty to Nadler never wavers. I always make him happy with my contributions. Yesterday, I obtained permission to explore the basement to study the Overlords' symbolic writings they left behind. I copied the symbols to translate them. It's my hobby, and except for the men's showers, I'm allowed unrestricted access to the base in my free time. I'm eager to show my latest findings to Jim. He's always surprised and delighted when I reveal information gleaned from using my special secret skills. He allows me to call him Jim in private and never in front of Miss Elly. She would throw a fit.

Miss Elly is not at her desk, so I peek through Jim's half-open door, and he waves me in. I close the door and approach his desk.

"Happy birthday, Jim. I brought you a present."

I lay the paper with my symbol translations on his desk in front of him. Jim pushes away from his desk and motions for me to sit on his lap. I sit facing him.

"I'd love a present. You," Nadler says, drawing me in for a kiss.

Jim lifts my skirt to push my panties down. His hands cover my behind, and he whispers what he'd enjoy for his birthday.

The door flies open, Miss Elly bursts into the office, sees something we never intended to share, and drops her papers on the floor.

I stand, yanking up my panties as Miss Elly grabs me by the arm.

"Go straight to your room." She pushes me out the door.

Nadler says nothing.

§

Miss Elly paces in my room, and I don't have to read her to know she's fuming.

"You little whore. Do you know what they call girls like you? A tease."

She struts around me, and she's so angry I expect her to slap me.

"Wicked girls like you make life challenging for decent men. They're weak, especially when you offer yourself up like a damn tramp. They can't control themselves. You're too young and a mess of trouble for men."

I want to defend myself, but I'm at a loss for words.

"I've known all along what a little whore you are, pretending to be so innocent. Men gawk at you, and you love it. Jim looks at you like you're special, and you use it to get whatever you want. He treats you like you're something special, but I can tell you, you're just a little piece of nothing, using powerful men to get your way. You've no idea how serious this is, and if anyone else had walked in, you would have cost Jim his career and more. You better keep your mouth shut."

She takes a deep breath.

"You have to go." She puts her hands on her hips. "Stay put until I say otherwise."

She slams the door on her way out, and I jump.

She never let me tell my side. Does she believe this is my fault? Does she think I seduced him? What could I say even if she let me speak? I'd protect him. Why is she so upset? The military culture enshrines free sex. Military women service any officer requesting their service. They can refuse them but seldom do. They can also offer their services. I've learned this over the past year.

Miss Elly bans me from Nadler's office.

§

I'm confined to my room except for unpleasant meals accompanied by Miss Elly. This afternoon, even my favorite books can't entice me to concentrate on anything but this awful turn of events, so I'm sulking on my bed when someone bangs on my door. Miss Elly.

"Come with me."

"Why?"

"You're going to meet with a security officer."

"Where?"

"In a conference room. Move it."

§

A stone-faced officer sits at the conference table, shuffling papers.

"Angel, we're sending you on a special assignment. You need to sign a Non-Disclosure Agreement or NDA. You already know the importance of keeping everything that happens on this base classified. Major Nadler discussed that with you. You understand what classified means?"

Why do I have to leave? What did I do wrong?

I nod. I understand its meaning, and I've always kept all secrets, including my own.

"Where's Major Nadler?"

"He's busy with other matters, so I'm taking over now."

He shoves the paper in front of me.

"What would I sign it as? My name's not Angel, and I have no last name or title."

The officer hesitates.

"I need a name; one I get to choose."

The officer sighs.

"A proper first and last name and a suitable title. Everyone here has a rank or title, so I want one too." Now's my chance to get an official name. "I want a paper giving me the right to live my personal life as I please, and the freedoms military women have, but not matching rules. I won't have sex with men who ask."

The officer stiffens, his eyes wide, but he says nothing.

"I don't believe you should hold me to the same standards or rules as the military women since I'm not one. I'm also not a civilian domestic, and y'all shouldn't treat me as such. These are my terms before I sign anything."

The officer nods. "And what have you chosen for your new name?"

"Zena," I say. "Daughter of Zeus. Zena Roberts. Zena, like the warrior, spelled with a Z."

He agrees.

§

It's been almost a week, and I haven't seen Nadler, not once. I'm meeting with the same security officer again in the same conference room.

"We've given you an official title, Special Consultant. I have your contract and your NDA. We're also providing you with identity papers since you have no birth certificate. You'll need those at Mountainview."

What?

"Why are you sending me away? To Mountainview? What's there?"

He clears his throat.

"You're needed there for an important assignment. They'll brief you when you get there, and you'll meet your new handler."

He's truthful, but I'm still exiled.

"We listed your date of birth as April 10, 2077, since you arrived here on April 10th, and the year indicates that you're fifteen—based on the doctor's determination."

He scrutinizes me.

"We left the parents' names blank. Do you remember anything yet?"

"No. I don't know who my parents were, and I don't know my birth date, so that's fine."

The officer hands me all three documents, and when I inspect the identity papers, they appear to be in order. I read the NDA. It forbids me to disclose anything I've witnessed or any task they required me to perform on this base—under penalty of prison. My contract stipulates our mutual responsibilities. I promise to behave professionally in my duties and to keep all matters confidential. All work product belongs to them. I must be honest and faithful in my conduct. They agree to protect me and allow me to live my personal life without interference.

They agree to my terms, and I agree to theirs. Among their three signatures, Nadler's name stands out.

I sign the papers with my new name.

CHAPTER 6

Eight years later ~ Central Control

I hate eating alone. Central Control's huge fifth-floor cafeteria teams with uniforms, and I'm the lone civilian allowed to eat here. On my first day at Central, three years ago, I arrived at the cafeteria for breakfast and left hungry after they informed me civilians weren't allowed. It was never a problem at Westview or Mountainview.

When I mentioned my experience to my liaison, Major Michael Corday, he immediately took me to the cafeteria and stood in line with me to inform the staff I was a consultant working with the military. When lunchtime came around, Michael insisted on accompanying me. By dinner, which we also shared, we knew we liked each other. It was easy talking to Michael.

All these people and I sit alone. Michael normally joins me for meals, but he took leave off base two weeks ago, and I'm eager for his return.

When they forced me to leave Westview eight years ago, it felt like Nadler had abandoned me. One day everything was great, and the next, I was exiled. This time they kicked me out of Michael's apartment three days after he left. But Michael should return soon.

High-ranking officers like Michael are given accommodations called apartments. Lower ranks and women's quarters are smaller and labeled rooms. We lived together for over two years, and now I'm in my old quarters, which I retained when I moved in with Michael, to keep my personal effects private.

I've come a long way since leaving Westview at fifteen. They assigned me to Mountainview, where I worked counterinsurgency for Central Intelligence for five years, the official group that engages me as a Special Consultant. My assignment was to investigate the leaking of their base activities to the Overlords. In my third year, after finishing my initial assignment, they transferred me to the Radio Room, where I worked for my final two years. Early on, as a hobby, I started collecting messages the Overlords transmit to their bases, and after studying hundreds, I discovered the schema for decrypting them.

The upper echelon at the main military base learned of my success. It was a huge deal when my handlers at Mountainview transferred me to Central Control to teach my technique for deciphering the messages to their elite team. It's the largest military base with its six floors and incredible size. The highest-ranking officers live, work, and make major decisions on the top floor. It's well known the lab on the fifth floor engages the smartest military experts. And they wanted me.

I smile, remembering how as a twenty-year-old, the immense size of Central Control overwhelmed me, twice the size of Mountainview, with its half-dozen floors and different way of life, at least on the top two floors. My orientation was Michael's responsibility, and he introduced me to Central's Radio Room to learn the ropes and get acquainted with the crew. Word of my schema decoding discovery proceeded me. When I was ready, Michael introduced me to my new handler, Major Morgan, and I became acquainted with his team.

I miss Michael. We clicked right from day one. We spent our evenings getting to know each other, and after a few weeks, he suggested I move in with him. Now, I sit alone in a sea of military personnel, missing Michael, realizing how much he's a part of my life.

Michael proposed to me a month ago. He informed me he wanted several children and planned everything without sharing it with me first. I was obliged to confess my secret; one I've kept for the last ten years, that I can't bear him children. Women on every base must receive a birth control injection every six months unless they are screened and have permission to conceive. I've avoided the shot because it's unnecessary.

At first, Michael was deeply troubled, but after consideration, he devised a plan. Michael decided he would marry, his wife would live in Valleyview, where all military wives raise their children, and I'd continue living with him. She would grant him the children I can't. I argued I wouldn't be his mistress because it would be unfair to his wife and children.

I'm willing to set him free and move on. If I let him sacrifice his dream, he'll resent me one day. Michael swore he loved me too much, wouldn't give me up, and would seek a solution. Out of the blue, he announced his plan for temporary leave and left shortly thereafter. I'd have moved on, but he insisted he loved me, so I'm willing to stay. It's been two weeks and counting with no sign of Michael.

This is our first stretch apart. Michael always shows up at the lab to escort me to lunch or dinner, standing there watching me and smiling until

I notice him. I haven't visited the atrium since he left. We often spent time there watching the seasons change, observing the moon rise, or pointing out the constellations. Most of all, I don't like sleeping alone.

Recently, the Radio Room staff informed us they're no longer receiving messages. Either the Overlords recalibrated the radio frequencies, found a method to block us, or discovered another mode of communication. Radio Room staff spend their hours trying to figure that out, but my workload has been considerably reduced. On slow days like today, I visit my second home, the library. New materials arrive periodically, so I'm on a treasure hunt for unread books with plenty of time to read in Michael's absence.

§

As usual, I'm alone in the library and I can hear myself breathing. I'm lost among the shelves searching for reading material when someone moves behind me. I see Colonel Wickmore standing several feet away. He grins at me, so I nod and resume my reading. I know his name, but we haven't officially met.

"You must be the Special Consultant I've heard about. Zena Roberts?"

"Yes, sir."

"You're a very attractive young lady. There's a horror film playing at the movie theater tonight. Accompany me."

"Sorry, sir. I don't enjoy horror movies."

I continue reading, striving not to appear rude, hoping he'll leave.

"Okay, then. The Officer's Club it is."

Michael never took me to the Officer's Club, warning me Club was too rough for me, a gathering where officers seek sexual pleasure and military women provide it.

"I've never been to Club, and I don't service military men."

"No, no, I wouldn't expect that. Nobody will bother you while you're with me. You're my guest. That's all."

"I'm sorry, but I'm afraid I wouldn't enjoy it. It's not something I'd do."

"Sure, but you eat, don't you? Tonight, we'll dine together in the Officer's Mess."

"I'm sorry, sir, but I'm in a committed relationship and can't accompany you anywhere."

I'm careful to keep my tone respectful to not offend this high-ranking officer. "My lover is off base right now, but he'll be home soon. I'm faithful to him, so it's a bad idea, even for dinner."

"Michael's not coming back anytime soon," he says. He smirks and reaches out to touch me. "So, be an obedient little girl and join me for dinner."

He grabs my left breast and starts fondling me. I drop my books and rush past him. Why does he think Michael isn't coming back? I'm not hanging around to ask Colonel Wickmore.

§

No word from Michael. The past two days held disappointment, and I'm starting to worry. I visit the quiet library, which appears empty, in search of an interesting read to keep my mind off him. A stimulating book of Nabokov's lectures on Russian literature looks promising, so I scan through the pages.

I'm slammed, face first, against the wall. Behind me, someone grabs my wrists, knocks my book to the floor, and secures my hands over my head, holding them tight with one hand.

Are they detaining me by mistake?

His free hand pulls down my pants. I struggle, but he presses against me, and I can't move. He unzips and presses himself against my bare bottom.

"So, my little lady. You're too special for me? I'll show you what a skillful lover I am."

That voice. Colonel Wickmore.

"I know how to please a woman and I'll show you."

With one foot, he spreads my legs. His free hand probes me while he whispers in my ear.

"You know you want this, baby. You've never known a real man like me before."

His crude words and hot breath churn my stomach and my face hurts where it smacked the wall. I close my eyes and wait for this to end. He touches me, and I don't want him to. It's my body, not his. At last, he walks away, and I'm relieved he didn't rape me.

§

My handler is often in the lab, but today I find him in his office.

"Major Morgan, I need to talk to you." I'm still trembling, and I'm dreading this.

"What's going on?" he asks, never raising his head.

I close the office door. "I was attacked in the library."

He stops and makes eye contact. "What do you mean, attacked?"

"Colonel Wickmore slammed me against the wall and assaulted me."

"He raped you?"

His face shows concern, but he shakes his head. He doesn't want to hear that a Colonel raped his consultant. I report what happened, and my face feels warm. This is not a discussion I wish to have with Morgan.

"I'm not returning to the library. He was there Tuesday and tried to get me to accompany him. I wouldn't, and he accosted me, but I got away, so I guess he's not happy."

Morgan sighs in relief.

"No problem. Avoid the library until this blows over."

§

I've avoided the library for two days now, but today my teammate requires a book in the library, and I know exactly which book, its location, and the page where I'll find the information.

"Major Morgan, I can't visit the library, even if it's a quick trip."

"Take Mick with you. With him there, the Colonel won't bother you."

I like Mick. I tell him the plan, and he accompanies me to the library where we seem to be alone, and I quickly locate the book we need. Someone enters the library as we're ready to walk out. Colonel Wickmore looms in front of us.

"Lieutenant, take a walk for about fifteen minutes. I want to talk to this young lady."

Outranked, Mick has no choice but to follow orders. I hand the book to Mick and signal I understand. Maybe the Colonel simply wants to talk or apologize. Mick leaves, and I attempt to follow him, but the Colonel blocks my way.

I try to push past him, but he rushes me again. This time I'm facing him when he slams my back against the wall, again securing my wrists above my head.

"You sure are a gutsy little bitch, aren't you? You belong to me to do whatever I want. Mind your station, young lady."

Mick returns a few minutes later to find me collapsed on the floor with my hands shaking, trying to pull up my underwear.

"Are you all right?"

I sheepishly describe the Colonel's actions, but Mick doesn't show the revulsion I feel. He shakes his head. When we reach the lab, I report the incident to Morgan, and he promises to notify someone.

§

My quarters still don't feel like home. Back in my room for weeks now, I miss Michael's apartment. Like other quarters I've resided in, this room contains a single bed, a modest dresser, a clothes rack, and a quaint bistro table. I could invite a female guest to share my table, but I couldn't offer tea or anything else. Rooms don't have kitchen facilities. Food is allowed in the rooms, but it's uncommon to bring it in. What's not allowed is male companionship. Men are not allowed in women's quarters. Women are not permitted in theirs unless they're higher-ranking officers and have apartments. I've been in both.

After each Wickmore incident, I record in my secret shorthand the date, hour, location, and how he assaulted me. In one entry, I logged a recent episode that occurred while on a walk around the rotunda, when Colonel Wickmore grabbed me. A week had passed since he last attacked me, and I mistakenly felt safe. He pushed me to my knees and unzipped. I threatened to bite it off if he put that filthy thing in my mouth. He let me go and walked away laughing. But I won.

I reported that assault to my handler, but Morgan advised me if the Colonel never forced me to service him, there was no crime. He suggested negotiating with the Colonel to make him happy. I scoffed at his ludicrous idea. Why would I do that? I included this in my report.

My log noted no assaults for two weeks before it happened again.

I'm the first and only female ever assigned to the lab, so I visit Comfort Rooms when nature calls, instead of using the communal men's room the officers in the lab and Radio Room share.

All Comfort Rooms have a bathroom, cot, and chair. They lock, and everyone is free to use them. These days I check around before entering. My log describes another incident that happened when I opened the outer Comfort Room door to leave, and Wickmore pushed me back in. The Colonel locked the door, I tried to escape, and I fought him. He pinned my arms above my head, and I couldn't move. He won.

My next log entry describes how I went over Morgan's head and straight to Commander Harris's office on the sixth floor and reported Colonel Wickmore's attacks. He suggested that I "be nice" to Wickmore, and while I'm at it, I should be nice to him too. But I didn't want to be nice. I wanted to be free.

I'm weary of his game, but I've avoided Colonel Wickmore for the last five days by being hypervigilant when leaving a Comfort Room and staying away from dark corners and hallways. So far, I've been successful at dodging him. At night I rest uneasily, fearing he might gain access to my room in the women's quarters. Maintenance crew members are the only males allowed in women's quarters, with notice, but certainly not during the night, except for emergencies. But the Colonel ignores the law, so I'm not safe. My sleep suffers, I have no appetite, and I can't anticipate his next move.

Michael hasn't returned, it doesn't pay to complain to Morgan anymore, and my colleagues understand what's happening to me. If someone was hurting them, I'd stand and fight even if I knew I'd lose. It's the right thing to do. My value here seems to have diminished now that work is slow.

§

Mick informs me of a meeting in the coffee room as soon as everyone's assembled. The coffee room, a quiet location with a large table frequently used for meetings, separates the lab from the Radio Room.

Everyone has arrived, and Major Morgan calls for attention.

"I have incredible news. They found a Book hidden in a wall safe at Riverview, written in the same strange symbols seen around our bases. Several experts attempted to decipher it without luck."

He nods at me. "But we have our own expert here with success translating these symbols."

"Do they have any guesses about the Book's content?" I ask.

"That's where you come in. Central Intelligence recognized the Book's importance based on how well they hid it. They want you to start translating it as soon as it arrives."

"When will it arrive?"

"They're making several backup copies. I'm aware it's a tough assignment, maybe even impossible, but if anyone can handle it, I trust you can. Once you're up to speed, you'll share your methodology with your colleagues."

Everyone stares at me, and my face feels warm. They're aware I've dabbled in translating symbols, but this is an astounding find. An entire book of their secret language. I might learn more about the Overlords and why I believe they're my enemy. Nobody else seems to share my strong disdain for them. My palms itch to start working.

"We could receive the Book in a few days. They're sending the original Book, so security will be tight."

§

Another week passes without Michael, and the Book hasn't arrived yet. The Colonel has attacked me again, this time forcing me into a vacant office. Whenever I believe it's over, he reappears. He, the hunter, and I, his prey. I've spoken to military women, and they all echo the same lame advice, give in, give him what he wants. High-level officers expect service at will, their will, not yours. Don't be difficult. Do whatever's necessary. No, this body belongs to me. I'm not military, and I service no one.

§

February will end soon, and Michael has been gone for nearly two months now. The Book remains in transit, and my days are full of resentment and fear. This can't be happening. I had everything, a prestigious job, an attentive lover, respect from my colleagues, and now I've lost it all. I want the Colonel to stop, but I've failed to make it happen. And I want Michael to return. He'll protect me. I don't know how to make that happen either.

§

My work area has never been cleaner. I'm preparing for the Book that should arrive soon. We're all present in the lab, including my handler, when an officer shows up and heads straight for me. Does he have good news about Michael?

"Ma'am, Colonel Wickmore requests your attendance in his office. I'm to escort you."

I freeze. What? I glance around. My comrades are suddenly very busy, their eyes avoid mine, and nobody says a word. Morgan steps over to hear what the officer wants. The officer repeats himself, addressing Morgan this time. Morgan sighs, shakes his head, and signals his okay to accompany the Lieutenant, given the Colonel made the request. Nobody says or does anything. I understand the Chain of Command, but I also understand common decency, and they all know what's in store for me.

I want to refuse, but I don't know the penalty for disobeying a senior officer's request. Could he put me in jail or somewhere where I'd be totally at his mercy?

I leave with the officer.

We arrive at the Colonel's office where, sneering, he ushers me into a back room. He closes the door behind him, muttering something about my being a good girl. I turn to face him, get up close, and he's surprised I'm so willing.

I bring my knee up hard.

Colonel Wickmore drops to his knees, holding himself and gasping for breath. I walk out, wish his receptionist a good day with a smile, and ask an officer in the hallway to point me to the General's office.

I barge into the General's office, waltz past the receptionist, and note the General talking on the phone at his desk. The receptionist, one step behind me, follows me in. The General shoos her away and holds up his index finger, requesting me to wait a minute. While he concludes his phone conversation, I survey his office. Two framed photographs, each showing a young soldier, are displayed on the shelf of a bookcase against one wall.

One soldier resembles a much younger Michael, but it makes little sense for the General to display his photo. A red flag flares up in my mind, but I chase it away. This isn't the time for it, and it doesn't matter. I'm leaving the military for good. I don't recognize the other young soldier.

The General hangs up the phone, and I ask, "Who is that soldier?"

"That's my son, but it's a very old photo. He's very successful now."

"You must be very proud."

"I am."

I pause to regain courage before my anger subsides and fear takes over.

"Colonel Wickmore has been assaulting me for several weeks now. The military promised to protect me. I apprised Commander Harris, but he failed to stop it, so I quit. I am done. Send me to a civilian base of your choice. I don't care."

I storm out without giving him a chance to speak, aware of how serious this can get. Military rules are clear on addressing an officer, much less the General, and I'm positive they would frown upon kicking a high-ranking officer between the legs, but I don't care what they do to me. I'm so done.

§

My room becomes my refuge for the next three days, and I sleep or stare at nothing, mulling over my situation. Mick sends me food every day, and on the first day, my meal tray includes a note informing me that the Book has arrived at Central.

On my third day, Major Morgan breaks protocol and knocks on my door, informing me I'll be leaving soon and that he needs to discuss my relocation. I open the door, and I'm a mess, smelling from not showering or changing clothes in three days. I haven't run a brush through my hair even once. He orders me to shower, change clothes, and meet him at his office.

§

"Sit. I have good news. The Book arrived two days ago."

"I heard."

"We've decided to transfer you to Cavalry."

"That's a military base. I quit. I'm going to a civilian base where I'll be safe."

"Commander Pierce will visit tomorrow to discuss the possibility of your transfer to Cavalry where you'll begin translating the Book."

I don't speak.

"He'll decide whether he'll accept you, and you'll decide if that's agreeable. Commander Pierce will take personal responsibility for your protection."

Michael often spoke about Commander Pierce. Twice a year, Michael spent the day at Cavalry, and when he returned, he'd describe how efficiently the base was run and how well he thought of Commander Pierce. I want to leave Central without forgoing translating the Book. It might be my one chance to answer plaguing questions. I'm unfamiliar with civilian

bases. Now I have a choice.
"Yes, sir."

§

Major Morgan summons me to his office. When I enter the room, he stands, and Commander Pierce sits with his back to me. When the Commander stands and turns, I'm astonished by how formidably attractive he is, especially in his dress uniform.

"Commander Pierce, this is our star, Zena Roberts."

It's against military rules to approach a Commander without permission, but that's exactly what I do. Major Morgan tenses as I walk over and offer my hand to Commander Pierce. The Commander takes it without reservation, smiles, and his energy surges to me like a lightning bolt traveling through our clasped hands. My face lights up.

"I'm delighted to finally meet you, sir."

I read him. He would indeed protect me.

§

The shuttle hasn't arrived yet, nor has my handler shown. Out of the corner of my eye, I catch Mick approaching me.

"I wondered if you were going to say goodbye," I say.

"I wouldn't miss it for the world. You know you don't have to leave."

"Yes, I do. I'm done here. Michael is gone, along with everything I've worked for."

Mick shakes his head. He knows how much this assignment meant to me.

"It's not gone, Zena. You still have the lab. Nothing's changed there. I know you're upset, but the Colonel won't hurt you now that Top Brass knows the truth. Major Morgan couldn't do anything, but the General certainly can. And if you leave, you won't be here when Michael gets back. It could be tomorrow. He won't let anyone hurt you. Give this another chance?"

"It's been two months. Michael promised to return in two or three weeks. Where is he?"

Mick shakes his head again and frowns.

"I peeked at the Book, and it's awesome. Have you seen it yet?" he asks.

"No, but I'm eager to translate it."

"Did you meet Commander Pierce?"

"Yes. Michael always said Commander Pierce is strict, no-nonsense, but fair. A decent man." I hope Michael is correct. "Major Morgan said the same. Cavalry doesn't have housing for another female, so it was up to the

Commander to decide whether to take me."

"Where will they put you? With the men?" he asks, grinning.

"I guess I'll find out," I say, matching his grin.

"Anyway, we both agreed. Commander Pierce said he'd personally see to my protection. They sent the Book with him."

I don't want to transfer to a civilian base. I want my prominence, I want Michael back, and I want this nightmare to have never happened. But it did.

Everyone at Cavalry will respect and trust me, and I'll make friends. Good friends. I'll take a lover and be so successful at my work they'll insist I stay. I'm alone now because I gave all I had to Michael, and he took it with him. That's a mistake I won't repeat. Maybe I've lost my prestigious job and my hard-earned reputation, but I'll find a home where I belong.

Mick hugs me and plants a kiss on the top of my head but says nothing.

"You know I care for you, Mick, and I'll miss you, but not Central."

With sad eyes, he nods and leaves.

Deep in thought, I jump when Major Morgan puts his hand on my shoulder. At that same moment, the shuttle arrives, and privates load my belongings into the second car. I'll be boarding the passenger car soon. Major Morgan hugs me and whispers.

"I'm sorry you're leaving. You've been an invaluable asset to our lab, and I've enjoyed working with you. I wish it wasn't ending this way."

Me too.

"You're always welcome here. I'll always hold a spot for you, should you reconsider and decide to return to us."

He kisses my forehead and squeezes me one last time.

I step into the shuttle, and I'm the only passenger, but I'm not bothered, with so much to reflect on—where I'm headed and what I'm leaving behind. Before the shuttle starts moving, a young soldier with a warm smile sits next to me. I welcome my pleasant, young traveling companion.

"First trip to Cavalry?" he asks. "If you're nervous, hold my hand."

The transit tubes run deep underground and there are no lights except a muted glow in the shuttle cabin. There's nothing to see but the dark tunnel, anyway, and the transit speeds by so fast it won't be a long trip. Transit trips always unsettle me, so even though he's teasing, I take his offered hand and snuggle down in my seat. He smiles, watching my amusement. It's a wonderful omen, and I enjoy holding hands with my young companion.

CHAPTER 7

Whooshing sounds echo in our passenger car, with a decreasingly low grind as the shuttle crawls to a stop, ending our hour-long transit ride to Cavalry. My fellow passenger stands, stretches, wishes me a pleasant stay, and disappears, but something odd about him triggers a red flag in my mind, like a warning flare. Red flags signal my brain that something's amiss, which often means nothing, but sometimes investigation becomes necessary. My excitement leaves no legroom for alarm or concern.

Two young officers greet me while a private removes my belongings from the shuttle cargo compartment. The officers escort me to an office for an updated photo to create a Cavalry lanyard. I'm twenty in my old lanyard's photo, taken almost three years ago when I first arrived at Central.

My new lanyard includes my current photo with my title and name, Special Consultant Zena Roberts, on its front. The information listed on the back contains my classification, a ranking of twelve, signifying my work as Classified, the highest security clearance awarded to a civilian. My lanyard records my work location as the Office of the Commander. So, I'll work near Commander Pierce daily.

Two privates escort me to the freight lift in an isolated back area with my belongings loaded on a hand truck. As the open lift rises, the view on the other floors scarcely changes with its slate-gray walls like a cavernous cave. On the fourth level, we cross the polished great floor to my accommodations. One private points out Commander Pierce's office suite and my nearby residence with the Police Center between them.

Cavalry is the smallest base I've seen, especially compared with Central, yet the walk from the freight lift to the opposite side across the rotunda is a respectable distance. All bases have circular builds, with a huge middle column extending from the roof to the basement. They call the area surrounding the column the "great floor," with all offices, living quarters, cafeterias, gyms, and various specific rooms, lining the perimeter.

From this distance, my modest dwelling looks habitable. They informed me there were no available women's quarters, and I expect disappointment, but when we reach my room and they open the door, I gasp. It's so tiny and appears partitioned off from a larger room. Next to the entrance, in the corner, stands a tall metal rack, complete with several hangers, and near the bottom, two small metal shelves to hold my belongings.

A modest cot dominates the room, leaving a narrow path to a bathroom. No space for a dresser means no drawers for my undergarments or lotions. Inadequate shelves provide insufficient space to store my CDs and treasures. The privates again explain women's quarters are unavailable, so this was their best solution with short notice. It's pointless to complain, meaning I'll have to manage. They move my belongings in, set them on the floor, and begin opening the boxes.

"I'll unpack, and I'll return the boxes I don't need. Thank you so much," I say. With no drawers, I'll need a box or two. I'm eager to meet my colleagues and settle into my new office.

We pass the Military Police Center and continue to Commander Pierce's headquarters. Inside, in front of the Commander's office, sits a military woman at her desk. She looks fortyish, with short, frizzy coffee-brown hair. Commander Pierce stands next to the desk.

"Squared away?" Commander Pierce asks. His welcoming but amused smile greets me.

"Yes, sir, I'm eager to start, sir."

His receptionist rolls her eyes.

"This is Specialist Cassie Reyes," he says, nodding at the receptionist.

Commander Pierce dismisses my escorts with a nod and indicates I should follow. He directs my attention to a break room, a long, narrow section bordered by cabinets separating it from the expanse of a larger room. The right side boasts a counter featuring a prominent glass window, providing a clear view into Commander's office. Clean cups next to a spotless sink complement a coffeemaker with its freshly brewed pot.

Voices chattering from beyond the break room grab my attention. As we enter a small open office, I spot two boxes next to a huge copier printer almost covering a table along the outer wall. One box might hold the Book.

Another set of cabinets creates a partition for the open office. Against them stands a table stacked with office items, under which two chairs are tucked. A long table against the outer wall hosts two computers separated by a short file cabinet. An officer sits facing one computer and turns toward us. Next to him stands a tall, lanky officer, holding papers, towering over a pleasant-looking military woman studying a clipboard.

"Seated, Major Paul Abrams, and standing, Major Thomas Williams,"

Commander Pierce says. "This is Specialist Jennifer Campbell. She maintains our supply cabinets. Need anything, ask her or Major Abrams."

Major Abrams stands. He is an attractive man, but his blond hair and pinkish skin are unusual. There are few blond-haired or reddish-blond-haired people. Some citizens have light skin, but most people are light brown, with brown or black hair. He's taller than me, like most men, but shorter than Major Williams, who is at least a head taller with brown hair and tan skin, even though I doubt he's ever been outside. Only salvage teams are allowed outside the base, and even they are forbidden by the Overlords—but quietly sanctioned by the Peace Force.

Specialist Jennifer Campbell, by comparison, is my height, with dark brown hair cut very short like all military women.

"We don't have available office space for you, so the computer next to Major Abrams is for your use until we find a better location." Commander Pierce pauses again, squints, and appears lost in thought for a moment. "You know how to use a computer?" he asks.

This restricted space won't allow me to spread out my materials.

"Yes, sir, but it's not necessary yet. My work requires a much larger work area. About this big, sir," I say, stretching out my arms. "And I require quiet and isolation to concentrate." I study my surroundings, disappointed in the lack of privacy and insufficient workspace. It won't serve me to appear demanding, but they must understand my terms are non-negotiable.

"I listen to music to help me concentrate. My CD player has headphones but might distract others. This busy, cramped office won't work for me, sir."

The officers trade patronizing grins, and Major Williams shakes his head.

"My assignment is complicated and requires concentration, so my environment must be conducive. I must be able to work." Exasperation builds, but I persevere, not accepting failure.

Major Abrams asks, "What about the kitchen table in your apartment, sir? We sometimes have meetings there but it's otherwise unused during the day." With folded arms, he seems to consider other options.

Commander sours at the idea but concedes, shaking his head, and he and Major Abrams direct me past the receptionist to stairs leading to a small landing. Commander unlocks the door, we turn and climb a few more steps, and we're in the largest apartment I've ever seen.

To my left, a table in front of the sink almost fills the small kitchen and is more than sufficient for my needs. Cabinets above a side counter form a wall next to the steps, and an opening above the counter allows observation of the stairs. A lonely coffeemaker stands unused on the counter near two used cups by the sink. It doesn't appear to function as a kitchen.

The enormous living room, in contrast, flaunts magnificent floor-to-ceiling windows dominating the entire exterior wall, presenting a breathtaking scenic view. From the kitchen, you can observe snow-covered mountainous peaks beneath a light blue sky with silvery billowing clouds.

Commander could entertain his entire staff in his living room. A long sun-faded turquoise couch, facing away from the kitchen, sits flanked by matching chairs, a loveseat on one side, and a single-seater on the opposite side. Two similar chairs, one facing the couch and its twin back-to-back facing the window, complete the set. The floor area in front of the windows leaves ample space for dancing.

The living room, immaculate and tidy, appears unlived in, with no personal items anywhere, nothing disturbed, and not a single book on an end table. No homey decorations or wall coverings. I envision myself dancing, my music playing, and bringing life to the forsaken apartment. Past the kitchen, a small hallway lined with a large metal wall rack ends with a set of double doors. The bedroom? A bathroom door stands open, revealing its purpose, next to a laundry room with its half-open door exposing a washer and dryer.

Commander agrees to surrender his apartment short-term, although I sense his reluctance.

We return to Major Abrams' office, where Major Williams waits alone. Commander Pierce removes a large bound volume from the smaller box on the table and ceremoniously hands it to me. It's the Book. I leaf through pages of familiar symbols that beg me to translate them. Major Williams opens the larger box and pulls out a console disc player.

"That came with the Book. Someone will install it in your quarters," Commander says.

Has he seen my closet-sized quarters?

"My room is tiny, sir, with no space for it. Can someone install it upstairs for now? It's an improvement over my portable player, and I'll be spending more daytime hours at work. Would that be all right, sir?"

Commander nods with an eye roll, and I sense his worry that I'm commandeering his apartment, and I can't blame him. I make a silent promise to be a worthy steward.

"We'll install it tomorrow," Major Williams says, returning the player to its box.

Commander frowns but nods.

Major Abrams shows me the supply cabinet behind his office, and I grab two legal pads and pens. I'm ready to get started. The officers appear surprised by my eagerness.

"You don't need to start right away," Commander says. "Get unpacked and learn your way around. We're flexible around here. We work seven days a week, but take personal time as needed. Notify Cassie if you're not coming in for the day. Our routine ensures office coverage, but that won't include you. The cafeteria is on the third floor, and you can visit anytime … without notifying anyone. Stay on the fourth floor except for meals."

"Is the library on this floor, sir?" I ask.

"Second floor, but if you need access to the library, I'll arrange an escort. We have restrictions, and our visiting civilians need an escort."

"What's on this floor, sir? What evening activities are available?"

"Not much for civilians on any floor. The Officer's Club and Mess are on this floor, but you don't have access. We have men's and women's quarters, offices, and next door, the Police Center," he says and shrugs.

"If you become acquainted with cafeteria staff, they might invite you to join their activities, but you'll still need permission. On the third floor, there are military and civilian quarters, a lounge, a game room, a movie theater, and the gym, but again, you don't have access." He studies me, inspecting me from top to bottom, undoubtedly deciding I wouldn't use the gym, anyway. My soft, round body differs from the thin, muscular military women. I move more like a dancer than a soldier, and my main forms of exercise include dancing and walking.

It's obvious they're unprepared for, and unwelcoming, an intrusion like me, but Nadler taught me to present a professional face and stand proud.

"Cassie will point out the women's quarters where you'll find the showers and laundry room. If you need anything, she's a valuable resource. Check with her for your doctor's appointment, and when ready, I'll arrange an escort."

Finding the women's quarters shouldn't be difficult, and visiting the doctor for mandatory contraception is unnecessary. Commander doesn't need to know. Nobody does.

"Incidentally, sir, who is my handler?"

Commander hesitates, appearing unsure. Am I his first and only civilian asset?

"You'll report to me. Need anything for your project, consult me or Major Abrams. Everything else, Cassie or Jen will assist you."

His rules are far too strict. I'm accustomed to much more freedom, and my handlers always made exceptions for me, and my contract allows it. It's too soon to challenge Commander. Today, my priority is to acclimate.

"I'd like to get started immediately—if that's okay, sir. I've looked forward to examining the Book from the moment Major Morgan described it. Unpacking can wait until evening. What time do you start in the morning, and how late do y'all stay?"

After Commander Pierce explains the work schedule, he mentions his housekeeper is scheduled for Friday afternoons, and she needs a couple of hours to clean his apartment, so I'll have to work around her. I head to the apartment with the Book and pad of paper held close, and Commander trailing behind me.

"One more thing, Zena, my bedroom is off-limits. I don't allow anyone, not even the housekeeper, in my bedroom." His brow wrinkles.

"Understood, sir. I'm that way about my personal space. My privacy is important, and I promise I'll respect yours. I'm professional."

He sighs, wishes me a pleasant day, and leaves. The Book takes its rightful position directly in front of me on my new worktable, where I dive right in. My work materials sit ready on the side while I examine the Book. Cassie unexpectedly stands before me, her arms folded.

"Commander's bedroom is off-limits. Nobody but he is allowed in there, and you wouldn't like the consequences for breaking that rule." She leaves without another word. What's in his bedroom that he hides from everyone, including the housekeeper?

A half-hour later, Major Abrams mounts the stairs and strides over, shaking his head with a cocky smile.

"Wanted to warn you in case nobody else mentioned it. Commander never allows anyone in his bedroom, except himself, not even me. He insists on that, and I'm unsure what he'd do if you broke that rule, but you wouldn't like it." He waits for my response.

"Thanks for the heads-up, sir. Commander informed me, and Cassie also warned me. Understood." My tone remains professional, and I offer a warm smile. I watch him leave.

I'm getting the idea Commander doesn't want me in his bedroom....

Engrossed in my reading, a burning in my stomach reminds me it's time to find the cafeteria. Steps nearest the office lead to the third floor, near the open cafeteria, where I'm bowled over by the smells of fresh-baked pies. A Military Police officer follows close behind me. I stand in line with my tray, waiting for the server to dish out the food and the challenge. Civilian staff have a separate dining area and are prohibited from eating in the cafeteria. My wait isn't long.

My server stands with her hands gripping her hips, glares as if I should know better, and says, "Civilians don't eat in the cafeteria."

From inside my blouse, I extract my lanyard, remove it, and present it.

"I'm Special Consultant Zena Roberts. I work in Commander's office."

That's all it takes. The server glances at my ID and returns it to me. Her entire demeanor changes, and she offers to send coffee to my table. She smiles when she brings the coffee, but no one else smiles my way. Officers seated at other tables watch me with suspicion. Major Williams and Jen Campbell lunch with several others a few tables away, watching me, but they don't invite me, even though there's room. I smile their way, nod, and turn to eat my lunch. The MP makes his rounds, trying not to be obvious, watching me.

CHAPTER 8

"Good morning, Cassie," I say, hoping to wear down her frigid façade with cheerfulness.

She glances up for a moment, says nothing, and then turns back to her cluttered desk. Okay, not an auspicious way to start my second day. This morning, I selected a black skirt, off-white blouse, and black vest, my most professional outfit, and twisted my hair into a tight bun to appear older and more mature. In the lab at Central Control, I liberated my hair after earning the respect and confidence of my colleagues.

In the break room, I equip myself with a steaming cup of coffee and peek through the counter window to view an unoccupied Commander's office. Upstairs, I find Commander and Major Abrams making conversation in hushed tones, drinking coffee with a saucer of dainty iced cake squares between them. Their sweet cakes, decorated with squiggly designs in different colored icing, look unappealing this early in the morning.

I hesitate, unsure if I should interrupt their morning custom.

"You're good. Sit," Commander says. He points to my chosen spot by the sink.

Major Abrams rises and steps aside, allowing me to slip past him. I retrieve my Book and papers and prepare my workspace.

"Sir, do you mind me storing the Book and papers in the bottom cabinet?" I point to my new storage location.

"You're fine," Commander says.

I sip my hot coffee and study Commander. Such a handsome hunk with those dark, piercing eyes, and short black hair begging my fingers to run through it. I imagine his full, luscious lips pressing against mine, and it makes me wish I was prettier.

The officers stand, gather their cups and plate of sweets, and leave without a word. I open the Book to my bookmark. A captivating guide, the Book details the Overlords' intent, and their step-by-step plan, including how they'll proceed, when they'll execute each step, and why. The century-old Book's excellent condition amazes me, and it's apparent they've completed several steps of their plan. I'm midway through translating the introduction, which summarizes a comprehensive six-point program or Master Plan.

§

Major Williams arrives with a worker carrying the CD player to install on a coffee table near a living room chair. Nobody seems to know who ordered it delivered with the Book. The young worker dawdles while Major Williams supervises. Why is Major Williams hanging around? Perhaps curious about me? They both venture to glance over now and then. Since Nadler rewarded me with my first player and music discs, music has been an important aspect of my life. The CD console, an immense improvement over my portable player, should yield many hours of pleasurable listening.

§

Armed with the handful of music discs I grabbed from my quarters after an early dinner, I continue translating the Book with my music playing in the background. I create notes in a cryptic shorthand of my own invention. Engrossed in my work, I'm unaware of the passing hour, and the Commander stands before me now, surprised to see me. I glance at my wristwatch.

"Sorry sir, it's later than I thought. I'll pack up and leave."

While gathering my materials, I remind myself to pay more attention to his schedule.

"I'll be hitting the track for an hour if you want to stay and continue working."

His relaxed stance eases my concern.

"I'd love that. Thank you, sir."

I welcome another hour.

Commander disappears into his forbidden bedroom, and minutes later, leaves wearing sweatpants, a tee-shirt, and running shoes, like Michael, who performed his mandatory workout three days a week. Then Michael returned to the apartment for a shower, often inviting me to join him. Where is Michael?

The hour flies by, and I'm lost in concentration, scribbling my notes while reading the symbols. I'm caught off-guard again when Commander bounds the steps, his face flushed and his shirt soaking from sweat.

"I'll shower, then let you out. Office doors stay locked during evening hours, so if you leave, an alarm sounds. Tidy up while I shower."

After stowing the Book and my papers in the cabinet, I switch off my music and store my disc with the rest of my collection. I ensure the living room is in order.

The bathroom door creaks open, and I glance up.

Commander strolls out of the bathroom stark naked, his still-wet bronze body glistening as he towels his hair dry. Did he forget about me? He presents himself in all his natural glory. He glances my way, and I gulp. My eyes are already full, so I avoid his and head to the kitchen table to wait. Minutes later, he joins me, wearing sweatpants without a shirt. Michael did that, claiming he needed to cool down after his shower, and I never minded. I enjoyed the show.

Commander escorts me downstairs, watching me. Does he fear I'll remark about his beautiful naked body? Without a word, he unlocks the office door, and I head for my tiny room, where I tumble naked into bed, fantasizing about Commander, naked.

§

At my worktable this morning, Commander and Major Abrams drink coffee and eat their bite-sized sweets, but Major Abrams bears a silly grin. Commander must have mentioned the previous night's events.

"So, enjoy your evening last night?" he asks. He smirks and eagerly awaits my answer.

"I went to bed early and got a relaxing night's sleep," I say, smiling.

"Understand you worked late last night. How'd that go?"

He's trying to entice me into a conversation I'm unwilling to engage in. He grins like a Cheshire Cat, waiting for my reaction.

"Well, I accomplished a great deal. After reviewing the symbols I'm familiar with, I created a plan."

Major Abrams' face drops in disappointment. Commander remains poker-faced.

§

After dinner, when Commander appears upstairs, he doesn't offer to let me stay, so I store my materials and wish him goodnight. Instead of enduring an unbearable evening in my tiny quarters, I set out to explore. Commander restricted me to the fourth floor, but it's quiet and appears abandoned. On the left side of the rotunda are women's quarters, Comfort Rooms, stairwells, offices, and meeting rooms. Past the suite of offices, a shadowy hallway cloaks darkened doorways. I pass the men's quarters, the Officer's

Mess, and another stairwell and circled back to Commander's office. Dead quiet, except for the echoing click of my footsteps.

An MP kept a visible presence at a distance all evening, perhaps supervising me or maybe making rounds. This won't work for me. Not a soul in sight, so where do they socialize? The MP enters the police station and claims his desk.

He watches me walk into his office, and I offer my warmest smile, hoping he's approachable.

"Hi, my name is Zena Roberts, and I work in Commander's office."

"Yes, Ma'am," he says with a questioning look.

"Do you have a name?"

He's not as forthcoming as I'd like.

"Yes, Ma'am. Sergeant Sean Martin. Can I assist you?"

He's so professional, so I must conjure up some captivating charm.

"I'm going stir-crazy with no one to talk to, and I'm afraid I won't last the night." I wink.

"Well, Miss Zena, we can't have that."

We chat all evening, and Sean warms up to me. I confess my love for music, and he shows interest, so I slip off to my quarters to fetch my portable player and a promising disc. Nights are so uneventful, so it's clear he appreciates my company. He grins when I offer to let him borrow my music.

§

It's Wednesday, my third day at Cavalry, but this morning I must dispute my restrictions. Commander works at his desk, and when he notices me through the break room window, I signal to speak to him. He nods, motions for me to come around, waits at his door, and then invites me into his office. Two visitor chairs face his desk, so I fill the first one and wait for him to address me.

"What's goin' on?"

"Sir, I want to renegotiate my restrictions and clarify my needs. I don't need supervision or protection, but if I'm harmed, I need assurance you'll take appropriate action. You're strict in your rules, and I'm protected here, but I need more freedom, not a chaperon, and I can navigate on my own."

Commander studies me, and although he's not smiling, I'm positive I've made my position clear.

"The rules stand. You need an escort. You're under my protection."

The matter's closed, but I'm far from finished.

"Okay, here's the problem, sir. My room is extremely tiny, with barely enough room to change clothes or sleep. I'm isolated all day because my work requires it, and I'm not complaining, but I need to socialize in the evenings and make friends."

"The rules stand. You need an escort to ensure your safety." Commander squints and I sense he's surprised at my tenacity.

I've failed to persuade him, so I scan his desk while preparing an effective defense. A photo on the far end of the desk displays five soldiers, triggering a red flag in my mind. A younger Dan, the officer who brought me to Westview, stands next to a younger Andrew. Were they members of the Commander's unit before he rose in the ranks? Does he know Dan and Andrew's current whereabouts? It's important to resolve my restriction issue, so first things first, and my red flag questions can wait.

"Understood, sir, but I'll be here indefinitely, and I can't live this way. My ability to perform my work will suffer, and I need to unwind and socialize after working in isolation." My eyes plead.

"It's inhumane to keep me under wraps like this. I'm under your protection because the military at Central failed to protect me, but you'd never allow that here." I pray that's true.

"In my ten years, I've had one incident beyond my control, and my contract protects my right to a personal life. I can handle myself, sir. Cavalry men are disciplined due to your leadership, and I'm safe here."

He studies me, appearing to reconsider. I inhale and hold my breath, slowly releasing it, waiting for confirmation that I've successfully presented my case.

"I'll consider it. Meantime, stay at the apartment tonight and listen to your music while I work out. Thursday nights, I attend the Officer's Club, so the apartment's yours tomorrow evening. I'll advise you of my decision on Friday."

The idea of staying at his apartment tomorrow evening pleases me. I'll be alone but with space to dance or exercise. I'll bring my drawing pad to sketch, so I snap a mental photograph of Commander to draw from later if I choose to, like I did when he came out of the shower.

That evening, after work, the apartment becomes my music chamber until Commander returns from the gym. This time when he exits the bathroom after his shower, I allow him privacy by turning my attention to the dark landscape, my back to him, searching for the moon.

§

Thursday passes slowly, but my workday finally ends, and I'm prepared for the evening, equipped with more music and my sketch pad. With Michael, I rarely enjoyed a whole evening singing and dancing with nobody watching.

After Commander leaves for Club, with my music softly playing in the background, I take out my sketch pad and begin another pencil drawing of him. I strive to preserve his sexy expression sitting behind his desk yesterday before the image disappears. I sketched Michael twice, but never shared it with him, not wanting to explain. He never showed interest in my art, anyway.

I set my finished sketch aside and I'm ready to party. My music blasts and my forgotten inner child sings and dances. It's been forever, but my body instinctively remembers how to move, and singing my well-known melodies revitalizes my spirit. Tired now, I swap my fast tunes with slower pop-opera ones. The couch invites me, so I curl up like a puppy to rest until my eyelids grow heavy, and away I drift.

I'm standing at the edge of a weathered back porch facing a summer forest. Beautiful blue jays and cardinals sit on branches chirping their sweet songs. Little brown sparrows flutter their wings and join the chorus. The air smells sweet, like freshly cut grass, and I extend my palm, dotted with little pieces of nuts. A tiny black and white bird lands on my outstretched fingers, chirps twice, and absconds with a nut.

My eyelids flutter open. Commander smiles down at me.

"I guess I wore myself out," I say, propping myself into a sitting position. "Did you enjoy Club, sir?"

"Affirmative. Ever been to Club?"

"No, sir. I didn't think they allowed civilians."

He nods and watches me gather my sketch pad and art pencils and stow my music.

At Mountainview, I was too young to attend Club. I was only twenty when I left. At Central, Michael discouraged me, claiming it was a social Club designed for men. The Colonel invited me, but I'd never willingly go anywhere with him.

"I'll take you some time. You'll meet plenty of officers and women there."

His eyes twinkle, and I sense there's more meaning behind those words.

CHAPTER 9

Friday, my day of reckoning finally arrives, and as promised, Commander Pierce summons me to his office to reveal his decision concerning his unreasonable restrictions.

"You're free to move around without an escort. Report any problem immediately, and I'll handle it. The library's on the second floor. There's not much else for civilians, but I'm sure you'll make friends. As I mentioned, the cafeteria girls may have a club or group you can join, or at least you'll learn what they do for fun."

"Thank you, sir. I'll visit the library this afternoon while your housekeeper cleans."

My library visit will be therapeutic, and a crucial part of my healing. After Colonel Wickmore's second assault in the library, I refused to return. A significant loss since the library was my lifeline, my second home, my escape, my sanctuary, and my teacher. I want that back.

§

The second-floor library appears empty—of people—but jam-packed with books, stuffed randomly on shelves. There's scant rhyme or reason to their method for shelving the books in these disorganized libraries. When visiting a disheveled library, I make it my mission to rearrange books by subject. Each time I visit that library, I reorganize more books.

After confirming no monsters or Colonels lurk in the aisles, I scour shelves for books I haven't read. I select several interesting books, including a book of poetry, another on Egyptian hieroglyphics, one discussing life after death, and Gibbon's classic *Decline and Fall of the Roman Empire*. And its companion, *Death of Democracy*. With my stack of books, I collapse on the antique medallion davenport near the entrance, depositing my selections beside me, amazed at how remarkably easy it was to conquer my fear.

An officer enters the library and stands at a book return table near the front. For a moment, an irrational fear bubbles inside me, but I chase it away. This isn't Central, and he's not Colonel Wickmore. He's a young, attractive man, exuding a confident alpha male swagger, reminding me of Nadler. He rummages through the stack of returns and glances my way. It's unusual to see a civilian woman reading in the library, especially one dressed in professional civilian clothes.

I catch his glance and smile.

He nods and moves closer, holding two paperbacks.

"Mind if I ..." he asks, nodding toward the couch.

I slide to my corner and wave for him to sit. With my books stacked between us, he settles on the far end of the modest sofa, and stretches out, manspreading.

"New here, aren't you?" he asks.

"I'm Zena Roberts, sir. I've been stationed here less than a week, working in Commander Pierce's office as a consultant on a special assignment."

"That so? What kind of assignment?"

"Sorry, sir, it's classified. Do you have a name?"

He chuckles and says, "Sure do. Lieutenant David Cross, at your service." He bows his head and waves his arm like a gallant prince. "So, Zena, that's an unusual name."

"I'm named after Xena the Warrior, but it's spelled like the Russian variant, meaning Daughter of Zeus. Have you been stationed at Cavalry long?"

"Yeah, I'm pretty much a fixture around here, I guess. So, a Russian lady warrior? Live up to your name?"

"I'm trying. Do you visit the library often? I love libraries. So much lost knowledge."

"Occasionally. What type of books are you interested in?" he asks. He leans over and flips through my selection, reading titles.

"Oh, science, philosophy, biology, and geography. I love reading about the supernatural or paranormal, and fiction. Whatever I find available. What books interest you?"

"Astronomy. Heard of the constellation *Serpens*? It includes two parts, *Serpens Caput* and *Serpens Cauda*."

"Sounds like your constellations have something to do with snakes. Serpent?"

His demeanor changes, and sounding intrigued, he says, "*Serpens Caput* is the snake's head, and *Serpens Cauda* is its tail." His eyes twinkle with curiosity. "How did you know?"

"Oh, I've learned a great deal from reading. So, is your interest in snakes or stars?"

"Both." He picks up one book from his lap and shows me the cover. "Have you read *The Girl with the Dragon Tattoo*?"

"Yes, several years ago. It contained ugly rape scenes, which I found disturbing, although, in the second scene, she gets revenge. I liked that."

"Good to know." He laughs. "What did you think of the tattoo?"

"I don't remember the dragon tattoo picture, but I've seen several books with images of tattoos, and I'm impressed with the talent necessary to create one. I love all forms of art, but I'm sure they don't allow tattoos anymore, or I'd get one ... a rose or a butterfly."

He studies my reaction with a twinkle in his eye. "I have a snake."

Is he being naughty, or does he have a snake tattoo?

"Where?"

"On my back. A snake tattoo covers my entire back."

"Show me. I'd love to see it. I thought the military forbade tattoos. Do they know?"

He laughs. "Yes, of course, but they made an exception for me. I was sixteen, and it was illegal, but they let me keep it. Instead of punishment, they sent me to military school. I was a rebel, and military school straightened me out. Found out where I belonged. And I don't show it to just anyone."

"I'm not just anyone. I was precocious, at least that's what I'm told, but they didn't send me anywhere to straighten me out. The military likes me the way I am. Not sure about here."

Lieutenant Cross holds up the other book, revealing the cover. It's another book I read several years ago, about a dominant and his submissive, and it left me with a sour taste in my soul. I make a face.

"I read that book and hated it, like the part where he whips her."

It's bizarre talking to this total stranger about rape, tattoos, and whipping, especially after my ordeal at Central, but he's so relaxed and non-threatening that I'm comfortable with him.

"What did you think of the book?" I ask, curious about the male perspective of literature I find offensive.

"There are many ways to express one's sexual desires. A group of us engage in a game we call Play. The woman maintains control, and whatever she says goes. If she says stop, he stops, and if she says no, that means no. It's consensual, and many women enjoy Play."

"So, they use belts?" My entire body cringes at the idea.

"Sure, belts, paddles, straps, if she agrees."

"Do women do it to prove they're tough like men and able to handle the pain?"

"No, to please the men, but they enjoy it, too. It's not what you think.

We have strict rules here, and you can't hit a woman without consent and no harder than she wants."

No harder than she wants? Sorry, that's wrong.

"Civilian women Play, and they're far from tough."

It would surprise him how tough we need to be to survive.

I cringe again. "Okay, this is ridiculous. Any woman who lets somebody whip her needs to be locked in a psychiatric hospital until she regains her mental health."

He laughs. "He doesn't whip her like you think. It's play, like a game, but nothing like punishment. Nobody hurts women. It's not allowed, and we don't want to hurt women."

"So, Lieutenant Cross, what's your function here?" I say, changing the subject.

"Salvage. We make certain everything brought in gets cataloged and squared away."

Two delightful and engaging hours race by before I realize the housekeeper must be finished and I should return to work.

"You know, I'm willing to show you my tattoo … if you do something for me first. Let me show you how harmless Play is, at least once."

"Sure, on the twelfth," I say, giggling.

"The twelfth?" He raises his eyebrows, looking hopeful.

"Of never."

§

The long afternoon finds me thinking about the officer I met in the library. He intrigues me, yet he talked about sex scenes I'd never consider. I shrug it off since I'll most likely never see him again, anyway.

For dinner, I should try out the second-floor cafeteria.

Mostly higher-ranking officers frequent the third-floor cafeteria, but the second-floor crowd has a mix of lower ranks and privates. They all seem to know one another, so officers rarely wear their rank. I distinguish higher-ranking officers from the behavior of others around them.

The aroma of fried onions, garlic, and mystery meat causes me to salivate and my stomach to grumble. The civilian staff behind the counter are friendlier and serve me with no problem. Military men at the tables, irrespective of rank, seem curious but more accepting of my civilian presence. Halfway through dinner, Lieutenant Cross sits across from me.

"Mind if I sit?" David asks. He grins, and I gesture, although he's already sitting.

It's an advantage for me to be seen with an officer—a greater chance others will accept me. A mixed crowd today makes me less conspicuous. A civilian server brings a coffee pot to the table, offering some to Lieutenant

Cross, but ignoring me, her attention fixed on him. He waves her off.

Funny, it looks like I've become invisible. I never drink coffee this late, but she could have offered. Peace Force members are known for their lack of manners toward civilians, who are almost always female on military bases, viewing us as second-class citizens.

The pecking order bewilders me, but it's not my responsibility to change our culture. Michael and I disagreed about our purpose in this world. His philosophy was to fight for what's right, and I insisted my work was my priority, so we had long engaging discussions about our beliefs.

"Where did you go?" Lieutenant Cross asks, squinting.

"Sorry, my mind wandered. I'm thinking about philosophical differences."

He tilts his head at me like I'm speaking in tongues.

"May I call you David in private? I'm used to addressing people by their given names."

Lieutenant Cross stares at me for a moment with a strange expression.

"Sure, but only in private."

Could it be unusual at Cavalry to call officers by their first names? We hardly know each other, so maybe he thinks I'm forward, but he said yes.

"What do you do for fun or entertainment besides Play, David?"

"Agora, right over there," he says, pointing to closed steel double doors behind him, across the great floor. "That's our second-floor club. It opens soon. Many of us hang out there."

"I've never been to a club. Do they have music and dancing? Do they allow civilians?"

"Sure, Agora allows everyone. The fourth-floor Officer's Club is exclusive, military only. Agora has music, conversation, and dancing. You've never been to a club?"

I shake my head. He lifts an eyebrow as if it can't be possible.

"Well, we're gonna change that."

We chat while I finish dinner, and when the doors to Agora open, David escorts me in. Music plays, and I'm in love. Agora sports a small dance floor awaiting dancers; behind it, a private tends a CD player on the counter. Tables and chairs line both sides of the dance floor. We passed booths walking in, reminding me of a soda shop like in old movies I've seen. It's a small gathering, but it's still early. David guides me to a booth where another couple joins us, a private and a civilian woman.

"Tim, this is Zena Roberts. Zena, this is Private Timothy Parker and his girl, Lauren."

I recognize Lauren from the second-floor cafeteria. A couple starts dancing, and I'm aching to join them. Tim moves in his seat with the music.

"Lieutenant Cross, do you dance?" I ask.

"Nope."

My hopes dashed, I turn to Tim, wondering if it's acceptable to ask him to dance since I'm not familiar with Agora's rules.

To my delight, Tim reads my mind and asks, "You dance?"

"I do."

David lets me out, and Tim and I head for the dance floor. Tim, a skillful dancer, knows many of the same dances I do, and we move in step like we've been dancing together forever. Others join us, and soon the dance floor is hopping. When we return to the booth, Lauren is gone. David stands to let me in.

It's late when the festivities die down and the crowd thins out.

"Time to say goodnight. Thank you so much, Tim, for dancing with me."

"Enjoy yourself?" David asks, bearing a knowing smile. I've been beaming all evening.

CHAPTER 10

Half asleep, another disturbing dream replays in my mind. Perching on the edge of my bed, I try to make sense of it. I was in a hospital bed holding a newborn baby wrapped in a pink blanket when a nurse asked about my plans for breastfeeding. A young man, his face out of focus, sat next to my bed, and I sensed he was my husband.

It's so bizarre because all I remember is living on military bases where they don't allow children, although I was the one exception. My childhood memories, before thirteen, were erased, but I must have seen babies and children at one point. To this day, I long to remember.

§

Upstairs, Commander and Major Abrams engage in their daily routine, munching sweet cakes with their coffee, and I wish them a good morning.

"You're cheery this morning," Major Abrams says, moving to allow me access to my spot by the sink.

"Yes, it's a beautiful day." After an evening of dancing and delightful conversation, it would be beautiful for me even if it poured drenching rain outside.

After retrieving the Book and papers, I pretend to work.

"Is that shorthand?" Commander asks. He eyes my papers covered on both sides in my cryptic scribble.

"It's my unique personal shorthand. I use it to keep track of the possible meanings of the symbols." Half true. "I write so fast in cursive I can't read my own writing, so my shorthand allows me to work faster and keep organized."

With the Book opened, I stare at the symbols as if I'm in deep concentration, hoping his questions will stop. I dislike lying, but Nadler said it was acceptable to lie, sometimes, but never to him. I've made progress translating the Book and begun outlining my preliminary report, but that truth must remain hidden.

The officers leave, taking their coffee cups and dessert dish with them.

§

Cassie spots me passing by her desk on my way to refill my empty coffee cup. "Zena, do you have a minute?"

"Sure."

"I spoke with Dr. Mitchell, and he reports you haven't checked in with him yet. When did you receive your last contraceptive injection? You must schedule a doctor's appointment. Get that squared away. I can schedule an appointment for you."

She never glances up.

"Thanks for reminding me, but I'll take care of it straight away. Where is his office?"

"Second floor, same side as the cafeteria. Ask anyone, and they'll direct you. You're certain you don't want me to make an appointment?"

"Thanks, that's unnecessary, but I'll check in with him."

In the break room, I fill my cup to the brim with a steaming hot brew. Commander enters with the same idea, and as I watch him fill his cup, I sip mine and study him. Such an attractive man. He takes a sip of coffee, and I'm envious of his lucky coffee cup pressed against those luscious, full lips. He stands so close that his aftershave intoxicates me as I fumble and search for a witty quip to impress him, but nothing clever comes to mind.

"So, it's been almost a week. Have everything you need?"

"Yes, sir, I'm managing quite well," I say, careful to maintain eye contact. "The library was easy to find, and I borrowed several interesting books for evening reading."

"Excellent. I like to hear that."

My mind fails me, and I'm desperate to appear more engaging, but I prefer to study his beautiful clean-shaven face and imagine tasting his delicious-looking lips.

"Zena?"

"Sorry, my mind wandered. The Book is so challenging, and I'm absorbed in its complexities."

Commander is my handler, and I must keep that foremost in mind. I excuse myself and hurry upstairs, redirecting my thinking to lunch with David.

§

When I arrive early for lunch, I'm greeted by whiffs of pan-fried pizza—three cheese, sausage, pepperoni, and vegetarian—all competing for attention. The half-filled cafeteria shows no sign of David. Tim lunches with a group of other privates. He notices me and nods as I exit the line with my pizza selection. I return his nod and choose a seat alone in case David shows up. Finished eating, I prepare to leave when David parks himself across from me.

"Given any more thought about our discussion?"

"You mean Play?" I ask.

"I'll show you there's nothing to fear, and I'll never do anything you don't want. You're in charge."

"I'm pretty sure it's not the twelfth yet."

He pouts. "Come on, we had fun last night, didn't we?"

"Yes. I enjoy your company. I enjoy talking to you and hanging out with you, but I'll never Play. It's not my way."

"What's your way?"

"I make love. That's my way."

"Sounds like I'm not the kind of man you want."

"Maybe not." My heart sinks, but I conceal it. He's playing, and I understand his game.

He leaves without another word.

§

When I return for dinner, David never shows up, so I join Tim and his friends. Their trays each boast a generous slice of apple pie with whip-creamed dollops, and although I don't eat sweets, the aroma of cinnamon apple delights my nose. We chat like old friends, and one by one each soldier excuses himself.

After dinner, I explore the second floor in search of the doctor's office. A door with a sign confirming it's the Infirmary opens to a small, empty reception area.

"Anyone here?" I ask, listening for sounds of human activity.

A young officer wearing a white coat emerges from an adjoining room sporting a warm smile and a regulation buzz cut, high and tight.

"Can I help you?" he asks.

"I know it's late, but I'd like to see the nurse, if possible. I'm new here."

"You must be Zena Roberts, the new consultant we were expecting. Need your shot?"

"No, not now. I'd like to speak with the nurse about a different matter."

"You're in luck. I'm Corporal Noah Turner, Dr. Mitchell's nurse. How can I help you?"

"Can we discuss a personal matter? Are you busy?"

"My patients always come first. Let's move into the examination room and talk there."

The examination room contains a single chair, so I climb on the exam table. An uncomfortable feeling grips me, recalling the first time I was on an exam table, exposed and embarrassingly examined.

"I'm not here as a patient. You're sure you're not busy?"

"I'm free. So, what brings you here?"

"I need some … information."

"Okay," he says.

He shuts the door and sits on the chair across from me.

"I'm aware of the rules about privacy, but I have questions about what some call Play."

"You're right about privacy, especially concerning another person's sexual habits, but if you have questions sexual in nature, please feel free to ask. I've heard them all."

His warm smile could melt a glacier.

"Have any women who Play ever sought treatment for sustained injuries?"

Nurse Turner looks up at me and leans forward.

"I'm not aware of anyone needing treatment. It's my understanding the woman is always in charge …"

Sure, heard all that before.

"Okay, I'm told it's consensual, and men never hurt the women, but it seems that with belts and paddles, they must … hurt them. Right?"

My stomach churns. Does he Play too?

"Why would you think that? They wouldn't Play if that was true. No one forces them."

He's so nonchalant as if Play is natural. He stands and walks over to me.

"If you don't want to Play, no one can make you," he says in a reassuring voice.

"I met someone who Plays, and I want confirmation I'm safe with him."

Nurse Turner's kind eyes put me at ease.

"Well, Zena, I'm sure no one abuses women on this base, and we'd never tolerate it. Even punishment is administered in a safe and tempered way. Stay clear of men who Play if you're not interested because they definitely are. That's my advice."

"Well, I appreciate your advice," I say, and slide down off the table.

"What about your birth control injection? Let's take care of that," he says. He turns and reaches into a medical cabinet.

"No, I took care of it at Central, and I'm protected. Thank you for your time."

§

In my room, absorbed in reading a library book, my eyelids grow heavy, and in short order, I find myself on a beach gazing out at the water, breathing the salty air. Hot sand squishes between my bare toes. Waves roll in, washing over pebbles. Off in the distance, seagulls take flight against a turquoise sky, their flapping wings almost audible. A man and two children, a boy, and a girl, sit in the sand nearby, industriously building sandcastles. When I wake, I know the familiar man is my husband, and the children are mine.

§

What I'm learning while translating the symbols in the Book amazes me, and I've recorded scores of notes for my preliminary report. The Overlords intend to cooperate with nature by altering human behavior to make the earth sustainable again. The operative symbol roughly translates to *The Great Healing, Regeneration,* or *Wellness.* It reads like utopian science fiction. However, based on known events over recent generations, their intentions run contradictory to reality. With luck, by translating the Master Plan, I'll understand my stubborn belief that the Overlords are my Enemy. I'm tackling the first section for translation, titled *Phase I—Infiltration.*

§

Mid-morning, I pass Cassie's desk on my way upstairs with a full cup of coffee.

"Incidentally, Cassie, I visited Nurse Turner yesterday."

"You didn't see Dr. Mitchell?"

"Not necessary. Nurse Turner attended to my needs, and we made plans for a follow-up visit." It's half a truth and a lie. No worries about getting pregnant since it's impossible, and it's my business, not theirs.

§

Back in the break room, setting my rinsed cup in the sink, I'm surprised by Major Williams standing in the entryway, waving me into Major Abrams' office.

"You've been here a week now. How's it going?" Major Williams asks.

"I'm learning my way around, sir."

Major Williams walks over, drapes his arm around my shoulders, and whispers in my ear.

"Wanna take a walk with me?"

"I should get back to work," I say, pasting on a fake smile.

"No worries. I'm pretty fast."

"That's not comforting."

I'm unsure he catches my meaning, but he laughs.

§

David has joined Tim and several others at their table, so I breeze past them with my tray. I smile and nod to everyone. I select an empty table and eat alone, ignoring David, and acting like I don't miss his company. After finishing my meal, he walks toward me, and I pretend not to notice him. He sits across from me.

"Have you checked out the library?" he asks. "They delivered a load of books yesterday, so they should be finished shelving them. Check them out."

"I'll do that. I should finish the book I'm reading this evening."

"Not going to Agora tonight?"

"I hadn't planned to. I thought I'd read or explore. Are you?"

"Sure. Wanna go with me?"

Like he hasn't been avoiding me.

"Can I bring my music? I have some decent dance tunes."

"Sure, why not?"

We plan to meet in an hour, giving me sufficient time to change from work clothes to casual wear and select suitable music.

§

I'm punctual, and when I return, I find David waiting. A small crowd has gathered in Agora, but the music hasn't started. I pass my music discs to the private who acts as disc jockey. David escorts me to his booth where Tim and Lauren join us.

A half-hour later, my music rocks Agora, and when we see couples on the dance floor, Tim and I join them and dance to several tunes. After partnering with two other soldiers, I rejoin David. A sweaty Tim sits across from David, but Lauren has left. We're deep in conversation when a civilian woman standing nearby catches my attention.

The plain, small-framed female with shoulder-length brown hair watches us, looking about to speak or cry. David, aware I'm watching her, appears annoyed, turns to her, scowling, and motions to her to leave. She does.

"Who was that?" I ask.

"Nobody."

"Well, she looked like somebody to me," I say, waiting for a better answer.

"We Played for a while, but she decided to end the game. Now she's ready to come back, but it's too late."

Am I the reason it's too late for her? But David and I will never Play. It's not my business to interfere, and she appears around my age, old enough to fend for herself. She's not a girl; she's a woman. He's free to Play with anyone he wants. David doesn't belong to me.

§

Because I arrived late this morning, I missed the morning coffee ritual. I'm reviewing the enormous, detailed information in the Book, including the Overlords' plan outlining the path to our ultimate destiny. From researching history in books and movies, I've studied life before the Overlords intervened—but how we arrived at the present circumstances remains unknown.

From my historical research, I learned the former inhabited world was vast, with hundreds of countries globally tied together economically but divided by religion, race, moral beliefs, different cultures, violence, and war. Greed triumphed over compassion and common sense. The earth was dying because of neglect and the worship of power and riches. No book references describe our descent from that world to this reduced one. Now, many laws govern our behavior: no personal wealth, religion, politics, war, mass shootings, hate-mongering, or conspiracy theories.

Also gone, as far as I'm aware, are sexual morals, art, theater, ballet, and interconnectivity by something called the Internet, social media, television, or radio broadcasts. Everyone is literate and educated, but from my experience in the quiet libraries, they seldom self-educate as I do. What happened to move us from the past to the world today is unknown. A tremendous gap exists between recorded history and present-day conditions.

The Overlords quelled war and rumors of war, including any disruption of domestic tranquility—whether from racial, religious, ethnic hatred, or political divisiveness—by rooting out the causes. Poverty, crime, drugs, alcohol, and civilian-owned firearms are all issues of the past, as are unwanted pregnancies and social stigmas arising from perceived differences between people. They transformed a world of deprivation into one of prosperity where individuality was replaced by unity and uniformity. A brave new world with free health care, abundant food, clean water, safe housing, and universal education. Shangri-La?

§

Major Abrams pours himself a cup of coffee, and cup in hand, I prepare to do likewise.

"Missed you this morning," Abrams says. He takes a sip and watches me fill my cup.

"Major Abrams, what do you do here?"

"I'm second in command," he says, standing a bit taller. "I'm also Chief Information Officer, and I collect data from each department and manage the flow of information."

"And what does Major Williams do?"

"He manages the maintenance team. They take care of any plumbing, electrical, or building problem."

"Your given name is Paul, isn't it?" I ask, stepping back, awaiting his answer.

"Sure, why?"

"May I call you by your given name, in private? We work in the same office, and you call me by my given name. Need we be so formal?"

Major Abrams stares at me like David did when I asked him the same question. Nadler taught me to address officers by their rank and surname in public and always address Commanders by rank even in private, but on other bases, I was allowed to call my comrades and my handler by their first names in private. I'm not privy to Commander's given name, and I'm too well-trained to be informal with him.

Major Abrams hesitates and squints while looking me over. One might think I asked him to cut out his tongue.

"I suppose it would be all right ... in private," he says, smiling like he's considering a private moment.

Major Williams enters, crowding the small break room.

"Zena asked to call me by my first name in private," Paul says with a wink.

Major Williams steps back, holding the same strange expression at first, then smirks and puts his arm around me.

"Take a walk with me, and you can call me anything you want ... in private," he says with a wicked grin. He's not taking me seriously.

"No, joking aside, may I call you Tom when we're in the office? But never in public. I understand the rules."

His expression changes, and I can't figure out whether he's offended or disappointed. There must be a strict rule for addressing officers at Cavalry, restricted to rank and surnames. When my co-workers at Central allowed me to address them by their given names, it broke the tension, making me feel like part of the team. Here, I'm not part of their team, but we encounter one another often.

"You can call me Tom, in private. But not Commander. He wouldn't tolerate it."

"Thanks, Tom. I understand, and I'm careful."

My minor victory and I return upstairs to my worktable.

§

David joins me for lunch, and over meatloaf, sweet peas, and mashed potatoes with brown gravy, we chat about Agora, my love of music, and dance. Our conversation turns into a lively discussion about a book I'm reading about the merits or disadvantages of democracy and freedom. After exhausting the subject, our conversation wanes.

"Have you considered joining me in Play?" he asks. He looks hopeful while displaying a naughty boy grin.

"I've been considering, but I'm not clear why I'd enjoy Play," I say.

"You should at least try it. No harm in trying, is there?"

"No harm?" I ask, folding my arms across my chest in defiance. "Belts, paddles?"

"I promise I'll never do anything without your consent, and I'll never hurt you if that's your greatest fear. It's Play, and it's fun."

"It doesn't sound like fun for me."

"Come on and give it a chance, and if you don't like it, I'll understand. I'll leave you alone, I promise."

I don't want him to leave me alone.

"Let me think about it." I need to change the subject before one of us walks away.

"Is there a hard rule against calling an officer by his first name?" I ask.

David shifts in his seat, and his expression turns serious.

"It's generally frowned upon, but there's no strict rule for military personnel, depending on rank ... but they expect civilians to be more respectful."

"Even in bed?"

"Well, when you're in bed, you'd be alone, so ..."

I laugh. "When you're intimate, making love, naked, must you still be so formal?"

"Can't say. I wouldn't know."

I make a sour face.

§

Commander stands at Cassie's desk.

"How was lunch?" he asks.

"Lunch was fine, sir. And afterward, I did some research on the second floor."

He accompanies me to the steps of the apartment.

"I have a poker game tonight, so if you want to stay in the apartment and listen to your music, it's no problem."

"Thank you, sir, but I have plans for tonight. Tuesday is poker night?

Rain check, sir?"

"Rain check, it is. Why do you use the second-floor cafeteria? Is there a problem with the one on the third floor?"

"No, sir, I was on the second floor doing research, and I decided to have lunch there."

Is he having me watched?

He looks like he has more questions but changes his mind. He stands so near that his intoxicating cologne makes my heart beat faster. David never affects me like this. Although Michael and I cared for each other, and our relationship was great, he never drove me wild like this. I try not to blush, and I smile. That's all I can manage. I excuse myself and run upstairs.

§

A nightmare leaves me sitting on the edge of the bed, my breath racing with my heartbeat. This terrifying nightmare was far too real. A dark figure wore a trench coat, but his features were in deep shadow. He intended to remove something from me I'd never surrender, and whatever the Shadow Man snatched from me would kill me. So, I killed him.

What does the dream mean? I believe the meaning of a dream lies in the telling—but I've nobody to share it with. Was my dream about David pressuring me to Play? But David isn't a dark, shadowy figure, and Play wouldn't kill me. I wouldn't enjoy it, but it wouldn't kill me. Could the Shadow Man represent the Colonel at Central Control demanding favors from me, and my refusal to surrender to him, so he stripped them from me? It didn't kill me, but something inside me broke. That's like a death. The nightmare was so real, and the ominous feeling won't leave me.

§

After a leisurely lunch, I ask David where to find the Radio Room, and he points to an open entrance near the cafeteria.

"Why the interest in the Radio Room?"

"When I worked at Central, I had phone conversations with the personnel stationed here, and I'm eager to meet them." I can't tell David about my plan to dig up information on Michael.

He seems satisfied, and it's partially true. When David leaves, I head for the open doorway. Inside, past the sergeant's office, I enter the Radio Room, and it feels familiar.

The crew members raise their heads, scrutinizing me as I wander into their domain. I'm a civilian and a female, and neither belongs in here. Their elevator eyes start at my legs and stop at my breasts.

"Hi, fellas. I'm Special Consultant Zena Roberts. At Central, I worked with several guys in our Radio Room and had phone conversations with Corporals Gary Morris and Justin Peterson. I'm eager to meet them in person if they're here."

A sergeant marches in, and I repeat my introduction. My reputation preceded me, and Gary and Justin approach me to shake my hand, exclaiming they are glad to meet me. I turn to address the sergeant.

"The Commander is my handler, and I work on the fourth floor in his offices. I'm here on assignment."

The sergeant nods and leaves, and I explore their operation. I planned to ask about Michael since he oversaw Central's Radio Room and often visited here. It's the wrong time. Instead, I ask if they are receiving any messages yet.

Gary frowns and shrugs.

"The Overlords have been dead quiet for months now," Justin says.

The sergeant reappears, and he's friendlier. I assume he called Commander.

I thank them for taking the time to speak with me and excuse myself, leaving them to resume their duties. On returning to the office, Commander stands at Cassie's desk.

"How was lunch?" He knows.

"I had a pleasant lunch, sir, and afterward, I stopped in the Radio Room to meet the staff. The sergeant was kind and allowed me to meet two men I had phone conversations with from Central. I didn't stay long and only wanted to introduce myself."

Commander sighs, a relaxed smile crosses his face, and he nods, seemingly pleased I'm forthcoming. It's a novel experience for me, having my handler aware of my every move. What else does he know about me? Is he privy to my relationship with David and our Agora visits? That's my personal life, and reading him would tell me, but I let it go.

§

A smattering of regulars fills Agora tonight, but the music hasn't started yet. Tim and Lauren haven't shown up, so David and I sit alone in our booth. He looks puzzled, and then apparently reaches a decision.

"You've never been to my office. Care to see it?"

"Sure." I imagine his office, visualizing a cluttered desk and maps hanging on the walls. Maybe some posters displaying different weapons. Or maybe a chart of our solar system.

The wide ramp near the cafeteria slopes to the main floor, to an unfamiliar section. David points out his elevated office overlooking an area resembling a docking bay. Several young privates, unloading a truck, stop and watch me. I wave to them, and they wave back. David redirects my attention by leading me to his office.

The entire outer side of the rectangular office has windows facing the docking bay. Even the entrance door has a window. His desk sits at the back of the room, facing forward with a visitor's chair in front of the desk. A windowless door opposite the entrance might be a bathroom or storeroom.

"What do you think?"

His sparse office is uninviting, nothing like I imagined. The plain office walls display a framed document hanging over another piece of furniture, a single bookcase with three books, and other artifacts. It doesn't appear he spends much time in his office, and I'm confused about why he brought me here. I glance around, trying to appear impressed, but I'm not.

"There's something else I want to show you."

He puts his arm around my shoulder and walks me toward the door opposite the entrance. He unlocks the door and enters, turning on the lights, with me following. The cream-colored room has white sheets draped over mysterious furniture. One, shaped like a doctor's exam table, sits next to exercise equipment. A pair of black leather straps and two paddles hang from a shiny black bar screwed into the wall. He left the door open, and I'm considering running.

David tells me this is where he likes to Play, explaining each piece of furniture or equipment and singing the virtues of Play. He's into it, and I'm ready to leave, but I refuse to show fear. After all, he claims it's consensual, and I'm not consenting. I force a fake smile, and when he's done trying to sell me on Play, I head for the door. He follows, turns off the lights, and closes the door.

"So, what do you think?" David asks.

"I'm not sure. Play's new to me. I'll need to give it more thought."

No, I'm sure.

Halfway up the ramp to the second floor, I spot a door displaying Overlords' symbols above it. The rough translation suggests this was a nursery or childcare room. Symbols often mean phrases rather than individual words, and they can differ in meaning depending on context. I might find other symbols in similar unexpected places, and I'm interested in exploring them. We part for the evening, and I head upstairs to the quiet fourth floor.

I stroll around the perimeter, searching for undisturbed areas. Alterations completed over the years covered up many of the symbols or obliterated them. After passing the women's quarters, I'm drawn to a wall in an unobstructed, hidden alcove. There is no evidence of symbols, but the wall slides open without warning, revealing a locked door. While I'm examining it, the door unlocks on its own with a muffled click.

I check around before stepping through the doorway. When I close the door behind me, the wall makes a faint grating sound, sliding back, concealing the door. A narrow wrought-iron platform, like fire escapes I've seen in old movies, leads to a set of steps that takes me down to another walkway that extends in either direction. Motion-activated lights illuminate my way.

On the third-floor level, I turn right, and the path leads me to another door. Dare I? It could open to a busy hallway, someone's room, or the men's showers. That would be terrible. I flash on a memory of a naked officer discovering me hiding in the men's showers when I was thirteen.

When I open this door, the wall retracts, and I peek out to establish my whereabouts. It's a deserted shadowy passageway, so I release my held breath and close the door behind me, triggering the wall to slide shut. Darkened offices line the hallway on either side, and I navigate by the soft illumination of the great floor lights, ending near the third-floor cafeteria. My luck persists—nobody's around.

Where do people socialize on this floor? I use the stairs to return undetected to the fourth floor.

CHAPTER 11

I loiter after lunch until the second-floor cafeteria is almost empty and the delicious cooking aromas are swapped for heady odors of hot soapy water. Angie, one of the cafeteria women, lugs around her soap pail and sponge, cleaning tables, wearing bright yellow rubber gloves.

"You know, Angie, my entire first week, I dined on the third floor, but it's so much nicer here. Everyone is gracious, and y'all work so hard to manage the cafeteria."

All true. Her face beams.

"Angie, by any chance, do you know any of Lieutenant Cross's playmates?" I look over my shoulders to ensure no one hears. "He talks about Play, and I'm interested in learning more from a woman's point of view."

She ponders my question while dunking her dingy orange sponge in a bucket of sudsy water, squeezing it.

"Two girls, Heather, and Sandy were his playmates once. I can talk to them to see if they'll speak to you. If you come back later, I'll let you know."

"Thanks so much. I'll be here early for dinner."

§

A half an hour early for dinner, I nod to Angie. She stops by my table with a pot of coffee and whispers that both women will speak with me. Angie steers me to a private room in the civilian quarters and promises to return soon. A few minutes later, she reappears with two brown-haired young women. I thank Angie. She smiles, winks at me, and leaves.

"Thank you for making time to speak with me. I'm becoming

acquainted with Lieutenant Cross, and he's asked me to Play."

"Oh," says Heather.

Sandy nods and sits back.

"Lieutenant Cross told me about Play, but I'm curious about Play from the female perspective. I respect your privacy, and I won't repeat anything you say to me. If you feel uncomfortable, please say so. I don't want to intrude on your privacy or make you uneasy."

"Okay," Heather says. Her timid voice warns me to tread carefully.

I give Heather a warm smile and touch her arm in reassurance—and to read her better.

"What do you want to know?" Heather asks while Sandy remains quiet.

"How did y'all meet Lieutenant Cross?"

Heather takes a deep breath. She looks to the ceiling as if praying, and then back at me.

"He was eating in the cafeteria and motioned for me to sit and talk to him. He explained Play and asked me what I like. First, some general stuff, then he started asking about … you know … sexual stuff. He asked me if I wanted to Play and, well, at first, I said no. Sometimes he acted like he liked me, and sometimes he ignored me. I wanted him to like me, so I said yes."

"It was pretty much the same for me," Sandy says, finally speaking.

I take Sandy's hand, putting her at ease, and make a connection to better read her.

"Did he take y'all to his Playroom?"

Sandy nods, but a surprised Heather fidgets, twisting a strand of hair between her fingers.

"Yes, that's where we started Playing. He told me to take off my clothes, but I was shy. I've had sex but never allowed a man to see me naked before. It embarrassed me for him to stand there dressed … and me, wearing nothing," Heather says.

"But you gave in?"

Heather glances down, then lifts her head and makes eye contact.

"Well, he said if I didn't, then we may as well leave. I wanted to stay, but he wouldn't give me more time, so I did it. That's the way he was. He'd ask me to do things, and if I didn't, he would insist we leave; but if I gave in, he was happy, and we'd have sex."

Heather worries her hands as she recalls and conveys her story.

"Heather, did you enjoy Play?"

"Sometimes, but not everything he wanted. I told him I wanted to please him, but he wanted me to do stuff I refused to do, so we'd stop. Then I'd never know if I'd see him again. He'd stop coming around for a while. After a while, I started doing what he wanted, hoping he wouldn't ask again."

Sandy says, "Yeah, that's the way he was. He had to have his way. I did everything he wanted, then he dumped me. Playing wasn't so bad, and the quicker you gave in, the sooner he'd move on to the next challenge."

"Why go along if it made you uncomfortable?" I ask Heather, who appears unsettled.

"When I did what he wanted, he was nice to me. We hung out at Agora, and I'd sit with him, and everyone knew I was his girl. I liked that," Heather says, her face crumbling as her eyes tear up. "I loved him, and I thought if I pleased him, he'd love me too. No matter how I tried to please him, it was never enough. After a while, I gave in to everything, even if I hated it. Then he dumped me cold. I hated myself for what I did, but I loved him."

"What about those belts and paddles? Didn't they hurt?"

"No, they look scarier than they are. Men have rules. They can't hit a woman harder than she allows. You can tell him to go easier. He never hurt me … too much," Sandy says.

I cringe, hoping it doesn't show.

"The spanking wasn't the worst—once you got used to the idea. It was the … other stuff he wanted me to do," Heather says.

So, to David, Play is a game about winning, not sex. Was dumping her part of the game and fun for him, or because he lost interest? Conquest and domination seem like dreadful ways to have sex.

"Are you ladies all right now?"

"I guess, but I don't go to Agora anymore. I'm not as shy about sex, and I regret some things I did, but not everything," Heather says.

Anything these women left out, I managed to read.

"Thank you for sharing your stories. You've both been very helpful."

"You should talk to Terry, the girl I replaced. Terry transferred to the third-floor cafeteria. She didn't last as one of Lieutenant Cross's girls. Terry fought him a lot, so he quit her, and she requested a transfer upstairs to avoid him," says Sandy.

It's clear David comes across as charismatic and personable, and all his *girls* fall in love with him, but he has a dark side.

§

In the bustling third-floor cafeteria, bursting with the pungent fermentation of sauerkraut and kielbasa, I ask a civilian worker cleaning tables where I might find Terry. She points to a slight woman working behind the counter. I approach her and suggest we have a conversation, but Terry replies she's busy. However, she agrees to meet with me when the lunch crowd leaves.

Eventually, the lunchroom clears, and I keep my appointment with Terry, meeting at a table far from others, even though the cafeteria is almost empty. I explain my reason for wanting to chat and promise to keep her confidence. She agrees to a conversation, but when I ask my first question about David, her expression sours as a disruption behind me catches her attention. She stands, so I turn around to see the head matron storming our way, and she's not happy. I stand to face her and offer my hand.

"You must be Joan Evans. I'm Special Consultant Zena Roberts, and I work in Commander's office. I'm glad to meet you."

She eyes me with suspicion, giving me the once over. This is an easy read. She knows who I am, but not why I want to speak with one of her workers. She doesn't take my hand.

"Is this about the punishment?"

Punishment?

"No, no, of course not. I'm engaged in some research and wanted to talk to Terry. It's a confidential matter, and if it's a bad time, we can reschedule."

She appears confused and unsure of her next move.

"Oh, I'm sorry, Miss Evans. Apparently, there's a different protocol at Cavalry than I've enjoyed at previous assignments. My high-security clearance has always given me free access to speak to whomever I wish."

Miss Evans scowls, so I offer my ID.

"Look, no harm, I'll speak to my handler, Commander Pierce, and I'm sure we can straighten this out. I certainly don't want to step on anyone's toes."

She appears nervous and scrutinizes me when I mention Commander.

"I need about half an hour, but I want to follow the rules. I know you're as serious about your job as I am about mine."

Miss Evans takes a step back.

"I apologize. I'm still learning the different rules," I say.

Miss Evans relaxes her stance.

"I suppose it's all right, but if we get busy, Terry needs to return to her job."

"Understood. If the cafeteria gets busy, I'll leave."

At that moment, a concerned-looking Major Tom Williams appears.

"Problem here?" he asks.

"No, of course not, sir," I say. "We're having a *civil* conversation. Get it? We're all civilians, so ... civil?" I giggle.

Miss Evans and Terry grin at my joke, and then Miss Evan's eyes narrow. Tom nods and leaves, and the head matron walks back to the kitchen. Terry and I take our seats to finish our interrupted conversation.

"Why the interest in Lieutenant Cross?" Terry asks, peering over her shoulders.

"Well, I'm getting to know him, and he talks about Play. I'm interested in your experience because it doesn't sound fun to me, and play should be fun for both parties."

I read her, and she's reluctant to discuss what David wanted of her.

"So, you worked on the second floor when you met him? Did you seek him out, or did he approach you?"

"He started talking to me, and he scared me at first because he has a reputation, but he was nice. Then he started talking about Play. I wasn't interested, and he acted like I was too immature for the game, anyway. I tried it to show him I wasn't. At first, it wasn't awful, but I didn't care for it. He asked me to ... do stuff that seemed wrong, and I refused. After that, he treated me like I was the problem. He said if I was mature enough, I'd please him, but I couldn't, not his way. I'd rather not discuss what he wanted."

David's previous two playmates shared enough, and I Paid Attention to what they omitted.

"I understand, Terry. I don't want you to divulge anything that makes you uncomfortable. How long were you with him?"

"Maybe a month, but I kept saying no to him, and I guess he gave up. One day, he told me he didn't want to see me anymore, but if I ever grew up, I should let him know. But if he found another girl, I'd be out of luck. It hurt, but I was tired of him telling me I wasn't sophisticated enough, so I stopped coming around. When I saw him with different girls, it was difficult for me, so I transferred here."

"Terry, I'm proud of you for standing your ground. You're one strong woman."

She straightens her shoulders and lifts her chin.

Terry made it sound more like a punishment than play. Which reminds me....

"What was Miss Evans talking about? Punishment?"

Terry lowers her head, and for a moment, I fear she's reluctant to speak.

"I had a problem with Miss Evans. She kept me on potato peeling duty so long my hands hurt. I refused to peel any more vegetables and insisted on doing something else. Miss Evans took me to the Commander and claimed I refused to work. He gave me two swats as punishment and told Miss Evans to rotate the jobs. She might worry that she'll get reported to the Peace Council for mistreating us. We don't have civilian support except for her. And if she's the problem ..."

I nod in agreement. Nobody wants to be arraigned before the Council or to expose our dirty laundry to the Overlords.

"I'm sorry, it's not my job to be anyone's advocate. It seems like the Commander handled it. Am I wrong? Has your situation improved?"

"Yes, and I'm treated better now."

"Well, Terry, thanks for your time. I'll let you return to your duties."

How could Commander punish this slight young woman? Commanders have the authority to punish anyone who breaks the rules, but why punish this civilian woman for refusing to peel potatoes because her hands hurt? My stomach flip-flops.

§

The small hospital room has another bed, however, it's empty. I'm alone in my hospital room, my belly contracting in mind-numbing pain washing over me in waves, and I swear to all gods I'm dying. No one could survive so much pain. The torment eases. I rest, and then it begins again.

The pain wakens me, and I'm in my tiny quarters at Cavalry. What the hell was that? I hug my abdomen, which feels normal. No pain. It was only a dream, but the agony felt real, and I'm drenched in sweat. My one memory of being in a hospital bed was with Andrew when he needed me, but his pain never touched me. Instead, he felt comfort from me.

§

Commander enters the break room and fills his cup, standing close to me, but this time his presence reminds me of Terry's unfair punishment.

"How's it going?" he asks. With a slight frown, he makes eye contact, and I suspect he has an agenda. Did Tom report my conversation with the head matron and Terry in the cafeteria?

"You've been here almost three weeks. Making any friends?" he asks. There it is.

"Yes, sir, I've met several civilian women and had interesting conversations with them." I'm honest, at least. What else does he know?

"Excellent."

He smiles, and I forget everything except the sexual tension I feel when I'm near him. I study his muscular frame and tan skin, a shade or two darker than mine, although I imagine it's been years since he felt the sun, if ever. His soft, full lips invoke daydreams about covering them with passionate kisses like lovers do….

The silence is awkward, and I'm unaware of how long we stand there, with me staring at him. I take a sip of coffee.

"Good, cooled down enough," I say, still savoring the warmth of his proximity.

I leave, my face warm. Rounding the corner, I steal a glimpse of him watching me, smiling.

§

In the cafeteria line, I inhale the tantalizing fragrance of onions caramelized in butter, combined with the steam from bubbling cauldrons of beef broth.

I choose a large crock of French onion soup blanketed with oven-browned Provolone cheese. David sits with Tim and two unfamiliar privates. He gestures for me to join them. They're engaged in animated conversation, and David neglects to introduce me. Ready to leave, the two privates stand, nod in my direction, and walk away. Tim departs, leaving me alone with David.

"So, who were those guys?" I ask. I don't need to read him to discern he's upset.

"From the salvage unit." His tone is curt. He avoids eye contact and stares at his empty bowl, biting his lip.

"Why didn't you introduce me?"

"No need. They're setting out tomorrow," he says. David clenches his jaw and frowns.

"Are you angry with me about something?"

"Should I be?"

David stares at me, so I shrug my shoulders and feign innocence.

"Anything you'd like to share with me, Zena?" He knows.

"I'm not sure. Can you give me a hint? A lot happens in my life."

"You've been talking to my ex-girls behind my back."

"Yes, I conducted my own research. You keep asking me to Play, but I don't understand the game and what's in it for me. How can I decide without information?"

"I told you everything you needed to know." He stays calm and relaxes his shoulders.

"Not what it's like from the woman's point of view, and it's still unclear why I would Play. It isn't my way, and making love is better."

David leans forward with his elbows on the table and his chin on his hands.

"You know I won't wait forever."

"Am I not worth waiting for? After all, you're asking me to Play, and I'm not sure I can trust you yet. Ever hear the expression *trust, but verify*?"

He laughs. "I think you're playing with me." He cocks his head and squints one eye.

"I don't play," I say.

CHAPTER 12

Major Tom Williams and Jen engage in playful conversation and laughter with Major Paul Abrams in his office. I wish them good morning as I pass them on my way to the supply cabinets to restock my legal pads and look for folders.

Michael often spoke of the Commander's Inner Circle, and it appears Tom, Paul, Jen, and Cassie comprise that Circle. Will they invite me in someday? Michael claimed it's an exclusive club, but obstacles like that never deter me.

Their devious smiles warn me of impending mischief.

I'm resting my hands on the open cabinet doors looking for folders when Tom slips in behind me. Jen stands several feet away, glances my way, and then resumes marking her clipboard. Tom wraps his arms around my waist, and his hands brush my hips as he pulls me to him. I move forward to discourage him, but he pulls me back with careful intent. His tender embrace kindles a fire inside me that I haven't felt in months.

As Tom holds me tight against his chest, his manhood presses against me. The warmth of his body mixes with the smell of his cologne and his gentle touch, and I'm reluctant to move away. With his arms crossing over me, they brush against my breasts. I can't breathe. He whispers, his breath warm against my ear.

"Let's visit the Comfort Room and get better acquainted." Tom's tongue lashes out and licks my ear lobe sending a chill through me, and I'm frozen, stuck to his warmth, thinking forbidden thoughts.

Jen, still standing there, wordlessly reminds me Tom isn't mine to enjoy. She bears a thin but muscular frame and a masculine manner, like a soldier. Yeah, she could wipe the floor with me in her sleep. I hear Commander's voice, and Tom steps away from me.

"Hey, Jen. Is it okay if I call you Jen?" I ask.

She lifts her head and shrugs, and if she's disturbed by Tom's behavior, she hides it.

"I don't see any folders, and I need them to organize my papers."

I grab two legal pads and a box of paper clips. Jen meets me at the cabinet, bends down, and rummages through a couple of boxes on the bottom shelf.

"How many?"

"I think three folders are plenty, now that I see where they're kept."

She isn't friendly, but not hostile either. If Tom was my lover and he behaved like that in front of me, it would end us. When I walk past Paul with my materials, he flashes me a conspiratorial smile and laughs. It may have been fun for them, but it's clear I need sex.

§

David didn't show, so after eating lunch alone, I explore the second-floor perimeter, this time hunting for doorways to the secret corridor. As I pass several Comfort Rooms, I relive disturbing memories of Colonel Wickmore dragging me into them, locking me inside. Before his attacks, I used the Comfort Rooms for its bathrooms, never for sex, but now I can't enter them.

§

David meets me for dinner, and after a light conversation, I debate asking him about something that's been on my mind.

"May I ask you a question?" I ask.

"You just did," David says, smiling.

"You mentioned several men on base Play, but can they have normal sex too?"

"Normal is whatever two or more people enjoy doing together, given it's consensual."

"Okay, sure, but can they have sex without Play? Do they?"

"Not me, but I can't speak for others. I don't see why not, depending on their tastes."

I pick at my food, mulling over his response.

"Wanna go to Agora after?" David asks.

"Sure, but I need to tidy up my work area. I'll meet you there when I finish."

§

David waits for me near the Agora entrance, and we grab our usual booth in the back. I didn't bring my music and don't intend to dance. Tim and Lauren join us, but I'm deep in thought, half-listening to the conversation. Another officer joins us, and David signals for me to scoot over to allow room. David moves closer to me and drapes his arm behind me. While the officers make conversation, I'm hyper-aware of his warm body close to mine and his arousing aftershave. My gaze settles on a young private and civilian woman in another booth. They are inseparable, his hungry mouth on hers. I want that.

The officer leaves, and I have no clue who he is, but David remains sitting close to me. Can he feel this too? I move my hand to his thigh and caress him with a light touch, and he shoots me a searing glance, but I feign innocence. David gives Tim his attention, and I gently stroke the top of his thigh, pretending to play with the material of his slacks. When he glares at me again, my gaze drifts to the kissing couple. I slide my hand down to his inner thigh, and, with a quick movement, his hand grabs mine, preventing further exploration. I look at David with pleading eyes. He gives Tim a signal I don't understand, but Tim grins, and he and Lauren leave.

"Do you ever kiss your women?" I ask. I focus momentarily on the kissing couple before turning to David. He studies me as if trying to figure out my game, but I'm not playing.

David leans over and his lips brush mine.

He opens his mouth slightly and kisses me harder.

My impatient lips have missed this so much that I quiver with pleasure. One hand combs through his hair while the other finds its way to the hardness between his legs. David scoots out of the booth, with me following close behind. He leads me to the backroom lavatory, where, with his lips still ravenous on mine, he removes my panties, and then explores me with his hand. He steps back, watching me as he unzips, and then he's inside me. My first experience with restroom sex.

§

We return to the booth with our spontaneous bathroom copulation replaying in my head, a short-lived, unique experience for me, but so hot my embers still smolder. It wasn't making love, but it was enough, and I feel an incredible closeness to David.

I had forgotten how much I loved a man's touch—with my consent. The Colonel at Central did plenty of touching—against my wishes, so it doesn't count. His abuse left me anxious, making sex undesirable, and I feared Colonel Wickmore had damaged me forever.

My body belongs to me again, and I'm free.

David watches me but says nothing. His eyes are unreadable, and Paying

Attention would reveal his thoughts, but I want to savor this evening in case it's the last.

§

Morning finds me with a brand-new outlook on life. I've successfully conquered my fear of the library and my fear of intimacy after Colonel Wickmore's brutal impositions. A feeling of empowerment flows through me, and the future is promising. I'm beaming as I easily translate one symbol after another and fill another page with my script. My last sip of coffee is cold, and I need a hot refill.

Chatter emanates from Paul's office, and as I'm filling my coffee cup, Tom steps into the break room and invites me to join them. Tom takes his seat, with Jen standing next to him. Commander Pierce sits to Paul's right, and everyone appears relaxed and in a jovial mood. Tom holds a magazine with a cover revealing it contains porn and offers it to me.

"Take a peek. We want your opinion on this," he says, smirking.

I accept the porn mag and skim through pictures of naked couples having sex in various positions. One page displays a woman with the aftermath of pleasuring a man on her face. I grimace in disgust, so Tom jumps up to see what's displayed on the page. He makes a gesture indicating fellatio, and everyone giggles, except me. Not amused, I flip through more pages. Another page shows a woman kneeling on all fours with someone spanking her with a hairbrush, and I'm able to hide my true feelings this time.

"Oh, oh. Someone's been a naughty girl," I say.

The group laughs. Finished, I hand back the publication to Tom, appearing indifferent.

"So, what did you think?" asks Tom.

"I'm not sure what you're asking. It's pornography, full stop."

Tom appears speechless.

"If you want to know if it's good pornography, I'm the wrong person to ask," I say, wiping my hands on my skirt. They all giggle again.

"Do you like sex?" asks Tom.

"Of course, but I don't use porn to pleasure myself. It does nothing for me."

Jen shakes her head and laughs.

Tom tries again. "You don't seem interested in sex, so we wondered if you like it."

"I don't service the military troops if that's what you mean, and as a civilian, I'm not required." I strive to keep my tone pleasant but professional.

"So, you don't have sex?"

"I didn't mean to imply that. I take … lovers. When I meet a gentleman, and I'm interested, and the attraction is mutual, then we have the Talk."

"The Talk?" Paul asks.

"Sure, we negotiate the relationship. We discuss what each of us wants or expects. For me, it's important to be exclusive, and since my relationships generally last a few months, my lovers agree to it. If they didn't, it wouldn't work."

"You discuss what you want or expect for sex?" Commander asks.

"Of course, that's an important part of it, but not all."

"Yeah, you won't find anyone here willing to have a relationship with you and meet your terms," Commander says. "That's not how it's done here. Sex is casual and doesn't mean anything. Nobody here is interested in … relationships."

One would expect this view from men.

"Well, Jen, aren't you and Major Williams … in a relationship?"

She shakes her head and giggles. "No, military women don't take lovers."

I believed Tom and Jen were an exception because there are exceptions to every rule. That explains why she didn't react when Tom approached me. I thought the rules might differ for the Inner Circle. David and I are starting a relationship, aren't we?

"I've never had problems finding a lover. My previous relationship lasted over two years."

The mood in the room shifts, and it's obvious without reading them. The men regard one another, speaking a silent language they alone understand.

"My relationships last awhile. Men often say one thing but do whatever they want."

I watch their curious reactions like they share a secret. Well, I have secrets too.

"That may be true elsewhere. Here, it's different, so you should change your thinking," Paul says. "Casual sex isn't so bad."

"For the men," I say, directing my attention to Jen.

§

I face a long, dull afternoon and fill the time listening to music. Should I submit my report too soon, it will raise eyebrows, and no one will understand my knack for translating the symbols when nobody else can. It eludes me how I'm able, but I've accepted this skill as another of my special gifts. They may not view it that way, and I need them to trust me. Whatever I can reveal now is common knowledge, so it won't matter much. So, no hurry. Nobody appears that interested in my work, anyway, and they don't expect results anytime soon.

§

David sits across from me, and I'm trying to follow our conversation, but I hear Commander in my head, saying *nobody has relationships here*. My dinner of vegetarian Chow Mein noodles tastes like twigs and straw. Don't David and I have a relationship?

He invites me to Agora, and I accept.

This time I dance. I enjoy dancing with Tim, but when we return to the booth, Lauren has gone. Why doesn't she stay when Tim and I dance? Tim excuses himself, and later I spot them on the dance floor. Lauren isn't a skillful dancer. I could teach her some moves, but she is always quiet, and it's difficult to form a friendship with her. Tim returns to our booth alone.

He and David carry most of the lively conversation, with me interjecting my opinions. I love the music, especially mine, and soaking up the energy and ambiance of Agora. People are welcoming, and it's so different from Michael's unseemly description.

CHAPTER 13

On a long-desired break this morning, I stretch my legs by exploring the fourth floor. It's my fourth week at Cavalry, and I'm continuing to learn my way around. At Central, Michael and I spent hours in the atrium, and it occurs to me that Cavalry may also feature one. A suite of offices appears uninhabited until an officer hurries out from a doorway, almost running into me. I ask if there's an atrium, so he invites me to walk with him. Beyond the suite of offices is a hallway that was dark when I last explored this floor, but today a soft light glows from its far end. He directs me to an arched doorway straight ahead. I thank him and walk toward the muted radiance.

This atrium, a quarter the size of Central's and shaped like a generous slice of pie, has floor-to-ceiling windows lining its imposing curved side. Full of flowering plants, fragrances of gardenia and honeysuckle flood my senses as I enter. A sprinkler system turns on, and the scent of water and wet potting soil permeates the air. A black leather couch facing the windows offers a relaxing view of acres of trees and sky, and like Central's atrium, the ceiling has immense skylights. The sky is cloudy today, but I imagine its beauty in the sunshine. I stroll along the entire window's span to the atrium's furthest side, then retrace my steps to view the breathtaking scenery again.

Most folks work at this hour, so I'm alone. On the opposite side of the base, the window scenery differs from the familiar view in Commander's apartment. Trees stretch out in every direction, covering the entire landscape. It's still March, and many deciduous trees have yet to blossom, but by summer, they'll be covered in a blanket of different shades of green.

§

When I stop for coffee in the break room, Commander stands by the coffeemaker, filling his cup. I grab a cup from the nearby tray, and Commander tips the pot toward me, offering to fill mine.

"Visiting the library again?" he asks.

"No, I needed to clear cobwebs from my brain and get my circulation moving again, so I took a walk and explored this floor."

I want to learn who he is, and everything about him. Instead, I study his lips, his deep brown eyes, his strong jawline, the small, almost invisible dimple in his chin, and his hefty, broad, inviting shoulders. I'm normally not one for loss of words. Nadler trained me to make conversation to glean information from subjects, and I was damn good at it. But now, I can't even form words, much less make interesting conversation, so I simply stand here with a dumb smile. His cologne makes me weak in the knees.

I want....

He nods and heads back to his office, and I float upstairs.

§

After dinner, David sits across from me, smiling.

"So, now that we've enjoyed sex together, it's time for you to try Play. I'll take you to my Playroom."

"David, we haven't made proper love yet. I still want to show you how I enjoy sex. Take me to your bed where we can leisurely make love. I promise not to hurt you," I say with a wink.

David leans back in his chair, flashing a wide toothy grin.

"Okay, let's meet back here in an hour."

In my quarters, I prepare for an evening of loving, and with my insides fluttering with butterflies I hurry downstairs where David is waiting in the cafeteria. With his arm around my shoulder, we follow the ramp toward the main floor. Midway down the ramp, David stops at the door with the symbols I translated to mean *nursery*. He unlocks it and turns on a light. We enter a room filled with boxes, bed frames, and a collection of miscellaneous items. This nursery is now a storage room. On my left, an open door reveals a bathroom.

Halfway toward the rear of the extensive room, it becomes a cozy little love nest. We descend four steps into a round, carpeted, sunken pit. Mirrored on the opposite side, four steps lead back up. The circular pit has built-in curved couches and, almost filling the center, a huge matching round ottoman larger than a double bed. The upholstery may have been a vibrant burgundy once, but age dulled it. David climbs the steps across from me, removes a white sheet from a tall set of built-in shelves, and brings it to the pit to cover the ottoman.

While David prepares our lovemaking haven, in my mind, the room becomes a nursery. Toddlers crawl around, playing together, struggling to pull themselves up or clambering on the furniture. I envision them holding on to the couches and ottoman to learn to walk under the watchful eyes of several mommies.

Now it serves a different purpose.

"What do you think?" David asks. He proudly waves his arm in the ottoman's direction.

"I'm imagining this was a nursery."

"What makes you say that?"

"The symbols on the door," I say without thinking.

David tilts his head, raising his eyebrows, and I'm reminded I must be more cautious. It's unlike me to slip up like that. My knowledge of the symbols is Classified.

I'm relieved when David pulls me down onto the ottoman and kisses me. He reaches under my skirt and slips my black panties off, and when he tosses them, they land on the edge of the round ottoman, half on, half off. I work to unbutton my blouse.

The door unlocks, making clicking sounds, and someone enters. I scramble to pull my blouse back on and peek out to see a grinning officer walking toward us. Are we breaking any rules? I turn to David, but he laughs and shakes his head.

"Oh, my, look what I found here," the officer says. He's enjoying this. He exudes an air of authority befitting a high-ranking officer but isn't wearing his rank. Why would we be in trouble?

"So, Cross, this your new girl?" he asks.

He addresses David, but his eyes fix on me. David remains silent, and I can't see what he's doing because I'm keeping my eyes glued on the intruding officer. My panties are still draped over the edge of the ottoman and catch the officer's attention. Black undergarments are non-existent in this culture. Military women are issued white underclothing, without exception.

My clothes are custom-made at a civilian base, and the officer seems fascinated with the novelty of my black underwear. He turns back to me.

"Well, sweetie, lift your skirt and show me what you got."

Why in heaven's name would I do that, and why in hell isn't David protecting me? I can't see David with my eyes still trained on this creep. If this officer is his superior, David can do nothing. I hate this.

The officer stoops to pick up my panties, but before he gets a good grip on them, I snatch them from him and slip them on in front of him. He stands there smiling, watching me. I pull my lanyard from my blouse and show it to him. He stands so close to me I don't bother removing it from my neck.

"I'm Special Consultant Zena Roberts. I work on the fourth floor in the

Commander's office. Commander is my handler and protector. I doubt he'd be happy to know you're treating me like this."

Whether or not that's true, I'll risk it. My bluffing might work. The officer laughs, steps back, and shakes his head at David, who stands next to me now.

"She doesn't Play?" he asks.

I glare at David, and he shrugs.

"Not yet, Frank, but I'm working on it."

"Well, I'll let you lovebirds get back to whatever," he says with a wave of his hand.

Frank, smiling, nods to David and leaves. I watch him walk out until the door locks.

"So where were we?" David asks.

He tries to pull me close to him, but I push him away.

"Why didn't you stand up for me?"

"Looks like you held your own."

"That's not the point."

"He was playing with you, baby. He can't force you to do anything against your will. The law is the law. We're friends, and I knew he wouldn't hurt you. Besides, if you won't do what I want, then he'll never convince you."

David laughs and then begs with pleading eyes.

"Let's leave," I say. "Anyone might walk in on us. Let's go to your room."

He laughs.

The joke escapes me until we arrive at his quarters. It's not a room. Lower ranks and women have rooms. He enjoys an apartment, and it's respectable, almost as large as the one I shared with Michael. Not as huge as Commander's lavish apartment, but I'm impressed. He's not part of Commander's Inner Circle, but he must be a First Lieutenant, a very high rank. I've been in First Lieutenant's quarters before.

He leads me to the bed, and I gaze up to discover at least thirty small five-pointed stars decorating the ceiling.

"Do they glow when you turn off the lights?"

"Yeah, but gotta leave the light on for a while."

He studies my face for a reaction. The fluorescent stars delight me.

"Wherever did you get them? They're perfect for decorating my room. It's tiny and plain, but I'd love to have stars shining on the ceiling, like sleeping outside under the stars."

"Our salvage unit brought them in a while back, and we'd have thrown them out."

My lips press against his. He pushes his greedy tongue into my willing mouth. Without his help, I unfasten the buttons of his shirt and peel it off.

I pull his undershirt out of his pants and over his head while planting baby kisses on his chest. He watches me remove my top and bra. Pressing my bare chest against his, I kiss him again. I undo his belt, unzip his pants, and leave the rest to him, and while he finishes undressing, I remove my shoes, skirt, and panties.

Naked, we kiss again. I move my lips to his neck and kiss my way down to his navel. He picks me up, sets me on the bed, and grabs my wrists, forcing my hands above my head. A panic starts in my belly, remembering Wickmore, and my whole body tenses. David releases my wrists and gently caresses my arms as his hands travel down to my breasts, where his tongue takes over, and his hands find other places to explore.

§

We rest on our backs atop the covers, and I stare at the dormant ceiling stars. David turns over onto his side, away from me. Did he forget about the tattoo? A sinister gray-black serpent covers his entire back. It coils up a gnarled tree branch with iridescent green leaves bearing forbidden fruit. Its crimson tongue flicks out at me as I toy with the skin on David's back.

As his muscles ripple from my light touch, the snake moves. The shadowy, airbrushed detail casts the viper's three-dimensional form as dangerous. It reminds me of the story of Eve. The serpent tempted her, forever changing her and her world. Realizing I found his tattoo, David tries to turn.

"No, no, let me see. It's beautiful. I love the artwork, with its vibrant colors and remarkable detail. What does it mean?"

"Don't know. I wanted the snake. I was sixteen. What kid knows about meaning?"

At sixteen, I knew a great deal about meaning. A snake could mean temptation by the devil, danger, or deceit. It can also mean regeneration, if not immortality. Whatever, David's serpent is beautiful. David relaxes and allows me to study his tattoo. I run my fingers along the snake's length from its tail to its head. I bend lower and kiss his viper on its scale-dressed head above its eyes, working my way down to the small of David's back. His waist dips slightly as he rests on his side, and that's where my lips need to be. He turns over, and we make love again.

Later that evening, David dims the lights to near darkness, and the ceiling glows with starlight. When I close my eyes to thin slits, I swear the stars twinkle. I ask David what the stars mean to him, we talk late in the evening, and I stay the night.

§

I'm late arriving this morning, and Commander and Paul are lingering at the kitchen table, deep in conversation that stops when they see me. Commander glances at the clock but says nothing.

"Overslept, sir. I had trouble falling asleep and didn't want to wake up." Last night I enjoyed a deep and refreshing sleep in David's arms, in his spacious bed under twinkling stars, instead of my tiny cot in my tiny room, so it's half true. I didn't oversleep, and I awoke smiling. So, none of it is true.

"Everything all right?" Commander asks.

"Yes, sir." I nod, turn to retrieve my work materials, and open the Book to one of my bookmarks. Like a mask, I slip on my professional face, spread out my papers, and sip my coffee, waiting until they finish theirs. They realize by now I can't work in their presence. The moment they leave, I crank my music as loud as I dare, savoring my memories of last night.

§

David, having to work late, doesn't meet me for dinner. After eating alone, I peek into the Radio Room to determine if the shift has changed. I want to inquire about Michael. After passing the sergeant's closed door, I greet two men seated at their consoles with their backs to me, engaged in conversation.

"Hi, fellas, I'm Special Consultant Zena Roberts. I worked in the Lab at Central Control and partnered with our Radio Room staff. I met your day shift recently and looked forward to meeting the night shift."

Another soldier sits further back alone, fidgets, and turns away.

"Central? Then you know Corporal Davies, transferred here from Central last year," one soldier says, pointing toward their nervous comrade.

A red flag flares up like fireworks. His face is familiar, and although his features bear a resemblance to Davies, he's not the Davies who worked at Central. Davies worked nights, but we had several conversations, and although I haven't seen him in months, no one can change that much. I stroll over to greet him, touch his shoulder, and Pay Attention. My hand jerks back. At Westview, he called himself Scott, the same Scott that Fischer whipped, and I helped escape through the secret magic corridor. So where is the real Davies?

"Of course, I remember. We spoke infrequently, but sure. It's Ryan, isn't it? How are you? I didn't realize you transferred out. How do you like working here?"

The impostor—Scott, aka Ryan Davies, seems to relax a little, and it's obvious he doesn't recognize me.

"You remember me, Ryan. Michael and I had a longstanding relationship until he left. I worked in the Lab next door," I say, playing a hunch.

"Sure. I know Major Corday, and I remember you, Ms. Roberts."

He confirms my suspicions—he does have connections to Michael.

"Oh, Ryan, please call me Zena."

§

The morning starts with a flash bang as thunder shudders the apartment, and I'm mesmerized watching the torrential downpour drenching the windows, sending rivers of raindrops snaking down the glass. In the distance, whirlwinds whip the branches of the trees, forming a wave sweeping across the landscape. Sudden lightning bolts startle me and send a rush of adrenaline throughout my body. As the thunderclap rattles the windows, I see myself running through the forest during a downpour covering myself and someone else with a blanket, and in a flash, it's gone.

A memory? A premonition?

§

The excitement from the thunderstorm, and my weird hallucination, lingers throughout my day, making me edgy, but by evening, I'm craving companionship. Agora is energetic, and I dance several times with Tim and then with an officer. Back at our booth, I notice Tim and Lauren have disappeared and David is smiling.

"Where'd everyone go?"

"To be alone, I guess. Should we do likewise?"

§

David's delicious lips taste mine, and when his mouth moves to my breasts, pleasure washes over me in waves. Naked, I stand beside his bed, reach for his hand, and guide it between my legs. My knees weaken, and I stroke his head, pushing him gently, hoping he'll understand. He lifts me and sets me on the bed. My body surrenders to his tongue, and I yield to the euphoric tsunami overtaking me.

I pull him close, and he urges me to turn over, but I long to watch his face as he enjoys me, and when I tell him, he concedes. David moves above me, and I witness his relentless desire dissolve into satisfaction. Drained, he rolls off, resting breathlessly beside me, his eyes half-closed. When he turns away from me on his side, his serpent tattoo comes into full view. The snake flicks out its wicked tongue but lets me kiss its head.

"I'm starting to think you only want me for my snake."

David turns toward me with a grin.

"True, but it's not this snake I want." I pet the viper, then move my hand to David's front.

"It's this one."

"Okay, that's good." David turns his back to me again.

My finger traces the tree branch and flowers.

"You need a butterfly in this scene. Do you think your snake would eat the butterfly?"

"Don't know, butterfly. Depends on how good she tastes." He chuckles to himself.

"I'm curious. Your tattoo would have taken several sessions to complete and must have hurt. Why did you get it?"

"I was sixteen, wanted it, so I got it. Pain is relative. Life is full of pain, and when you choose the pain, you become its master. Why do you ask so many questions?"

"That's how I learn. I'm not a fan of pain and avoid it, but sometimes it's impossible. The worst pain comes from a broken heart."

"Wouldn't know, because I don't have a heart."

I grab his arm, pull him onto his back, rest my ear on his chest where his heart should be, and listen to the beat, beat, beat.

"Oh, you're right."

He smiles like he's charmed by me.

"So, David, I'm imagining you at sixteen, and I'll bet you were naughty. Did you purposely look for trouble?"

"Me? I was wild, undisciplined, angry at the world, and found ways to irritate my parents. But that stopped when they sent me to military school. Best thing that happened to me. Gave me focus." He nods to himself.

"Why were you so angry?"

"Don't know. Growing pains? Testosterone? I wanted my life to have meaning and importance, but I lived in a world with children playing children's games. I had tons of energy and no way of applying it. Military school was tough, offering both physical and mental challenges, and I loved it. Worked hard, joined the Peace Force, excelled in Officer's Academy, rose in the ranks, found purpose and focus."

"Purpose and focus have been a priority for me, and I'm also good at my profession, but I don't remember having the same drive. Maybe it's different for women."

"Sure, that's why men rule the world," he says.

With that, he snickers, and I deliver him a soft punch in his arm.

"Men are full of themselves, but they'd suffer without us. Behind every successful man stands a good woman."

David chuckles. "Yeah, we don't think the same."

"You wouldn't be alive without your mother growing you inside her body, pushing you into the world, and giving you life, not to mention feeding, bathing, and caring for you."

A shadow passes over David's face, his smile fades, and his eyes glaze over, hinting he hides a veiled story.

"I doubt I'd do well in the military. It's hard enough for a civilian woman to work with men who consider themselves superior. We know better."

David's broad smile reappears, and he cocks his head.

"So, kitten. What were you like at sixteen? I'm betting you were a good little girl, always wanting to please." He grins.

At sixteen, I lived on Mountainview, having worked on an assignment for a year. I was obliged to play a part, with everything an act, a game. My mission was to convince people I was an innocent, irreverent, cocky teen who was angry and broke the rules—the way David behaved without acting. I needed to gain their confidence so I could learn their secrets for the upper echelon.

"Yeah, I guess that's true, but I'd get in trouble sometimes because I wanted to learn everything I could. I had to learn boundaries."

David doesn't answer. His soft snoring confirms he's sound asleep. With the lights turned down, I watch the ceiling come alive with fluorescent stars.

§

David wakes me early and informs me he's scheduled for an all-day training. Every military base requires training exercises to keep service members in peak condition. He claims it's exhausting, and we can rendezvous for lunch tomorrow. I kiss David and whisper I'll miss him and hope he enjoys training. Is he taking training or conducting it? I don't ask. I dress, grab my lanyard, and leave.

§

As I approach the office, a young private brings in a large box and deposits it in front of Cassie's desk. Cassie sees me and points to the package.

"You got a delivery from Melbourne Ridge," she says.

The garment department on Melbourne Ridge makes my civilian clothes. Commander exits his office with papers and hands them to Cassie.

"Stevens, take the parcel and escort Miss Roberts to her room."

We make the short trek to my room. I stand at my open door while Stevens empties the contents of my allotment on my bed, then leaves, taking the empty container with him.

With my new clothes stowed in the laundry basket to be washed later and my lotions stored on the shelf, I grab my keepsake box holding my treasures. I remove the top item, Michael's undershirt. He left it for me to wear when I missed him at night. Michael, gone for three months now, not a word. I hug his shirt to my face and try to remember his smell.

Michael's undershirt covered another shirt, Dan's. I never learned his surname, or I've forgotten. The photo on Commander's desk shows a younger Dan and Andrew. I need to ask Commander if he knows where they're stationed.

The shirt Dan loaned me ten years ago fits tighter around my bust and no longer covers me sufficiently. Washed and worn to bed a few times, it ended up stored in my keepsake box. A pocket-size container, hiding at the bottom of my treasures, contains Andrew's cross necklace. As it dangles from my fingers now, I recall the day he loaned it to me, and how Andrew needed me to care for him.

He promised he'd find me when he had two sturdy legs, but he has yet to find me after a decade. I don't need his care now, but I miss him. He would have been proud had he found me at Central Control and seen how successful I became. Would Andrew be proud of me now? I grip the necklace tight, imagining the day when I can return it to him. I've replayed that scene in my mind countless times over the past decade.

§

Back at my worktable, I'm lost in organizing my preliminary report. The section on *Infiltration* is intriguing. In preparation, operatives root themselves in key positions of authority. The Book refers to them as *Seeds*. One section I'm working on details the construction of their bases from the ground up, including the water system, air filtering, and power grid.

The Master Plan depicts how bases will be built with two basements. A subbasement will shelter enslaved workers while they erect the walls and lay the floors. A central column will house an elevator for delivering building materials and food to the workers. Bases are circular with outer and inner walls with a maintenance corridor running between them. The upper basement will be used for storage.

While bases will vary in width and number of floors, they will all be built primarily underground. Three subterranean tunnels will extend from each base. The largest tunnel will connect the main floor to the surface for transferring materials from or to the outside world. A smaller tunnel extends from the corridor to a central hub. A third tunnel (or set of tunnels) will interconnect each cluster of bases for high-speed underground travel.

The Master Plan also describes advanced crystalline technology used instead of electricity produced by our old inefficient power plants. We retrofit all salvaged appliances with their new technology, providing clean energy. There was no reference to crystals in my reading of history.

My music today streams as tranquil as a dark, placid river, relaxing me and allowing my subconscious to filter out the world and let the symbols speak to me. Something slams against the window from outside, making me jump. It stains one windowpane with a hand-sized brownish-red smear that slowly drips down the glass. A bird?

The view outside captures my attention, with forests carpeting the foreground while mountains punctuate the panoramic view, with puffy white clouds drifting across the azure sky, shape-shifting. They morph from elephants to horses to an old man with a white beard.

I can almost smell the pungent perfume of lush green forests and feel the sun's warmth caressing my skin. I imagine a rogue wind whispering her sweet secrets into my ear. The eternal music of nature lulls me into transcendence ... reminding me of something. I yield to the imagery and float with music in my ears and a symphony in my head.

Voices whisper to me, but their words mystify me. The voices blend into one emanating from beyond the mountains, unnerving and perplexing me. Am I losing my mind? Am I hearing things? I shut off the music and listen. Nothing. I'm in the physical realm.

CHAPTER 14

Instead of my usual attire, a white blouse and navy-blue skirt, this morning, my ensemble includes a spanking new pair of black dress pants, complemented by a beige tunic blouse tied with a red sash at my waist. Cassie notices me with disapproving eyes but says nothing. With my cup of coffee, I proceed upstairs, greeted by Commander and Paul engaged in conversation. Paul stands, letting me slide past him. I retrieve the Book and my papers from the cabinet, sip my coffee, and wait for them to finish their daily routine before beginning mine.

"Training was successful yesterday. Cross is certainly proficient at his job. He really whips the men into shape."

I almost choke on my coffee and struggle to clear my throat as my eyes tear up. Paul glances at me.

"He should oversee all training since he gets such excellent results. He's a natural leader," Paul says.

"Cross can handle both. He spends too much time hands-on and should trust his team to shoulder more. It's their job. No complaints. He works hard and is the best, but he needs to relinquish some control now that he's moved up. What's it been, three years? Let's shove off so our little lady can work."

Commander winks at me, and they stand, ready to leave.

"One of your new outfits?" Commander asks. He noticed.

"Yes, sir."

"Haven't worn pants before, have you?" he asks, standing to leave.

"No, sir, not here."

"Very nice," Commander says as they leave.

A red flag warns me that something's amiss. Yesterday the big smear on the window was visible from my table, but today, it's gone. A closer inspection proves me correct: no smear or telltale sign indicating it was ever there. Did I imagine it?

§

The sweet, nutty aromas of baking pies tempt me while standing in line as I choose a mystery meat dish. I eat alone until halfway through my meal when David joins me.

"How was training yesterday?" I ask. He looks rested.

"We accomplished a lot, but I'm glad it's over for now. Miss me?"

"You know I did, but my clothing issue arrived yesterday, so I stayed busy all evening."

"Nice outfit. Never seen you in pants before. I'd like to pull them down right now and …"

"Here, in front of everyone?"

"Okay."

I shoot him the stink eye.

"So, Agora tonight—or my place?"

"Your place."

§

David waits for me at his office and escorts me to his apartment. I prepared an intimate bag that includes a toothbrush—in case I stay the night.

"You may pull my pants down now, provided you kiss me first."

He plants a kiss on my moistened lips. I step back and reflect, aware of who David is and his treatment of his women, but with me, he's different. With me, he's kind and playful, and he lets me lead when we make love. He's gentle and generous. With me, sometimes he forgets to hide and reveals his true self, the darkness, and the light, the lover his playmates will never know.

I don't have to pretend I'm something I'm not to please him. He's not jealous or controlling or demanding, and it's easy. I realize this can't last, knowing he'll want to Play, not with me, but with someone, but he's mine for the moment, and I intend to enjoy every minute.

I pull him close, my mouth seeking his, and offer my tongue. His hands explore me. He removes my clothes, lifts me, places me on the bed, sheds his clothes, and then joins me. David flips me over on my stomach. He massages my back, and I relax. I feel his hands travel to my behind, where he caresses me. He suddenly lifts his hand, and I sense what he plans to do.

"Stop."

He freezes, and I turn over and pull him down to me.

§

David turns to rest on his side, away from me, like he always does. I trace his snake tattoo with my fingers and then with my kisses. He doesn't move. I follow the contour of his hip with a soft touch, and when my hand arrives at his butt, I pull back and smack him, not hard, but it makes a thwack. He jerks and turns his head toward me.

"You know, you just assaulted an officer."

With a healing touch, I massage his wounded behind, then plant soft kisses over the damaged area until he spins around. I crawl into his arms and stay the night.

§

I'm so engrossed in drafting my preliminary report, that my morning coffee sits forgotten—not even a sip. So many questions require answers. One section of the Book uses a glyph that translates to *Plant* or *Root*. These *Seeds* interact in secret with one another and their environment. Not only on local levels, but on provincial, national, and global ones as well. Like an invasive vine, the seeds grow, intertwining with sister seedlings, forming overwhelming powerful networks, a sinister Secret Society, a Deep State.

I'm curious about the point in history when these events happened, perhaps in the late twentieth or early twenty-first centuries. History books might provide clues to support this. I dump my cold coffee in the sink and head downstairs to the library.

I hunt for historical information from the twentieth century on, anything at all. The collection is poor, the history books are scattered, and the magazine selection is worse. I search shelf after shelf until hunger pangs distract me, reminding me it's lunchtime.

David sits sipping his cup of coffee in the cafeteria. I wave and load my tray with a colorful spring salad sprinkled with balsamic vinegar, accompanied by a fresh-baked baguette.

"The library's a mess. Who do I talk to about getting it organized?"

"Looking at him."

"Oh." My face warms, and I flash David a sheepish grin.

"Nobody uses the library that much. Hasn't been a problem. Scientists or technical people take books that interest them. I'll bring it up at the next high-level meeting."

"You're invited to high-level meetings?"

David grins. "Yeah, sometimes they want to hear what I have to say."

"It would make my job much easier. Are there history books or magazines not kept in the library?"

"Well, porn magazines wind up in the Officer's Club or porn room in the library."

"That's all you think about, sex?"

"Sure, when I'm with you."

"That's sweet, but what about history books? Or old news or educational magazines?"

"What exactly are you after?"

"Anything historical from the late twentieth century on."

"Why do you need them?"

"For my project."

"Which is about …"

"Classified. I'd need my handler's permission to discuss my project with you, and he's not here."

David grins again.

§

Sunday morning, I inform Cassie I'm taking a personal day. I return to the library to sort through the books, moving all the fiction into one section, a simple task since I'm not interested in organizing them. I won't waste the morning alphabetizing books by title or arranging them by author. My book shuffling consumes my morning.

At lunch with David, I recount my library labors.

"You don't waste any time, do you?"

"By sorting the books, it's easier to find the volumes I'll need, so I took today off."

After lunch, I revisit the library, and half an hour later, two privates show up to help. At dinner, when I join David, I thank him. He shrugs and explains their need to provide room for the incoming batch of books soon to arrive from the next salvage run.

§

This morning, Commander watches me squeeze past Paul and take my seat behind three old books stacked on the table.

"They delivered these for you this morning. You requested books on the late twentieth and early twenty-first centuries?" Paul asks.

"Great. I'm interested in recent history."

I thumb through the pages of the books and study their titles.

"Hopefully, these books will help with translating the symbols. I lack a frame of reference for certain symbols, so the books may prove useful."

"Had you asked me, I'd have made certain you got what you needed," Paul says.

Did I offend him? He is the Information Officer. I casually mentioned my needs to David, and he made it happen.

"Oh, it was spontaneous. It occurred to me while poking around the library, but these books aren't critical at this point. I wanted them handy to browse at my leisure," I say, hoping to smooth feelings. Neither asks about my contact. Do they already know?

Paul shakes his head, and I promise myself I'll request information from him first. It's ill-advised to step on toes, but I'm uncomfortable with so many rules. I've always worked independently, and my handlers never interfered. They allowed me to work without constraint, and I delivered.

"Cassie reports you took yesterday off. Were you sick?" Commander asks.

"No, sir, I'm fine. I had things I wanted to do and needed a whole day."

"Anything interesting in the library?" Paul asks. They know.

"I learned the layout and moved all the fiction books to one section, making it easier for people interested in fiction and those who read non-fiction. Easier for me."

"In the future, if you plan to take off, give me notice," Commander says. He doesn't sound angry, merely annoyed.

"I'm sorry, sir. When I first arrived, you instructed me to inform Cassie should I need a personal day. Perhaps I misunderstood. But you're correct, of course. You're my handler, and I should have informed you. Next time, I'll check with you first. I'm still getting familiar with the different practices here."

The officers finish their coffee and then depart. I switch on my music, something uplifting and energetic. I begin my research and crack open the yellowing pages of the old books.

§

At dinner, I thank David for the books. He shrugs. David mentions he's attending a poker game this evening. We've spent so much time together, and I fear becoming dependent on him as I did with Michael. I need my freedom, my own friends, and my individual space. David leaves, and I head for the Radio Room.

Corporals Anthony Brooks and Jacob Carter engage in conversation at their posts at the front of the room, with Ryan Davies at his post toward the back. When Davies spots me, he raises a porn magazine, flashing the cover like he's warding me off. I chat with Anthony and Jacob but glance over at Davies occasionally. What's he doing here? Does he know Michael's whereabouts? If I Pay Attention, I'll know the truth, but he's so jumpy I'm afraid if I get too close, I'll spook him if I'm not patient. We're not going anywhere. Eventually, he'll realize I'm not a threat and warm up to me. He might remember how I helped him—escape.

CHAPTER 15

My eyes open, and with my room immersed in eerie darkness, I crank my light up as high as possible. The brightness can't chase away another awful dream. I'm left shaking and drained.

I stood in the rain, staring down at my grave. The name on the tombstone was blurry, but I knew it was mine. I was dead, but I felt the rain and smelled its earthy, dank musk. Near my grave were several others—my husband's next to mine, and those of my children and grandchildren. Their names were indecipherable, but somehow, I understood the headstones of the marked graves were of my entire family. My tears mixed with the rain, and I was bidding my final farewell. In my dream, I awakened on a hotel bed, aware it was a dream, but knowing it was an awful truth. I cried out in anguish. My cries rattled me awake.

Turned up bright, my light chases the shadows from my tiny, coffin-like room. Was my dream a premonition? It can't be the past since I'm only twenty-three and have never married. Is it my future or my fear of the future manifesting in my dreams? Why am I tormented by such vivid and disturbing nightmares? A cloud of doom hangs over me.

§

My dreary dream followed me through my long day, and tonight I hope David's sexy playfulness helps me forget the gloom of the day. In his apartment, I toss my overnight bag on a chair, and we settle at his table nursing cups of hot tea.

"How do you see your future?" I ask.

A puzzled David squints at me.

"You ever wonder about your life in twenty, thirty years?"

"Nope, I live in the present. Do you?" he asks.

My dream crosses my mind for a moment, then fades away.

"No matter how my future turns out, I want to be free."

"You're not free now?" He wrinkles his forehead and sits up.

"I mean outside. I want to live free outside with Mother Nature."

"No such thing. Everyone answers to someone, even off base. We're safe here and as happy as we choose to be. Could be far worse. You gotta make the most of what you're given. There's no guarantee our life would improve living off base. You're as free as the institutions allow, plus Mother Nature is unforgiving, and she doesn't care about you. How would living outdoors be superior to what the Overlords provide?"

I cringe at the mention of the Overlords.

"Don't you ever want to venture outside and breathe fresh air, feel the sun on your skin, feel the rain on your face? Don't you want to smell flowers? Watch caterpillars build cocoons, then emerge as butterflies? Free to flutter away? Eavesdrop on birds talking to one another?"

"Birds can talk?"

"I'm serious. I observe the outside world every day but can't enjoy it."

"Have you ever been outside? Wild animals and nasty insects that bite you live out there. And ..." His eyes narrow, and with a warning glare, he says, "... snakes."

I giggle. "I need to worry about them inside here, too."

David laughs.

It's a lot to consider. I always believed freedom was preferable, and I accepted that truth without question. The weight of this overwhelms me, and feeling trapped like this frightens me. I recall Plato's *Allegory of the Cave* about prisoners chained together in an underground cave where they could only see what their captors wanted them to see. Like the people on the bases, the prisoners lived their entire lives believing what was shown to them.

In the allegory, one prisoner escapes and discovers a different reality outside the cave. Even though some soldiers leave for salvage runs, and from reading, we know what the outside world was like, everyone believes we're fortunate, confined to the bases. I was outside for a short time, but now I yearn to be as free as the butterflies.

"There's a movie tomorrow. Science fiction. Wanna go?" David asks.

"What's the movie?"

"*Terminator*. A robot travels to the past to kill his adversary's mother."

I can't tell David I've seen the movie because I want to see it with him.

"Sounds like fun. Do you believe in time travel?"

"It's just a story, but I hear it's violent. That a problem for you?"

"You'll be there if I get scared."

CHAPTER 16

April came and went, and the view from the apartment windows allowed me to watch winter melt into spring. The mountainside turned from brown to green, their trees leafing out into a magnificent emerald carpet. I often visit the atrium to observe its view from the opposite end of the base. The days are longer, and the sunshine is brighter.

I'm far along completing my preliminary report, and I've covered both sides of the papers from three more legal pads, some filled with my thoughts or questions. Most of it shapes my report, all recorded in my special script. At long last, I'm feeling at home here.

The passages in the Book I'm translating this morning disturb me. Their plan includes reducing the world population by maintaining a negative birthrate, asserting overpopulation is unsustainable. Without enough food to feed everyone, they'll decrease the numbers. Other passages discuss upsetting the normal order by supplying the needs of their bases by taking from agriculture, banking, and commerce, driving big companies out of business, and diminishing government power. All able-bodied disenfranchised individuals will resettle on specific bases. It claims the refugees will cooperate because of widespread famine and devastation.

Other sections advocate sterilizing women from all over the planet, although they'll take healthy women to bear offspring for them. Some qualifying male refugees will serve as sperm donors. The Master Plan documents the need for genetically suitable females, young women of all races, from all countries—echoing our old antebellum breeder plantations, twentieth-century American Eugenics programs, and the "strong and pure" Master Race initiatives of the Third Reich—but why?

§

112

I'm eager to see David tonight. We meet almost daily for lunch or dinner or both.

Agora is a frequent haunt, and we've seen two more movies, both violent science fiction films I've seen previously. We spend hours in his apartment talking and sometimes making love.

David answers the door on my second knock. We lose our clothes and fall on the bed, our lovemaking urgent tonight, and then it's over. I cuddle in his arms for a while, and then David turns his back to me as he does. Satisfied, I start at his neck and plant little kisses while I whisper what I love about him. David seems distracted.

"Mm-mmm, I love your smell and this part of your neck."

I nuzzle and kiss his neck, lingering before moving down to his broad shoulders.

"And I love your tattoo, your venomous serpent."

I brush my hands over his back.

"I'm crazy about the way you make me feel, and I love this part right here."

I caress the small of his back.

"I love you, David. You're a good man. I love watching you with your team; and how they respect and follow your lead. I love your strength and self-discipline. And I love you because you're so naughty. Most of all, I love the way you love me." I'm ready to make love again.

A change washes over David, and he stiffens, then moves away from me. A darkness falls over him like a blanket, alarming me. Did I say something wrong? He gets up for the bathroom, and when he returns, he dresses, avoiding eye contact.

"I forgot I need to get up early. Inspections tomorrow, really early." He's lying, and it's the first time he's ever lied to me. He's told me many things uncomfortable to hear, but he's never lied before.

"Did I do something wrong?" Did I break something between us? Aren't we friends? He should tell me if I did something wrong.

David watches and waits with a weak smile. The message is obvious. After freshening up in the bathroom, I dress, and David shows me out. No kiss goodnight, nothing.

§

In the morning, I'm still disturbed about last night's events. Something's wrong between us, and I don't understand it. We had a wonderful evening, and then something changed. When David meets me for lunch, his darkness from last night has lifted. My senses alert me, and I'm baffled, but from the way David behaves, we seem okay, although he avoids eye contact.

113

"Can't make it for dinner. Crazy schedule. Meet me at my office tomorrow after dinner?"

I sigh in relief. He must be preoccupied with work issues.

"Sure, sounds great. Is everything all right?"

"Why wouldn't it be?"

He never kisses me or shows affection in public. Nobody engages in that behavior, so it must be another rule. With a reassuring smile, he leaves.

§

Thursday crawls by like a sleepy snail with David on my mind all day, and evening can't arrive fast enough. I choose a sexy, casual outfit, with black tights and a short skirt to please him. Tonight, I'll read him to discover what's troubling him. Maybe I can help.

David stands by his desk facing away from me. He turns his head, sees me, and waves for me to come in. My heart beats faster. He doesn't move, and when I enter his office, it's clear why. A civilian woman sits in a chair in front of him with her mouth on him, giving him something I don't.

David's hands caress her head, and he's talking to her the way he talks to me when we make love. He's enjoying himself, and when he's ready to release, I hear him urging her to swallow for him. I can't look away. Why is he doing this? I'm frozen, watching him give her what's mine. When he pulls back and zips up, he stands there and watches me with a satisfied grin, and I can't speak.

I turn away to leave, taking one last glance, unable to hide the pain in my eyes. I've broken my most important rule: *never let them know they hurt you.*

Never.

CHAPTER 17

I run up the ramp and two sets of stairs with an overpowering desire to cry or scream. Blind to my surroundings, I reach the fourth floor. Numbness overtakes and engulfs me, but it won't last, and when it wears off, I'll need to be alone.

Across the hall, Commander and his team are leaving the office, and I remember it's Thursday, their Club night. Most of my music CDs have found their way to Commander's apartment, and a couple of them are perfect for soothing my breaking heart.

"I'm sorry to bother you, Commander, but would you mind if I run upstairs for my music? I know exactly which ones I want."

"Why don't you join us at Club? You said you've never been. We're headed there, so walk with us, and I'll get you in," Commander says.

I'm in no mood for Club or merry military members. My heart breaks, and I need to suffer alone. No, I don't. Damn it, I don't want to bear this pain alone. It's time to move on, and that's what I do best; I move on.

"I'd love that. Thank you, sir."

Tom and Paul wear knowing smiles, but whatever's in store for me will be the cure.

I had passed by the Club's unmarked closed door on a previous exploration across the rotunda. Now, Tom pulls the door open to the hearty sounds of officers and military women chatting and laughing. Inside, the officers gather at small round bistro tables on both sides of a narrow pathway leading to the back. We brush past them to a modest square platform perfect as a small dance floor.

A long tavern-style bar with high stools extends from the dance floor almost to the front, and an officer behind the bar serves drinks. No alcohol, of course, since it's forbidden on all bases. The sound system rests on a cabinet alongside the bar wall beneath an enormous mirror in an ornate gold frame. Beyond the dance floor, Tom and Paul take their seats at a reserved, long rectangular table. Commander accompanies me to the bar across from the table and signals the bartender.

"Mack, meet Zena Roberts. Zena's my guest tonight."

Commander Pierce nods at me and leaves to join his team at the long table. Three military women join them, and I recognize Specialist Jen Campbell, but not her two companions. One tall, thin woman with short light brown hair is muscular like Jen but has a masculine air. Her shorter friend is thin, not as brawny, and appears more feminine and attractive.

"So, what kind of music do you play here?"

Mack inserts a disc, and the music blares, but it's not to my taste.

"So, Zena, right? Like the daughter of Zeus. Russian?" Mack asks.

"Or like the warrior." My standard reply when I'm asked about my name.

Mack looks me over, and I doubt he believes the warrior part since nobody ever does.

"So, Mack, do people dance? I noticed the small dance floor."

"No, most officers play pool or find female partners," he says, pointing at a pair of pool tables near Commander's party.

Four officers and a military woman sit at a table across the pathway near one pool table. They notice me, and the officers yell out.

"Yo. Twelve o'clock high. Fresh meat," a deep voice says.

"Hey, little girl, wanna sit on my lap? Got a big surprise for you," an unseen officer says.

"You can sit on my finger," says another.

"I got a better idea. Come on over here, open your mouth, and close your eyes …"

They all laugh.

I ask Mack to allow me to sort through his music stack to search for familiar artists or music. I flip through several discs, ignoring the catcalls from across the aisle.

The tall, tough-looking woman from Commander's table pulls up a stool next to me.

"Hi. I'm Mary Jo. Commander says you work in his office."

"Yes, I'm Zena Roberts. I've been on base for a couple of months, but it's my first time here in the Officer's Club. How do you tolerate their vulgar language?"

"You'll get used to them. If you're nice to the officers, they'll treat you better. They're teasing you because you're new … and a civilian, an easy target."

"Okay, I'm not sure I want to know them."

"They're harmless." She nods their way. "You used to eat in the cafeteria, but I haven't seen you there lately."

Yes, of course. She and the other woman lunched with Tom and Jen.

"You already met Jen, and Lynn sits next to her. Lynn and I are Commander's girls, his only girls." She nods toward the Commander's table.

That's unfortunate news, but after David's display of deception, I'm not feeling much love for men—even Commander.

"Yeah, Commander has specific needs." She stares straight into my eyes.

I play innocent.

"Have you heard of Play?" Mary Jo asks.

Crap. It's everywhere. "Play? I'm not sure what you mean. Like playing pool?"

"No, not quite." She laughs. Mary Jo is marking her territory, so I'll help.

"Some officers enjoy spanking women, sometimes with belts or paddles or whatever the girl wishes. The girls enjoy it too. I like it relatively hard, and Commander loves that."

I wince, and Mary Jo beams.

"He loves getting head, and I'm the best on the base. You know what I'm talking about?"

I want to play dumb, but I doubt she'd believe it, so instead, I nod and make a face. The Inner Circle must have told her about my disdain for giving head. Again, it pleases her, so she continues to mention acts Commander enjoys. I feign shock, and a big smile crosses her face.

Mary Jo moves close to me, looks around to see if anyone is watching, and slips her hand under my dress to the inside of my thigh. "If you'd like to take a walk on the wild side, Lynn and I can show you how it all goes down."

"Thank you for the invitation, Mary Jo," I say, discretely removing her hand. "Perhaps another time." I smile.

Mack joins us.

"So, you don't like oral?" Mary Jo asks. She grins at Mack, and he smiles.

"Well, I've never tried, so I wouldn't know."

Mary Jo raises her eyebrows and draws her head back. It's her turn to be shocked. Mack shakes his head.

"How did you manage that?" Mary Jo asks.

"No one ever asked me."

"Don't have to wait for us to ask," Mack says.

Okay, two against one.

"The guys across the aisle, the ones teasing you, they Play," she says, like a warning. With that, Mary Jo leaves and joins the taunting men at their table, and they burst out laughing. She resumes her now-secured position at

Commander's table, followed by bellowing laughter, and my stomach clenches like a fist.

A soldier from the table of teasers strolls over, slides onto the stool next to me, and asks Mack for a soft drink. He sizes me up.

"Hi, I'm Sergeant Greg Wolf. And your name is Zena?"

"Like the warrior," Mack says, handing Greg his drink.

"Zena the Warrior. Never heard of her. A mythical comic book character?"

"Sure, a fearless female superhero," I say.

I sense Greg is planning mischief, so I Pay Attention. He sips his drink and squints at me.

"So, you're new here. First time at Club?"

I nod.

He slides his hand over my knee and caresses it while trying to move to the inside, his eyes on mine. I scoop up his hand and hold it.

"I don't know you well enough."

"You're right, and I'm trying to fix that. Why don't you and I take a little walk and become better acquainted?" His deep baritone voice is soft and seductive.

I'm not interested. "I don't Play."

From Greg's table, a tall, lanky soldier with a devious smile joins us. Greg stands and moves behind me, so I stand, sensing a twinge of trouble.

"This is Sergeant Eric Jackson," Greg says. "Works with me. Eric, this is Zena."

Eric smirks as his eyes undress me.

What do they have in mind? I scan Commander's table, and he obviously sees what's happening. Is he waiting to see if I can handle myself? Greg moves behind me and pulls me to him, holding me by the waist.

"You have sexy legs," Eric says.

My tights are semitransparent except for the crotch. David enjoyed the see-through material.

"What's that you're wearing covering your legs? They extend all the way up?" Eric asks.

"They're called tights, and yes, they do."

"Let me see."

Seems like there's a theme among Players. "I'd rather not."

Greg's hand creeps down my thigh to the hem of my skirt, and I sense it's Eric's job to distract me. I reach behind me to grab Greg's privates and give them a firm squeeze.

"I suggest you change course, soldier," I say in a loud whisper to guarantee he receives my message.

Greg laughs and releases me. "You play rough," he says.

"I don't play." I offer a reassuring smile and take my seat.

Eric rejoins his table, laughing, but Greg parks himself next to me. After we discuss Club, his work, and Play, he returns to his friends.

The men's room must be through a door between the two pool tables because officers make brief visits alone, but I don't notice one for women. When I ask Mack for directions to the ladies' room, he tells me women use Comfort Rooms, but I won't use them, so I'll have to hike across the rotunda to my quarters. No problem, but will they allow me back in?

I'm not supposed to approach Commander in public, so I walk over, stand close to the table, and watch Commander with pleading eyes until he invites me over. Mary Jo and Lynn have left, and Tom, Paul, and Jen sit across from him, their backs to the room. I approach him.

"I'm sorry to bother you, sir, but I need to ... use the restroom. Will they let me in when I return from my quarters? It's still early."

"No, you're fine, but you don't need to go to your quarters. There are Comfort Rooms nearby. If you have any problem getting back in, have them see me. You'll be fine."

"Sir, I don't use the Comfort Rooms. Long story."

Commander glances at Paul with a telling smile.

"Well, my private room has a bathroom, and it's close by. I'll take you there."

He winks at Paul, wraps his arm around me, and leads me out of Club to a Comfort Room in front of the men's quarters. Commander has a keycard, and Comfort Rooms don't require them, so it's private. Besides, I'm safe with him since he's my protection. Inside, he points me to the bathroom, and I hurry to use it. When I exit, he takes his turn, giving me ample opportunity to check out the room.

A tall bench, much like a doctor's exam table, sits near wall cabinets. Suspended from the ceiling, two ropes with large rings dangle several feet away. A private exercise room? David's Playroom springs to mind. I recall Mary Jo's comments and realize what this is.

"What do you think of my Playroom?"

Commander startles me, his footsteps silenced by the plush burgundy carpet.

"What's the exam table for?"

"I like to Play. Do you know what that means?"

"I've heard about it." I shrug.

He says, "The girl bends over the table for Play ... and sex."

"And the rings?"

"Likewise, for Play and sex ... for holding on."

A huge belt hangs on the wall near the rings. I gasp and stop breathing for a second.

"That's for show. I don't use it." He laughs. Commander grins, enjoying my discomfort.

I scan the rest of the room. There's nothing else but a single chair. I turn around and almost bump into Commander standing behind me. I gulp and step back to a safe distance.

"You haven't said what you think." His voice is soft.

"It's not suitable for lovemaking, but that's not what you use it for, is it? Do all men on this base Play?"

"No, just a few of us. You met Sergeant Wolf. He and his friends Play."

"I know."

Commander raises his eyebrows.

"Do you ever make love? Is Play your only way to enjoy sex? I mean, can you make love?"

He cups my face with his hand, sending a bolt of electricity through my body. The temperature in the room becomes several degrees warmer.

"Are you asking me to have sex with you?" he asks.

"Make love. No, I mean, I'm not asking you to … do you want to, sir?"

"I want to have sex with you," he says.

I brace myself.

"Okay. Let's go to your apartment and make love in your bed. I call it lovemaking, but if you want to call it sex, it's fine."

Did I say too much? What if he only Plays? He said he wants me.

He steps back, and he appears to be deliberating.

"There's one problem. Nobody's allowed in my bedroom but me."

"I won't peek at your stuff because I'll be too busy kissing you. You kiss, don't you? It's a deal-breaker for me if you don't. I love to kiss, sir. It drives me …"

His lips find mine, and at first, his kiss is soft, but then his hunger takes over, and a moan escapes me. I want him, but not here.

"Return to Club with me, finish your drink, then leave. I'll follow after a few minutes. Wait for me in front of the office."

In the distance, Commander walks toward his office, where I'm eagerly waiting, and it's clear he doesn't want anyone to catch us together. Mary Jo said she and Lynn were his only girls, so this will be another secret arrangement.

Most of my relationships were clandestine out of necessity. Secrets are my way of life, and it makes sense for Commander to protect his privacy and avoid scrutiny, especially given my civilian status.

Commander nears his office and my heart beats faster. When he reaches me, he unlocks the door, and we're inside. He ushers me upstairs and into the living room where he kisses me again and directs me to remove my panties.

"Can we move into the bedroom to be more comfortable, sir?" It's a risk I'm willing to take. I kiss him hard, then pull back and wait.

He hesitates, and for a moment, I fear I've made a mistake, but then he guides me to his bedroom. After a quick peek around to make sure that no whips or chains hang on the walls, I give him my full attention. I pull my blouse over my head and remove my skirt. His eyes focus on my tights, which hide little. He smiles, turns me around, draws me closer, and runs his hand over my bottom through the material of my tights.

"I like this."

Me too.

With my help and insistence, he removes his clothes. He stands naked, watching as I linger, pulling my tights seductively down and then off. Then I remove my bra and stand naked before him, my gaze on his face. He nods in approval. I kiss him again, this time pressing my bare skin against his. His gentle touch triggers a feverish response, and I want him to devour me.

I slip from his embrace to recline on the bed, inviting him to join me. His lips find mine again, and we explore each other. My body aches for him to pleasure me, but I can't ask. He knows I won't do the same. He reads my mind and works his way down, and I surrender, reaching a thunderous climax. I pull him on top of me, and he takes his time.

Satisfied, he rolls off me, but my gaze stays on him. I'm here in his sacred bedroom, the forbidden chamber, his inner sanctum, in the arms of an amazing, gorgeous, sexy man, and David is forgotten.

I make a trek to the bathroom to freshen up. Commander takes his turn, and when he comes back, he's surprised to catch me still here, stretched naked across his bed.

"We're not finished, are we?" I ask.

§

The bedroom doors stand open, and the morning light seeps in, illuminating the empty spot where Commander slept, the sheet and blanket turned back. I reach over to his side to feel the cold sheets, remembering how we woke earlier this morning and made love again before drifting back to sleep.

Commander Pierce doesn't talk much, but he can read my mind. I'm wide awake now, in his queen-size bed with the bright white sheets and navy-blue extra soft blankets in his forbidden bedroom.

David had his chance. Why did he hurt me like that? Because I said I loved him? I'll never do that again. I make mistakes, but I learn from them.

I fix my eyes on the clock on Commander's dresser. It's early, my bladder is full, and I need to dress and leave before Cassie and Paul show up. Commander's not in the living room or kitchen, so maybe the bathroom?

I knock on the bathroom door, it opens, and I'm face to face with Paul, his eyes wide and mouth gaping open. He steps aside for a better view and says nothing, but his eyes scan me from head to toe. I push past him and slam the bathroom door. After taking care of business, I use Commander's toothpaste with my finger as a brush, stalling for time, hoping Paul will leave.

What now? My clothes are in the bedroom, so I grab a towel, wrap it around me, and peek out the door. The towel doesn't cover much. Paul is sipping coffee in the kitchen, glances my way, then back at his cup. I sprint to the bedroom and hurry to dress.

Commander remains at large, so I join Paul at the kitchen table. Neither cup of coffee on the table is for me, but I slide one cup close to me and sip it while watching Paul, who smiles, shaking his head.

"Where's Commander?" I ask.

"Phone call."

We both sip our java, studying each other, not uttering a word.

Commander vaults up the stairs and encounters the two of us drinking coffee in silence.

"I'll get another cup," Paul says.

Paul stands to leave, and he and Commander trade smiles like they share a secret, but this time I'm clued in. I wait until I'm certain Paul is gone before excusing myself. When I reach Cassie's desk, Paul is emerging from the break room with another cup and a pot of coffee. They must have a lot to share.

§

In the third-floor cafeteria, I dawdle over a breakfast of banana bread, fresh and hot from the oven, hoping the men will have left before my return. Unable to procrastinate any longer, I stop by my room, grab clean clothes, hit the shower room, and proceed to the apartment.

From the break room, I glimpse Commander in his office, so it's safe to start my day. Settled at my worktable, I find it impossible to concentrate. My head spins. I've fallen down the rabbit hole where nothing is the same.

§

For lunch, I opt for the third-floor cafeteria, refusing to deal with David after his despicable behavior. Tom and Jen sit with their friends at their table, ignoring me. Do they know I spent the night with Commander?

Back at the office, Commander is engaged in conference with Cassie at her desk. As I pass by, he nods but refrains from smiling or otherwise acknowledging me. I bump into Paul in the break room for my mid-afternoon coffee run. He teases me with a naughty smile, so I ignore him, fill my cup, and then leave.

To avoid David, I'll have to distance myself from the second floor, which means avoiding its cafeteria, Agora, my social circle, and maybe even the library. I'm still uncomfortable in the third-floor cafeteria, but there's no David and his horrid behavior. I'm in limbo without my friends or hangouts, and I can't tolerate staying in my tiny room.

CHAPTER 18

Another strange dream jolts me awake. This time I was a little girl, and my mommy and daddy were fighting. Scared, I pressed my hands against my ears, trying to block out their angry words. I hated listening to them. I jumped when Daddy slapped Mommy and cursed her, then I jumped again when he left, slamming the door. Mommy cried in her bedroom, and I cried in mine. I hated him and hoped he never came back. Something traumatic erased my childhood memories, so could this be a suppressed memory?

The week crawls by with Commander showing no interest in me, so perhaps it's a one-time deal. Maybe I didn't impress him. He's polite when I'm around him, but reserved. Cabin fever makes my evenings especially rough, so once, I visited the Radio Room, making sure David wasn't around first. Twice I went to the atrium with a book to read, but it became dark too early, so I fell asleep there.

Last night, I explored the corridor again. After descending two flights, I opened a second-floor door and entered a hallway near the Infirmary. People were nearby, so I retreated to the corridor and backtracked. Not wanting to end up in Agora, I postponed trying others. I saw more doors on the third-floor level, but I didn't feel lucky, so I returned to the fourth floor.

This morning I'm greeted by a friendly Commander and Paul, but they leave before I'm settled in at my worktable, and I'm still unaware of how he feels about me. I focus on translating the Book to keep my mind off Commander.

The Book is growing much more disturbing. This section's title is *Cultivation*. A symbol meaning *Transplant* describes the activity of low-level agents. Undercover, they'll capture, isolate, and remove Bad Actors from society—murderers, rapists, drug dealers, and such. They'll move the Bad Stock to secret work camps for slave labor to construct concealed housing complexes, which we now refer to as bases. They use a glyph that means *Storage*. In the end, they would allow no one to live freely outside the camps or bases.

It's late afternoon when Commander appears.

"Zena, I'm hitting the gym tonight. Stop by after I shower? I'll watch and let you in."

"I'd like that, sir."

He tells me when he'll expect me and leaves.

§

It's Thursday, Club night, and I'm invited. Last night, I met Commander at his apartment. After brief lovemaking, he warned me to check if I had my lanyard so I didn't get locked out, and I knew the evening was over. This is new for me. My lovers always engage in conversation with me after sex, or we cuddle. Nobody's ever summarily dismissed me, leaving me feeling like a whore. David never did that.

I longed to spend the night in Commander's spacious bed and wake up to the beautiful sunrise. Instead, I went to the atrium, where I must have fallen asleep. I remember closing my eyes and then opening them to a blinding light. In the distance, hovering over the immense forest, was a huge luminous disc. It was flying away from the base, and when I blinked, it disappeared. I wasn't sure if it was a dream, but it startled me awake.

In my reading, I learned the middle columns in all the bases were used as an elevator during construction, but I never understood how the Overlords accessed them. I left that fact out of my report and never told anyone. What's the point since they're not using them anymore? Are they?

Officers congregate outside Club, and when we weave our way in, it's bustling with chatter and activity. Commander and his team continue to the long table while I seat myself at the bar. Mary Jo, Lynn, and Jen join the team at the exclusive table.

Mack watches me claim my spot and strolls over to greet me.

"What'll you have, girlie?" he asks. He knows my name.

"I'll have water. Thank you, Steve."

"My name's not Steve."

"My name's not girlie."

I smile, hoping he has a sense of humor. He responds with a smile.

I hand Mack my music discs. He shuffles through them, reads the labels, and picks one to play. The recording dates from the 1970s. The player blares soulful strains of "*Maggie May*" by the incomparable Rod Stewart, and I know the words and sing along, keeping my voice low to avoid attracting attention. Mack stands behind the bar, observing me.

When my song finishes, Mack asks, "Where do you get your music?"

"Oh, my handlers gift them to me because they know how much I love music. I've been collecting CDs for years. The salvage units bring them in."

Friends in high and low places with access to their salvage treasure trove give me music CDs before cataloging, but I keep that to myself.

"They share books with me too, but I had to leave them behind."

"What subjects interest you?"

"Any kind of science, history, and occasionally fiction."

"Science? Which discipline?"

"Several, but I don't claim to understand most of it, especially books on string theory and quantum mechanics, but I enjoy reading them, anyway. I'm also interested in books about paranormal experiences or clairvoyance. The eggheads snatch up the most interesting books, but they lend them to me. Philosophy and behavioral science are my favorite subjects."

"Eggheads?"

"You know, very smart people who live in another dimension in their heads, able to grasp complex concepts I can only flirt with."

"You don't like eggheads?"

"Not true. I'm in awe of them because I'm different, too, in other ways. I worked with several very intelligent men at Central."

"What did you do at Central?"

I walked into that one. "It's Classified, and I can't discuss my work."

Mack nods.

"What do you do at Cavalry besides tend bar?"

A voice behind me asks, "Mind if I sit?"

Greg moves into view, so I motion toward the stool.

"So, you came back," he says.

"Yeah, I couldn't stay away. How do you like my music?"

He shrugs. We have a brief conversation, but before long, he stands and slips his arm around me. "So, do we know each other well enough now?"

I smile but rebuff his invitation with a shaking of my head.

Greg sits down, and we make small talk until Mary Jo appears at his side and whispers in his ear. He glances at me with a question I don't understand, so I shrug, he stands, and then they stroll out. When they return to Club half an hour later, Mary Jo doesn't resume her position at Commander's table. Instead, she joins Greg and his friends. Lynn and Jen have also vacated their honored spots. Will they ever invite me to the table?

When Mack approaches, I beckon him to come closer.

"So, Steve. How do the Overlords get to our bases from theirs?"

"I assume they travel the same way we do, with jeeps and trucks. They deliver truckloads of food and supplies as needed. Why do you ask?"

"Do they use aircraft like in the movies?"

"The movies are great fantasy, but they aren't real."

Was the flying disc a dream? My attention shifts to Commander's table.

"Are Mary Jo and Lynn members of the Inner Circle?"

Mack laughs.

"No, no women allowed. They are Commander's girls, the only girls he enjoys. Major Williams fancies Jen for now. The Inner Circle has three members. Majors Williams, Abrams, and Matthews. You haven't met Major Matthews. He's on family leave, but we expect he'll return soon."

"And Cassie? She seems like she's an important asset to the team."

He laughs again.

"No, as I said, no women. Four men made up Commander's Inner Circle, but one passed a few years ago."

"Was he old?"

"No." Mack laughs, but a dark shadow drapes over his face.

CHAPTER 19

Sean keeps me company at the Police Center, my newfound Radio Room friends make time pass, and exploring the corridors keeps me busy. I miss David and Agora and dancing with Tim, but another week flies by, and I still find it difficult to fill my evenings.

My assignment keeps me distracted and engaged. I stare at my open Book, trying to digest what the symbols suggest. The Master Plan describes their strategy for Good Actors—healthy, young, fertile women. It describes advanced genetic engineering and designer gene-splicing technology. They'll relocate Good Stock, as they label them, in secret breeding camps, thus ensuring the Good Actors will be fruitful and multiply with healthy stock. They intend to blend the divergent races into a monochromatic standard issue to eliminate racial differences, prejudice, and violence. Based on my observations of base personnel, they're close to reaching this goal. I'm uncertain how society on Overlords' bases compares with ours. Nobody I've spoken to knows.

Late in the afternoon, Commander drops by and invites me to visit him after work—as if he's tasking me with running an errand. I agree to rendezvous with him. It seems he wants sex on Wednesday, then we attend Club on Thursday. The rest of the week, I don't exist for him.

§

The Commander escorts me to his apartment, my office by day, our love nest by night. He becomes amorous and draws me to him for a long and welcome kiss. I want to please him, and after our lovemaking, I remain in his arms, my head on his chest. I don't want to let him go because when he gets up—it means it's over for the evening, so I snuggle closer, not wanting this to end. I trace the length of his arm muscles, then brush my fingers across his chest. I plant kisses along the route and inhale a mix of his faint body scent, aftershave, and sex. His warmth calms me, and I ache to stay in his arms forever. In bed, the Commander becomes a different person, attentive, warm, sweet, and almost playful.

"Hey, now, don't you be falling in love with me," he says.

It might be too late, but I won't confess it because I won't repeat that mistake.

"Don't be silly, sir. I'm using you for my pleasure," I say with a wink.

He smiles, allows me to remain a while, then excuses himself, and it's over.

§

Thursday—Club night, I'm still not invited to the Commander's table while the other women take their place. Mack and I chat. Men approach me and I rebuff them. Greg stops by and we talk, and then Mary Jo steals him away. I like Mack. Somewhat standoffish, he's warming up to me. He seems to know everyone but doesn't stand around talking to anyone. He observes them, studying the officers like they're bonobo monkeys in a lab. Sometimes, they act like those incessantly horny hominids. I'm pleased he finds me interesting enough for conversations, but he doesn't approach me, and he doesn't seem interested. I miss Agora.

§

The week races by. Research monopolizes my workday while my preliminary report sits idle. The Book speaks to their reuse of recyclable materials. They planned to infuse it with ultra-high-density compressed greenhouse gasses extracted from the atmosphere, providing a sustainable, inert, and energy-efficient building material.

According to the Book, they'd utilize it for everything, including building additional bases, in the open since nobody would remain to interfere. They'd use it in a specialized membrane for filtering the earth's waterways, saving the remaining wildlife. They'd go to extreme lengths to cleanse, protect, and preserve Earth's ecosphere, something my ancestors didn't care enough about, according to my research. That is—until the Overlords took over.

My legal pads are overloaded with my script, so I need to restock. Paul and Commander are deep in a work-related discussion, so I nod and slip by to the supply cabinet. With my acquired legal pads clutched to my chest, I sneak past to avoid disturbing them.

"Find everything you need?" Paul asks.

"Yes, sir, I'm good. Thank you, sir."

Commander asks, "Are you free tonight? I want to see you this evening. Same time?"

Why does he discuss our evening plans in front of Paul? What else does Paul know? Does Commander discuss everything with him? I'm not ashamed, but still, I'm very private.

"Yes, I'm free tonight, sir." I nod. I'm sure Paul knows plenty. But still.

§

It bothered me all afternoon, and now snuggled in Commander's arms after making love, I brace myself to ask a question. I may already know the truth.

"Paul knows about us. Do you share everything with him?"

Commander hesitates. "He knows we're having sex if that's what you mean."

"But do you talk about our private moments?"

"We have sex," he says. He pretends he doesn't understand what I'm talking about.

"Do you discuss personal things? I'm a very private person and can't express myself freely if you share details of our intimate moments with others. They don't need to know, and it would embarrass me."

"I've told no one anything personal, and if it bothers you, I won't say anything. I want you to feel free to express yourself in any way you want."

He's mocking me, but I read him, and he's truthful.

§

In my room, thoughts about my evening with Commander lull me into a deep sleep, and before long, I slip into another strange and disorienting dream. I'm standing next to a car crash with the front end of the car twisted and crunched. The driver sits trapped in the driver's seat, with half his body crushed. He's alive, but he can't survive the severity of his injuries. He beckons me to come closer to him, asks me to hold his hand, and in a weak voice says he doesn't want to die alone. When I take his hand, a white light flashes, blinding me, and something enters my body and embeds itself deep inside me. The light dims, and the driver releases my hand, his body lifeless. I have my first Knowing. He has given me something extraordinary, a Gift.

My dream hampers my concentration all day, making work challenging. It's only a dream, but this Gift would explain my special skills, the abilities no one else seems to have. The car is comparable to the ones I've seen in movies. My dream reminds me of Andrew's accident, but this is far worse. This poor creature died.

I look forward to an evening with the Thursday night Club crowd. I long to dance, but no one dances at Officer's Club. At least Mack is interesting to talk to, and I need a friend.

§

Club hops with activity tonight with officers playing at both pool tables, and voices ring loud over the clacking of colliding balls. The officers at Greg's table are boisterous but refrain from yelling anything crude. I brought some mixed music discs and now hand them to Mack.

"How are you today, Steve?"

Mack appears to enjoy our little game.

"I'm fine, girlie." He flips through the CDs and selects one.

Commander doesn't invite me to the table, and Mary Jo still retains her place of honor next to him. They don't talk much, but she's there if he desires. I imagine he requests her services between our love sessions. It's pointless to expect him to be faithful since I won't Play, but at least he's considerate and spares me. If our relationship changes, I can broach the subject. I never asked for David's loyalty, but we made love so often I thought it unnecessary. We had a genuine relationship, and he was more than my sex partner—at least, that's what I believed. It was perfect with David—like we belonged—until it wasn't. I miss him.

Greg stops by for his usual chat about art, music, cafeteria food, and whatever. I like him, and we have lively discussions, but it's not long before Mary Jo abandons her coveted post and claims Greg for herself. Why does she do that? I'm not going anywhere with Greg. We're friends, that's all.

"Where are you?" Mack asks, snapping me out of my trance.

"Mack, do you think dreams mean anything? Can dreams reflect events that happened, but we forgot about them? Is that possible?"

"Dreams are your brain reorganizing while you sleep. Sometimes your fears show up in your dreams, though. Why do you ask?"

"I've been having weird dreams about people and places I can't possibly know. They seem so real, more like memories than dreams."

"Even memories are unreliable. I wouldn't worry about it. I've read studies about that. What do you dream about?"

"A different way of life."

§

It's only Monday, but Commander invited me to his apartment again. We meet at the door at our usual time, he lets me in, and in his living room, he pulls me close, kisses me, and whispers in my ear.

"Let's try something different this time. I want to Play." His voice is soft and gentle, but I'm not fooled. He unbuttons his shirt, and I shudder at the thought of a belt and how he'd use it.

"I don't want to Play."

He pulls me back to him; his shirt is open now.

"I'll be gentle. Let me spank you a little. I won't hurt you. You tell me if it's too hard."

His breathing quickens and his face becomes harder and more determined, but his touch remains gentle. I back away. Everyone claims Play is consensual, but I'm locked in Commander's apartment where no one can hear me scream.

"If you want to be with me, sometimes you'll have to Play." His tone is gentle but firm.

"Isn't that what you use Mary Jo for?"

He steps back, acting surprised, then ignores my question and repeats everything about Play I've heard before. The woman is in charge and can stop whenever she wants, and so on. We haven't been together long, and we don't have a relationship. I can't Play his way, but even if I mustered up the courage to try, he'd never respect me or want more. I want more. A change washes over him, and his expression hardens with a desire I've not seen before.

"You want me to go to Mary Jo?"

His voice is now flat, almost angry.

"I'm not going to Play."

Commander Pierce pulls away, sits on the couch, and cradles his head in his hands. Moments later, he stands, and his face softens.

"Okay, maybe it's too soon. Come here."

He pulls me close again and kisses me with such passion that my body melts in his arms. He carries me to the bedroom. Afterward, he dresses— my cue to leave.

§

I'm invited to Club, so I meet up with Commander and Paul at our usual time. When we arrive, I take my customary seat at the bar. Mary Jo and Lynn assume their regular seats with Tom and Jen, and again I question if they'll ever invite me to Commander's table. Mack plays my music, and I chair dance and sing to myself. I've learned most of the lyrics to my songs, and Mack watches me, smiling. We chat until Mary Jo slides in beside me.

"Where do you get your music?" she asks. With deference, she indicates to Mack she would like a glass of lemonade.

"Oh, I've been collecting for years. It's one of the perks of my services."

Commander approaches the bar, something I haven't seen him do before, and stands between us, putting his arms around us both.

"I want to Play. Anyone interested?"

Commander grins at me first, and when I shrink back, shaking my head, he turns to Mary Jo, his eyes twinkling. Of course, she's delighted to accompany him, and she tilts her shoulder, lifts her chin, and smirks as they leave with his arm around her.

I watch until they're out of sight, ask Mack for my music discs, and march out, head held high. At my first stop, the Police Center, I ask Sean for my portable player, apologizing that I need it for the evening. On to my quarters, where I ditch my party music for my Somebody Done Somebody Wrong ballads. At my last stop, the hidden wall to the secret corridor, the wall moves, and the door opens for me with a touch. Concealed inside, I sink to my knees, collapsing into a ball, heedless of the dusty walkway. My tears are frozen, refusing to fall—I'm far too angry to cry. How could Commander do that in front of everyone, especially me?

I need an isolated place to scream or cry and curse the darkness, Commander, and Mary Jo. How could he choose her over me right in front of my face? Is he doing to her right now what I refused to do? Does Mary Jo know I've been with Commander? I shouldn't be mad at her since she had him first, but I am. I'd like to scratch that smug grin off her face.

Without paying attention to where I am, besides the pits of hell, I stumble down three flights of stairs. The pathway ends with a door, but I don't hesitate to open it. The wall slides back, revealing a dark, deserted storage room dimly lit by the corridor lights. Stacked boxes fill half the room, leaving plenty of space for me to vent. Excellent—an isolated retreat for listening to my melancholy songs and beating my chest with nobody to hear me scream.

I shut the door and the wall closes behind me, plunging me into complete darkness, except for a tiny red dot near the ceiling across from me. With my CD player clutched in one hand, my free hand explores the air for anything solid. No time to panic. The entrance wall should have a light switch. I test the floor ahead with my foot, finding it free of obstacles, and with care, extend my hand to explore in front of me as I cautiously step further into the room, touching nothing near me.

A door creaks and movement inside the storage room disturbs the quiet. I'm not alone. A beam of light scans the room, but boxes obscure the light source.

Without warning, a brilliant spotlight targets me.

"Hands above your head."

Blinded by the light, I obey, my heart racing.

Overhead lights switch on, revealing an officer standing a few feet away, his gun pointing at me. Male voices whisper in low tones, but I can't discern how many. I'm focused on the gun.

"My name is Special Consultant Zena Roberts, and I work in the Commander's office."

Damn, Commander won't appreciate this.

A younger officer moves to my side, removes my portable player from my hand, examines it, and, convinced it's not a weapon, hands it back.

"I have to search you."

He pats my sides, back, and between my breasts, using the side of his hand, and then he starts at my ankles and works his way up.

"Sorry, ma'am."

He stands, extracts my lanyard from inside my blouse, and reads it with it still around my neck. He nods to the officer with the gun and steps back.

"What are you doing in here? How did you get in?" asks the older officer, returning his gun to its holster.

I point in the direction where I entered, where the wall should be, but I'm confused. Shelves cover the wall behind me, as well as the adjacent one. I spin around, but no matter how I turn, I find no evidence of where I entered. I couldn't have moved that much.

"There was a door." My voice sticks in my throat as I search for answers. "I entered from the corridor. I swear a door was behind a wall … but it's gone now."

Several more officers enter, with David among them. Behind him, Commander appears, looking unhappy and as puzzled as I am.

I'm ushered into a small interview room and allowed to sit while they hammer away with questions. They stand over me, staring down to intimidate me. Standard procedure.

Commander stands quietly off to the side, observing the proceedings.

David watches, his arms folded, squinting in my direction, and Frank, the creep who asked to peek under my skirt, stands next to him at parade rest. I've seen neither in a while.

The officer with the gun introduces himself as Lieutenant Philip West but neglects to introduce the officer who searched me. They alternate grilling me, repeating the same questions, but expecting different answers. I learn the secured room opens with a special passkey, and when the motion detector went off, it alerted Security, who dispatched officers to the scene.

Lieutenant West asks, "How were you able to obtain a passkey?"

"I didn't have a passkey. I accidentally discovered an entry point from the corridor."

"What corridor?" the other officer asks.

I need to lie. It's dangerous to confess that my misadventure began on the fourth floor or that I've explored the corridor several previous times.

"On the second floor, I was searching for an isolated area to listen to my music alone. I like to sing loud sometimes and didn't want anyone to hear me. I was near the library and took some stairs down."

While exploring once, I discovered steps I assumed led to the main floor.

"I noticed an open door, entered, closed it behind me, and found myself in the corridor. I encountered steps, so I followed them down and continued along a path that ended at a door, so I opened it, thinking it was my way out. A wall opened, and once I was inside, it closed behind me. I couldn't see anything. It was pitch dark, and I couldn't find a light switch."

I catch my breath and think. Nadler taught me to never show fear.

"Someone trained a spotlight, and you pointed a gun straight at me. You know the rest."

David watches me, but I don't read him. I never expected to see him again so soon, and it sparks painful memories of what we once shared, all I lost, and how he hurt me. At least David wanted to spend time with me, unlike Commander, who uses me when it suits him. Now here they stand before me, both of my disappointing lovers. I miss David.

Lieutenant West says, "Let's take a walk, and you can show us the corridor entrance."

"I wasn't paying attention to where I was going, and I'm not sure where I began. The second-floor layout is unfamiliar, and I don't have my bearings yet. I'm very upset right now. Tomorrow, when I'm not such a mess, I'll try to retrace my steps, but right now, I'm overwhelmed. Nobody has ever drawn a gun on me or frisked me. This is difficult for me."

My hands fidget, with the right degree of shaky. I let out a long sigh.

We agree to meet the next day, buying me time to polish my story.

Commander orders me with him, and we take the elevator to the fourth floor in silence. We're both quiet the entire miserable march across the rotunda. I'm so rattled I can't read him or tell if he's angry, but I sure am. Stone-faced, he escorts me to my room. I imagine him returning to Club to inform his team of my misadventure.

In my room, I peel my clothes off, wash up, and sink into my cot. My head spins, and I don't know what to tackle first. David and his betrayal, Commander and his cruelty, or the corridor and that miscalculation? My heart aches, and I've never been jealous before. When my lover wants to move on, I'm always gracious and set him free. Nothing ever wounded me so deeply before. This is a unique experience.

I sink into a deep, restless sleep, but a disturbing dream wakes me in the middle of the night and puzzles me more than the others. I'm inside a cabin, and the view from the window shows nothing but woods. Muted sounds of the forest and an earthy smell fill the bedroom. The wrinkled face in the mirror can't be mine. My long hair is gray, almost white, and my eyes are tired and sad. I watch myself remove my clothes, collapse into bed, and wait to die.

CHAPTER 20

Cassie yells up the stairs, informing me of Lieutenant West's arrival. He's early this morning, and when I read him, I discover he's already met with Commander. An officious Lieutenant West escorts me to the elevator, where we descend to the main floor and walk past the infamous storage room. The door secures with a lock requiring a passkey.

"Who has access to the passkeys?" I ask, keeping my tone professional.

"Security."

"When you enter the storage room, does it immediately trigger the alarm?"

"I'm supposed to ask the questions."

I crank out a sly smile. He hesitates, rubbing his chin.

"The alarm sounds after a delay sufficient for someone with a passkey to enter and deactivate. They turn the light on, alarm off, and perform their duties. When they're finished, they reverse the process."

West escorts me to his office and motions for me to sit.

"Let's run through this once again. You were searching for someplace isolated, descended stairs, discovered an open door, and entered, but you can't remember where it was."

"Yes, sir, that's correct. I'm unfamiliar with that area except the library, but that's all, and I wasn't paying attention. I should know better, but I guess I made a discovery by accident. That's helpful, isn't it?"

"We'll see. The problem is, I'm having a difficult time believing you because workers are continually active in that section, and nobody's seen any doors at the bottom of the stairs."

West pauses for a moment and eyes me with suspicion.

"Why would you close the door after entering an unfamiliar corridor?"

Good point.

"Out of habit? I was absorbed in my music and not thinking. I hoped it'd be clearer to me today, but it's not. Believe me, I'll not do that again."

I switch on my feminine charm, but West is professional. He sits there and studies me.

"I understand you have high clearance. Is there something I should know? Is your work connected to this discovery?"

"I can't discuss my work without the Commander's permission. He's my handler."

"Well, I spoke to your handler, and he tells me your work has nothing to do with any corridor. You're translating a book created by the Overlords. So, let's try this again."

"Well, it isn't directly related to my assignment, but I'm used to having full rein on a base because it's how I learn. In fact, I discovered the symbols from exploring, which is how I got interested in learning how to read them. I recognize exploration and tracking symbols can be dangerous, but I'm usually more cautious."

I fake exasperation and defeat, it works, and West warms up to me.

"Well, you're correct. Exploring can be dangerous. If you need to explore, get Commander's permission, and he'll assign someone to escort you. Don't do this on your own."

"Is Commander very upset with me?"

"Nah. Nate's a good guy. He's more concerned about your safety, but don't tell him where you heard that."

"Nate?"

"Sorry, Commander."

"Is that short for Nathan?"

"Sure."

I freeze. A red flag? Michael mentioned his brother's name was Nathan. Coincidence? Michael talked about his brother, his half-brother, Nathan, who was sixteen when his birth mother died, so they sent him to live with Michael and his mother. Michael was a year younger, and they didn't get along. Nathan was quiet and kept to himself, whereas Michael was outgoing and liked everyone. Nathan was studious, had personal goals, and wanted to take charge. Michael also had goals, but he wanted to change our world. There might be more than one Nathan. But still....

"We're done. I'll take you back," West says. He opens his door, then we head to the lift.

"I'll take the stairs instead of the elevator, for the exercise," I say as we near the ramp.

Lieutenant West nods, laughs, and then leaves. David stands outside his office and turns my way, so I hasten up the ramp.

§

My weekend has been hellish, but I've avoided confronting Commander. He hasn't mentioned our debacle at Club or afterward. I'm avoiding that conversation, but I long for a confidante—someone who cares for me, someone on my side. Like I thought David was. I'm so angry with him; I want to hurt him. No, I want him to realize how much he hurt me. To understand he destroyed a friendship I valued.

It's a dreary Monday morning, and I'm late getting to work again, intending to avoid Commander and Paul. Cassie stops me at her desk and informs me Commander is convening a high-level meeting with his team in the main conference room. They expect me to join them in an hour for a briefing on my project.

They'll conclude their high-level business before I arrive; at least it worked that way at Mountainview. If they invited me to a briefing, they would request me to present my part of the discussion, my assignment. Sometimes my handler would speak for me, and I'd explain anything he couldn't answer—although sometimes they'd direct their questions to me. When I finished, they dismissed me.

Cassie instructs me to bring the Book, a notebook, and a pen. I know the drill but thank her anyway. She gives me directions to the conference room, and upstairs I prepare for the meeting. This is the first time they've shown interest in my work.

§

Before entering, I knock, announcing my presence, knowing if I'm too early, they'll instruct me to wait. A long, massive, polished conference table with seven seated senior officers greets me. The number of officers present doesn't surprise me, but who they are, does. Commander Pierce heads the table, flanked to his left by his second-in-command, Paul. Frank, the creep who wanted to peek under my skirt, sits to his right. David sits next to Frank and seeing him startles me and triggers a fluttering in my belly. Tom sits next to David. Across the table, to Paul's left, is Lieutenant West, which I would expect since he's Head of Security and he already has insight into my project. To his left is Mack, and it's clear bartending is not his day job.

"Many of you have met our consultant, Zena Roberts. She's working on a special project. Zena, describe your project to the group," Commander orders.

Standing at the foot of the conference table across from Commander Pierce, I hesitate, and I glance at each expectant face.

"Sir, I'm confused. Could I speak to you in private?"

"If you have a problem, say whatever's on your mind." He drums his fingers on the table and bites his lip.

"I'm sure it's okay for me to speak since you requested it, but I work for

Central Intelligence, and I'm always concerned about disclosing classified information."

The officers sit back in their chairs grinning.

"They all have the proper clearance," Commander says. "Let me introduce you then. First Lieutenant Frank Kelly, here on my right, heads Supply Operations, responsible for food and non-food distribution. His team supplies and manages the cafeteria and Officer's Mess and the distribution of office supplies and personal products. Next to him is First Lieutenant David Cross, Head of Salvage Operations under Major Daniel Matthews. Matthews is away on leave visiting his family, and you'll have the opportunity to meet him soon. Next to Major Abrams is Lieutenant Philip West, who you have already met, and I'm sure you're aware he's Head of Security. And of course, you know Mack, First Lieutenant Vincent Reed, my Senior Science Officer, an expert entomologist ..."

"Bugologist," Tom interjects with a grin.

I've been to a few high-level meetings, and they never introduced attendees. In previous meetings, I knew who the base Commander and my handler were, but no other officers. It makes sense they include First Lieutenants in high-level meetings.

"So, brief us on your project."

Alice experienced this after she ate the cookie and shrunk. Or was it the drink?

"Thank you for the clarification, Commander."

Straightening my shoulders, I ignore their patronizing smiles. With my head held high, I hold up the Book.

"Workers found this Book hidden behind a false wall at Riverview. It's written in a symbolic script known exclusively to the Overlords. We've found these cryptograms on all the bases. Architectural modifications removed some, while construction covered or destroyed others. Many remain, especially on the lower levels, including the first basement, where there's little construction."

I pause and pass the Book to Mack on my right.

"It was while exploring that I first became interested in the hieroglyphics. I translated several symbols as a hobby, and over the years, I've kept my interest in them and built a small vocabulary. This find, the Book, is remarkable. It contains so many new pictograms to learn, increasing my knowledge and symbol vocabulary. Our expert cryptologists examined the Book but failed to translate it. But I have a unique, natural gift for translating symbols. Not all symbols represent individual words. Like in English, certain symbols represent ideas or phrases that are interpreted depending on the context. You can imagine that, without a Rosetta Stone, it's a tough assignment, but I love it, and I'm very excited about this opportunity. It's arduous and often painstaking. Nothing worthwhile comes easy, I always say."

I never say that.

"I'm sure we'll learn a great deal from the Book. We hope to understand how the Overlords reason and perceive things by mastering the symbols and their nuances. My main area of interest is studying the Overlords and gauging our importance to them. I've spent several years decoding their radio messages, within their cluster, with considerable success. History is another subject of interest, and I believe it benefits us to look back—to see where we're headed. As they say, 'past is prolog.' I'm reminded of what Solzhenitsyn wrote in *The Gulag Archipelago*. He says if you dwell on the past, you'll lose an eye. If you forget the past, you'll lose both eyes."

I pause, letting it sink in.

Tom leans over the table to Mack and, in a loud whisper, asks, "What's a salsa shit, son?"

Mack shakes his head.

I hear muffled laughter, but I ignore them.

"My personal goal is to tie events from our past to our present to predict our future. My goals work well with those of Central Intelligence."

I sit.

After dinner, in my tiny room, I'm a caged animal with no space to pace. Fury builds inside me and needs release before I go mad, and my coffin-sized room won't contain me. My insane energy sends me downstairs to the main floor, where I stand watching David move around in his office. It's safe to assume he doesn't have his dick in some unfortunate woman's mouth. The door stands open a few inches, so I barge in, and David stops near his desk in the same place he stood that awful night, and the rage I've held in rushes out.

"You took a beautiful friendship and ruined it. I loved you, but not the way you think. It was your friendship, your companionship, I wanted. I thought you cared about me."

I stop for a breath and exhale some of my anger.

"David, you were exactly what I needed. Never judging or criticizing, I could be myself with you. I loved how we were together. Don't worry. I'm not in love with you—if you're afraid of that. I wasn't expecting a future with you."

I raise my voice, but David remains silent. He locks his eyes onto mine like a petrified rabbit.

"Why didn't you just say you wanted to move on? I would've let you go. Just say you preferred to Play, and you couldn't with me. Were you afraid I'd make a scene and not let go? No, letting go is what I do. Your friendship mattered to me. Why did you hurt me like that? You couldn't get me to Play, so you pretended to care for me? Then dumped me so you could watch me burn. Is that your game?"

David flicks his tongue in his cheek, lets out a deep breath, and shakes his head no.

"I'm so angry with you, but I want you to know I loved you in my way, and you're better for it. I won't bother you again, but damn it, I had to tell you this. Now, I'm about to make another huge mistake."

I turn, and without a backward glance, I storm out of his office and fly up the ramp and two sets of stairs to the fourth floor. From the midpoint between the office and my room, I see my timing is perfect when I spot Commander returning from the gym.

As Commander approaches, he notices my face but says nothing. With his sweaty arm around my shoulder, he guides me to the apartment. Upstairs, he showers. I wait in the muted living room light, staring out at nothing. He emerges from the bathroom, wearing a towel. He beckons me and, in silence, shepherds me to his bedroom.

Sometimes sex feels like comfort.

CHAPTER 21

A ll my red flags demand attention. Another crazy dream escapes me, and in a meditative half-sleep, I visualize the General's office. The photograph of a young Michael, next to one showing the soldier the General claimed as his son. Then, there's the photo on Commander's desk with the five soldiers. I make a connection between the middle soldier in Commander's photo, which resembles the soldier in the General's photograph of his son. Two others are Dan and Andrew. Might the last two soldiers be Paul and Tom? What does that mean?

Lieutenant West referred to Commander as Nathan, and Michael has a brother with that name. Michael told me they didn't get along. Nathan fell in love with a woman, Macy, and planned to marry her. One day, Nathan came home and entered Michael's room without knocking. Michael was on the bed with a naked Macy riding him, and Nathan walked out without a word. A week later, he joined the Peace Force. He was eighteen. Michael said he also joined when he was of age, but they chose different paths. They kept in touch over the years, but they weren't close. Neither of them ever courted Macy again, according to Michael.

When Michael spoke of Nathan, he had nothing flattering to say, but after his trips to Cavalry, he'd rave about Commander Pierce in awe of him. He'd tell me Pierce was strict but fair, a decent man, and his subordinates respected and loved him. He praised Commander Pierce's Inner Circle and always had complimentary comments. How can Michael's brother Nathan and Commander Pierce be the same person?

I suspected Michael's purpose behind his trips to Cavalry was to visit the staff in the Radio Room, and that's possible, but it makes more sense he would visit his brother. And it finally dawns on me why the General would display a photograph of Michael. If the young soldier shown in the companion photograph is Commander Pierce, then the General is their father. Why wouldn't Commander mention his brother, Michael? He would have known about me, wouldn't he?

At my worktable, I find it difficult to concentrate. I need answers to my questions.

§

I'm relieved not to run into David on the main floor. When I find Lieutenant West's office, he's alone at his desk, and without waiting for an invitation, I sit across from him.

"Do you know Major Michael Corday from Central?" I ask.

"Of course. Everyone knows Commander's brother."

There it is.

"Were you aware Michael and I had a relationship and lived together at Central?"

Lieutenant West nods and then squints as if it was common knowledge.

"Sure. Michael spoke of you often. He was quite enamored with you."

"And the General, he is Michael and Commander's father?" My voice shakes, which gives him pause.

"You didn't know?"

And answered my question.

"I wasn't sure."

West's little office feels warmer and smaller, and, luckily, I'm sitting. It's time to change the subject.

"I'm embarrassed that I didn't realize the officers I knew at our meeting were upper echelons. I'm overly cautious about discussing my assignments."

"Don't worry about it. Your briefing impressed everybody."

He is too kind.

"Thank you. I should take a break from my work occasionally and pay more attention to my surroundings."

"You're doing fine."

I need more intel before West lets this slip and Commander learns what I discovered.

§

Finished for the day, I stop by Cassie's desk.

"By the way, Cassie, Commander mentioned in the meeting there's another officer on his team, a Major Daniel Matthews."

"Yes." Cassie sighs but doesn't look up.

"I noticed a photo on Commander's desk showing five men. I'm guessing Commander is one, and maybe two others are Tom and Paul. Is Major Matthews in that picture?"

She bristles at my referring to Tom and Paul by their first name.

"Yes." She crosses her arms.

"And the fifth officer in the photo?"

"That's Major Andrew Jenkins. He's no longer with us."

Mack mentioned four officers comprised the Inner Circle, but one passed away.

I choke. Andrew is dead?

"How did he die?" It takes great effort to keep the grief out of my voice.

"I never said he died. We don't talk about it."

Cassie's stony countenance fades into sorrow.

I slip away before she can witness my breakdown.

In my room, I allow tears to stream down my face, my pillow muffling my sobs. It can't be true. Please don't let it be true. Andrew, I can't lose you before you find me.

I retrieve my treasures and dig for the little box holding Andrew's cross necklace. My hands tremble as I open the box. I clutch Andrew's necklace, kiss it, then hold it close to my heart. It's all I have left of him. He promised he'd find me. Now that'll never happen. My head throbs like it might explode, and my heart aches like it might burst. He was here. I missed him. And I'll never see him again. I can't breathe.

Grief is my companion all evening and night, and my tomblike room becomes my refuge. I doze when I'm exhausted, then wake and cry again, but when sleep takes over, I dream about Andrew, and by morning I'm numb. How long has Andrew been gone? Was his death recent, and what happened?

After breakfast, I learn about their memorial room on the fourth floor. The mahogany door bears a gold sign embossed with the words *Cavalry Memorial*, and inside, two rooms join a short hallway. A waiting room greets me first, but the second room displays wall plaques, so I wander over to the most recent plaques and browse until I reach the last one. His name: Andrew Jenkins. The dates below read: 2063—2096. He died four years ago. Why didn't I know, and why couldn't I sense it? Why didn't I try to find him? Four years. Kneeling in front of his plaque, tears run down my cheeks, and I can't fathom how I still have tears to shed.

I want to talk to Andrew, but I can't form any words.

§

I walk in late again, and Cassie doesn't roll her eyes like she often does when I disappoint her. It's difficult to concentrate on the open Book before me. My excitement for this Master Plan and its foreboding wanes.

Andrew is dead.

What happened to civilization occurred so long ago, before my time, and I should care, but right now, my sorrow overshadows everything. I need to learn how Andrew died.

The hours drag by, my music plays, and I remember Andrew. Mack tends bar at Club tonight, and he'll have answers.

§

I crash Club unaccompanied and have no trouble getting in now that they know me. At the bar, I wait for Mack to come over. Commander notices me from his table, surrounded by his privileged Inner Circle, but I turn away as Mack approaches.

"Well, Lieutenant Reed, why didn't you say something?"

Mack smiles and shrugs.

"I liked it better when you were Steve."

Mack laughs and moves closer to me, planting his outstretched palms on the bar.

"I'd like a closer inspection of the Book. It's an unbelievable find."

"Okay, so now you like me for my Book instead of my impeccable taste in music."

"I never said I liked your music," he says, teasing me.

"I learned a great deal in that meeting. And I've met everyone there, but I was surprised you're all part of the high-level team. I'm wondering what else I should know. This Major Matthews, he's coming back soon? I'm excited to meet him." Mack has no idea how excited.

"You'll have to wait. Heard he won't be back for a couple of weeks."

"The fourth member of the Inner Circle, you said he passed, and Cassie said the same. How did he die?"

I work to sound nonchalant and to stifle my grief. Mack drops his shoulders and frowns.

"Nobody talks about it, so if I tell you, keep it to yourself."

"I can keep a secret, and I'll consider it classified."

Mack smiles, then leans in even closer, so nobody else hears.

"Jenkins put a gun to his head. Blew the top off. Major Matthews found him, and they all took care of the body. It was unbearable here, and nobody wants to remember, so don't bring it up, especially to the Commander or his team. They all took it hard, and it's best left alone."

I can't speak. My heart races and a queer feeling in the pit of my stomach makes it hard to breathe. Darkness found Andrew, and he couldn't reach the light. I take a deep breath and push my pain aside.

"I'll never bring it up. Thank you for telling me."

Mack nods, straightens, and folds his arms.

Part of me is desperate to leave, but I can't tolerate being alone. I'm so tired and I'm spiraling headfirst down the rabbit hole, where nothing's the same, everything hurts, and everything's upside down. This was never supposed to happen. Andrew should have found me. I want a world where David and I enjoy each other. Where we have fun, and I have him, and Andrew is alive, somewhere. I don't recognize myself anymore. What in hell's name is happening to me? I'm not the person I'm supposed to be. I'm stronger than this.

Greg joins me, and I purposely flirt with him, putting my hands on him, stroking his arm, then his thigh. I want to fight. I want Mary Jo to charge over and attack me for screwing with her sex toy, but she won't. It's not allowed, and she knows better, but something needs to give.

Mary Jo slithers over to rescue Greg from my clutches. She says nothing, and I've lost my nerve. I don't want to fight. I want to stop the pain. Mary Jo glares at me as they walk away.

Commander approaches and grabs my arm. "Let's take a walk."

We plow through the crowd, his arm around my shoulder. He steers me to his Playroom, unlocks the door, and inside, he removes his top shirt and then his undershirt. He wears that hard expression, meaning he wants to Play. At first, I entertain the idea of allowing him to hit me, to kill the pain inside me, but I want to fight.

He moves in to kiss me, and I back away. He moves closer again.

"I want to Play. Come here. I won't hurt you."

"I want some things too." Rage bubbles as I grit my teeth and step back, but it's my sorrow fueling my anger. "Play isn't among them." I summon my courage with a deep breath. "So, have you heard from your brother lately? You know, Michael? Or is he *not* your brother?"

Commander steps back, his eyes wide.

"You know he is," he says as if I should have known, his tone almost apologetic.

I wasn't expecting that.

"Well, I do now. I found out very recently. I've been here over three months, and not once did you speak Michael's name. Not once did you mention your brother."

He shrugs, feigning innocence.

"You never brought up his name either," he says. Commander retreats, takes a deep breath, and exhales. "Zena, I thought you didn't want to talk about him."

"So, when you brought me here for sex, you didn't think I needed to know?"

"Why would I talk about Michael when I want to have sex with you?"

Oh, he has all the answers.

"You knew it would hurt Michael, especially what you wanted of me."

"Hey, wait a minute. You came to me. I brought you here to use the bathroom. You checked out my Playroom and then told me you wanted to have sex with me."

My mouth drops open. That's not how I remember it.

"Oh, so it's my fault you made me betray Michael."

"Hey, I didn't betray Michael. He knows me, and you knew you were Michael's girl when you came on to me. You know it's what you wanted."

A burning rage slithers up my spine.

"I'm no longer Michael's *girl*, but he's still my friend, and he's still someone I care about, and sure, he knows you. You're the last person in the world he'd want for me. And if I had known who you were, I'd never have let you touch me. I'd never hurt Michael that way."

"Come on, I can't believe you didn't know. If you're feeling guilty now, that's on you. I took what you offered. You're a grown woman. If you're gonna do it, own it."

His eyes are cold now, and we're both furious.

"I didn't know you and Michael were brothers, but you did. Were you getting revenge for what he did to you twenty years ago with Macy?"

His face flushes, and he shakes his head like he can't believe I'd say that.

I hit a nerve. One point for me.

"Look, you uppity bitch. Don't blame me for your problems. You lead men on, tease them, and then cry foul. You know what they call girls like you? Cock teasers. Men approach you, and you act sweet and flirty, and then you turn them away. You get what you deserve."

"Uppity bitch? You think so? I told you; I don't service military men because I don't have to. I'm a civilian, and if they can't figure that out, it's their problem. Plenty of military women will fuck them, but I won't because I'm not a whore."

"No, you're worse than a whore. You lead men on and give them nothing."

"At least I don't hit women with belts to get my kicks. First, you hit them, then make them kneel before you like you're a fucking king to watch them suck you off."

Commander's face burns bright red now.

"Shut up. Or I'll slap you right across your face." He's suddenly in my face with his open hand raised.

I step forward, glaring at him, daring him. Suddenly, shaking, I change my mind—I don't want him to hit me. My tears defy me and burst down my face even though I forbade them.

Commander lowers his arm and turns away. He grabs the shirts draped on the coat rack and dresses, glaring at me while undoing his pants to tuck in his shirttail, and then opens the door. He holds it open for me and waits.

I escape downstairs with tears flowing down my face. I'm ready to explode when I reach the main floor, but hold it in. David's not in his office. Agora isn't an option because I'd hate for anyone to catch sight of me like this. My last stop is David's apartment.

When I knock on his door, it opens, and I stand there, unable to speak. When David sees my tear-streaked face he stands back, and then opens the door enough to allow me passage.

He closes the door, and I fill his arms, even though he might not hold me. He does.

"I just learned someone dear to me from my past is dead, and it hurts too much. It can't be true. I don't know what to do."

It's true. He guides me to his bed where I slip off my shoes and fall into it fully dressed. He removes his shoes, snuggles next to me, and holds me while I cry.

I've never let anyone see me sob like this.

CHAPTER 22

On my breakfast tray, two sunny-side eggs glare at me above a strip of bacon, mocking me with its greasy sneer. It's Friday morning, David's nowhere in the second-floor cafeteria, but I'm among friends. I pass by Tim, and he waves. Several others wave too. Everyone seems pleased I've returned to the second floor.

I grit my teeth at the prospect of working today, reluctant to be around Commander, but I'm here to do my job, and he's my handler, so I have no choice. News of my argument with Commander undoubtedly reached the office. Cassie doesn't miss much. Fortified with coffee and smashed runny eggs, I head to the fourth floor. Instead of going to the office, I turn toward the Memorial Room across the rotunda. Inside, I'm alone as I approach Andrew's plaque.

"Good morning, Andrew."

I plop down on a bench facing the array of wall plaques and stare at his. At first, my words lodge in my throat. Andrew is gone, and I never believed in the afterlife, but I yearn for a heart-to-heart.

"Well, here we are, Buddy, reunited finally, except you're not here, are you? I wish I could feel your presence, to know some part of you remains, existing somewhere in this chamber. But no matter. This conversation is one-sided where I do the talking, and you listen."

I draw on my resolve with a deep breath.

"You promised you would find me, but did you even try? Were you concerned about me after you left Westview? It's been ten whole years now since you left for rehab. How long before you forgot me?"

Another deep breath.

"I'm angry because you know I'd have been there for you in a heartbeat. I'd have sat with you in your darkness until you battled your way out, as often as you needed. Why didn't you find me? You promised."

My tears won't come, and I fear I've exhausted my reserve.

"Four years. I kept your cross necklace all this time, and you've been dead four years? It doesn't belong to me. You said it was a loan until you found me. Who should I pass your necklace to? Dan isn't here, so I haven't seen him yet, but I still have his shirt. Poppy, I wanted to show you what I've made of my life. I wanted you to be proud of me." Poppy was my name for Andrew when he ordered me to brush my teeth or get ready for bed. He loved it when I teased him about it.

"I'm so tired, Poppy, and I try so hard. Everything is falling apart, and I need you now. I can't stand losing you, and it hurts to let you go. You promised."

Andrew never saw me as weak or broken because he needed me to be strong. Now I need him. No, now I need someone, not Andrew. He wasn't strong enough to fight his own battles, so how could he possibly help me fight mine?

"Okay, Poppy. It's time to say goodbye. Andrew, I love you, and I wish you were here, but I need to let you go. I hope wherever you are, you find peace. I don't need you, and I've stood strong until now, and I'll continue because I choose to live. Why did you do this? It hurts that I can't bring you back. Goodbye, Poppy. You know I love you, but I won't be back."

I leave the chamber, proceed down the hall, and walk out the door, taking my sorrow and stuffing it down deep with my rage where they can keep each other company. I have work to do.

§

Cassie glances up when I pass her desk. I'm late enough to miss the coffee clutch with Commander and Paul. I skip my morning coffee to hide upstairs until lunchtime. Unable to work, I turn on melancholy music and remember and try to forget. I'm alone with my sorrow. Down the rabbit hole where left is right, right is wrong, and everything is turned upside down and inside out. Michael is still gone. Andrew is dead. Dan? Commander threatened to hit me. David? At least we're friends again.

CHAPTER 23

Saturday passes without conflict, and today I can focus on translating and keeping my mind off my troubles. I reorganize my preliminary report, adding new information. The Book refers to something called *Readiness*. But readiness for what? The Messiah ... the Rapture ... the Apocalypse? Some Big Event? An expected epic cataclysm that changes everything.

Most symbols translate without difficulty, but some seem impossible to decipher, mystifying me, and I'm struggling with them.

§

So far, my plan to avoid Commander and his team has been successful, but when he comes upstairs after lunch and sits across from me, it's clear my luck has run out. I set my writing aside and offer my full attention.

"We need to discuss a few things. We need to talk about Michael, for starters. I'm busy now, but I want you to come back after dinner so we can sit down for a long, serious talk."

Does he think I'd have sex with him now?

"This isn't about sex. I need to ensure we understand each other because it's obvious we don't. We've both had time to calm down and reconsider."

My expression must have given me away, or maybe he reads minds too.

"I'll come back after dinner, sir."

§

Everyone has left for the day except Commander, who waits for me. He escorts me upstairs, locks the door, sits on the couch, and invites me to sit next to him.

"A few days ago, we exchanged some nasty comments. We could've avoided that whole mess if we had talked about certain subjects. You're upset about Michael, and I'd like to start with that."

High-ranking military men never apologize or admit wrongdoing. They try to fix their transgressions, and it's clear he wants to fix this, and so do I.

"Michael talked about you, so, sure, we knew who you were. The General transferred you after Michael left you high and dry and you had problems with Colonel Wickmore, who harassed you. I left you alone for as long as I could. Not because you were Michael's woman. I was waiting for you to make the first move. Your interest in me was clear, but you seemed shy. So, I waited. Then it seemed you were waiting for Michael, and you weren't friendly toward the team or approaching me. When you flirted with me in my Playroom, I took what you offered. I wasn't hiding anything from you. You didn't bring up Michael, so I saw no need to."

"He's your *brother*. Why wouldn't you mention him? Especially if you knew we had a relationship at Central. I don't understand."

"Okay, why didn't you? You may not have known I was his brother, but you had plenty of opportunities to bring up his name."

"I don't discuss my personal life. I transferred here for a fresh start and didn't want to bring any of my old baggage. But if I had known you were Michael's brother, I'd have asked you about him. I wanted to understand why he never returned, what happened to him, and whether he was safe. When he left, he asked me to wait for him. That was five months ago. Where is he?"

"I don't know his whereabouts. Michael takes leave every couple of years. He takes a leave, and no one hears from him for several months. We're used to that. He's fine, I'm sure, or I'd have heard some news. When he comes back, he'll explain himself to you."

Such a lame explanation for five months of uncertainty.

"The General is our father, and I'm aware you met him. Michael and I grew up military."

He sighs. "I shouldn't have called you a bitch."

"Uppity bitch."

He nods.

"You need to understand that when I choose to Play, I can get agitated. It's the wrong time to attack me. In fact, there's no good time to attack me. I'm not accustomed to anyone talking to me that way, especially women. Had we been in public, you wouldn't have been so lucky. Look, I want you to be my girl. I realize it's different with you. Different from my usual. But I enjoy you, and it's clear you feel the same. I want you as one of my girls."

Had I not been sitting, I'd have fallen over. His *girl?* Like his property? Or like his woman? Michael often called me his woman. Is that what he's saying? What about Mary Jo?

"Sir, I have relationships, not arrangements. I'm typically involved with someone for at least a few months. Michael was the exception. It isn't difficult to have an exclusive relationship for a few months. When it's time, we go our separate ways."

"If you want an exclusive relationship with me, I can grant that, but you'll need to Play. You can't ask me to give up Play. I don't need it every time, but I'll expect it from you when I do. Or I keep Mary Jo. I won't sneak behind your back. If you want exclusive, you Play."

"No belts?"

He hesitates so long it seems I lost him. "No belts. Not until you're ready."

Okay, that will be never. It appears we're both hoping to prevail without compromising.

"But I'd require an actual relationship for me to even consider Playing."

"What does that mean?"

"We'd spend evenings together, learn about each other, and have fun together, but no sex."

He frowns. "How much time?"

"An evening now and then, to chat or listen to music. No sex. We can enjoy sex nights, but I wish to stay overnight those evenings, not make love, and then be dismissed like a whore."

I enjoy negotiating.

"And if we're exclusive, Mary Jo and Lynn can't share your table at Club while you ignore me. I won't flirt or leave with anyone, but if I get the chance to dance, I will."

Commander hesitates, then shrugs. "That sounds fair."

"How about Tuesday night, then?" I ask. Tuesday night is poker night. I'm testing his resolve.

"How about Monday night after the gym? That's tomorrow."

"I have plans for tomorrow and business to attend to."

"What business?"

I need to know where I stand with David, but I can't tell Commander, and I can't juggle two lovers.

"Personal things."

§

Monday night, after eating dinner alone, I head to Agora, searching for David. He no longer eats in the second-floor cafeteria. At the door, Tim catches me and pulls me away.

"Zena, you shouldn't go in there."

"Why not?"

Tim hesitates, and it's clear he doesn't want to tell me.

"Look, Zena, Lieutenant Cross has a new girl, and he's been with her for a while since you stopped coming around."

That's not the news I want to hear.

"I understand. What's her name? Do I know her?"

"Her name is Mary. She's all right."

"Okay, thanks for telling me. I've moved on too, so it's fine."

He nods and steps aside. It's early, but a crowd is gathering already. Several smiling soldiers greet me. I haven't attended Agora in a while, so I stop to chat with familiar faces and then turn my attention to the booth. Our booth. David sits with a plain civilian woman.

"Hello, my name is Zena. I'm a friend of Lieutenant Cross."

David stiffens and frowns. I hold out my hand, and Mary takes it.

"I'm Mary." That's all she says.

Mary appears timid and unassuming. She's not good-looking, and she's noticeably quiet. I sit across from David for a while, smiling as graciously as I can manage. Mary relaxes, and so does David. I'm not claiming my man. I'm letting him go. We chat for a little while, and I take my leave, wishing them a good evening. I don't want to stay.

§

Tuesday drags, but my workday comes to an end. For my evening with Commander, I comb through my CDs for music he might appreciate. Our conversation can include work, but not my past, and not Michael. I should review some questions to ask. What was his mother like? Does he enjoy music, or what does he think of mine? I won't mention Play unless he does.

My black blouse drapes over my breasts and the top of my pants; from what I can see in the mirror, it's not bad. Commander expects me at the office door soon.

§

One of my favorite singers belts out my beloved songs. This is our Getting to Know Each Other evening, but Commander pulls me close and kisses me without allowing me to remind him this is our no-sex evening. He takes me to his bedroom, removes my blouse and lanyard, and then kisses my neck.

Change of plans.

This time, after making love, he invites me to join him on the couch. I restart my music and join him.

"What do you think of Celine?"

"What?"

"The singer. Her name was Celine Dion. This music is old but timeless."

"It's … nice." He nods.

"Would you rather listen to music with male singers? Or something a little edgier? My collection is large and includes several genres."

"No, this is fine."

"So, did you like growing up on the civilian base? Did you see your father much?"

Commander smiles and cocks his head.

"I grew up on Valleyview with the military wives and children. Didn't you grow up there too? Were your folks military, or just your uncle?"

Michael must have related to Commander my Mountainview cover story. There, I worked undercover with everyone believing my handler was my uncle, who insisted on taking custody after my father's death, having lost my mother years earlier. I can't tell him I woke up in a cave at thirteen and was taken to live on a military base.

"I grew up military. Did your father visit often?" I ask.

"Infrequently, as a youngster. As a teen, he visited more often. Didn't like to be around little ones, I guess."

Michael told me his father visited often during his childhood, but I'll keep quiet.

"So, what made you decide to become a Commander?"

He sighs. "Any man of substance strives to be his best. What made you want to become a Special Consultant?"

"I got drafted." I laugh. Our conversation is not heading in the right direction. Men normally like to talk about themselves. This one prefers to ask questions. "The military discovered my special skills and wanted to use them, so they made an exception for me."

"Why didn't you enlist in basic training?"

"I enjoy my freedom and don't want to be bound to anything. And I hate the idea of being used as a sex object to service men I detest. I maintain agency over my body. I give the military enough. How long have you served as Commander?"

"Eight years. Two years before that, I was Second in Command, learning the position. My Commander retired, so I assumed his command."

Commander's handheld buzzes, so he excuses himself.

"Sounds great, but I can't. I have … company. No, I can't bring her." He laughs. "You'll find a fifth."

I can't hear what the other person is saying. Commander paces with his back to me.

"Sure, but next time. I made a promise. Besides, we play every week."

When Commander turns toward me, I motion to him it's okay, but he signs off.

"No, I made a promise to you."

"And I'm releasing you from your promise. This was fun, but you want to—play poker? Please, I'm fine."

I smile to show him I'm okay with his preempting our evening.

"Where's your poker game?"

"Major Abrams' apartment behind my Playroom. Are you sure?"

"Yes, please. Go have fun."

Commander calls back with his change of plans. We part company, and once he's out of sight, I realize I have a long free evening.

§

The second floor appears abandoned, and Agora is almost empty. On the main floor, David is in his office, but not alone. He's opening his Playroom door and ushering Mary into it. I'm unsure how, but I'll have to get used to this. Back on the fourth floor, in front of my quarters, when I reach into my blouse for my lanyard, it isn't around my neck. I forgot to put it back on after Commander and I made love.

The fourth-floor men's quarters include four apartments. It's quiet when I approach the first apartment and when I knock, there's no answer. The second one, no answer. The third is more promising since I can hear muffled voices when I get close, so I knock, and Paul opens the door.

"You decided to join us?"

"No, I need to see Commander. I left my lanyard behind by mistake."

He steps aside to let me pass. Commander stands by the poker table where his team sits. They're playing a version of strip poker. The men all sit fully dressed, but three military women stand in different stages of undress. One has nothing on top. Another still has on her bra. The third stands with her back to Commander, with everyone encouraging him to take her bra off—everyone but me. Once her bra is free, she whispers something to him, and he reaches around and cups her small breast in his hand. He sees me and quickly takes his hand away.

"Sorry to interrupt you, sir. I left my lanyard in the office and can't get into my room."

I pretend nothing's wrong, but everything's wrong. He left me to play with these disgraceful whores. Paul offers to escort me to retrieve my lanyard. The entire walk across the rotunda, I hide the volcano raging inside me. Every time I manage one step forward, I'm thrown two steps back. We share an uncomfortable silence on our trek to the office, and when Paul lets me in, I tell him my lanyard is in the apartment. He grins and unlocks the door. I search the bedroom, find the lanyard on the floor, and fix it around my neck. We leave, and I'm done.

156

CHAPTER 24

Images of Commander removing another woman's bra and touching her sear my mind, so working remains difficult. The days drag, and I avoid Commander by arriving to work late and leaving early, and lucky for me, he stays away while I'm working. We had made love a couple of hours earlier, and he needed to fondle another woman? It's past time for me to let go.

After an endless workday and eating alone, I have lots of energy. I dress in my cutest casual attire, with my black blouse cut low to show the right amount of cleavage. My skirt wraps around, and I'm wearing my see-through tights. If I'm careless, my skirt might open a bit and show my thigh or some of my ass. I could be careless.

My spot at the bar waits for me, and I plan to ignore them all night with my back to the Commander's table. I hand Mack my music and wait for someone to join me. Meanwhile, Mack leans on the bar facing me. The first song plays, and I sing the lyrics to myself.

"What's this song about?" Mack asks. His face twists in a grimace, and it's clear he finds this specific song disturbing. Wait until he hears the rest.

"Dishwalla's *Pretty Babies* is about turning our children into sex objects. Dressing them like little tramps for men to crave."

"That never happens. Why do you listen to this kind of music? It's troubling."

"Good, because it's meant to be. This music is over a century old. It happened often in those days, and it undoubtedly still happens now."

"No, not true, because we have strict laws to protect our children. No one would dare harm a child that way. The Overlords rid us of the evils of the past."

I'd love to educate him on how wrong he is, but I'm not angry with Mack. Let him live in his delusion. They don't allow children on military bases, but they allowed me. The officers may be clueless about the Truth.

I sing the last verses of the song, but when the next track starts, I remember the lyrics about a woman putting a gun to her ear. If anyone listens, it will hit home, so I pretend not to notice and sing along in a low voice, not wanting to call attention to myself. I stare at my hands clasped in front of me.

"And in this song, the woman wants to die?" Mack asks. He hunches his shoulders and shakes his head.

"No, she wants to live. She's caught up in a prison of pain and wants to be free. That's my take."

"What kind of music is this?"

"Edgy, isn't it? Not all of my CDs are about falling in love or broken hearts. I have different styles of music, something for every occasion."

"I don't like this, so I'll change it to something else."

"Okay but play the sixth song first. It's my favorite."

He concedes and I sing along, "… *remain a child in your arms forever.*"

After playing my favorite song, Mack removes the CD and plays the next disc, a collection of love songs and heartbreak by various artists. After hearing the first melody, Mack relaxes and nods at me.

A commotion at the door gets everyone's attention, and their eyes follow an officer strolling up the aisle. He stops and talks briefly to officers on his way to Commander's table. I'd recognize him anywhere.

Dan stops to speak to Greg, then saunters up to Commander's table. Mary Jo, Lynn, and Jen abandon their seats to mingle as if on cue while Commander and his team greet Dan with welcoming smiles. He gives Commander a bear hug first, then walks around to deliver Paul and Tom hearty hugs before taking his place next to Commander.

Dan looks the same, but older. Will he remember me? I keep my eyes glued to him as they blissfully talk and laugh together. Something unfamiliar flutters inside me. I'm happy for them but unhappy for myself, and I don't understand why this hurts.

"The Circle is complete again," Mack says.

"Why did the women leave?"

"They don't belong there now, and they know it."

Mack watches the head table. The air has changed with a vibration shift, but its meaning eludes me. I turn around to watch, and Commander notices me and signals me to join them. I approach the table where Commander motions me to walk around to his side.

"This is Major Daniel Matthews. I mentioned him at our briefing. And Dan, this is our Special Consultant Zena Roberts. She's here from Central working on a project. I'll bring you up to speed tomorrow once you're settled."

"Zena? Michael's woman?" Dan asks.

"She was," Commander says.

I study Dan. His bearing is different than I remember. I want to ask if he remembers me, but a clenching in my bowels warns me against it. He's not the gallant hero I remember, the one person to protect me and put my needs ahead of his own. I'm not the same either. Angel grew up. Dan scrutinizes me, and I touch his arm. The image of him at Westview saying goodbye becomes sharp in my mind. The memory is still there, but he's not remembering.

Dan's eyes narrow and settle on my hand on his arm.

"Sorry, I had to see if you're real since I've heard so much about you. I guess you are."

He smiles but appears displeased. The Inner Circle is unaccustomed to brazen women.

"Well, Miss Zena. This should be interesting," he says, but I doubt he means it.

"I'll let y'all get back to your reunion. Welcome back, Major Matthews, sir."

I return to my seat at the bar. They continue boisterously laughing and talking while I fight the tears and sorrow welling inside me.

David saunters up the aisle, stopping to chat with Greg, then heads to Commander's table. I've never seen David in Club before, and he looks out of place. David acknowledges Commander with a nod, gives Dan an enthusiastic handshake, and joins the group. I turn back to my music. I glance now and then, trying not to be obvious as the evening wears on.

David stands to leave, notices me, and joins me at the bar.

"So, this is your new hangout?"

"Only on Thursday."

"How are you getting along?"

"Better." That's a colossal lie. "I met your boss."

"You're always welcome at Agora. You love dancing, and I doubt you'll be doing that here." He scans the room and the small vacant dance floor.

"If Tim joined us, there would be dancing. But thanks, I'm sure you'll see me down there. I miss it."

David leans over and kisses my forehead. "Take care." And he's gone.

Mack lifts his eyebrows, staring at me.

"You know Cross well?" he asks.

"I used to frequent Agora downstairs and sometimes sat with him. We're friends."

Mack shakes his head in disapproval.

"They dance down there, and that's where I belong."

"Nah, I'd miss you," he says, but doesn't sound like he means it.

CHAPTER 25

Commander and Paul have lingered at my worktable, surprising me. I purposely delayed coming in to avoid them. It appears Commander is waiting for me. He nods at Paul. While I gather my work materials, Paul rises and leaves, and Commander stays.

"I guess you're a bit upset about the other night."

"Sir, I wanted to talk to you about that. I've decided I don't want to be your girl. I don't see it ever working since we're so different. We both work here, and you're my handler. It's never a smart idea to mix work and personal life."

Commander shakes his head.

"Well, think about it. We enjoy each other." He grins and then becomes thoughtful.

"It wasn't what you thought, and I didn't know they invited girls. We were having a bit of fun, and it meant nothing. I never have sex with women at poker games. Not my thing. The guys were egging me on, and I went along with it. I don't see why you're upset."

"Maybe because you passed up an evening with me to play poker with your friends and fondle that little whore. I'm not upset. We're a bad idea, and I'm clearly not enough for you. The base teems with men, and I'm sure one will find me enough. Who knows?"

"Little whore? Military women are accommodating. They're upright women doing their duty. That doesn't make them whores."

"Isn't that the definition?"

"You accommodated me, so what's the difference?"

Did he just call me a whore?

"There's a huge difference, but I suppose if I don't want to be your whore, I'll need to stop accommodating you. Either way ..."

"As I said, it meant nothing to me." With that, he sighs and leaves, shaking his head.

A sickening feeling courses through my body, starting from my pelvis and working its way up to my chest. I've never felt ashamed about my sexuality or my relationships. It's not wrong to share myself with men I care about, and it's not dirty. It isn't.

§

The afternoon drags. The Book is open in front of me, my notes scattered on the table, but my concentration flew out the window about an hour ago. It's still early, but it's doubtful I'll accomplish anything, so I close the Book, gather my papers, and stash everything in the cubbyhole shelf. With my music put away, I make sure I'm leaving the apartment the way I found it, grab my empty, rinsed coffee cup, and head downstairs. Paul is in the break room when I drop off my cup, but he avoids eye contact and leaves without a word. Strange.

It's time to learn more about Davies—Scott, and his connection to Michael. Why is "Davies" here? At Central, I couldn't confirm my suspicions about Michael, and Paying Attention could have revealed everything, with so many opportunities, but I allowed them to pass. He had his secrets, and I had mine. Our lives together were wonderful, so it didn't matter. But now I want to know, and I've brainstormed a scheme for determining his whereabouts.

§

In the main floor's transit bay, the Transit Officer sits at his desk in front of a computer.

"Hi. I'm Zena Roberts. We met when I arrived four months ago."

The officer nods in recognition. "So, Zena. What can I do for you?"

"Well, I'm working on a special project. I have level twelve clearance and would like to look at your transit records. It wouldn't take long, and I'll just take a couple of notes."

I flash my lanyard, even though he's aware of my clearance. He stands and allows me access to his computer. The seat is still warm. I thank him and stare until he gets the message and waits outside his office.

First, I search the database for Davies' transit records. He has one entry, traveling alone, with nothing unusual about his trip. The date means nothing to me, with zero noted anomalies.

Next, I search Michael's records for the past three years. Several entries show his ingress and egress. He's almost always alone, but the dates give me pause. Unbeknownst to me, Michael always traveled here on the same dates every year, June 23rd, and January 5th. Every year. Nothing unusual, except for the last entry. He arrived on January 4th and stayed until the 6th.

Michael was here for three days? He left Central on January 2nd, so where was he before arriving here? Why did he stay at Cavalry for three days? He returned to Central since no other transit destinations depart from Cavalry, but never stopped to visit me. He must have taken another transit somewhere else from Central, but that data isn't available on this system.

One last search—of my transit record. I haven't seen the nice young officer who traveled here with me since that day, and I want to learn his name. The passenger manifest shows my arrival on February 28th, but my name is the only one listed. It shows I traveled alone.

$$\S$$

Last night I lay awake contemplating my discoveries; nothing about Davies, and a mystery about my fellow traveler. And Michael? What is significant about his travel dates? It appears I'm more clueless about him than I thought. I'm not sure why it even matters now. He could have returned with no one informing me. Michael and I are finished, but I need closure. Why did he want me to wait for him, promising we would be together? Then nothing but unanswered questions.

This morning, I have my table to myself. I need a plan to fill in the missing pieces, and my coffee cup needs a refill.

$$\S$$

A red-faced Paul storms into the break room, breathing hard, as I pour my coffee.

"You approached Sergeant Masters for the use of his computer to search transit records."

He bellows so loud I'm sure they can hear him on the entire floor. His cold eyes narrow into slits.

"You need access to anything, check with Commander Pierce or me first. You get permission, and we make proper arrangements. Do not act on your own."

Cassie sure is getting an earful. I imagine her smiling.

"Do you understand me?"

"Yes, sir."

He leaves in the same storm.

CHAPTER 26

The extra chairs at my worktable sit empty, so my morning chats must be over. My personal life has become a disaster. I keep making mistakes, silly mistakes. In this strict culture, the instant I believe I figured it out, the deeper I fall into the rabbit hole. From Paul, I get the cold shoulder all week. Commander and I avoid each other. David's never in the cafeteria. Even Tom ignores me, and I've yet to run into Dan. I'm avoiding Club, but I miss my conversations with Mack, and loneliness gnaws at me like a beaver felling a tree.

Trying to comprehend the meaning of symbols distracts me from my out-of-control life. The Book describes something called *Jamming*. Chaos will result from the failures of governments to govern when farmers can't feed the masses and industries can't provide jobs or goods. Businesses— from banking to bakeries—will collapse. Pandemonium will strike a blow worse than destructive warfare. The chosen, destined for captivity on bases, will become a Noah's Ark of humans instead of animals. The remaining population will perish without fertile females for propagation. Globally, wildlife and plant life would achieve an astonishing comeback, like hitting a planetary *Reset* button—their symbol, not mine.

§

I need more than working, eating, and sleeping. I need someone to talk to, a friend or companion. The main floor is full of activity, with military men performing their duties. I slip past security offices to almost nonexistent activity and discover an office with an open door. I peer in and see a familiar face. Mack doesn't ask me in, so I invite myself.

"You here to give me a blow job, girlie?" He's not serious because he knows better.

"Nope. I didn't know you had an office down here."

Next to Mack's desk is a bookcase filled with various science books. One title catches my eye, so I select it.

"So, you understand string theory?" I ask, holding the book up to him.

"Sure. Don't you?"

"I've read about it but don't understand it. Chaos theory, multi-verses. Sounds so science fiction. It's beyond my level of comprehension," I say. "So, Steve, what do you do down here?"

"That's classified, girlie."

"Touché." I laugh.

"Can I ask you something?"

"Sure." He grins.

"Do you know Major Michael Corday? Does everyone know him?"

"The whole team knows Commander's brother. He comes here twice a year and loves to brag about you. You could say we knew you intimately before ever laying eyes on you."

"Intimately? You mean the type of person I am or …"

"Both. Michael loved to share. I probably shouldn't tell you this."

"No, please do."

"He talked about how smart you are, how pretty, and how much you love sex. And what you like."

What? Michael discussed our lovemaking? That explains a lot.

§

I stuff my anger toward Michael down with my rage over the Colonel's mistreatment and sorrow over the loss of Andrew. It's getting crowded in there. How dare Michael discuss our intimate moments. Did they laugh and compare notes? Did they rate their women on performance? Are all men like this? Wasn't my relationship with Michael special? Commander promised he didn't discuss intimate details of our lovemaking.

Commander and Paul remain at the table this morning, and when I arrive, I pretend nothing's wrong. Paul gets up and leaves without a word, but Commander stays.

"So, are you still angry?" he asks.

"I have a question."

I hold my breath for a moment, then summon up courage.

"Word has it, Michael was very descriptive about our private sex life."

"Yeah, Michael liked to brag about you." He nods reflectively. "Only said good things. Made you out to be perfect."

"That's why he cheated on me every time he came here?"

His eyes widen. "Hey, come on. Guys don't consider that cheating. It means nothing."

"He cheated, and he lied, and it meant something to me."

"Michael loves you, but maybe he loves his freedom more. He hid it from you because it meant nothing to him."

Commander winks and stands, watching me for a moment, then leaves.

§

My eyes are open now. I was dreaming again. No, it was a nightmare. The Shadow Man troubled my dreams, seeking something from me. The feeling of being hunted won't leave me, but I wasn't afraid in the dream. Again, killing him was my only option. It was so dark, but I wasn't afraid. What does it mean? Is it about killing off what plagues me, or is my subconscious trying to show me something? Whatever Shadow Man desired was deep inside me; if he took it, I'd die. Who's trying to take a piece of me?

My tiny room feels more like a coffin than usual. I try to shake off the ugly feelings. When I check my hair in the bathroom mirror, my reflection appears the same, yet I feel like I'm unraveling.

"Who are you?" My mirror image stares back at me in silence. "You were fearless and understood exactly what's required and how to accomplish it because you were in control. You did whatever was necessary. Nothing stood in your way. You had a purpose, remember?"

My reflection glares back at me.

"Who are you now? How did this happen? I don't recognize you. Why are you making so many mistakes? We're better than this because we know. We have the Knowing."

The woman in the mirror has transformed. No wonder Dan doesn't recognize her because I don't either. She's flying without a flight plan. An important piece to the puzzle is missing. A piece she doesn't know but needs to know. I need to know.

§

Concentration doesn't prove to be a problem today. I'm wrestling with a difficult passage in the Book because the symbols make little sense. There's no frame of reference for these symbols, and they confound me. One symbol flashes in my mind like a neon light, demanding my attention.

My Shadow Man dream still haunts me, suggesting a link between the nightmare and the symbol. Does the symbol represent Shadow Man, death, birth, sacrifice, or gift? This differs from the red flags, but it screams importance. Something inside me begs me to pay special attention to this.

The Book speaks of the *End*. The glyph means both *end* and *beginning*, depending on the context. But the end of what? The beginning of a New

World Order? The Master Plan predicts what will happen as the free-range population dies out. With the land restored to nature, the entire planet becomes a paradise free from want, disease, and worry. The Overlords demand two things of us: obedience and to be fruitful and multiply—on their terms. Sounds like it promises a utopia for many, mainly males, but an empty existence for me.

It's July already, with summer in full bloom. The heat never penetrates the base, and I can't measure if our summer temperatures register as blistering as they once were. Several articles in old magazines warned about dangerous levels of global temperatures. They called it Global Warming or Climate Change—even the Book references it. The Overlords, determined to heal the planet, must have succeeded.

This is conflicting for me, knowing they're my enemy, and yet they may have saved the planet. It's difficult to marry these two ideas. When I was younger, I believed the Overlords may have killed my family. Although I have no memory, it would explain my hatred of them. I've never heard of Overlords killing people, but I remember telling Nadler they were all dead—my family, my people, all dead. Another event may have wiped them out, but I've never had a clear memory. Only dreams.

Nobody's been in the Memorial Room, so I raise the lights and find Andrew's plaque. I stand in silence, recalling when Andrew fell into a dark spell and I tapped inside his subconscious without his knowledge, searching for the source of his torment. His pain danced like flickering flames of a fire, so I pressed on his thigh, relieving his pain, but darkness and sadness remained. I concentrated below his level of awareness and caused him to fall into a dream state to recall a comforting childhood lullaby. The light returned, and his suffering eased.

To my knowledge, no one else can do this, and it confounds me how I can. Ten years later, and still no answers. I stopped joining, after Andrew left, never wanting such an intimate connection ever again. It made me feel so close to him, so much that my heart broke when he left. Jim Nadler didn't have the magic to heal it. Andrew's cross necklace didn't have any magic, either. But Andrew's promise kept me strong enough until I could stand on my own.

This rawness is alien. David and Commander are two men I love in different ways, and I can't have either. Andrew is gone forever, Dan is no Prince Charming, and Michael didn't love me enough to stay. The fury over the Colonel's injustice smolders inside me. It's getting tougher to make it through my days. I care for Mack, but he's not where my heart is. I'm tired, and my own darkness is peeking out from the edges, taunting me, waiting, eating away at me.

CHAPTER 27

From Paul's office, male voices boom with laughter, and I recognize Dan's voice. With my cup filled with piping hot coffee, I stroll over. Dan sits next to Tom, leaning back, his legs stretched out. Paul sits at his desk with Commander to his left. They're reveling in idle banter and continue despite my presence.

"So, she gave you head?" Paul asks Dan.

"Yeah, she was pretty good."

"Swallow for you?" Tom asks.

"Like a champ."

Tom turns his attention toward me as I change my mind and pivot to leave.

"Zena. Gotta question. Why don't you like to pleasure men?" Tom asks.

"Beg your pardon, sir?" I don't please men? I stare at Commander.

Paul says, "He means, why don't you give head?"

Should I tell the truth? Why not? I don't need to reveal everything.

"Well, sir. When I was younger, a man exposed himself and tried to force my head down. Another one invited me to view porn. The video showed a woman performing fellatio, and he ejaculated on her face. It was so disgusting I resolved I'd never do it, and I haven't."

Dan smirks and shakes his head in mock disbelief.

"Why didn't you try it? You might like it," says Dan.

"I was too young to understand anything about sex."

Dan raises his eyebrows, and his smile disappears. The other men's expressions also become serious.

"How young were you?" Dan asks.

"Thirteen."

Dan pales. He peers at the others, who all shift in their chairs.

167

"What happened to these men?"

"Nothing, I didn't tell."

All four officers gawk with incredulity.

"Did they touch you?" Dan asks.

"Yes."

"They should've stripped and whipped them both and then sent them to prison." Dan shakes his head and pounds the armrest with his fist.

I flinch. After all, I let them. Should they punish me too? The officer told me we'd be punished. I let it happen. I cringe, wishing I had kept my mouth shut.

"Who did this? Why the hell didn't you report it? The Peace Force has zero tolerance for criminal behavior. They're the worst of the worst, hurting a child like that," Dan says.

"He warned me they would punish us."

"You know better now, don't you? We protect our children. That's our greatest responsibility. Because you didn't tell, those men are free to hurt other innocent girls. Damn it, you should have told someone." Dan slams the armrest again, and I wince.

That can't happen since military bases don't allow young children. Except for me. Who could I tell? Nadler was a top-ranking officer, and the other officer might have been as well. I want to run and hide.

"Who were these men? We could still track them down, although it must've been several years ago. Damn it, I wish you had told an adult." Dan pounds his fist again, and I flinch again.

Why is he so furious? Nadler taught me how to be his woman. Now what? It must remain a secret. Why didn't I keep my damn mouth shut? I could kick myself.

"I can't remember their names." Half a lie. I know Nadler's name well, but he would expect me to protect him. I'm complicit, so lying is my only option.

Dan leans toward me, eyebrows furrowed.

"You realize children are not responsible for the actions of adults? You're an adult now and don't have to be afraid. Whatever happened is on them. They own it, but it's your responsibility to protect other children by reporting what you know."

I snap back to the present. My responsibility? They enforce the rules, not me. I have a job, and I do it. Let leadership change the world—like Michael. He'd have done something.

"It was so long ago. My memory's hazy, and it's over now."

Dan shakes his head, and I realize it's not about me. It's about military pride and their reputation for handling injustice. Does he blame me for their failure? Can they be so naïve?

"No, it's not over. Those men are pedophiles who prey on innocent children. They molested you. If someone has sex with a child, even if she's willing—it's still rape," Dan says.

"Statutory rape," Paul says. "No matter whether they forced you or convinced you, they had no right. You were a child."

Dan took care of me at the stream and never touched me when we slept in bed together. He respected my innocence. This is hard to digest. If my young age made me innocent, then everything they did to me and asked me to do was wrong, wrong, wrong. Not only forbidden sex but everything that happened. In addition to those officers, several others followed. Like my first lover at Mountainview. We lasted a mere three months because he discovered my age and was aware it was wrong, not because he thought me childish, as I believed. He wasn't protecting me.

"Didn't anybody ever teach you this?" Commander asks.

My whole body shudders. These men, the ones who molested me, were my teachers.

"Where were you raised? Where were your parents? Did they know?" Dan asks.

I'm mortified. What have I done? What possessed me to spill my secrets now?

"It's over, and I don't want to talk about it anymore."

In the break room, I dump my coffee in the sink and leave the cup. I don't want it now. I can't share the awful truth with anyone. They swore me to secrecy, and that's my life.

§

The evening can't come fast enough after spending the better part of my day worried somebody would come upstairs to interrogate me about my molesters. Somebody like Dan. The rest of my afternoon is consumed by mulling over this new information.

They raped me; several men raped me, according to Paul's definition. Some lovers may have been unaware of my age. But even as an adult, the Colonel assaulted me several times, recently, and the military did nothing. What is wrong with me that makes it okay to abuse me but nobody else?

CHAPTER 28

I'm pouring over the Book, trying to translate symbols that have evaded me. A section in the Master Plan mentions bringing females to the bases to produce offspring for the Overlords, and I'm reminded of Monday's discussion with the Inner Circle about sex with children. I've re-read that passage several times, and I'm reading it again. I can't determine whether they're kidnapping children, young fertile women, or both. They don't specify the age, but age would factor in the degree of their compliance. Older women would be reluctant to allow their bodies to be used as incubators. Young women, or girls raised in the Overlords' culture, might be more accommodating. It doesn't address acquiescence outright.

Do they rape unwilling women? Or seduce them the way I was? What incentive would these women have to carry babies? Would the ones who bear the children nurture and raise them? It doesn't appear so. Do those newborns belong to the women who carry them, by either biological rights or law? It isn't clear at all.

The Master Plan states a special team will care for infants while another team will care for pregnant women. But who comprises the teams? They'll care for everyone, especially the children, who they'll teach the Overlords' ways. Nobody knows what happens on the Overlords' bases, and nobody knows whether this plan was even implemented.

Babies continue to haunt my dreams. In the middle of the night, incredible pain roused me from another dream about childbirth. I woke before the baby was born. Why do I keep dreaming about giving birth, and why so much pain? I can't get pregnant.

I need someone to talk to, and I'm eager to see Mack tonight.

§

His door is open, but I knock. Mack is working at his desk and motions for me to enter, but to give him a moment. I browse his bookcases and select a book, *I am a Strange Loop* by Douglas Hofstadter. His earlier book is nowhere to be found. I scan a few pages to see if I remember anything, and it appears as complex as I recall.

"You can borrow that if you like but remember where it belongs." Mack glances up for a second, then resumes focusing on his paperwork.

"I read it a long time ago."

Mack looks up in surprise with an unconvinced smile and cocks his head.

"Yeah, what's it about?"

"Well, it's mostly way over my head. It was easier to read than his previous book *Gödel, Escher, Bach*, which was very difficult to read. I understood the words, but the concepts perplexed me. It was always a mystery where he was headed with it. The *Strange Loop* was easier to follow, but I admit I puzzled over that one, too. This is too highbrow for me."

"Do you know who Gödel, Escher, and Bach were?"

"Gödel was a mathematical genius known for his *Incompleteness Theorem*. Escher was also a mathematician and an artist who created mystifying drawings of realities folding into themselves, morphing back to their original form. A strange loop. Bach was a musician obsessed with numerology who composed fugues that folded into themselves."

I giggle to myself, then say, "That statement is unprovable."

"Very good. You surprise me."

"Because I'm a woman?"

"No, I know you're very intelligent."

"Do you have any knowledge about how the Overlords treat their women?"

"Not much at all. They imposed our laws stipulating the treatment of women and children. The laws prohibit assault or harm to anyone. You can't hit anyone without their permission, and sex must be consensual. We protect women and children, and they mandate corporal punishment for men who abuse them."

"Why would anyone grant permission for someone to hit them?"

"In training or practice. For those who Play, it's always consensual. Even corporal punishment is consensual, but the lower ranks prefer to get it over with, rather than suffering imprisonment or appearing weak to their comrades. It's a matter of pride. Naturally, high-ranking officers are exempt."

What? Wickmore is above the law? So, some pigs are more equal than others.

"High-ranking officers are exempt from punishment?" I ask in disbelief.

"From corporal punishment. They are generally demoted depending on the severity of the crime. Or kicked out of the Peace Force. Depends on the offense. For lower ranks, when you break the rules, you pay the price. Why do you ask?"

"You can refuse punishment?"

"Sure, but nobody does. Even civilian girls would rather tough it out. But Commander takes it easy on the Civies. Err ... civilians."

"How often does Commander punish civilians?"

"It's rare, I'm sure. Punishment is rare. We all know the rules, and we follow them."

"The Overlords. They punish their people?"

"Don't know, and I doubt anybody does. I assume they're more liberal."

This is news to me. I thought we made our own rules, but we sure don't follow them.

§

Last night, an awful dream about the sinister Shadow Man unnerved me. This Shadow Man was different—larger and darker somehow, and this time the victory was his. He touched me, drawing something from me, my life force, perhaps. A white light flashed, blinding me, and I stepped outside myself, watching my body drop to the floor. My hair turned white and wispy. My skin wrinkled, dried out, turned to dust, and the wind took my remains, scattering them. I awoke in a sweat. A warning?

The clock seems to have stopped unless I'm in a time warp where everything moves in slow motion. My workday refuses to end, and although I've listened to music all morning, now I want quiet. I abandon toiling over my report and dodge translating the Book because I wish to be elsewhere.

Footsteps sound on the stairs, and my breath catches. I've been avoiding Commander for the last two weeks, arriving late, leaving early, and drinking coffee in the cafeteria so I don't run into him in the break room.

Commander sits across from me.

"Haven't seen you lately. Avoiding me?" he asks.

A chill washes over me at the sight of him.

"Yes, sir. I mean, no, sir. I'm not avoiding you. Never, sir. I've been busy working."

"Good. Since I'm your handler, it would make it difficult if you avoided me," he says. He eyes me with a raised eyebrow. "Which you're not."

"No, sir. I mean, yes, sir."

When he's near, part of my heart lobbies me to run away, but another part wants me to climb into his arms and stay there. He's unhealthy for me, and we have different wants. He wants a plaything, and I want him.

CHAPTER 29

The last section of the Book suggests it will take a few decades for widespread pollution to end, in part, due to drastic reductions in population. Its Master Plan estimates this may require three or four generations or between fifty to eighty years. The symbol used for humans also disturbingly means *Crops*. As the environmental cleanup ramps up, the climate will be restored to normal pre-industrial levels. The planet will begin healing, with rain forests regenerating, ocean levels decreasing, rivers and lakes running pure again, and weather patterns calming and stabilizing. The earth will become healthy again.

A few symbols continue to be extremely difficult to translate, and I struggle to decipher their meaning. My mind is blocked, so I stand gazing out the window, letting my thoughts clear as I relax and concentrate on my breathing. Taking deep breaths, I release them with slow, steady exhales and visualize birds flying free with their outspread wings flapping the wind, letting them soar over mountains and trees.

As I continue to relax, I let my mind fly free, and the symbols appear behind my closed eyes. When I reach out to touch one, it turns into a butterfly that circles me before fluttering away. The second symbol remains out of reach. It rotates several times before dissolving into tiny minute specks that float away. Then the voices surround me, so many voices all competing for my attention. I try to isolate one, but it's impossible. They blur together, all speaking at once. My relaxation deepens, and I hear one voice, but the words have no meaning.

"Are you all right?"

My body tenses as I notice Commander standing close to me. The voices recede, and my breathing normalizes as I return to the real world. My face feels warm and flushed. What did he see? I wait until he speaks again.

"Zena, are you all right?"

"Sorry, sir. I'm lost in thought, concentrating so hard I didn't hear you."

"Don't be sorry. You were acting strange. I had no idea what was happening."

He raises his eyebrows in a show of concern.

"Oh, sometimes I get so deep in concentration I block out the world." I force out a small laugh. "It's part of the process. That's why isolation is necessary for me. Some symbols are very difficult to decipher, so I use a technique called free association. I free my mind and pay attention to my uncensored thoughts. Sometimes it works, but not always. Not this time, but I'll keep trying."

Commander stares at me but seems satisfied with my answer.

"Did you need something, sir?"

"No. Just checking in before I head to lunch. Carry on. Don't want to interfere with your process," he says with a wink.

I imagine Commander, at lunch, relating to his team about his crazy consultant, with her free association. I retreat to my table. Commander never checks on me, so what did he want? I'm too flustered to read him, but no matter. Concentrating is an exercise in futility now. Commander makes me so nervous. He'll never be for me, but I can't control the way my body responds to his presence. They say time heals everything. Right now, my stomach wants lunch.

§

The second-floor cafeteria is busier than usual, but I'm able to find a table alone. My mouthwatering dish of mac and cheese, which I call Cheddar-Whatever, is browned around the edges and garnished with a side dish of steamed green beans and toasted slivered almonds. I'm devouring my lunch when the sound of rowdy men several tables over catches my attention. A civilian sits with a salvage unit, and he's a sight I've never seen before. He's dressed in an olive-green shirt and matching pants, and over his shirt, he wears a tan vest with several pockets. Everyone seems to know him, and I'm curious.

I flag a passing soldier.

"I've never seen a male civilian on base. Who is he?"

"That's Blake. He's a scout for this unit. He knows the terrain better than anybody, so he's been traveling with them."

I study Blake, wondering what he could tell me about the outside world. Blake is rough and ready. He sits differently than the military men, is more relaxed, and doesn't worry about appearance. That's clear by the way he picks his teeth in public. A Wild Man. He wears a bored expression until his eyes meet mine. I wave. He ignores me and turns away. How rude. I ignore him for the rest of my meal but glance up every so often to see him watching me. He's not a handsome man, but I'll bet he has interesting stories to tell about life outside.

§

Mack's office door is open, and without knocking, I stroll in. Dan stands inside talking to Mack, catching me off guard. Mack appears uneasy and watches me as if trying to caution me.

"Major Matthews, I thought I heard familiar voices, sir. So, Lieutenant Reed, this is your office? I imagined you worked on the second floor, sir," I say, feigning innocence.

Dan clenches his jaw.

"I'm so sorry to intrude. This is so rude of me. I'm afraid I wasn't thinking." I nod and turn to leave.

"What are you doing down here?" Dan asks. He folds his arms across his chest.

"Just exploring, sir. I'm curious to see what's down this way, besides Lieutenant West's office. I wondered what else I'd discover on my walk."

Lying is never smart and they frown on it. My lies might catch up to me.

"You need an escort down here. Stay upstairs instead of running around empty hallways. Stay out of trouble," Dan says.

"You're right, sir. There's nothing down here, anyway. Have a nice day, or evening, rather." I nod to both officers and disappear.

§

The meanings of some new symbols in the Book mystify me. I trust they're important since they repeatedly occur in the last stage of the Overlords' plan. I sense it's detrimental for us and fail to understand it, but deep inside, my purpose seems connected somehow, yet I'm clueless about how.

The Book indicates they plan to re-educate most of the *Crops* in storage. After confining everyone to the bases, universal cultural training of children born in captivity will obliterate notions of freedom, individual rights, and personal property. Competition for land, territory, food, money, and power will cease to exist, with religion and politics forgotten. It's a Golden Age of modesty and respect for the planet with no emphasis on the individual. It's another kind of death—the loss of hubris that makes us human.

Could it mean the end of humanity as we know it? Where we're nothing more than an agriproduct to them? A ticket to a Golden Age? The price of admission to Utopia? The steps, not only to Parnassus but Shangri-La itself? It sounds less like Heaven on Earth and more like a living hell.

Commander has been leaving me alone, so I try meditating again. With soothing music playing in the background, I waltz to the window and attempt to drift away, but something catches my eye. Outside, in the little window well, a strange, fuzzy creature has attached itself. I move closer to examine the mystery. An elongated ball of fuzz is growing in the window's corner, almost out of sight.

With my face pressed against the glass, I peer down at my discovery. It appears to be a cocoon, almost a pinkie finger long. How could a caterpillar scale the base this high? And why is she outside this window in the middle of July? Wouldn't she have morphed into a butterfly and headed south by now? It might be alive or maybe a failure of nature. It's hard to tell, but it's intact, so I'll have to keep my eye on it. My discovery should interest Mack. Right now, my body craves caffeine, but my coffee cup is empty.

After pouring my coffee, I peek through the break room window to watch Commander at his desk, concentrating on the papers in front of him, frowning. My cup almost overfills, but I catch it before burning myself and making a mess. It's too full, so I take a sip. Ouch, too hot. Blowing on the steaming brew, I continue watching Commander. He must sense my gaze because he raises his head, looks my way, and grins. I turn away to move out of his view. That ship has sailed. He's not for me. I need someone who wants only me. Not forever; nothing lasts forever.

Paul walks into the break room, grabs a cup, and stands at the coffeemaker. After filling his cup, he turns to me, studies me for a moment, shakes his head, and leaves. What the hell was that? Dan returns, and now I'm an outcast? Is Paul still angry because I investigated without his permission?

Before I sip my coffee to a reasonable level, Tom enters the break room. What is this, Grand Central Station? Wait, what? Where did that come from? I draw a blank. Central Control? No. Tom gawks at me like I'm an alien from outer space. I hope I wasn't thinking out loud. Tom joins Paul, the laughing starts, and my skin crawls.

§

The second-floor cafeteria is almost deserted. While staring at nothing, lost in thought, I catch Lieutenant Frank Kelly approaching from the corner of my eye, and cringe.

"Well, Miss Roberts. It's nice to see you again. May I join you?"

I nod, and my curiosity piques. We haven't talked since he asked to peek under my skirt.

"How are you this evening? Don't see you often down here," he says.

"No, and I don't remember ever seeing you in the cafeteria."

"I take my meals in the Officer's Mess. Fourth floor."

"That makes sense." What does he want?

"I came off as a bit crude the first time we met."

"A bit crude?"

"Thought you were Cross's girl. No excuse, but he never hangs with nice girls like you."

"That's how you treat women? Or only civilian women?"

"We play around, but it means nothing. The civies ... I mean, civilian girls who Play, just play along, and nobody's hurt."

"I don't Play."

"So, I hear."

I sigh, studying him. I understand he won't apologize, and this is as close as he'll get.

"You delivered a very detailed briefing, captivating everyone. I reckoned you were intelligent but hadn't realized how exceptionally sharp you are."

"It seems Major Williams thought it was a joke."

"Nah, he likes to tease you. Have you been to Agora yet?"

"Yes, I went with David, and I loved dancing, especially since meeting Tim. He's a fantastic dancer, but I don't remember seeing you at Agora."

"Haven't been in a while. I don't dance," he says with a cautioning wink and a smile.

"So, where is everyone?" I ask.

"Poker game. That is, provided I find a fifth."

"Is it a hard game to learn?"

"No, I can teach you." He teases.

"Then I'll be your fifth."

Frank laughs until he realizes I'm serious.

"I'm a quick study."

"Okay, let's see what the players think."

When we reach Frank's apartment, Lieutenant Philip West and his assistant, Corporal Jason Edwards, are already seated with cards and poker chips in front of them.

"Zena's gonna join us. She wants to learn to play poker."

"We playin' strip poker?" asks Jason.

"No, not tonight," Frank says, giving Jason a disapproving glare. "Zena, you sit next to me, and I'll teach you how to play."

The four of us sit, but there's still an empty seat. Someone knocks. Frank opens the door, and David enters. When he sees me, his eyes grow wide. Women don't play poker, or at least not with officers.

"We playin' strip poker?" David asks. He grins and chuckles.

"No, Zena wants to learn the game, and I thought it would be fun," Frank says.

After explaining the rules, Frank sits next to me for the first few hands, giving me hints. We don't play with chips until I learn the ropes. He shows me his cards and advises me what to do with mine. The others also offer advice. Frank soon realizes I can handle this on my own and moves away so we can't see each other's cards, and we play with chips. I have an advantage and can sense when they're bluffing, and I could read what cards they have if I Pay Attention, but that's cheating. I'm here to make friends, not win at poker.

That means I lose a lot.

But then everyone loses since there's one winner each round unless there's a tie. I learn how to bluff, and it's easy since I habitually hide my emotions, anyway. The joking around and teasing is fun, and we're all enjoying ourselves, but my pile of chips is decreasing. I never realized losing at poker could be so much fun.

I have a win-worthy hand, and everyone folds except Jason and me. My chip stack has dwindled to three chips. I avoid reading Jason, but he's practiced at bluffing. He tosses five chips into the center pot, and to see his cards, I must do the same. I don't have five chips.

"Frank, can I borrow two chips?"

I look at Frank with puppy eyes.

Frank laughs. "Sorry, not allowed. If you can't match, you must fold."

They're all waiting.

Jason scrunches his face. "You know what. If I win, you can do something for me. If you win, you don't owe me anything. How confident you feeling? You probably got this, but who knows?"

I'm tempted to cheat. I have a decent hand. The other officers smile or shake their heads at Jason. They know something I don't. Jason can't lose, but I could lose more than I want.

I fold.

The game's over for me. I had a full house, aces high.

I ask Jason, "What did you have?"

"Game's over," Jason smirks. He was bluffing.

They invite me to their game next week.

§

I'm almost finished translating the Book, but I'm alarmed about the planned conclusion. I don't completely understand everything, but what I grasp unnerves me. The Master Plan claims individuals living in this Brave New World will be oblivious to anything other than their Gilded Cage and whatever knowledge their Captors plant in their minds. Plato's Cave 2.0? The glyph means *Overlords* and the truth of their intentions confirms an Awful Truth. They never completed their plan, that's clear, but their success will prove catastrophic for everyone. I'm dragging my feet, finalizing my preliminary report until I decipher those last symbols. How will I disclose this to Central Intelligence? Worse, how will they respond? Kill the messenger?

All week, I've checked on my cocoon and noticed no change, but it should be changing. A cloud hangs over me as I stare at my possibly dead cocoon. I so wanted to watch nature spring forth life from my vantage point. Suddenly, there's a tiny movement. Okay, little one, hang in there.

§

When I knock on the door, Frank answers. I've been eager all week to play again. David and the other officers smile when they see me, and Jason invites me to sit next to him.

"I'm looking forward to taking all your chips," he says with a wink.

"Or I'll take yours this time." I wink back.

Game on.

Frank is the first dealer. He deals us each five cards face down, and everyone tosses in two chips to start. We take turns discarding unwanted cards and getting new ones. I study their faces searching for tells, learning how they bluff. They're skillful, so I pretend I'm clueless and unsure how to proceed. I toss two more chips into the pile when others do.

David, West, and Jason are still in, and it's David's turn to bet.

He says, "I'll raise five more."

West folds.

Jason calls.

I hesitate and fidget and bite my lip before betting my five chips.

Jason shows his hand; two pairs.

David has three Jacks.

I show mine; three Queens.

All eyes are on me.

Frank laughs.

"You taught her well," West says to Frank.

David squints at me. "Need to watch this one. Her second time playing, and she bluffs like a pro."

I act innocent and touch my finger to my chin. "Does this mean my ladies beat your gentlemen?"

"Yep, kitten, that's what it means. Lucky hand, good bluff," David says.

The players moan and pretend they're upset as I rake the chips from the middle of the table to my spot and take my time adding them to my stacks.

§

Last night was fun and I look forward to the next poker game. Frank's not so bad, after all. He and West watch over me, whereas David and Jason love to tease me.

It's easier to concentrate on the Master Plan today, and it seems the tide is turning. My coffee cup is empty, so I head to the break room with my mind on our next poker game. I've barely poured my coffee when Commander spots me from his office and gestures for me to come around. When I circle around, he's waiting at his door.

"Michael's back. He'll be here tomorrow morning."

CHAPTER 30

Seven months ago, I kissed Michael goodbye. Seven months of worrying about him, my world becoming unglued, discovering his deception, learning to live without him, and now he's back. My pacing makes the apartment feel smaller, and I'm eager for his arrival, so I dump my cold coffee, and with my empty cup in hand, I head downstairs.

I ask Cassie if Michael has arrived yet, and she gestures toward the Commander's office. From the break room, I peer through the window. Michael stands, his back to me, his light brown hair and lighter skin contrasting his brother's dark features. Commander notices me, says something to Michael, and nods in my direction. Michael turns around and rushes out with a beaming smile while I hurry around to meet him.

His handsome face lights up like the sun when he sees me. Like it always did. He wraps me in his arms and tries to plant a kiss on my lips, but I turn my face away, aware Commander is standing there, making this awkward.

"We're in public," I say, whispering to remind him.

Michael smiles and stares at me like he can't get enough, pulling me close, his lips brushing my ear.

"I missed you so much, sweetheart, and there's so much I want to share with you, and you won't believe where I've been," he says, whispering in my ear. "I understand you're unhappy right now, Zena, but when you hear what I've done, you'll forgive me."

Michael turns to his brother. "I need to talk to my woman. May we use your apartment?"

Commander frowns but nods.

Michael and I head upstairs, and in the living room, he pulls me to him and properly kisses me. He squeezes me tight like he's afraid to let me go, and then steps back for a better view. My feelings bounce all over the place like ping-pong balls. I'm happy to see him, angry he left me, relieved to see he's healthy, but hurt because he looks so good and I'm a mess.

Michael appears comfortable in the apartment, and he's surprised I am as well.

"I work here. The kitchen table is my desk, and the apartment is mine during the day."

My work materials remain stowed, anticipating Michael's visit. He's finally here.

"You work in Commander's apartment?" he asks.

"Yes, your brother is my handler. They didn't have an office for me, so here I am."

Michael regards me with concern for a moment, then paces, taking in this latest information. Did he think I'd never learn he and Commander are brothers? He pulls me to the couch, where we sit with knees touching, facing each other.

"I solved our problem. Two women were willing to be surrogates, and they're both pregnant. I'm having two sons, both healthy. My mother and sisters will raise the boys, but you and I will visit them. I don't expect you to act like their mother, but you can bond with them and be an important part of their life. Return to Central with me, and I'll show you—everything will be like before. I love you so much. This is the answer to everything." He studies my face.

"There's more," he says. He lowers his voice, glances at the stairs, and then around the apartment. "I visited an Overlords' base, and it's incredible. They're decent people who believe in high morals, treat people with respect and dignity, and have a fair society that's all-inclusive. They're respectable people, good people. Keep this confidential. I fear I've said too much."

"Your secrets are safe with me, Michael. I'd never reveal anything you share with me. I know about your connection to Davies, or I should say, Scott," I say, whispering close to his ear.

Michael's face turns ashen gray, reaffirming they're involved somehow.

"How do you know? What do you know?"

"No matter. I've told no one, and I won't. Your secret is safe. What are you planning?"

"Scott's my friend. My mother knows him, and that's all I can say. I can't talk about it, but you must trust me. Come back with me today, and I'll explain everything I can."

I'm eager to learn more about the Overlords, and Michael may be the key, but I'm gripped with fear. The Overlords are my enemy, and I sense deep inside that it would be a grave mistake.

"No, Michael, everything's changed. Didn't your father tell you what happened to me? I'll never go back to Central. You don't understand."

"The General explained Colonel Wickmore took an interest in you, gave you a hard time, and that's why you left. But I'm back, and the Colonel will never bother you again. I've always taken care of you, haven't I?"

"Until you left."

"Yes, but next time we'll take leave together. Every time."

"And my work?"

"We'll figure it out. We'll overcome any obstacle in our way together."

He pulls me close, but I push away.

"You don't understand. The Colonel didn't just give me a hard time. He assaulted me repeatedly. You won't even want me anymore when I tell you what he did."

"I'll love you no matter what, and nothing you tell me will change that. What's on your mind, sweetheart? I didn't expect you to be faithful while I was gone, so don't be concerned."

"No, listen. I don't know what they told you about Colonel Wickmore, but it was horrific. He hurt me, over and over again."

"Okay, tell me everything. You'll see, I'll always love you, no matter what."

My blow-by-blow account starts with the Colonel approaching me in the library and ends with the sexual assault the following day. I share my fear of rape and my refusal to revisit the library. I steel myself and study Michael's face, but he hides any emotion.

Next, I describe how Mick accompanied me for my next library visit, how the Colonel dismissed him and then assaulted me. I describe the Colonel unzipping and forcing me to my knees and how reporting the abuse to Morgan was fruitless.

Michael grimaces and shakes his head, and I take another deep breath.

I disclose the Comfort Room assaults, and his mocking laughter when I resisted.

Another deep breath. I've told no one the complete story, keeping it buried all these months, festering, and now it all spills out. Michael's unflinching expression is hard to fathom.

My anger rises as I relate the futility of reporting Wickmore to Commander Harris, enraging Colonel Wickmore, and making the following assault worse.

Giving Michael a moment, I watch his reaction. He keeps himself in check, and I draw another deep breath and exhale. I describe how the Colonel dragged me into a stockroom and threatened to tie me up if I didn't cooperate. He had a rope.

I take another deep breath. Michael remains unwavering. I can't read his feelings without Paying Attention, and I lack the energy for that.

It's harder to discuss the additional assaults. Still, I make certain he learns every dirty detail, including how vulnerable I felt, never able to anticipate ensuing attacks, always on edge, and worried about my safety.

And nobody helped me. I swallow hard.

I recount the worst incident. Colonel Wickmore sent an officer to my Lab to fetch me in front of everyone. No one raised a finger to help me, although they understood what was in store for me. Tears stream down my cheeks. Their silence was worse than anything the Colonel planned.

"I assume you know the rest."

Michael nods, then wags his head as if he's shaking off my story.

"I'll take care of this, sweetheart. He won't get away with this."

His voice stays calm, and I don't understand how he remains composed when I want to scream my lungs out.

"I kept a journal of his assaults at Central and prepared a statement, which I never shared with anyone here. No one from Central has shown up to investigate, hear my side, or take my statement. I've been waiting."

Michael says, "I'll take care of this, baby."

I take him at his word. He wipes away my tears with his fingers and pulls me close.

"There's something else," I say. "And I want you to hear it from me."

CHAPTER 31

Michael tilts his head forward, his eyes locked on mine, giving me his full attention. I take his hand and ready myself to break this uncomfortable news.

"You didn't mention everything when you talked about your brother, and it was almost four months before I discovered he and Commander are the same person."

Michael winces like a spanked puppy and offers me a guilty smile.

"I had no idea you would end up here," he says.

Yeah, that makes it better.

"Well, your brother and I had already been together when I discovered that regrettable fact. Otherwise, I'd have never betrayed you."

Michael releases my hand and jumps up. "What? No, what do you mean, together?"

"You thought I'd never have sex?"

"No, of course not, but my brother?" He paces in little circles, waving his fist in the air. "Damn it, damn it to hell."

"I didn't know he was your brother."

"Zena, I don't blame you, but he knew you were my woman. He knew how much I loved you. Damn him, he knew. It's my fault you didn't know, I get that, and I can't blame you."

His hands shake, and he makes a fist again like he wants to hit something or someone, but not me. He knows he can't fight with his brother, the base Commander. Rules apply, even for family. It takes a minute, but he eventually calms down.

"Okay, it happened. Are you two still together?"

"No, it's over, and it didn't last long. You can't fight with him."

"I know, babe. Don't worry. I know how to handle this. Come back with me, and I'll forget about it. Zena, none of this is your fault."

I conceal the minor fact Commander and I continued our involvement after I learned the truth. Family is important. I don't want to alienate brothers, since I'm done with them both. It's important to preserve their bond, shaky as it is.

"You don't understand. I can't go back to Central. The Colonel is still there, and no one's investigating it."

"I'll take care of it. Give me your statement before I leave. I'll fix things. Leave it to me."

Paul knocks, although we left the door open. He glances from Michael to me.

"Commander wants you both to join him for lunch. Be ready in five minutes."

It's not an invitation. It's an order.

§

This is my first occasion to dine in the Officer's Mess at Cavalry, and Commander's private dining lounge features a floor-to-ceiling window view behind a large rectangular table flanked by captain's chairs seating eight. Commander and his Inner Circle take their seats, with Commander assuming the middle seat facing the door, with Paul at his right and Michael to his left. I'm at the end, next to Michael.

Waiters in white jackets serve us, and we dine in relative silence, but the officers all watch me. Are they afraid I'm not versed in proper etiquette? The one useful lesson Miss Elly taught me was courteous table manners. Even Michael appears surprised … and relieved. We always ate our meals in the cafeteria. Was he afraid I'd embarrass him? He never invited me to the Officer's Mess.

With dishes cleared and beverages served, the conversation can begin. Commander won't ask his brother where he's been since that's private, so they engage in casual banter. How is the General? Anything new at Central? Cavalry? The conversation winds down to an uncomfortable silence.

"So, you couldn't keep your hands off my woman," Michael says. He stares at his brother, his chin raised. He doesn't sound angry, but I know him, and he's controlling his anger.

I long to hide under the table, but etiquette says no. Paul covers his mouth and coughs, Tom shifts in his seat, and Dan shakes his head. Commander appears unbothered and smiles.

I study my water glass and consider throwing it on Michael to cool him off. Doesn't he realize everyone now knows I told him? This isn't the proper venue for personal discussions. He didn't react this way when I disclosed the Colonels' repeated assaults for several weeks.

"You knew how I felt about her, Nate. Two years, you listened to me talk about how important she was to me, how much I loved her."

His voice remains low and as respectful as he can manage. Commander is his brother, but he's still the base Commander, and Michael needs to watch himself. He understands the rules and the consequences, so he keeps calm. Commander sits back, smiling.

"Hey, Michael, it was nothing. She means nothing to me. I wanted to check out for myself what you were always crowing about. You raved about her so much. We had a little fun, and I didn't break her." He grins and I wonder what he means.

Commander's sharp words plunge like a knife deep into my heart. It was nothing? I mean *nothing*? Michael cares more about his brother touching his sex toy than he does about the Colonel assaulting me. The officers grin and exchange knowing glances.

I stand, knocking my chair over.

"It's time you both grew up. I'm not some fucking sex doll you're talking about. I'm human, I have feelings, and I'm sitting right here. So, I mean nothing to you?" I ask, glaring at Commander, keeping my voice low but seething with venom.

"Well, you could keep that to yourself. Maybe it meant nothing to you, but it meant something to me."

Michael grabs my arm and begs me to be quiet.

"The two of you are brothers, and it's high time you both grew up and set this silly squabble aside. You're men, so act like it. You're family, and you're so lucky to have a family."

Michael's ears burn scarlet, and it occurs to me his stories may not be entirely true.

His voice sharpens. "Stop talking."

It's an order. I storm out.

§

Back in the apartment, slumped on the couch, I want to scream. I screwed up, but I loved Commander, and he announced to everyone I meant nothing to him. I wanted him. Michael only cares about his own needs, and neither one cares about me. I'm cut to the bone. I cared for Commander, and I embarrassed him, and I knew better, but his cruel words cut so deep. Michael needs to deal with the Colonel, and my behavior didn't help. This time, I butchered everything.

I have an overwhelming impulse to find a sharp knife, press its point at my wrist, slice my arm up to my elbow, release the pain, and see my own blood. To watch my pain leave my body. Instead, I stifle my tears and muzzle my screams, not wanting anyone to hear me. I hate them; I hate them all. Their smirking faces. Commander and his cruel words. Michael's behavior. Damn it, Michael must bring the Colonel to justice. I curl up in a ball and wait.

§

Paul yells up the stairs, informing me Michael is leaving. I grab my statement from its hiding place and rush downstairs. Michael wears a pained expression, but he pulls me to him and kisses me in front of his brother and everyone else, and I let him.

"I'll deal with the Colonel, and then I'm returning to take you home. Zena, I love you."

I slip him the envelope containing my statement.

"Michael, I'll keep your secrets, and I love you too. I'm sorry about this afternoon," I say, hanging my head.

He lifts my chin, peering into my eyes. "Yeah, me too. It's all my fault."

He hugs me again.

I watch Michael and Commander leave, my heart heavy. When they're out of sight, I run upstairs and curl up on the couch, my world shattered into pieces, and my pain unbelievable.

§

Two sets of footsteps on the stairs. Commander appears with Paul following behind him.

Paul has a leather strap in his hand.

CHAPTER 32

I stare at the strap. A sickening wave of weakness travels from my racing heart to my feet. Their serious faces warn me this won't be a pleasant visit, and a crazy panic boils up inside me. How can my life get any worse?

Commander stands in front of me frowning, his eyes cold, and he lectures me about rules and behavior and my unacceptable conduct. My heart thunders in my chest, almost drowning out his words as he commands me to address them by their proper names and always maintain decorum. I'm staring into his eyes, this man I loved.

He informs me he must punish me for my inexcusable outburst, although he doesn't want to, and hopes he never has to do this again. Commander tells me, as my handler, he won't punish me himself. He has delegated the administration of my punishment to Paul, who dislikes me and will get profound pleasure from hurting me. I don't speak.

I'm aware the law decrees no one may hit another person without consent, but I won't test it. The sting of the strap can't compare with the numbing pain roiling inside me. Commander takes my silence as permission and calls Cassie upstairs to bear witness. Once upstairs, she asks me if I'm menstruating, and when I indicate I'm not, she steps back and nods. So, humiliation is part of the punishment. I don't want Cassie here, but I doubt I have any say.

Commander stands close to me and having finished lecturing, orders me to put my hands on my head. He takes both of my wrists and places my hands behind my head. His eyes are cold and empty. He's doing his job. He tells me to spread my legs a little for balance. How hard will Paul hit me?

He steps back and signals Paul, but I'm not ready for it. The strap stings when it strikes my behind, and although I tried defiantly not to cry out, a shriek escapes me as I jerk from the impact. It's worse than I expected. My face crumbles and tears well up. I stare at Commander with disbelief and sorrow. How can he do this to me? How many times will he hurt me?

Commander signals Paul again, but this time to stop, and I sigh in relief. As he removes my hands from my head, he warns me next time will be worse. Next time he'll do it himself and won't go easy on me. But he hopes there won't be a next time.

He dismisses me.

I flee the apartment, head held high, with tears begging for release, but I suppress them until I find sanctuary.

My tears hold fast as I descend three flights of stairs to the main floor. No David anywhere, but I run into Frank. My tears break free, streaming down my face.

"What happened?" he asks. His voice is gentle but worried.

I can't answer, and I struggle to keep my sobs from attracting attention, so I shake my head. He takes me by the arm and guides me to his apartment, where I sit on the bed because it's softer than a chair. He sits beside me, his arm draping my shoulder, watching me until I regain my composure. I decide I'll be honest, no matter how humiliating.

"I got upset and blurted some things I shouldn't have, and they punished me."

Frank nods and shrugs. "Oh, first time?" Frank asks, sparing me humiliation.

I nod.

"How many?" he asks. His tone remains unconcerned, yet I sense sympathy.

"One, but it really hurt."

Frank smiles and gently strokes my head. "That's the point of punishment."

My tears start again, so Frank gives my arm a gentle squeeze, and I'm glad I'm not alone.

"I was looking for David. Do you know where he is?"

"No, but stay here and rest. I'll find him."

Staring at nothing, I want to disappear, to run away, but there's nowhere to run. I'm too exhausted, anyway. No one's ever punished me, and no one's ever treated me like this. I'm a consultant, an expert, and they're treating me like a delinquent child simply because I lost it for a moment, with sound reason. I can't believe this.

§

The door opens, and Frank returns with David.

"Hey, kitten, what's goin' on? Heard you got punishment."

David sits on the bed, consoling me, and pretends to inspect me.

"You're okay. How many swats did you get?"

"One."

"Yeah, Commander goes easy on civilians."

"He had Major Abrams do it, and he didn't go easy."

"That's odd. Commander always carries out punishment. It's part of the job." He brushes the errant strands, wet from tears, from my face, and with gentle hands, he strokes my hair.

"Well, he's also my handler." And he was my lover, but I can't say that.

David nods and cups my chin.

"Someone should have taught you the proper way to behave around Commander and his team. You're a smart girl, but if you need instruction, I can teach you."

His gentle scolding causes more tears to well.

"They taught me, but I guess I got too comfortable working so close to them, but it'll never happen again."

David tenderly rubs my behind, then wipes away the fresh tears rolling down my cheeks.

"Listen, kitten, I have to return to duty but stop by the office later, and I'll be there."

§

True to his word, I find David working in his office, and he takes me to his apartment, where we talk for a while. He turns off the lights, and we lie under the fluorescent stars.

§

Morning arrives too soon, and the idea of encountering anyone in the office sickens me. I procrastinate before heading for the office. I hate them all, and the thought of Cassie's gloating or facing Commander or Major Abrams fills me with dread.

When I build up the courage to enter the office, Cassie glances up, then resumes her work while I conceal my feelings, pretending nothing happened, and head for the stairs.

Cassie whispers, loud enough for me to hear. "You got it easy."

I pretend deafness and keep walking. Commander and Major Abrams aren't upstairs, and I sigh in relief. I prepared for an extremely uncomfortable experience, but even though I've been spared, I can't concentrate on work. With music playing, I perch on the couch, arms folded, hating this apartment now because every day, it will remind me of their mistreatment. I don't care if I "got it easy" because these people should be my support, not my enemy. I owe them nothing.

The morning creeps on, and I hurry downstairs and out of the office at noon, ignoring Cassie. In the second-floor cafeteria, I sit alone, nursing my coffee and misery. The scout, Blake, sits at a table, talking in a loud voice and laughing with four privates. He glances my way, catching me watching him, so I turn away. I'm not in the mood for him. I eat with purpose, keeping my eyes focused on my plate. How can I work now?

Approaching the office, my heart skips a beat. Major Abrams stands talking to Cassie by her desk, so I brace myself, steady my breath, and without acknowledging them, I stride past and head upstairs. Nadler always said: *Never let them see your belly.*

I hate it here, and I'm unable to function. I stare at my papers and the Book, but all I see is my private suffering.

§

It's been four days in hell, but I've succeeded in avoiding both Commander and Major Abrams. Cassie ignores me, and I'm grateful. Work is impossible, I don't care about the Book, and I hate this apartment. I spend most of my time listening to music and monitoring my little cocoon friend. I don't know how long it takes for caterpillars to turn into butterflies, so I'll be patient. The library might yield information, but I lack the energy to make the trip. I have faith she's in there doing what caterpillars naturally do to morph into beautiful, fragile butterflies.

On my worktable, the Book and several pages of my scribble are on display even though I haven't added a single line of my script since Michael showed up. Instead, one page flaunts an elaborate doodle of my cocoon with an emerging butterfly. Footsteps on the stairs alert me I have company, and through the counter opening, I observe Commander ascending, so I flip my legal pad over, hiding my drawing. He sits across from me.

"Thought I'd check in on you. How's your project coming along?"

"I'm making good progress, sir." My voice is steel, and my eyes are daggers. *Never let them see your belly.*

"Good. You've been coming in late."

"Yes, sir. I don't want to intrude on your morning ritual, sir."

A slight smile crosses his face. "It's no intrusion. Everything okay?"

No, my life is upside down, you punished me after your cruel words, and I hate you all.

"Yes, sir," I say, avoiding his eyes.

"If you need anything … for your project, ask. That's why we're here."

"I have everything I need for now, sir."

The coldness has disappeared from his eyes, but not my memory.

"Excellent. Carry on."

He seems about to speak but turns to leave with a nod before my first tear falls.

§

After lunch, instead of returning to work, I visit the library, hunting for new books and a distraction. Several workers are busy adding shelves for crates of new arrivals, making a noisy commotion, so after selecting a book, I retreat to a back room for peace and quiet. The quaint chamber invites me, offering a quiet and perfect spot for reading and resting my anguished soul.

An old high-backed upholstered wooden rocking chair matches a small sofa, both appearing sculpted from a deep, dark wood, aged from an era long ago. I close the door, slip off my shoes, tuck my legs under me, and settle on the sofa for an enchanting read.

My book, Maya Angelou's memoir, *I Know Why the Caged Bird Sings*, tells the tale of a young black girl growing up in the old South. I'm like a caged bird, too, but her world differs from mine, in the outside realm, in a different culture. In short order, I escape into Maya's story.

My eyelids grow heavy, and my concentration falters until the sound of a creaking rocking chair and soft humming snaps me to attention. I blink to focus my eyesight. A strange old black man, ancient like the mountains, hums unfamiliar tunes to himself and seems lost in thought as he sways back and forth in the rocking chair. He clutches the upholstery on its massive carved arms as if holding on for dear life. His knuckles turn white as his beard, counter-pointing his ebony skin like night and day. His humming stops, as does his rocking. He clears his throat.

He begins humming another tune and resumes rocking. Songs without words, only melody, as if courting Death to free him from his ageless burdens.

His eyes open, piercing, like onyx beads.

"Caroline!" he says. "Caroline, oh, no, it can't be."

My face warms. Who is Caroline? He must be at least eighty, and I've never seen anyone that age on a military base since most men retire by age seventy. But here he is, a treasure since almost everyone alive today was born on bases. This gentleman must have been born off base, in a different era, knowing a different way of living. I hope he's lucid. It will be exciting to learn everything he's willing to share, so beguiling to behold, sitting all prim and proper in his stately old rocking chair—humming.

"It seems you've mistaken me for someone else. My name is Zena Roberts. To whom do I have the pleasure of speaking?"

"Well, ma'am. Ms. Zena Roberts," he says with solemn dignity, "I'm Thomas Miller."

He glances sideways a couple of times, although we're alone in the room, and whispers like a naughty boy. "But you may call me Tommy."

"Very pleased to meet you, sir."

"Tommy," he again whispers.

"I'm very pleased to meet you." I correct myself. "Tommy."

He cackles his creaky old laugh upon hearing his name. He then falls silent, eyeing me up and down—as if trying to match me with faded images in his mind stored long ago.

"Where have you been? I've been waiting for you. Time's running out, you know."

"Well, … Tommy. My work keeps me busy, I'm afraid."

"Caroline was never afraid," he says.

Sadness settles over him, enveloping him like a shroud. "You're not Caroline, are you? Couldn't be. She'd be older than me—but here you are, this pretty young lady, reminding me so much of Caroline. My dear, old friend. I can't believe how much you look like her."

"Tell me about Caroline. It sounds like she was very special to you."

"Caroline was magic," he says. He wipes a tear from his eye. "I loved her ages ago when everyone lived free in the world before they sent us all to these dang blasted bases."

"How did you meet her?" My gaze can't leave this man's face.

"Caroline entered my world when I was fifteen. We lived in a farmhouse in southern Ohio. Pops was a Baptist preacher. Hellfire and brimstone, he'd always say. Yessiree. Then Caroline showed up on one glorious summer day, the nineteenth of June, I'll never forget. Pops found her walking along the side of the road in the middle of nowhere, carrying a suitcase. He was driving home from church when he spotted her and slowed down to offer a lift, and getting late, he invited her to eat with us. Pops called our housekeeper to set another place for supper."

"What about your mother? You don't mention her."

"Moms passed the year before. Nana, our housekeeper, stepped up as a substitute mother. A good Christian woman in her forties, she'd been with our family since my birth."

"I'm so sorry. Losing your mom must have been difficult for you."

"During supper, we learned Caroline had no family, job, or anyone waiting for her. Pops suggested she spend the night—as the Christian thing to do—and Nana mentioned she needed extra help with the chores. Pops asked Caroline if she'd consider staying on to help Nana—in exchange for room and board."

I can't help but smile. Of course, she said yes.

"Thought I died and went to heaven when Caroline agreed to stay." Tommy glances over both shoulders and smiles.

I'm tickled, imagining his delight.

"Caroline became my companion, confidant, and teacher, even though she was only twenty. She was an artist and taught me to draw. She loved music and nature."

Tommy's eyes close for a moment, savoring his memory.

"I joined the army when I turned eighteen and begged Caroline to wait for me, but she made no such promise. I never saw her again."

The afternoon slips away, and I must show up at the office to avoid more trouble.

"Tommy, may I visit you again to chat about the old days?"

"That would delight me, Ms. Zena."

"Would tomorrow be all right? Same time, the same place?"

He nods.

CHAPTER 33

I'm shunning Commander and his Inner Circle, so I've avoided the Officer's Club for over a month. Agora is hopping, and I'm feeling restless, with dancing in mind. Tim, dancing with a civilian woman, notices me and invites me to join him.

His dance partner walks away, and Tim and I move like we belong together. After several dances, we take a break and mingle, and I check out who's in Agora. David sits with Mary. When I wave to them, David signals me over. I slide into the booth across from them.

"You have lots of energy tonight," David says.

"Yeah, I have a lot to burn off."

"Well, that's certainly one way to do it."

I laugh, thinking of another. He smiles because we're thinking the same.

"So, kitten, what's goin' on?"

I glance at Mary, my replacement. I'd never share my business with her. David doesn't sit very close to her. What does that mean? Is he still seducing her, or are they beyond that? The first time I saw them together was over a month ago, so probably the latter.

"Nothing. My world keeps changing, and I struggle to keep up."

What does he see in Mary? She's mousy, slight, unattractive, and so quiet, sitting there waiting. For what? She never speaks, and what would they talk about if she did? My dark side peeks out. I still want him.

Tim drops by the booth, so I scoot over. He wraps his arm around my shoulders, but I squirm away. He knows I love dancing with him, but that's all I can offer him. I peek at David and spy a possible glimmer of jealousy. I could play that, but I don't play.

David encourages Mary to dance with Tim. She shakes her head no, appearing reluctant to leave me alone with David, but she needn't worry.

He's no longer mine. She finally surrenders.

A slow number plays and Mary embraces Tim as they dance.

"Now's our chance. Let's take a walk," David says. He slides out and waits for me.

Why not?

§

In his apartment, David makes us each a cup of tea, and we sit across from each other at his two-seater table. Could he be lonely for conversation? Mary can't be engaging at that.

"Okay, what's goin' on? Looks like you lost your best friend," he asks.

"Well, since you're my best friend, I hope that isn't true."

David shifts in his seat and frowns.

"My life is upside down. My assignment is increasingly more difficult, and my progress has stalled."

David stares into my eyes, and we stop talking. He stands, pulling me to him, his mouth covering mine. Does he think this is the reason I'm here? We undress, and I love how familiar this feels. We stroll over to the bed, holding hands. In his arms, I'm mindful of my love for him, but I know better than to repeat those words.

§

I snuggle in David's arms, and I know I can stay. We chat about stars and the meaning of life until he turns over. He's sound asleep.

With the light dimmed, I snuggle close to him. In the morning, nothing will have changed. But tonight, I have the luminous stars above me, and David with his sinister snake beside me.

§

After lunch, I visit my second home. The library is quiet with the workmen gone, and when I enter the back room, Tommy Miller sits in his rocking chair, humming. Taking my seat on the sofa, with paper and pen in hand, I'm ready to take a stroll into the past.

"Folks today say they love living in these here bases—but ..." Tommy says. He glances again over his shoulders even though we're still alone. "They don't know what they're missing, living free, out in Nature, off the land, fresh air, sunshine on your bare skin, living in concert with wild animals. All we had, for better or for worse, in God's country."

"God's country?" I ask.

"Why, nobody today even knows that there is an Almighty God."

Tommy sighs and rocks harder in his rocking chair.

"Now, the role of God, like everything else, belongs to the Overlords. Our Keepers, our Captors." He again glances over his shoulders. "More like they be our masters, and we be the help, if not the slaves."

I imagine the Overlords with whips and us bending to serve them.

"But Lord, how things changed. After the world fell apart, after the plague, the pandemic. Billions died, and the rest—chaos."

The Book never mentioned a plague, but it describes constructing bases with slave labor.

"Nations fell, businesses collapsed, crops failed. Mother Earth was dying and dragging us to the grave with her like the garden statue of the Commander, dragging Don Giovanni kicking and screaming off to Hell."

Tommy stops rocking, growing silent. He whistles tunes from an old Mozart opera.

"That's when the Overlords took over. They rounded up survivors and demolished the cities, herding everyone into camps. To create work colonies. To build their bases. For our own good—they said. For our protection, our wellbeing."

The Master Plan speaks of a final phase with the glyph that means *Harvest*. After they cleanse the planet, some *Grand Event* will unite the recently bred human slaves with an *Offering*, ensuring both their health and that of the planet. It promised harmony if not happiness, and the glyph used for this jubilee means *Renaissance* or *Re-birth*, but like the ancient Chinese Yin-Yang, the same symbol also means *Death*.

"Was everyone forced into the bases? I've heard there are villages out there still today."

"The lucky ones hid, and life was hard for them, but they were free."

I can't remember anything before Andrew's accident. The idea my people lived somewhere free outside is exciting. I hunger for more information. I want to learn everything.

"Yessiree." Tommy wheezes and coughs. "Like in Pharaoh's time, but nobody's alive today who remembers."

I glance up at Tommy.

"Except me," Tommy whispers, then pauses. "And you, Caroline, my sweet Caroline."

Tommy leans back and whistles another old song in my collection— Neil Diamond's *Sweet Caroline*.

"You're saying the Overlords didn't build our bases—we did? Slave labor?"

I'm aware of this from my translations, but I'm hearing it happened firsthand.

"Yessiree." Tommy wheezes again. "Built them with our own hands— from our own garbage." He laughs so hard he has trouble catching his breath.

I stare into his eyes, fixated, as he explains how vast ocean pollution created dead zones the size of continents, killing off almost all aquatic life. Meanwhile, levels of greenhouse gases in the atmosphere soared into the red zone. There was no turning back as Earth's climate settled into its death throes. This chaos allowed the Overlords to seize political control of the planet. They harvested all the plastics and garbage from the ocean's dead zones within a few years. With advanced technology, they pumped greenhouse gases into a witch's brew of ground-up ocean garbage and concrete mix—to make perfect building blocks for the bases.

"Tommy. Do you remember how it was? Back in the day, before ..."

"Before the Apocalypse?" His eyes twinkle like black diamonds.

"Yes, before the Overlords took over. What do you remember most?"

"Sneaky snakes," he says. "Slimy bastards."

"Why do you say that? People revere the Overlords now, don't they?"

Tommy peeks over his shoulders and whispers, "They don't know." He leans forward and glances side to side like he's telling a secret.

"Young folks are plain ignorant, or stupid, not knowing, not reading. Not keeping our history alive," Tommy says, staring me straight in the eye.

"Not you, Caroline. You need to keep the history alive. In here, where it counts." Tommy thumps his chest.

"You had the freedom to go anywhere you wanted. To live in a city, country, or out in the desert if you so desired. We weren't all equal yet, but it wasn't like this, with women treated like second-class citizens, and used for one thing."

"For sex," I say. I nod in agreement.

Tommy nods. "Then thrown away like a used tissue."

His words hit a nerve, sending an odd chill up my spine, remembering how cheap and used I felt when Commander finished with me.

"Let me ask you, Caroline, how do you like it, all cooped up in these cages? Don't you long for freedom? To smell the fresh air, dance naked in the rain, chase butterflies during the days, and watch lightning bugs at nightfall? Lie on Mother Earth's cool bosom in the evenings to gaze at the stars and wonder what's out there? To wonder if we're alone in the great big Cosmos with billions of stars and planets like ours?"

Tommy laughs. "Ha! Of course, you do. Don't you, Caroline? You miss it too. You remember. In here." He slaps his chest again, leans back, resumes his rocking, and starts humming an old boyhood tune. "The awful truth is we're not alone—not anymore, are we?"

"Yessiree." Tommy closes his eyes, rocks, and nods off for his afternoon nap, my cue to leave.

CHAPTER 34

Cassie informs me there's a scheduled meeting, and I'm to arrive in an hour. When I attend, everyone sits in their usual places, and again I'm at the foot of the table across from Commander. This time I'm ostracized by Commander and his Inner Circle, who mean nothing to me now. At least Frank, David, West, and Mack are still my friends.

"Zena, do you have anything to contribute?" Commander waits.

I stand. "No, sir, not currently. I'm making slow progress."

"Okay, fine. I've decided I'm too busy to act as your handler. I've discussed this with my team and decided to assign someone who can spend more time helping you."

My ears perk up and I scan the faces, all watching me. Someone else in the room? Like David or Philip West? Or even Frank. They could move me down to the first or second floor. I'd miss the view, but nothing else. David's office has space for another desk or table. Yes, this is great news.

"I've decided Major Abrams is the best fit for the job and has access to any information you'll need."

What? My legs become wet noodles, and I sit before they fail. I gulp and regard the other faces at the table. David and Frank know Major Abrams punished me, and now he is my handler? Sweat forms on the back of my neck and shoulders, and the room temperature rises, but my face won't betray me. Major Abrams' eyes avoid mine. He must be enjoying this.

"Do you have any problem with that?" Commander asks. He watches me, squinting.

Yes, of course, I do, but you'll never know.

"Outstanding idea, sir. Major Abrams is very intelligent and knowledgeable. I'm sure he wants this project to succeed as much as I do. He'll do a great job."

Just when I thought things couldn't get worse. Spiraling headfirst down the rabbit hole.

"Excellent. Meet with him tomorrow and discuss how you'll proceed. He'll report to me. If you have any problems or need anything, he'll help you. Okay, that's all. Dismissed."

I want to run out of the room, but I take my time leaving with my head held high and my heart scraping the bottom of my stomach. *Never let them see your belly.*

§

My papers are meticulously organized, but Major Abrams won't appreciate my efforts since he can't read my shorthand script. I could fabricate anything. What choice would he have but to believe me? I'm filled with a minute amount of power, but I can do this. I've done worse.

Major Abrams arrives at our agreed hour, and I'm prepared. I don't stand up. He's on my turf. I motion to him to take a seat. He stares at my stacks of legal-size papers scrawled with my script. He appears concerned, no doubt overwhelmed by my mountain of work, and he can't read a single scribble. Abrams grabs a stack of my papers and waves his hands.

"What is all this?"

"My notes."

"Can you translate all this to English?"

"Well, it is English, but I understand your point. If anything happened to me, you would have virtually nothing. My entire work effort for the last six months would be for naught. I should document the fruit of my labor," I say, smiling.

"I'll get you set up with a computer right away. You can move downstairs to my desk."

He closely watches my reaction and must be aware I hate him.

"It would be more productive if I stayed put. Can we get a laptop and set it up here? The computer would fit on the shelf in the evenings. You'd be cramped, and require privacy to visit with your comrades, and I'd be a distraction. I'd hate to impose on you. Besides, I'm used to quiet isolation to concentrate and work. I'm sure Major Williams can find me a laptop with compatible software and a memory stick or two."

Major Abrams scratches his head.

"Yeah, I'll talk to Tom. I'm sure we can do that."

"Great. We'll make a great team since we both desire to put forth our best effort."

You sorry bastard. Good thing you can't read minds.

CHAPTER 35

Tommy Miller appears weaker than usual.

"Oh, Caroline. Why didn't you wait for me?" Tommy's voice has a sorrow to it I hadn't heard before.

"Tommy, I ... I'm not ..."

"We'd have been happy on the farm together, you know," he says. "Remember how much you loved nature? The wildflowers, the butterflies, the birds? It could have all been ours, Caroline."

"But ... Tommy."

"You never told me what you were running from, why you were hiding. I wanted to be your hero and save you."

Tommy grows quiet. He falls asleep in his rocker, leaving me alone to ponder what our life would have been—had I been his beloved Caroline.

§

My morning coffee grows cold while I'm immersed in weaving everything together—my study of the Book, interviews with Tommy, and library research. Some material connects, but not all. The Master Plan is aspirational, not a historical document. It's important not to take Tommy's story as fact; my history books are incomplete. Still, it's clear the Master Plan was underway but never concluded. Somewhere along the way, they changed course. But why? Ultimately, we were never meant to live on the bases they designed for themselves, not us.

A week has passed, and my work suffers. Major Abrams made certain I received a laptop computer and thumb drive. I told him I needed to organize my documentation before committing to the computer. None of that is true. My preliminary report, in my shorthand script, is almost finished. I'm not eager to give Abrams anything, much less my report. When I'm ready, I'll type my report and submit it. When I'm ready.

Major Abrams bounds up the steps. My worktable remains ready in case anyone pops upstairs without notice. He appears pensive as he approaches and sits down across from me.

"Checking in." He bites his lip. What could be on his mind?

I say nothing.

"How's it going? Need anything? You've been quiet. Haven't seen much of you."

"I've been working, as always. I'll let you know if I need anything, sir."

My voice drips ice cold, but polite and professional.

"Have you started working on the computer yet?"

"No, sir. I have an outline ready and will start typing soon. Sir."

I stare deep into his eyes, hoping to unnerve him.

"Good, I'm looking forward to seeing something. Carry on."

§

Before lunch, I drop by the library to visit my old friend. Tommy sits rocking and humming. I sit on the sofa across from him, studying him, waiting for him to realize he has company. Tommy appears asleep, except for a slight rocking and his soft humming.

"It's Caroline, Tommy." I lie, hoping to reach him. "How are you?"

Tommy keeps his eyes closed but nods. He sings familiar words about being a motherless child in his gravelly old bluesy voice. What is Tommy trying to tell me? Is he dreaming? Or dying? There's so much I need to ask him.

"Are you all right?" I ask. "Do you know where you are, Tommy?"

He hums another familiar song about trouble in his way. What's Tommy trying to say? Why are my red flags all firing at once? Is he warning me of danger? He doesn't open his eyes.

"Tommy, it's Caroline. Tell me what I need to know. Am I meant to do something?"

He hums a bit, then sings a song about letting his people go. Is this code? Or biblical babble? I have better luck with the symbols in the Book.

"What should I do, Tommy? Please, tell me."

He nods, his eyes still closed, clears his throat, and resumes rocking and humming.

"Am I supposed to go somewhere, do something?" I ask, kneeling at the foot of his rocker. "Please, tell me."

After a silence, Tommy reaches for my hand and sings a song lamenting about not being able to stay here by himself, and I experience a Knowing that neither can I. A sudden chill floods the room. Why can't I stay here by myself?

I grab a colorful afghan draped over the back of the sofa and cover Tommy's lap, leaving my old friend to his field of dreams.

§

The cafeteria buzzes with twice the usual number of soldiers. All seats are filled except for a single empty chair—across from Blake, the salvage unit scout.

He invites me to sit.

"Well, what'd I do to deserve this honor?" he asks.

"This is the last available seat."

I'm eager to learn everything about this civilian. Where he comes from, and what he knows about the outside world. I take little bites of food. I'm hungry, but more for information than food. We finish eating in silence.

"So, Blake. You're a scout. How did you get that job?"

"Wanna join up? Could use an assistant. Be nice to travel with a maiden handy. But I ain't sure I'd share y'all," he says while staring at my breasts.

"No, I work upstairs, but I'm curious about where you're from and how you ended up with the salvage unit. Are you from a village? I've heard about hidden villages out there."

"Why y'all wanna know so much?"

"I have a curious nature, and you're different, like me. Everything about you is different. I don't fit in, but it seems you've made friends."

Blake licks his lips.

"Whatcha do around here? Y'all ain't dressed like no kitchen wench."

"No, I'm not. How did you get involved with the salvage unit?"

Blake flips me a half smile.

More troops enter the cafeteria with nowhere to sit, so I stand and suggest we take our conversation elsewhere. Blake stands. We deposit our dirty dishes in the plastic tub, stack our trays on top of the trash bins, and head to the ramp.

As we proceed down the ramp, I stop and turn to him and say, "If you won't answer my questions, I'll get back to work. I don't have time for games."

"Okay. Joined the unit three years back. They needed a scout, and I know the woods. Why y'all so curious 'bout me?"

"I'm interested in outsiders, and there's a great deal to learn about you and your people."

He's playing with me, but I won't reveal anything until he does. The first-floor docking area is empty, and I slow my pace to avoid venturing far from the ramp. The offices and storage areas ahead are off-limits.

"Okay, I'll tell y'all everything, but let's go over there." He points to some large boxes, suggesting he wants to sit. He pulls me behind stacked boxes, hiding us.

"On your knees for me, girl. I'll tell y'all whatcha wanna know. Come on, how 'bout takin' care of me with that purdy little mouth of yours."

He tries to push me down, and I panic.

"No, stop. I won't do that. That's not why ..."

His backhand cuts short my words. The force pushes me back, and I taste salty blood. The corner of my mouth burns like someone cut me with a knife. I straighten. He sees the mess he's made of my face and shakes his head.

Moving closer to him, I put my hands on his shoulders, surprising him. He's even more surprised when my knee comes up fast, and he doubles over in pain. I scramble out of striking range and then stagger to the ramp, covering my face to hide the blood. I race up the ramp, hoping to avoid contact with anyone, to take cover in my quarters, to clean up and heal. My face feels numb and puffy like it's swelling.

One of David's friends sees me, so I turn away, but it's too late. He rushes to my side and forces me to face him so he can see what I'm hiding. He moves my hand covering the injury, spots the blood, and inspects my face for damage. Too late, I can't hide this. I glance at my bloody hand. I've seen blood before, and it doesn't bother me, but seeing the smudges of my own blood on my fingers is strange. The soldier guides me up to the cafeteria, which now has an empty seat, and he orders me to sit.

"Hey, what happened here?"

"Clumsy me. I fell and hit my mouth. I'll run to my room and clean up. It's not bad."

He's on his radio making a call. Shit, I don't want this. Military and civilian staff surround me. Mary hands me an ice pack and directs me to hold it on my face for a few minutes.

"It will reduce the swelling," she says.

I thank her with my eyes. This feels strange. No female ever tended to me like this, not in my memory, anyway. What now?

David shows up, moves the ice pack aside, and examines my face.

"Okay, kitten, what's goin' on? Heard you had a fall."

I nod, trying to shrug it off. He checks my face and then confirms the rest of me is unhurt, with no blood or scrapes, and nothing is torn. He leaves, talking on his radio on his way to the first floor, but I can't dwell on that.

Commander and the doctor join us. I've never had so much attention, and I hate it. I want to disappear to my room. The doctor declares I'll live and praises Mary, saying the ice pack was a great idea, and she beams. Commander asks what happened, and I don't dare lie, so I don't speak. This lie could backfire and hurt me, and I can't risk that. They already punished me once, and I'm not sure what David will find.

Commander takes me by my arm. I turn and nod my thanks to Mary and the doctor. Commander escorts me to the freight lift, where I remain quiet on the way to the fourth floor and across the rotunda. At the office, he leads me upstairs. I'm still holding the ice pack and applying it until the cold gets too uncomfortable. I sit on the couch, wishing this was over.

"Okay, what happened? I'm told you fell and hit your mouth. That's not what I see here. Who hit you?"

I bet he's seen enough busted lips. I mumble it hurts to talk and wince with each word. Commander nods. Major Abrams comes upstairs. David soon rejoins us and squats down to my level. "Who hit you?"

I stare at my bloody hand. David rises, disappears into the bathroom, brings back a wet washcloth, and hands it to me. With soft dabs, I wipe the blood away from my face, cringing, exaggerating my pain, and then clean the blood from my hand.

"Okay, who hit you, kitten?" His voice is softer but insistent.

I shrug and hang my head. If I tell, they will whip Blake, and I already evened the score. Commander and Major Abrams watch me, waiting.

"Did one of our soldiers do this?" David asks.

I shake my head no. I can't let them question or accuse any of my friends.

"The visiting units then." David isn't asking.

"There are two units in. I'll question them all, but you'll make it so much easier by telling me right now." He raises his voice, his patience waning. I'm trapped. No one should pay for my stupidity. I must come clean. David ignores my pleading stare. He stands and announces he'll gather the troops and start the questioning.

"Wait," I say. I'm out of options.

David turns to me with a cocky, knowing look. He won, and I'm sick to my stomach. He moves in close and squats again.

"The scout. He wanted me on my knees for him. I refused ..."

"So, he struck you," Commander says.

I nod. It's out now, but I feel worse.

David nods. He stands, turns away from me, and radios someone. Commander orders me to accompany them. I hadn't noticed, but Dan has joined the group. Paul heads downstairs to his office, and the rest of us descend to the main floor. We proceed to an area I've never seen, a large room, and I recognize barracks like the ones at Westview. Soldiers line both sides of the barracks, standing at attention. Blake stands in a casual stance near his unit.

Commander pulls me to his side, and I want to shrink into nothing.

"Somebody hurt this girl. Smacked her right in the face. You all know the rules. We never hit a woman without her permission, and this one doesn't enjoy getting hit."

His voice thunders deep and resonating, commanding everyone's attention.

"One of you needs to step up. Who did this?"

He knows the answer. I stare at the floor until Blake steps up and confesses. He walks forward and stands about four feet away, facing us. Commander watches him and waits.

"That's how we handle womenfolk when they tease y'all, then refuse to give y'all your due. Gotta train 'em, right? Can't be teasing," Blake says.

What? I glare at him. I never promised him anything. He promised to answer my questions. Commander glances at me and shakes his head.

"Take off your shirt."

Blake removes his vest and shirt. If he's afraid, he hides it. Another soldier takes Blake's clothing. At Commander's order, he turns around and puts his hands atop his head. I can't bear this and can't stop it.

"Commander, I can't watch this," I say, my voice squeaking.

"Matthews, get her out of here."

Whatever he does after that, happens after I'm out of earshot.

§

My mouth no longer hurts, but I purposely arrive late to work this morning to avoid Commander. Yesterday, I took the rest of the day off to heal my mouth. When I enter the office, Commander stands at his door, orders me into his office, and then closes the door. Will he punish me, too, for lying? I didn't lie to him, but I wasn't forthcoming.

"Why didn't you report what happened right away? My job is to protect you. That's why you're here." He doesn't sound angry.

"I handled it, sir. I kicked him between his legs. We were even. I knew I could avoid him. He couldn't come upstairs looking for me."

"I don't understand you. You came here for protection, and when you get in trouble, you keep quiet. You act on your own."

"I got even. He knows he can't get away with hurting me. I punished him."

"That's not how things work here. I'm glad you got away, but you can't let these things slide. He belted you a good one. That's against the rules, and everyone knows it. Why were you with him, anyway?"

I don't speak.

"You could enjoy any man you desire. You don't have to associate with the … with Blake. Come to me, and I'll take care of you." His voice is softer.

"I'll never go to Blake. He hit me, and I'd never have sex with any man who hits me. Or watches someone else do it."

CHAPTER 36

My blurry eyes try focusing on the clock. It's morning, and I was dreaming. I stood on the edge of the time horizon, watching my life unfold: a husband, babies, friends, our lives out there where nature lives. It flashes by too fast. Was I visualizing my future? I can't get pregnant, but will that change?

§

The last few sections of the Book talk about the complete takeover, and whatever they've planned doesn't include us. A remaining handful of symbols hide their meaning, and it baffles me how most of them are so easily understood, but these few are incomprehensible, their meaning alien to me. No point of reference, and no clue. Maybe Tommy might give me insight, but he appears to be losing ground, and his words often mystify and scare me.

§

Cassie's not at her desk when I enter the break room almost colliding with Major Williams. The coffee pot is empty, and I need an afternoon caffeine boost.

"Well, hello stranger."

With nothing to say, I try to move past him, but he blocks my way.

"Hey, why so unsociable?"

"I need to get back to work, sir," I say, avoiding his eyes.

The chill in my voice appears to disarm him. He nods and leaves. I'm searching the cabinets for a coffee canister when Cassie steps into the break room.

"Commander wants to see you in his office."

Her voice offers no hint if I'm in trouble. What did I do now? I set down my empty cup.

"We're out of coffee." I watch her reaction.

Cassie shrugs and informs me she'll let "the girl" know. I didn't know we had a girl.

In Commander's office, he gestures for me to sit.

"Central is sending someone to meet with you tomorrow."

At last, someone's investigating Wickmore's attacks on me. Justice, after all. I've been waiting months for this. Michael kept his promise.

"Lieutenant Daemon Fischer. He's your new liaison, and they want him to oversee your work. Not sure you've had a liaison before, but since you're not working in direct contact with Central Intelligence, they want you to have an overseer."

Fischer? Also known as Ivan the Terrible because he loves inflicting pain. I never liked him. It's been at least eight years since I was booted out of Westview, and I didn't miss him once. I'll never forget how he whipped Scott.

"What time should I expect him, sir?"

"He's scheduled to arrive in the morning. Someone will notify you when we're ready for you. Abrams and I will meet with him first. We'll be working together. So, midmorning."

With that, I'm dismissed.

Daemon Fischer? What does he want? So, Fischer is a liaison for Central Intelligence? When did that happen? Strange how hearing his name reminds me of home. But I have no home. Westview wasn't home.

§

I've been pacing all morning, waiting for Fischer, trying to detect his evil presence, but I can't. My music fails to calm me, and it's difficult to sit still, so I pace. Is he here to take me away? I hate it here sometimes, but they say the devil you know is better than the one you don't. Well, Daemon is certainly one devil I know, and I must contend with devils here. I've made friends here, and David might realize he cares for me and return to me.

Music doesn't speed up time, and neither does pacing. Major Abrams shows up, alone.

"Zena, Lieutenant Fischer has arrived. I'll escort you and introduce the two of you."

The words, Dead Woman Walking, come to mind as we cross the rotunda to the conference room. It's melodramatic but tickles me, and Lord knows I need to lift my spirits.

Fischer aged well, graying at the temples, but still harboring his inner darkness. I extend my hand, and he smirks because he's aware of my abilities. He takes it, anyway. I hold his hand for a second, then pull back fast. His face registers fear or concern. I'm not sure which. That was fun.

Commander and Major Abrams trade alarmed looks.

"I guess Miss Roberts didn't mention we know each other," Fischer says. He grins, checking me out.

"Neither did you," says Commander, crossing his arms.

I don't notice Commander and Abrams leaving. I keep my attention focused on Fischer, reading him. He has mellowed, with his dark need to hurt people weakened. He can't hide it from me, so I trust my reading.

We sit across the table, scrutinizing each other.

"Hello, Zena. You didn't like 'Angel'?"

"I'm more of a warrior than an angel, wouldn't you say?"

"You look good. It's been a long time. You were what, fifteen?"

"I was, and you've … aged a lot."

He laughs. He wants this to work, but I don't care.

"You've been stationed here a while, and I'm not sure you're aware, but Colonel Wickmore retired. He's gone, and it's time for you to come home."

"I don't have a home. So, the Colonel retired? Was there an investigation?"

My teeth are grinding, and I'm afraid if I bite my lip, I'll bite it off. Justice doesn't exist.

"There was. The Colonel says you were enjoying the game. He swore once he had you, you responded to him. He insists he never raped you, and all touching was consensual."

"No one asked me."

"They didn't think it was necessary. Some women like men to chase them."

"My statement?"

"They read it. You described how he forced you into rooms, but you didn't detail any sexual abuse, just that he did what he wanted. It's over. The embarrassment of the investigation forced him into retirement."

I stare at Fischer. I want to hurt him, but he's not the target.

"Michael's back, you know. You can resume the life you and Michael enjoyed before. I talked to him, and he still wants you."

"Michael and I are finished, and I'm never going back to Central. I can't believe anyone there would believe that crock of shit. They knew me. If a woman can't move or if she's threatened with punishment, does that mean it's consensual? In what universe?"

Steam must be blasting out of my ears.

"Colonel Wickmore stalked me for nearly two months, messed with my brain and my body, making me afraid to do anything, even sleep at night. I never knew when he'd attack. I don't fuckin' believe y'all fell for his crap."

"You can handle yourself. Why didn't you handle this situation? You know you're capable. You have … skills. Why not use them?"

"Because he's crazy, and you can't deal with insanity. He's a sick, perverted bastard who changed his tactics as fast as I did. He had to win, and he wasn't taking any prisoners."

Fischer smirks. He tricked me into revealing myself. He's good, and I'm out of practice.

"Okay, Zena, look. You don't have to return to Central. Well, you will until you pass on what you've learned to their team. Then we want you to join us at Westview. Commander Nadler wants you back with us."

"Commander Nadler? When did that happen?"

"Five years ago. He's head of C.I. He wants you hands-on, back home."

"That wasn't my home."

"Hey, Nadler treated you like royalty, and he was damn good to you. I would have whipped your sorry ass for helping a prisoner escape. But he covered your ass instead. He cares about you and wants you back."

Sure, he covered my ass because he coveted my ass.

"This is a difficult time. Translating the Book is all-consuming, and I can't do both."

"You can work part-time on the Book, and interview with us as needed. As you know, it's not full-time. You'll have all your former privileges. I understand, here, you don't have the freedoms you're accustomed to, that Commander Pierce is strict. I spoke with him and Major Abrams. They make no exceptions, and if you stay here, you follow their rules. I heard you received punishment."

He's not gloating and almost sounds sympathetic. Who would have told him? Michael doesn't know, does he? Did Abrams or Commander discuss my punishment with him?

"Yes, I deserved it. I got upset and spoke out of line, but I learned from that, and I understand the rules and follow them. It won't happen again. Besides, they gave me one swat. First offense. First and last."

"I'm glad you're growing up and learning how to follow orders and behave yourself, but you're always welcome back at Westview, and I'll tend to your needs myself."

When I give him the stink eye, he realizes I'm reading him and laughs. He's still hardcore.

"This is my last assignment. I'm staying here until I'm finished, then I'll transfer to a civilian base. I don't belong in the military, I'm not happy, and I didn't choose this life. It's time to experience life among people like me."

"There are no people like you, Zena," Fischer says and chuckles, then he turns serious. "Central Intelligence won't let you go. You're too valuable and know too much. I know they let you down. That's why they made me your liaison. Someone needs to stay in touch with you and make sure you're happy and safe. I have C.I. behind me. At Westview, you'll be safe. Can't guarantee happiness, but we'll work with you."

I can't win this. How far would they take it to stop me from leaving? They know their secrets are safe with me. Do I only matter to them, providing I deliver?

"I need to finish my project before I'm ready for another change, so I'll get back to you. I need more time."

CHAPTER 37

The quiet back room in the library appears strangely different. The rocking chair has disappeared, and an old lavender-colored couch covered in a faded paisley flower print has replaced the sofa. No rocking chair and no Tommy. The chamber has a different vibe, old and dusty instead of quaint and cozy. Even the air feels like its soul was sucked out, though all base areas smell fresh from air filtering.

§

Not a soul in sight on the main floor. Mack won't be in his office. It's Thursday, and he'll be bartending at Club. Lieutenant Philip West's office up ahead has its door half-closed, so I knock. Someone moves, and the door opens.

"Well, Zena, what are you doing here?" his assistant, Jason, asks.

"I was hoping to find your boss."

"Is there a problem?"

"Not yet," I say.

From behind me, someone approaches.

"Zena, do you need help with something?" Lieutenant West asks.

"Hello. I was taking a walk and thought I'd stop by."

"Yeah, you shouldn't be back here unless you need security. Let me escort you out. I'll catch you in the morning, Corporal."

"Yes sir, I'll lock up. Good night, Zena."

"So, what's goin' on?" Lieutenant West asks.

"I wanted to see you."

"Sure. How can I help?"

"No, I mean, I wanted to see you. For companionship."

West smiles like I'm wasting his time. "I don't socialize except for poker. You should find someone else to hang out with."

I sense the disappointment in his soft words. His eyes tell me he doesn't want me to go.

"Well, I thought a private conversation in your quarters would be fun."

His eyes sparkle. "Are you offering to have sex with me?"

"Depends on your answer."

"Yes."

"Then let's go."

§

West nuzzles my breast. It tickles, but I'm unsure if he wants to make love again or if he's just playing. His radio beeps, and he jumps up to answer.

"When? Who all's there? Give me a few minutes. Did you notify Commander? Copy. I'll check it out and see if there's an issue here. Give me fifteen. Out." West dresses in a hurry.

"What happened?"

"Gotta go. It's probably nothing. Someone turned off the storage room motion detector. No one's scheduled to enter, so I need to check it out."

"It went off or got turned off?"

"Turned off."

"Why is that a problem?"

He finishes dressing without answering.

"Get dressed. Lock up. Make sure you have your lanyard. I don't have time right now."

§

I'm dressed, my lanyard hangs around my neck, and I peek out to ensure nobody's around. I pull the door closed and test it. It's locked. I'm certain West was referring to the storage room where he found me the first evening we met. I try to discover what's happening, but security officers swarm outside the storage room like agitated bees protecting the hive. Why was the motion detector turned off? Someone asks if they found the passkey, and red flags flare up. The corridor. I have a hunch.

In the Radio Room, Anthony and Jacob attend their posts—but no Davies.

"So, where's Davies?" I ask.

"Still early, so he could still show. He's got a new gal. Could be with her," says Jacob.

"Anything unusual happening here?" I ask.

"Yeah, we got a partial on a message. Took us by surprise. It's been so long since we picked up. It was short and then repeated twenty minutes later," says Jacob.

"Did you pick it up the second time?" I ask.

"A partial. We were setting up the recording system, and it started again," says Anthony.

"Can you decode it?" asks Jacob.

"Not a partial. I couldn't determine where the message starts without the heading sequence," I say. "I'll check back later or tomorrow to see if you catch a complete message."

CHAPTER 38

No one would have heard me screaming in my isolated quarters. I'm awake now, and my heart pounds with a chilly sense of danger. Tommy appeared in my dream as a strong, young, healthy teen. He kept repeating, "Time is running out. You need Caroline." Why would I need Caroline? She must be long dead by now.

§

Nestled at my worktable, I bring out the legal pad with notes from my interview with Tommy. It's all script except for his name at the top, TOMMY, in large letters. I'm so lost in thought I didn't hear Major Abrams come upstairs. He spots the legal pad before I turn it over.

"So, who's Tommy?" he asks. He squints at my notes.

"Someone I interviewed."

He sits across from me. "Interviewed? Why?"

"He's about eighty years old, and I wanted to learn about life outside." I wish he would stop asking questions. I don't want to speak to him, especially not about this.

"There's nobody stationed on this base that old. Not sure about a civilian base, but certainly not military."

He raises his eyebrows and tilts his head.

"What's his full name? What does he look like?"

"He says his name is Tommy Miller, but I couldn't tell his rank because he was wearing an old robe and sitting in a rocker. He has mahogany skin, snow-white hair, full lips, and dark eyes."

"Where did you see him?"

"In the library, in a back room."

"And you talked to him?"

"Yes."

"And he talked to you?"

His incredulous expression spooks me. I sense he thinks I'm playing with him, so I giggle and roll my eyes.

"I have a good imagination," I say.

"Okay, so who is Tommy? Come on."

"I thought of an old friend and absentmindedly wrote his name. I don't remember why."

"You shouldn't lie."

"It's not a lie. I'm playing with you, that's all."

§

On the way to lunch, I stop in the Memorial Room to visit Andrew. As I read the inscriptions on the plaques, walking down the line to Andrew's, something catches my eye, and I stop cold. The name on the plaque is Major Thomas Miller, and he died two decades ago.

§

No word about last night's events, and I'm curious whether Davies ever showed up for work. When I visit the Radio Room, Davies is absent again.

"No Davies? Did he show up last night?" I ask.

Anthony glances at me and says, "No, never showed. Nor today. Haven't heard a thing. Could be sick. Don't know."

Jacob says, "More like lovesick." He laughs.

"Did you guys record any more messages?"

Anthony says, "No, quiet all evening."

"Has anyone checked on Davies? I'm concerned."

"Naw, but I suppose we should. We cover for each other, but Davies could be in trouble. After my shift, I'll pop by his room and check on him."

I leave with a theory, but I must be sure. I need to talk to David. He'll know what to do.

§

David's nowhere in the almost empty cafeteria. Agora, in contrast, is hopping, so I peek at our booth. No David, but a waif of a woman sits there alone, and it's not Mary. I search for Frank or any high-ranking officer. Mary sits with a private, appearing to enjoy herself. Does this mean David is free? I turn to head down to his office, but as I pass the booth again, he's sitting next to the plain woman, his arm draped around her shoulders. I stand a few feet away. David sees me, and another scene flashes in my mind. When I sat with David in the booth. A young woman stood where I'm standing, about to cry, as if her entire world had ended. David dismissed her. Said she was nobody. Now I'm that woman.

David appears puzzled, and I'm frozen.

I can't move.

I can't speak.

David will never be mine.

I'm that pathetic woman.

David starts to stand, but I break free of my virtual prison and flee Agora. Bile rises inside me like a volcano, burning and threatening to erupt. I make it to the fourth floor. At my door, I fumble with my passkey with shaking hands. My eyes are blurry with tears. Inside, I lock the door, tear off my clothes, and crash.

Tears streak my face, soaking my pillow. Darkness surrounds me, closing in, and the pain is a hundred sharp swords piercing my heart. I scream into my wet pillow to muffle the sound.

I've lost David and everyone else I ever cared for. Fischer wants me to serve the pedophile who took my innocence, made me love him, and then cast me aside. I've lost everything, and I hate everyone, and I'm tired of all these secrets. I try so hard. Oh, Andrew, I understand how the darkness took you, and I'm so sorry.

My sobbing leaves me exhausted, and with my face buried in my tear-soaked pillow, hugging it for comfort, I fall into a deep sleep and dream.

I'm standing in a corner, trapped. In the dim gray blurry half-light, David, Commander, Paul, West, and Mack amble forward like zombies, stumbling into each other, melting like wax figures on a stove, morphing into Colonel Wickmore, who is joined by Michael.

The smell of scorched flesh sears my nostrils. They morph into Nadler, who extends his hand, reaching out to me, with panic scrawled over his face as the skin on his hand boils and burns off with sharp crackling sounds. Behind Nadler's charred remains, Dan and Andrew fuse into a solitary figure from my nightmares. The Shadow Man's laughter turns to a hideous ear-piercing shriek as he forces me to my knees with his hands so tight around my neck I can't breathe.

Right before I pass out, he becomes a hideous serpentine creature winding and coiling, squeezing, and hissing. With a silent scream, I kick and push with all my might. Fear overtakes me as I feel him reaching into me, trying to take what's mine. The room spins, and I feel myself falling.

A silent blinding flash of white light cloaks me, and I can breathe. The serpent has vanished, and the delicate scent of flowers perfumes the air. I emerge into a peaceful, glorious, sunlit field of wildflowers with millions of monarch butterflies fluttering around me, welcoming me back. Streams of long-forgotten images cascade before me like a parade.

My mom. She raised me alone after Dad left when I was twelve.

Stinky, our black poodle, and Tweety, my canary who flew away because I left the cage door open.

My first crush, first kiss, first driving lesson, first love, and first heartbreak.

Aunt Linda's death from cancer, my sisters getting married, my own wedding.

Giving birth, twice. Trish and Jamie.

Our first tiny house, which we outgrew, and our bigger house which we filled with love, noise, fights, laughter, and more love.

The car accident and receiving the Gift.

Killing the Shadow Man.

Having to leave my loved ones.

The cabin.

All night long, one dream after another. Ten hours, I sleep, and ten hours, I dream, and in the morning, when I wake, I understand. They weren't dreams.

They were memories.

I know who I am.

CHAPTER 39

I comb my fingers through a tumbleweed mess framing my puffy red eyes. I half expect my mirror to reflect my eighty-year-old self with gray, almost white hair, and wrinkles. Instead, I'm thrilled my image greets me with clear, smooth skin, long dark brown hair, a smile revealing a mouthful of natural teeth, and my eyes, although bloodshot, sparkle again. My naked body flaunts breasts no longer overtaken by gravity, perching above a flat belly, without stretch marks or pouch from pregnant months. My supple, tan body stands youthful and strong, and this face, different from the first time I was twenty-three, isn't beautiful but is acceptable. Special Consultant Zena Roberts had no clue how special she was.

My throat burns, and I regret screaming so much into my pillow, so with closed eyes, I bid the Gift's energy to spring forth to heal my discomfort. When I open my eyes, they're no longer red, and my throat no longer burns. Zena had no idea how to use the Gift's regenerative power.

Rebecca Daniels.

I whisper my name, and it sounds strange on my tongue after ten years, of not knowing my real name, not knowing who I am.

Becky. Born Rebecca Brooks in 1950. Named after the old Hebrew name, Rebecca, meaning *noose*. Russell Daniels and I celebrated fifty years of marriage, but he wasn't my first love. That was Kevin Roberts.

It's odd that Zena chose Roberts for her surname. For eight months, Kevin was my soul mate, the love of my life. I intended to love him forever. Then he broke my heart in two. No, into pieces, and I was hanging on by a thread, wanting to die because my life was meaningless without him.

Then Russ caught my eye and charmed me with long walks on the beach, intimate dinners, and tender lovemaking. He became my glue, putting me back together. Our love, different—a quiet love, steady and

220

giving, sharing, and forgiving, lasted a lifetime.

We were blessed with two precious children and watched them grow up and have children of their own. Our grandchildren became adults and gave us sweet great-grandbabies.

Russ was seventy-five when a stroke seized him in the middle of one night. In 2030, when I turned eighty, I left my family, not to die, but for rebirth—courtesy of the alien Gift.

No clue or sign of Rebecca exists in this tiny room. The clothes, memory box, and music CDs all belong to Zena. The drawings created in her short lifetime are tokens of her life, not mine.

I left behind every picture of my family, every drawing my babies drew for us, and every reminder of my former life. All that remains are memories; of giving birth, Trish and Jamie playing on the beach, and even the memory of my parents fighting. It all happened decades ago.

The cemetery dream of me standing before my family's graves, mourning, and saying my final goodbyes, can't be a memory. As Zena, I never visited the graves; some of my family were alive when I made my journey to the cabin for rebirth.

The car accident dream? I was seventy when I witnessed the accident. When I took his hand, the alien creature in the crushed car entered me, bestowing me with the Gift, and sought to force me to deliver it to the Overlords, unknown in those days, and gift it to them. My resolve was stronger than his, and he lacked the power to overtake my body while I still lived. My survival was pitted against his need.

During the short time the alien lived inside me, I learned of their plan involving a hundred other aliens. More are coming from their dying star, all needing sentient bodies to live on Earth—but they need the Gift, without which they'll perish. Their alien biology involves bringing a host body close to death to inhabit it, using the Gift somehow to make the transition.

I was old with death knocking at my door, but I felt reluctant to answer it. One of us had to die; I believed it should be him. It became my purpose, my destiny—to avoid the Overlords at all costs. My life depended on it.

The Tracker haunting my dreams, the one I killed, was real, and thanks to the Gift's power, I saved myself.

Symbols in the Book, which eluded me before, make perfect sense now, and I'm aware the Gift enables me to translate them. The Gift protects me, keeps me healthy and safe, and made rejuvenation possible in 2030, but is it possible my rebirth took sixty years? How did I fall asleep in the cabin and wake in the cave in 2090?

Zena needs to report to work, but it's impossible to function until I reach some clarity. I'm required to notify Paul before taking personal days to avoid making waves. It's a dreamlike experience entering the office for the first time yet knowing it very well since Zena's memories are also mine.

"Morning, Cassie. I'm taking a personal day and wanted to inform you."

I offer my friendliest smile. Cassie glances up, squints, tilts her head, and nods, without a word. In his office, upon seeing me, Paul turns and offers his full attention.

"Major Abrams, sorry to disturb you, but I slept poorly last night and need today off."

"You all right?" He scrutinizes me like he's unsure it's me.

"A bit more sleep, and I'll be good as gold."

Paul flashes me an odd look, and I remind myself this is the twenty-second century, and my figures of speech are over seven decades old, from a different world.

"Take care of yourself," he says. He resumes his work, dismissing me.

I remove a pad of paper and a pen from the supply cabinet as quietly as a mouse and slip past Paul, tucking the paper behind me. When I pass Cassie again, she ignores me. I need coffee and breakfast.

§

The cafeteria offers an unfamiliar dish called Pumpkin Steel Cut Oatmeal, but its savory spiced aroma, like pumpkin pie, delights my nostrils. Its sweet, nutty flavor tastes delicious, but the coffee is stronger than I like. I scan my surroundings and recognize the cafeteria, too, with different eyes.

My special shorthand fills the page. Mindful of the time, I rush to finish before the lunch crowd shows up. Thirteen-year-old Zena had no memory but believed she had a purpose. Where was she going? Never to the Overlords to deliver the Gift. She understood they were her enemy, although not why, but I do.

I envision the cabin where I slept to await rebirth, but I planned to be reborn as a grown woman, young, but not a child. It's difficult enough to obtain a new adult identity. As a child, it would be harder to explain the large amount of money from selling my house, hidden in my suitcase, a considerable amount of money. Where did it go? It would be useless now since the Overlords provide everything. Nothing makes sense. I needed to remember everything to keep myself safe and achieve my purpose. Did the Gift make me forget?

Military personnel drift into the cafeteria, so I gather my materials and retreat to my room. On the bed with my back pressed against the wall, I continue my pursuit. I separated from my path and became entrenched in working for Central Intelligence for the last ten years, but it was all unnecessary. My goal was to learn everything about the Overlords, unaware I knew the answers the entire time.

It's a waiting game until the aliens die out, provided I keep myself and the Gift safe from the Overlords. They require the Gift to survive, to inhabit the bodies of young adults they breed in captivity.

Countless alien entities wait for human vessels. The one hundred aliens already occupying aging human bodies will need renewal, which requires the Gift. My Gift. Without it, they die. It's them or me. The fate of humanity hangs in the balance, and I have my thumb on the scale.

According to the Book, the Overlords took measures to stop the pollution and destruction of the planet to save Earth for themselves. Powerful humans were unconcerned, and those who cared were marginalized. Greed, plus the need for power, replaced salvation for the planet and mankind. Overlords may believe in community, charity, respect, and decency, and their laws exist to benefit all *their* kind, but these are my people, and we inhabited Earth first.

The Overlords may deserve to inherit the earth, but if it hinges on my actions, they will fail. I am human, I want to live. The Gift is mine now.

§

I awake mid-morning, having spent half the night trying to find solid ground. Several pages of my legal pad comprise my musings, but I'm far from finished. I comb through pages of an older art pad, searching for clues. The butterfly in one drawing reminds me of the cocoon. In a way, I've emerged from the cocoon sheltering my memories. Why did I forget? I'm not safe here, and I needed to understand that. I need more time.

Paul turns to me when I enter his office.

"I need another day. I stayed up late again last night, overslept, and still need to resolve some personal matters, so I'll report for work tomorrow."

With a nod, Paul gets up and walks me to the front desk.

"You need to see Commander first."

Paul knocks on Commander's door and motions to him, then he opens the door and waves me in. Inside his office, Commander gestures for me to sit, and the door clicks shut behind me.

"What's going on?" asks Commander.

"I have some personal stuff that needs my attention because I'm not sleeping well, and concentration is difficult, but I'll come back tomorrow."

Commander leans back, tilts his head, and squints.

"What kind of personal stuff? Something I should know about?"

I read his concern and decide to speak my truth, not everything, just what's safe.

"My liaison, Lieutenant Fischer, insists I involve my former team at Central with my project. I told him I'd never return to Central, and he informed me Colonel Wickmore retired, but without an investigation, not a real one. Everyone believed the Colonel's lies. He also told me the head of C.I. wants me to join him at Westview when I'm finished at Central. I told

Fischer this was my last assignment, and I'm staying at Cavalry until I've translated the Book."

Commander nods.

"Fischer says they'll never release me because I know too much and I'm too valuable. I need to decide my next steps, and I can't concentrate with all this weighing on my mind."

"What happened with the Colonel? Word is you needed to leave after Michael left because Colonel Wickmore harassed you." He eyes me with casual concern.

"The Colonel began assaulting me two weeks after Michael left when I turned down his dinner invitation. He attacked me several times in the following weeks. After informing my handler and complaining to Commander Harris, it continued, and they did nothing."

"Wickmore raped you?" Commander asks, keeping his voice soft and sympathetic.

"No, he didn't seem capable of it. Maybe he believed attacking me would arouse him enough to … but he couldn't."

Commander looks me over.

"What did he do?"

I exhale with a deep sigh and close my eyes to steady myself.

"That's irrelevant. No one's doing anything about it."

"He hurt you?"

"Yes, he hit me. He was rough and touched me without my consent."

"No need to feel shame. Senior officials expect women to be willing."

"I wasn't willing, and it wasn't consensual. It wasn't sex. It was abuse and unlawful. What he did is irrelevant. Men think if a woman enjoys sex with one partner, it's no big deal if another man unlawfully forces her. Military men believe women should always be willing, and if she isn't, she deserves abuse. That's a problem. If I tell you how he hurt me, you would just dismiss, excuse, or justify it."

Commander leans forward like he's about to say something.

"That predator terrorized me for weeks. I was afraid to go anywhere, afraid he was somewhere waiting for me, afraid at night, thinking he'd get access to my room. It affected everything in my life, my work, and my sleep. Eating was difficult. My stomach was nervous all the time. You and I differ in the way we see things. You will never understand the importance of my retaining agency over my own body, to be able to protect myself and feel safe. This was worse than rape. I know." I sigh, and my body feels like a weight has lifted. "Besides, it's all in my rear-view mirror now."

"What? What does that mean?"

"It means it's behind me, and I'm not going that way."

Commander shifts in his seat. I request permission to leave, and he nods. I spend the morning into the evening working on my mystery.

CHAPTER 40

Commander and Paul have already left the apartment when I report to work. Their coffee cups sit on the counter, rinsed, and turned over to dry. My first task is to inspect the windowsill. My heart beats faster. It's gone. The cocoon is gone. No sign of it, no residual evidence. I check all the windowsills. No cocoon. Was it ever there?

I dive into my work.

Today I'm plunging ahead to fill in my preliminary report, which requires serious effort to type my prepared shorthand notes. Central Intelligence needs to understand my assignment's importance and how far I've progressed, for leverage. I plug away, compiling my report until hunger pangs hijack my attention.

§

From my corner table, I can view the entire third-floor cafeteria. I finish eating and list items in cursive that puzzle me: the cocoon, smear, voices, dreams, and Tommy.

If the cocoon wasn't real, what does it mean? The smear that splayed on the window disappeared the next day. It led me to the voices, but Zena didn't know how to filter them. When I Pay Attention, I can isolate and understand the aliens' voices.

My strange dreams? Most were memories, except the cemetery dream and the dream of the Tracker finding and killing me. Zena called him a Shadow Man. Was my subconscious warning me of looming danger? What does it mean? Please, not another Tracker.

Tommy appeared real. Why did I hallucinate this long-dead military officer, and what could his warning mean? Why can't I stay here by myself?

225

The biggest mystery remains. How I got from the cabin to the cave decades later. Did the Gift erase my memory to lead me to the Overlords? I've long forgotten my destination, but I was drawn somewhere.

I'm finished working in this environment. It serves no useful purpose, and I already know more than I can learn here. This isn't my destination. This base is the last place on Earth I'd choose to hide. But I must solve these mysteries before knowing how to proceed, before taking on Central Intelligence. One matter at a time.

My work captivates me, and the afternoon races by with me in deep concentration, crafting my report. One symbol I struggled with becomes clear—the snake-like symbol representing the alien's home world. David gave me a magazine article from 2014 showing a high-resolution image of the *Pillars of Creation* taken by the Hubble Space Telescope—in the constellation *Serpens*. The article discussed dozens of exoplanets in the *Serpens* constellation, with the closest one to us a mere 39 light-years away, orbiting a tiny yellow star you can see at night with the naked eye, *Lambda Serpentis*.

The article also discussed how, since antiquity, people have used snakes both to cure afflictions and to poison enemies, depending on their use. Snake mythology tells of a serpent brought back to life by another serpent, only for the reborn serpent to be killed by Ophiuchus, the god of medicine. As if snakes possess the Gift of Life by which they resurrect the dead through their bite. Like my Gift restores me. I missed the connection then, even after Tommy referred to the Overlords as *sneaky snakes*. Coincidence? Einstein said coincidence is God's way of remaining anonymous.

I'm the catalyst for the alien's change of plans. Without the Gift, the aliens couldn't inhabit human bodies, which forced them to abandon their original plan. It was still necessary to breed humans until they recovered the Gift, keeping us on bases for future use. As standbys? Had their plan come to fruition, today, aliens in human form would occupy all the bases. With sufficient genetic diversity, they might require even fewer humans unless more aliens are coming. Another Tracker?

Or, God forbid, another alien with the Gift? This would be alarming news. If I remain hidden until the aliens all die out, it might save humanity, provided I alone possess the Gift. If another alien arrives with the Gift, can I defeat him too? I want to live, but I'm not eager to fight, and facing another alien life-form sends shivers up my spine. Zena believed she'd have an advantage if she knew the Truth. She was dead wrong.

CHAPTER 41

I've made significant progress on my report over the past few days, but no progress on my mystery, and no clue where to search. I spend evenings in my room or the empty cafeteria with my legal pad containing the list. Most of my dreams are memories and easy to interpret. Tommy? Where does he fit in? He tried to warn me with his dark sentences, but about what? Who is Caroline? She must be long dead, so how does she fit this puzzle? The greatest mystery remains how I awoke in the cave, an afternoon drive from Westview—in a jeep. Where is Westview? The cabin was in southern Ohio.

All week, I arrived at work to find Commander and Paul drinking their coffee at my worktable. Each morning, I slip past Paul, retrieve my materials and computer, and resume typing my report. But this morning, Cassie informs me of a conference room meeting I must attend.

As soon as I enter the conference room, I notice Fischer. Commander heads the table with Paul to his left and Dan to his right. Lieutenant West sits across from Fischer. I read the seriousness of the group and my stomach somersaults.

Fischer flashes his trademark fake smile as I sit next to him in the only available seat. He pulls two photos from his jacket pocket and places them before me. One is a photo of Davies from Central. The other photo shows Scott. I inspect both pictures and when I look up at Fischer, I show surprise. There's no doubt they are two different men with similar features.

I tap the photo of Davies.

"This is Corporal Davies from Central."

I tap the second photo.

"Who is this? I mean, he claimed to be Davies, but he's obviously not."

"How well did you know Davies at Central?" Fischer's eyes narrow.

"He worked nights, and I worked days. I didn't know him very well, and I was unaware he transferred out."

"You went to the Radio Room on several occasions, didn't you?" Lieutenant West asks. We haven't been together since the night Scott vanished, nor have we talked.

"At Central, I visited the Radio Room often during the day, sir, as part of my job."

"And here?" West asks.

"Yes, sir. I popped in once during the day to meet the day crew, and then I met the evening crew and visited them several times."

"Why? What was your business there?" West asks.

"No business. When I was lonely, I'd go there for company. It was quiet, and I never interfered with their work."

"You were friendly with the night crew?" asks Fischer.

"Yes, with Anthony and Austin, but Ryan was frosty."

"Why? You two have a problem?" Fischer asks.

"No, sir, no problem. He seemed like he didn't want me to bother him, and he'd sit there absorbed in porn when I visited, so I avoided him."

"Didn't he seem different from the Davies at Central?" West asks.

"I didn't work with Davies at Central. As I said, I worked days, and he worked nights. My days were busy with my assignments, and I spent my nights with Michael, so I didn't socialize like I do here. I wouldn't have spent time with Davies since he worked nights, anyway."

"Why did you inspect his transit record?" asks West.

I'm taken aback. How much do they know?

"When I saw him, something seemed off, so I thought I'd investigate. It gave me an excuse to check out the transit records, but there was one record for Davies with no anomalies. Nothing unusual, so no concern."

Lieutenant West rubs the back of his neck and squints at me.

"Why didn't you report your suspicions?"

"Nothing was unusual, and it was a gut feeling. I mean, he seemed familiar, and it had been a long time, so I assumed I was mistaken."

"Well, Zena, it's obvious our Davies isn't the corporal you knew from Central. He's an imposter. Had you alerted us, we might have learned who he was and his purpose here. Why didn't you tell someone?" asks West.

West sounds angry, but when I read him, he's just tired and frustrated.

"Things are different here. They reprimanded me for viewing the transit records. Even with my high-security clearance, I don't enjoy the same privileges here that I've always had. My assignment here is to translate the Book, not investigate. I'm expected to stay in my own lane."

"Fine, but you could have reported your suspicions. You didn't have to investigate yourself."

"Yes, sir. I never point a finger at anyone without proof. Just having a feeling about someone is insufficient. It's easy to misjudge people, so I avoid snap judgments. It's wrong to put someone in the spotlight without probable cause."

Fischer wears his poker face.

"Also, I used my access for personal reasons, which I couldn't justify, so I wanted to keep it to myself."

"You checked the transit records for Michael and yourself?" West asks.

"Yes, sir."

"Why?"

"I learned Michael and Commander were brothers, and I had personal reasons to search Michael's transit records. Then I checked my own record because I traveled here with a young man. I never saw him again and wanted to learn his name, so I looked him up since he was so nice to me."

"Who was this young man?" West knows the results of my search. He doesn't ask questions without due diligence.

Red flags warned me when I watched the young man stand to leave. Something about his uniform was off.

Suddenly, it hits me. Above one pocket, I see the words *U.S. Army*. The face comes into focus. It's Jamie. My son. Now long passed. He served four years in the Army. Another hallucination? Zena didn't recognize him.

"I don't know, sir. The transit record shows I traveled alone."

Everyone shifts uneasily in their seats, glancing at each other. Dan and Commander have been quiet, but Dan watches me.

"It didn't occur to you to report that?" asks West.

"No, sir. I got in trouble for checking transit records and thought it best to let it go."

Paul bites his lip.

"You knew a transit passenger wasn't on record and didn't say a word? I can't believe that. Why wouldn't you say something?" Paul asks.

"You were angry at me, and I was scared," I say, keeping my voice soft.

Paul crosses his arms and looks away, shaking his head.

Dan finally speaks. "Why didn't you report this to someone else?"

I glance at Fischer. He doesn't need to know everything.

"I decided to stick to my assignment and not make waves."

West glances at his notes. "Any idea who turned off the motion detector?"

"I haven't talked to anyone or heard anything. I've been busy with my own issues."

"What issues?" West stares at me.

"I've had personal issues, and I haven't been downstairs since that incident."

West appears to be attempting to read me, but he can't.

"That's all. You're dismissed."

CHAPTER 42

I'm triple-checking my nearly completed report because I want perfection. The days have flown by, and I've made certain I'm compiling enough information to leave the impression I've deciphered a substantial number of symbols with success, with more important material remaining untranslated. Commander and Paul linger at my table this morning, so I try not to slurp my hot coffee. Their plate of petite cakes sits untouched, and I stare at an orange one. Paul notices and offers me the dish. I pluck the orange cube, take a bite, savoring its creamy citrus tang, and wash it down with coffee.

"How's the project?" Paul asks.

"It's going so well that I plan on submitting my report to you by the end of this week. Maybe sooner, but I make no promises. Don't want to jinx it."

"I'm looking forward to seeing something."

I nod and resume typing as Paul rises to leave. Commander nods Paul's way and leans forward.

"Seems you recovered from your setback. Made any decisions?"

"I plan to stay here for now. I can't handle more change. But Fischer won't agree."

I close my laptop lid.

"Do you send C.I. reports about me? Did you inform them you needed to punish me? Fischer knew. Did you tell him?"

Commander's eyes widen. "Fischer asked me about it."

"Did Michael know?"

"Sure, Zena, we spoke before he left for Central. He knows the rules."

"He knew you were going to punish me, and then he left?"

"Yes. What did you want him to do? Stay and watch?"

"No, sir. Thanks for telling me."

I attempt to work on my report, but concentrating is futile, so I stare at my notes, pretending. Commander takes the hint and leaves.

§

The packed cafeteria is noisy, but I'm so focused on my mystery list that it doesn't register, and I don't remember eating. After removing my dirty dishes, I set my tray on the garbage can lid, and back at my table, I catch Mary Jo standing near my table holding my legal pad. With an amused grin, she skims the page.

"Could I have that back? Please."

A wicked smile crosses her face as she steps back and acts like she can read my scribbles.

"Come on, Mary Jo. Give it back," I say, trying to grab my notepad.

David approaches, stands beside her, and the color drains from Mary Jo's face. His eyes are hard, and he says nothing, but when he extends his hand, Mary Jo surrenders my legal pad. David scans the page before glaring at Mary Jo, and after a brief pause, with lips tightly pressed together, he shakes his head and dismisses her.

Mary Joe says, "Yes, sir. Thank you, sir." Head down, she slinks back to her table.

David hands me my legal pad, and we both sit.

"Thank you. I was about to go ballistic. You saved us both."

David chuckles. We both know how that would end. With someone crying. Me.

"What's going on? Haven't seen you lately."

"I'm busy these days," I say.

David stares at me like he's trying to gauge what's different about me.

"Don't see you at Agora anymore. Where do you hang out?"

"Sometimes I stay here until they turn out the lights, and I frequently visit the atrium. Often, I stay in my room."

"You know, you're always welcome at Agora. Tim misses dancing with you, and several men have asked about you. You can sit with me anytime."

"David, a lot has changed. I've changed. I can't pretend it doesn't bother me to see you with other women."

David raises his eyebrows and sits back, his eyes on mine.

"Okay, meet me at my apartment instead, and we'll talk there."

"You don't understand. I accept that you'll never be mine and that you're not meant for me. Your lifestyle has no place in my world, and I don't fit into yours. I'll always value our friendship, and I have no regrets. But it's over."

The sight of David brings back many wonderful memories, and I still have feelings. I can't afford to be distracted by pipe dreams, though. I'm different, and I must move on. Neither of us speaks. I turn to a clean page and start doodling.

"Okay. What's going on?"

"I found out something that bothers me. Remember my punishment?"

"Sure."

"Michael came here planning to take me back with him to Central. I hadn't seen him in months. It was hard seeing him, and difficult detailing how a Colonel assaulted me after he left."

David cocks his head. I never spoke of the Colonel or Michael with him.

"After Michael left Central, a Colonel started assaulting me, abusing me sexually. It continued for weeks. When I couldn't take it anymore, I quit, which is why I'm here. The Book arrived, and they offered to send me to Cavalry to translate it."

David frowns, looking disturbed.

"I told Michael the entire story. It was the first time I spoke of it since coming here. I cried while telling him, but I felt he was the one person who would care. It was like reliving the trauma for me."

David studies my face.

"Commander invited us to lunch, words were said, and I lost it. It's not like me. I always control my emotions, but I broke down and spoke out of line this time."

I stop to take a deep breath.

"Michael knew they were going to punish me. Michael knew … I hate belts. I had a traumatic experience as a child and cringe at the sight of them. Michael knew and understood. He knew I was upset and how awful it would be for me. When he kissed me goodbye, he said he loved me and would return for me. Then he left, knowing."

David squints and runs his fingers through his hair.

"What did you expect him to do? He can't tell Commander not to punish you. You broke a rule, and that's what happens."

I slump back in my seat. He doesn't understand.

David leans forward. "What did you want him to do, kitten?"

"What you and Frank did."

He sits back.

"If he couldn't convince his brother not to hurt me, he could at least have stayed to catch me after. To comfort and care for me, like you did."

David shakes his head and bites his lip.

"I've taken risks and sacrificed for people I hardly knew because it was necessary. Because it was right. I'm willing to make great sacrifices, but this was no sacrifice for him. He knew I'd suffer and left, never saying a word."

Heat rises within me.

"All he had to do was stay and comfort me. What kind of love allows a man to leave?"

"I don't know," David says, swallowing after a pause. "It's pretty harsh."

CHAPTER 43

My thumb drive holds my twice-edited report, and I'm satisfied with the results. Unaware Commander and his team are meeting in Paul's office, I walk right in.

"I'm sorry. I'll come back later."

"You're fine. What do you need?" asks Paul.

"I have my preliminary report, as promised," I say, holding up the thumb drive.

Paul inserts the memory stick into his computer and brings up the directory. Leaning over his shoulder, I show him which files he should send to Central Intelligence. Some files in a subdirectory contain work in progress, so I suggest he copy those files for backup. When Paul realizes the significant amount of work provided to him, his mouth drops open, and he eyes me in surprise. He opens one document to find a sixty-four-page report.

"The other documents supplement the preliminary report."

Paul opens the other two files in that directory. Commander watches and gives Paul a signal. Paul nods. The printer hums into action, and my reports spit out. Paul retrieves the copies, separates them, and hands a copy to Commander. Paul's face hides what he's thinking, so I read him. He's stunned by the professional quality of my writing and the volume of it.

"Noticed Lieutenant Cross sitting with you at lunch," Dan says. "What's going on there?"

"We're friends, that's all."

"Friends, huh?"

"Yes, sir."

"Cross doesn't have female friends. He likes to Play with the domestics."

"Yes, sir."

"So, you Play now?"

"No sir. I'm not a domestic."

"Stay clear of Cross. He likes to manipulate civilian women."

"I'm not his type, and he knows I won't Play, sir."

"If he's spending time with you, then he'll have you in his Playroom before you know it."

"I've seen his Playroom, and I'm not interested."

Tom's face lights up. "You've been in Cross's Playroom?"

Commander shifts in his seat behind me.

"For about five minutes. He showed it to me, and then we left."

The men exchange glances.

Tom shakes his head and smirks. "So, he showed it to you?"

"What's the problem if Lieutenant Cross did talk me into Playing? I'm an adult."

The men all blink in astonishment.

"If I'm not interested, nobody, not even Lieutenant Cross, can convince me. I'm stubborn. But that's irrelevant because I don't Play, and he doesn't want me to."

"You're fooling yourself," says Dan.

"No sir. I'm certain about this, sir."

I turn to Paul. "Sir, I've reached a decent breakpoint, so I'll take the rest of the day off to regroup and let you read my report."

No one speaks as I turn and walk away. Now I have leverage.

§

After dinner, with kitchen duties finished, they turn down the lights, making it too dark for writing, so I gather my papers, take them to my room, and proceed to the atrium to reflect on what I know. It grows dark earlier now, and I don't have much daylight left.

With my head resting on the comfy arm of the couch, I close my eyes and visualize my first day. I was near Westview when Dan's unit found me. The jeep trip to Westview may have taken an hour or two, but we weren't traveling at high speed. I envision the scenery, but nothing seems familiar. Forest everywhere. It could be anywhere.

§

It's dark and I'm awake. The stars twinkle above me through the atrium's glass ceiling, and I remember where I am. I feel my way to the wall and follow it to the hallway leading to the great floor. It's so quiet, with nobody around, not even an MP, and although they've dimmed the lights, I can see.

My watch reveals it's midnight, so it's no wonder nobody's around. I must have slept for a few hours. When I reach my room, I remove my lanyard and swipe the keycard. Nothing happens. I try the handle. Locked. I try the keycard again. Nothing.

The Police Center appears closed, and the MP's office is locked. Commander is likely asleep and wouldn't hear me knocking on the office doors. Well, Paul is my handler, so he can handle this situation. I make the trek back to the opposite side of the rotunda.

My knocking produces a sleepy Paul, his hair tousled, wearing nothing but sweatpants.

"My keycard isn't working. I can't get into my room."

Paul scratches his head and invites me in.

"Can I use your bathroom?"

"Yeah, sure." He points toward the bathroom. Moments later, when I emerge, Paul is talking to someone on his radio. He has turned the light up, and while he chats, I walk around.

A familiar-looking cross necklace drapes the corner of Paul's dresser mirror, hanging over a plastic-protected photo of two young civilian men. I turn the necklace over. Inscribed near the cross top is a "P" and the notation "2/5" is engraved near the bottom. The picture, yellow with age, was taken outside in a front yard. One man appears strangely familiar. I sense I know him from somewhere, but I can't remember.

"Williams will send someone to examine your lock first thing tomorrow morning. You can stay here tonight."

"Who are these two men?" I ask, pointing at the photo.

"My father and uncle, taken before I was born. My father retired, but my uncle died years ago, and I never met him."

Paul squints and points toward a loveseat. "The couch is small and uncomfortable, but you're welcome to share my bed."

"I'll need an undershirt," I say. "What is your father's name? And your uncle's?"

Paul opens a drawer and rummages for an undershirt. "My father is Timothy Avery Abrams, and my uncle was Johnathan Daniel Abrams. My uncle joined the Resistance, but my father chose the Peace Force."

"Your uncle died free."

Paul smirks and cocks his head.

"You think we aren't free?"

"I'm not, but I guess it's all relative."

Paul shakes his head and hands me the undershirt.

§

The light in this unfamiliar room is dim, and I don't recognize it. Someone lays next to me, snoring softly, and I want to see who it is, but my heavy eyelids won't open, and I can't move. Am I dreaming?

"Jade, Babe. Where are we?"

The bed moves as someone shifts, sits up, and turns toward me. I try to focus on his face, but I don't recognize this person through my blurry eyes.

"Who are you? Where's Jade? Where am I?"

The young man comes into focus and slips back out.

"Zena, wake up. You're dreaming."

The voice is unfamiliar.

Who is Zena?

My name is Caroline.

CHAPTER 44

I'm awake, but I can't tell if it's morning yet in the dark apartment. The heat of his close body and his hot breath on my neck remind me I'm not sleeping alone. An unwelcome hand creeps up my backside under the undershirt, so I push it away and sit up.

"Paul. Behave yourself."

Paul turns up the light and rolls out of bed with a broad smile.

"Can't blame me for trying, can you?"

He and his naughty smile head for the bathroom.

"Don't take too long. I need to pee."

§

Paul escorts me to my room, where two men work on my malfunctioning lock. One worker requests my keycard, which he swipes, the lock clicks, and he opens my door.

"You should be fine now, ma'am."

"What was wrong with the lock?"

"The crystal expired, so we replaced it. Should last much longer. You're fine now."

Paul nods and crosses over to the office. I need a shower, clean clothes, coffee, and breakfast. In that order.

§

"Good morning, Cassie. How are you this morning?" I ask as I pass by her desk.

Cassie eyes me with disappointment and then returns to her paperwork.

237

With a fresh cup of coffee, I head upstairs to where Paul is relating last night's events as I glide into my seat.

"That little couch must have been uncomfortable. Should've come here. There's plenty of room," says Commander.

"Well, Paul didn't have to sleep on the couch. We shared the bed."

Commander stares first at me, then glares at Paul. He knows Zena slept naked.

"Major Abrams lent me one of his undershirts, and we went right to sleep. It was late."

Commander drops his shoulders and exhales.

"Do you have nightmares often?" Paul asks.

"What?"

"You were moaning in your sleep like you were being chased. You opened your eyes, stared at me, and then fell back asleep."

"I don't even remember dreaming. Did I wake you?"

"It's fine. You mumbled something about a jade. Not sure what that is."

I shrug.

§

Now that I've finished my preliminary report, I can step back and continue working on the mystery while I wait to hear from Central Intelligence. Tommy was a hallucination, so why did I believe he was real? What did his message mean? Why did he call me Caroline, and why is she so important since I couldn't have known either of them, could I?

Paul bounds up the stairs, my report in his hands.

"Zena, I'd like to review your report with you."

He plops down in the seat next to me, looking serious and perhaps angry, so I turn my papers over and push them aside. I close the laptop to make room.

"This report is impressive. Why didn't you give anyone a hint about how far along you were, of what you discovered? This is an immense amount of work."

He slaps my report against the table and glares at me, so I read him. He's more hurt than angry and keeps his voice low.

"You must have known the importance of this ... for months. You've been working with me for several weeks now and ... not a word."

It won't serve me to be defensive, and it won't help to remind him how they've treated me, the patronizing, the punishment. Then he becomes my handler, adding insult to injury.

"This is how I've always worked. I submit nothing until I verify my facts. This is a huge deal, and it's not smart to jump the gun."

"You should have shared your progress. We believed you were

struggling and understood this was a difficult assignment, and we didn't expect much. But this?" He slaps the report on the table again.

I sit quietly, waiting for him to calm down.

"Are you disappointed?"

"No, babe, but you must keep me informed."

He sits back.

So, it's babe now?

"While you're calming down, can I ask you something?"

Paul sighs then flips me a nod.

"Last night, I saw that photo of your father and uncle. Can you tell me more about your uncle? You mentioned he was part of the Resistance. Why did he choose to join them?"

"No idea. J.D. was the unconventional one in the family. Had to do things his way."

J.D.? Jade?

"What did he do in the Resistance?"

"Don't know. I was a youngster, but I heard he had a band of followers."

"Is that how he died? Fighting the Overlords?"

"Before my time." With a pensive expression, he asks, "Why are you so interested?"

"He looks familiar."

"Not likely. He died off base, and you weren't born yet."

"Did he have children that looked like him?"

"No, my father told me J.D. had a woman ... Caroline was her name, but he never mentioned children."

I choke on my own spit.

"Is she still alive?"

Paul shrugs.

"They likely took her to a civilian base. Most likely died there."

CHAPTER 45

I stand at the apartment window, allowing myself to fall into a transcendental state, with my music playing low in the background. The voices come, initially in a stream of chatter, until I filter them. Excited voices speak of making plans. I can't determine what they're preparing, yet there's an urgency. It sounds like terrific news for them. I listen to one voice after another, learning nothing of value, and let them recede. While in this meditative state, I attempt to assemble pieces of my puzzle. I conjure an image of the cabin where I hid for rebirth.

My suitcase sits by the couch in the cabin's quaint but quiet living room. An open window brings in cool air, but no sounds from the surrounding forest. I've returned tired and defeated, and I want to hide out in isolation to regroup, but I sense I'm not alone. I close the window and search for further evidence that someone else has been here.

A young, bearded man wearing jeans, a flannel shirt, and heavy boots enters the cabin and cautiously approaches me. He is unarmed, and I imagine he can discern by looking at me I'm unarmed as well. Three more bearded, similarly dressed men follow him in.

One of them carries a rifle, but it hangs at his side. Unnerved, I read them. They are rough but seem more troubled by my presence than I am of theirs. The leader signals them to stand back, then demands my name, and I tell him my name is Caroline.

When he asks me what I'm doing in their cabin, I say nothing. He picks up my suitcase, drops it on the couch, opens it, and tosses out my clothes, then searches until he finds the hidden compartment hiding my money stash. He grabs a handful of bills and gives them to another man, his eyes never leaving me. The man with the money leaves accompanied by the one holding the rifle....

"Zena?"

I open my eyes.

"Zena, are you all right?"

Paul stands next to me, eyeing me with a worried look, but I take a full minute to recover.

"I'm fine. I was meditating."

§

So, Tommy was telling me I am Caroline. I was born Rebecca in 1950, reborn in 2030, and called myself Caroline. Then I was reborn again in 2090 and named myself Zena.

Caroline was the one who walked into the cave, and I'm the one who walked out.

§

Clouds float across the blue sky above the mountains. It's late September, and green leaves are starting to turn. Relaxed, I stand gazing out the window and wait for the voices.

Jumbled voices fill my head until I whittle it down to a few. They speak of one called *Mana-ta-ah*, due to arrive soon, in the next few weeks. Voices claim he will track down the Gift, wherever it is, and the New Dawn will begin.

Another Tracker.

A sudden chill rakes over my body.

ABOUT THE AUTHORS

Gerry Conrad is an outsider artist from Cleveland, Ohio. To cope with the isolation of the COVID-19 pandemic, she envisioned a dystopian adventure of a young woman set in the future. At night, Gerry would relate the next installment of her story to her husband, writer Sam Conrad, who encouraged her to write it down as a novel. Together, they spun the tale into *The Awful Truth* series as a parable for our time.

www.ingramcontent.com/pod-product-compliance
Lightning Source LLC
Chambersburg PA
CBHW070558120726
47909CB00007B/2380